FUGITIVE SHERIFF

FUGITIVE SHERIFF

EDWARD MASSEY

FIVE STAR
A part of Gale, a Cengage Company

GALE
A Cengage Company

Farmington Hills, Mich • San Francisco • New York • Waterville, Maine
Meriden, Conn • Mason, Ohio • Chicago

LIBRARY OF CONGRESS CATALOGING-IN-PUBLICATION DATA

Names: Massey, Edward, 1942- author.
Title: Fugitive sheriff / Edward Massey.
Description: First edition. | Farmington Hills, Michigan : Five Star Publishing, 2019.
Identifiers: LCCN 2018032075 (print) | LCCN 2018047007 (ebook) | ISBN 9781432854997 (ebook) | ISBN 9781432854980 (ebook) | ISBN 9781432854973 (hardcover)
Subjects: | GSAFD: Western stories | Historical fiction
Classification: LCC PS3613.A819327 (ebook) | LCC PS3613.A819327 F84 2019 (print) | DDC 813/.6—dc23
LC record available at https://lccn.loc.gov/2018032075

First Edition. First Printing: April 2019
Find us on Facebook—https://www.facebook.com/FiveStarCengage
Visit our website—http://www.gale.cengage.com/fivestar/
Contact Five Star Publishing at FiveStar@cengage.com

Printed in Mexico
1 2 3 4 5 6 7 23 22 21 20 19

Two pioneer women made this book happen.

One foundered in the snows of Hilliard in 1869 and survived to become the second wife of my great-grandfather.

The second makes the daily sacrifice to support my writing that began when she handed me a bound volume of blank pages.

ACKNOWLEDGMENTS

John Nesbitt, Tiffany Schofield, Evaluators at Five Star Publishing, Hazel Rumney, Ann Gordon, Just Write Chapter of League of Utah Writers, Western Writers of America, Western Fictioneers, Lieff Cabraser Heimann & Bernstein, Friends, Family, and a rich tradition of survival.

★ ★ ★ ★ ★

I: Simms Pins on His Star

★ ★ ★ ★ ★

CHAPTER 1:
JULY 24, 1883

Deputy John Willford Simms reviewed the facts once again. A prisoner sat in the county's new jailhouse. Two members of the gang who robbed the express roamed free. U.S. Marshal Eire and his two special deputies showed up yesterday to demand Sheriff Simms arrest his deputy. That deputy stood on a ladder at six a.m. driving nails in siding, avoiding the marshals instead of helping the sheriff to protect the jail, because he shared this little yellow house with his second wife. The facts agreed with his father's prediction, "Something will happen."

Sheriff Luke Willford Simms had told his deputy to skip the dedication of the new jailhouse. Mayor Eldridge had insisted upon the ceremony to open this year's Pioneer Day celebration. Deputy Simms had almost whooped at his father's words when the mayor overruled him. "I *was* a pioneer, and this jail is not the place for Pioneer Day."

Sheriff Simms had worked hard to leave his accent in the England he had emigrated from thirty-six years before, and he had never referred to his own trek across the plains. On Saturday, his accent sharpened the unstated reminder of the mayor's arrival by train. He had also managed a play on Brigham Young's "This Is the Place" proclamation—all packed into a single sentence that left unremarked that he had settled in these mountains before the territory created Summit County. Nobody had more right to decide where to hold the annual holiday festivities celebrating their heritage, and nobody had more right to refuse to make a show of the dedication of his new jail for that purpose.

Sheriff Simms accepted and shared the values of a community that respected authority. A mayor's authority blanketed a man's right and a sheriff's common sense. The banty rooster of a mayor had the chance to listen to a wise and careful man, but he ignored the sheriff's final words, "Something will happen. Someone will get hurt."

It galled John Willford that his father kept him from the U.S. marshals rather than send him out to capture the two ruffians on the loose. He had insisted he could stay away from the marshals by keeping a lookout. He pounded his upset into the siding, and the more he sweated, the more he enjoyed the sunshine, and the more his ambivalence toward missing the dedication shifted. He meant to thank the sheriff for the time to finish his work.

"Almost done?" The distinctive voice of Sheriff Simms interrupted his thoughts.

"If I believed that to be a sincere question, I'd tell you." Deputy Simms paused to survey the work left to do. "I ought to finish in the next couple of months, what with this extra day."

"I was asking about today." The sheriff's voice carried up from behind the deputy. "And I know what you were thinking. The fact I can walk right up behind you means keeping a lookout isn't the safest way to approach this."

"I knew you were there. There's no other house on this street. I heard you walk up." John Willford turned to see where his father stood. "I could be done for today. Why're you asking? You need me at the ceremony, right?"

"You don't fool me," said Sheriff Simms, shaking his head, "and you best not fool yourself. We're dealing with forces beyond willful men. It's best to avoid them."

John Willford considered asking if he should avoid the forces

12

or the willful men but held his tongue. He had heard the sheriff's teaching untold times; the most important part of action is good judgment. His father's teaching did not tell him how to prevent a jailbreak and run from the marshals at the same time. "Pa, you been the law here thirty years or so. I don't think the marshals are going to be so ready to go against you."

"Twenty-nine," Sheriff Simms said. "The marshals don't aim to go against me."

"You know what I mean." John Willford climbed down the ladder and turned to his father. Sheriff Simms gave a slight shrug, and the two men, like two tall trees, stood for a moment in silence, a sturdy oak and a lodgepole pine rooted in place. The sturdy oak said, "Well, I'll deal with it."

"Well," Sheriff Simms repeated his son's word with deliberate emphasis. "You must admit, on the plain language, it's you they're going after."

"Nobody's been after me yet," said John Willford.

Sheriff Simms shook his head. "God could have given me a boy with good sense."

His father's exasperation amused John Willford. "And me a father, considering you're planning to guard McCormick alone. You know Hopt and Elsemore will try to break him out."

Sheriff Simms took in a deep breath like he had to start over. "When Marshal Eire and his two bounty hunters from Kamas showed up here yesterday, things changed. Eire's been on the job more than a year now, and he hasn't arrested anybody. I make it that's why he hired the Williams brothers. He didn't tell me. He told me he has an obligation to let me know they are working in my county. He wanted me to arrest you. Seeing's he's federal and I'm county, that's plain cheeky. I don't count those marshals for much initiative, but I've been thinking once they see you're not at Eldridge's celebration, they'll figure out to look for you at your two houses. Leave town. Go to Wanship.

Bishop Roundy needs telling those marshals are snooping around."

"From what I read of Eire, he's a bit of a retiring man, and those Williams brothers for damn sure don't worry me," protested John Willford. "Hopt and Elsemore worry me. Especially that Hopt. People say he's crazy."

"In that regard, nothing's changed," Sheriff Simms said. "I know they'll try something. I have Orson to watch McCormick inside the jail. Woodside can help me outside. We'll take care of what comes up. What those boys need is a good thumping."

"All purpose law enforcement," John Willford chuckled. He started to break down his ladder to take to the shed. "If you asked me, it's worth the risk with those marshals to make sure everybody's safe. Sometimes things don't go the way you'd like." Sheriff Simms turned to walk down Fifty North toward Main Street and the new jailhouse. He waved his right hand, the back of it signaling goodbye. John Willford called, "If you asked me twice, which you didn't, I'm about as pleased to celebrate this new jailhouse as the mayor."

The sheriff stopped walking, turned around, and replied. "I don't consider it special. Why should you?"

"Hah! You don't consider none of your achievements special."

"Any," corrected the sheriff.

Long since used to a father who taught with every word and action, a style he had tried to adopt with his own children, John Willford took in the correction without comment. "You know, sometimes being humble ain't what it's cracked up to be. Sometimes it makes it hard on others." The sheriff raised his hands to show a willingness to hear more. "Being proud of this new jailhouse'd make it all right for the county to be proud of it."

"Meaning the mayor's right in his argument with your father?"

"You know I'm not going to take sides against you," said John Willford, putting the ladder down to take an unencumbered step toward his father. "It did take you ten years."

"The jailhouse's not much to go on about," said Sheriff Simms. "Three cells and a little bit of an office for me and you deputies. It didn't take a year to build, stone and all."

"Yeah, nine years in the deciding." John Willford smiled, more out of frustration than in humor. His father had thumped who needed it with his walking stick and dragged them off to the old rock schoolhouse to sit in the little desks until Miss Lorimer enlisted his wife to convince the sheriff of the need for a jail. Then it took nine years and a robbery. Shootings didn't count enough. The taking of property, robbing one ore wagon, and the board of county supervisors agreed to build a jailhouse in the county seat. "You won't say, but you're as proud to have that jailhouse next to the courthouse as you are of any actual act of law enforcement. It deserves celebration. Hell, even before it's dedicated, you're using it—and for the taking of property."

Sheriff Simms returned to touch John Willford on the shoulder with his walking stick. "Son, I don't much disagree. A barrel-maker ought to be proud of a new stone jailhouse serving a whole county. But look at what I'm looking at. When those marshals tumble to the idea of searching for you, it doesn't do for you to be around."

"I could be up Chalk Creek fishin'." John Willford realized he was in the middle of a losing argument. His voice trailed off.

"Then go fishin'." Sheriff Simms shrugged. "But it's safer to go to Wanship. Like I said, Bishop Roundy needs a warning."

Mayor Eldridge rang the triangle, and the festivities began two hours after the bishop blessed the pancake breakfast. "Brothers and Sisters, Ladies and Gentlemen, I am overflowing with joy at the sight of such good attendance for my . . . er . . . our celebration. We thank the bishop for announcing our breakfast in all the Sunday meetings. We thank the Relief Society sisters for bringing their husbands and families. We are in attendance here because we are blessed. Our little community has not had much to celebrate this last year. Since we built the stone schoolhouse it has been a community center. This stone jailhouse behind me signifies another great milestone in our community. What better reason that Pioneer Day should be a day of celebration and joy?"

When the mayor began to talk, some people looked up at him, some paid attention to their plates, and some treated ringing the triangle as a signal to go to the serving table again. Two men appeared to be part of that group. They finished eating and stood.

"Celebration that at long last we have a jailhouse. Joy that it is a sturdy one, made of stone. With the occurrence of Saturday's robbery, we are grateful it is here ready for use.

"To that use, we owe the benefit of our own, great Sheriff Luke Willford Simms. He rode right out there with his posse of deputies and nabbed the ringleader. For the first time he returned with the culprit to a secure place to incarcerate the man who had robbed our community."

Mayor Eldridge paused to look over his constituents bowed to their pancakes. He smiled. The two men moved to each side of the serving table fronting the steps of the jail. The mayor did not see the men each grab one of the Relief Society sisters and reacted only when a commotion arose as each hauled his captive toward the steps.

"Gentlemen, stop that ruckus," the mayor admonished from the podium.

"Sorry," Elsemore shouted and dragged Sister Margaret up the steps. "Just a minute."

With the mayor's first remarks, Sheriff Simms surveyed the

crowd for the three U.S. marshals. Nowhere to be seen. Loud voices snapped his attention to the mayor and his tormentors. The two men had pulled the Relief Society sisters into position as shields and by now had reached the top of the steps in front of the door of the jail.

Sheriff Simms gripped his long, black walking stick and stood. He scanned the crowd once more in search of the U.S. marshals. Finding no one, he ran up the steps and behind the mayor to block the door.

Hopt pushed Sister Cora past the mayor and up the steps. Sheriff Simms raised his walking stick. Hopt saw it, crouched below Sister Cora's waist, and pulled her closer. Then he pushed her to his left, toward the right-handed sheriff. Sheriff Simms held back his stick, concerned not to hit Sister Cora. The fear in her eyes held him a moment longer before he reached to push her out of the way.

Hopt faced Sheriff Simms alone on the top step of the jailhouse. He rose to his full height and stood six inches short of the sheriff. He raised his pistol, angling it above his shoulder, and aimed at the sheriff's heart.

Sheriff Simms waggled the fingers of his left hand, beckoning Hopt to hand over the gun. He held his right arm, cocked ready to swing. Hopt disregarded the beckoning hand. Simms swung his walking stick, aiming to smash into Hopt's hat an inch above the left ear.

Albert Hopt pulled the trigger.

CHAPTER 2:
JULY 24, 1883

No one thought it unusual to hear a gunshot at a July 24th celebration. No one thought anyone would shoot Sheriff Luke Willford Simms. No one remembered anyone ever shooting at Sheriff Simms. For several seconds no one counted, no one did anything.

Sheriff Simms stiffened and toppled into Hopt. Hopt stumbled at the force of the glancing blow. The tall man's fall almost knocked him off his feet before he stabilized and pushed the sheriff aside. The sheriff continued his path to the concrete, and Hopt moved forward again.

". . . oh, my God," exclaimed Mayor Eldridge once breath and wit formed words.

Hopt stepped to one side of the door frame, waiting for someone to come out. Deputy Orson hesitated like everyone who had seen this unthinkable event. Now recovered, he raced to the body of his friend, his brother, and his sheriff.

Hopt stepped behind Orson and turned to hold his gun pointing at the backs of those looming over the sheriff. With his left arm, he motioned to Elsemore.

"Git over here. You don't need her anymore."

Hopt pushed through the door before Elsemore arrived. He scanned the wall. A ring of keys hung on a hook next to the gun rack.

McCormick edged back from the bars to the center of his

cell. Hopt unlocked the cell door and reached in to grab him by the elbow.

"We gotcha; let's git."

The three ran down steps behind the crowd surrounding the sheriff. McCormick patted Hopt's arm above the elbow of his free hand. He motioned toward the crowd and made two downward motions with the flat palm of his hand. The three commenced to walk.

Deputy Orson stood over the sheriff. Numb and slow, he twisted to look at the dumbstruck mayor. He spotted the Relief Society president and yelled, "Where's Seth Parker?"

She did not answer. Deputy Orson grabbed the first boy he could find. "Go find Seth."

"I don't know." The mayor recovered his voice and croaked his answer after the boy had departed. "What should we do?"

Woodside scanned the crowd twice upon hearing the gunshot before he recognized the commotion at the mayor's podium. He pushed through the crowd and saw Orson.

"What . . . ?" Woodside did not finish the question before he saw the sheriff. He asked Orson, "Can you handle this?"

"Yes."

"I best go after John Willford."

Seth Parker pushed through more than a hundred men, women, and children around the picnic tables set on the broad main street in front of the jail. Few had seen it happen, and the crowd surged in to watch Seth attend to the sheriff. All had depended on the man who lay on the top step to give direction and provide a sense of safety. Curiosity, confusion, and fear abounded. Three men who had no family to protect walked toward the livery stables.

U.S. Marshal Jacob J. Eire and his two special deputies pulled up at the south end of town an hour after the pancake breakfast began. Eire directed them to separate and take their stations north and east to guard against a possible fleeing John Willford Simms. Marshal Eire waited an hour to let his special deputies reach their outposts and settle into their watch.

Sound travels far in the thin air of that desert in the high valley. Before Marshal Eire nudged his horse into a walk up the length of Main Street, he heard a gunshot. He congratulated himself. The Pioneer Day celebration offered a perfect cover for his mission. From under the bluff, he turned the last leg onto the long, straight main street. To his great surprise he could see all the way down the vast, brown space dotted by a house or building here and there to the courthouse and the jailhouse. He could see the tables from the breakfast and a podium. No one stood at the podium, and no one sat at the tables.

Halfway up the street Eire caught the angle that allowed him to see the crowd. He continued to the jailhouse, looped his horse's reins around the hitching post, and pushed through to the top step. When he opened the screen door, he saw a tall, lean man and an older man with a deputy's badge standing over a body spread out on a table top set down on a desk.

"What's up?" he called from the door.

The tall, lean man looked at Eire's badge and asked, "Got a name?"

"United States Marshal Jacob J. Eire, but you can call me Marshal. Do you?"

"No need to call you anything," said the older man. "You're doing no good here."

"I asked, what's your name?"

"Seth Parker."

"And him?"

"Deputy Clive Orson," said Seth Parker.

"Least you coulda done is be here to help," said Deputy Orson.

20

"That Sheriff Simms?" Marshal Eire pointed to the body.

"Don't you recognize the man you met yesterday?" answered Deputy Orson.

"Yeah," said Seth Parker. "Sheriff Luke Willford Simms."

"What happened here?" asked Marshal Eire.

"They shot the sheriff," said Deputy Orson.

"Who?"

"The gang that robbed the express," said Seth Parker.

"That one on Saturday?" Marshal Eire considered an extra moment. "What'd they do?"

"What'd they do?" Seth Parker repeated. He took a ceremonial step to the side and pointed to his friend. "They shot the sheriff. The gang busted into the mayor's celebration to take Lester McCormick and shot the sheriff."

"The sheriff never mentioned him," said Marshal Eire.

"He wasn't asking for your help," Deputy Orson said. "He should have."

"Say," Seth Parker spoke up, "they might have robbed some mail along with that money. That'd make it your jurisdiction. Go catch 'em. And be quick about it."

"Where's your other deputy?"

Seth Parker and Deputy Orson exchanged glances.

"Other deputy?" asked Seth Parker.

"Doin' your job." Deputy Orson looked surprised at his tone of anger and caught himself. He stopped and breathed a few times and resumed. "We know why you're here."

Marshal Eire nodded and pointed between the two men at the dead sheriff on the desk. "We're here to see him about our federal duty." Eire stopped, and no one moved or talked. "If that express robbery falls under my authority, the court or the U.S. attorney will assign it to me. Until he does, I'll do the duty I've been assigned. I ask again, where's your other deputy?"

"Out patrolling the county." Deputy Orson used the exact

phrase Sheriff Simms had used when he could not find his missing deputies. He thought a moment and added, "Both of 'em."

Marshal Eire straightened his holster, his coat, and even his tie. "I know my duty. My deputies are at the north end and the east end of town. I'll go back down to the south end. We'll wait. Your deputies are apt to ride in one of those ways. One of my men, or me, will meet up with them and tag along back here."

"Sounds like an ambush," said Deputy Orson.

"Not at all," said Marshal Eire. He smiled. "We're here to help."

CHAPTER 3:
JULY 24, 1883

Deputy John Willford Simms grew up a son, a Latter-day Saint, and a deputy. He respected authority and followed orders. He put away his tools, visited both his wives, and left Coalville before the Relief Society sisters began serving breakfast. Defiant thoughts about his father sending him out of town had no place, even as thoughts, and melted away as Indigo set a steady, unhurried pace to Wanship. No need to weary a good horse or worry a good man.

Deputy Simms followed the Union Pacific. When the trail veered to bring it near the Weber River he stopped to let Indigo drink. Simms stuck his face in the water and felt the shock of the cold. He liked the rushing, tumbling river that raced down the canyon taking its name. Up here, close to its source, the river seemed an outsized title for a stream calm as could be and not twelve feet wide bank to bank.

With all the time spent looking at not much to see, John Willford rode into town early enough for a late lunch. His blue roan had the advantage of munching grass at each of his watering stops, and now John Willford's hunger added up to breakfast and lunch. Wanship offered one place to eat—Mother Burden's rooming house.

Deputy Simms crossed to the little table at the back of the room, a seat with a clear and unobstructed view of the door. He respected his father's judgment, and if his father was going to use caution with the U.S. marshals, John Willford would use caution, too. The thought brought back his fear that those marshals had pushed his father beyond caution by causing him to send off his best deputy. It also reminded him he needed to figure out where to sleep at night. He decided he'd leave around twilight and use the protection of darkness to return to Coalville.

He didn't know much about it yet, but those marshals were in town to grab him because of the Edmunds Act. They'd be apt to watch the two houses he shared with his wives. He amused himself thinking he'd go back to the jail and sleep in a cell. That would be safe.

Made hungry and a little irritable by the eight-mile ride to Wanship, Deputy Simms thought the young woman slow in filling his order and belligerent when he asked her if the beef she brought filled his order for steak. The long chew on difficult-to-cut meat convinced him he could not eat it. He decided to order another potato.

John Willford searched the dining room for the waitress. The lip of the front door wavered. He watched, hoping that a new customer would draw her from her hiding place.

The waver stopped a moment before the door burst open. Deputy Woodside plunged in.

Deputy Simms jumped to his feet, knocking the sorry beef and the good potato off the table. He yelled his question on the way to the door. "Did the marshals take my father?"

"The marshals did nothing." Woodside's shaken look had more to it than the look of a man who had ridden hard. Talking challenged him, and, when he did, he answered a question not asked. "Nobody coulda done nothing."

Indigo carried John Willford to the new jailhouse in less than two hours. Deputy Woodside urged his horse to keep up, but twice times eight miles at that pace was too much to risk such a good animal. He let his horse fall behind halfway to town.

John Willford kept pounding along the South Hoytsville Road. Crossing Hobson Lane, a little trail to the west, triggered the realization those marshals might be paying more attention to him than to his father. His father had sent him to Wanship to avoid the marshals, and he better damn well have wit enough to do it now when his father needed help.

Deputy Simms pulled Indigo to a stop and reversed his steps back to Hobson Lane. He turned further west to the path that ran parallel to the Weber River. He rode as fast as he could to the narrow trail that led east to South Main Street. Coming in from the west gave an unobstructed view. His guess had proved right. Anyone wanting to ambush him would go further south of town to find a narrower spot.

A block from Center Street, he dismounted and walked Indigo to the jailhouse. He dropped the reins and ran up the steps. He had no idea who was in there, but his hard riding had told him what he would find when he strode through the door.

He found Sheriff Luke Willford Simms spread out on a table Seth Parker had told one of the boys to retrieve from the breakfast and place across the sheriff's desk.

Seth stood behind the desk. The day he set up the livery more than ten years before, the town declared Seth the vet, and Sheriff Luke Willford Simms made him the coroner. Neither doctor nor vet, Seth had served his designated role and now stood coroner to Luke Willford's murder. Deputy Clive Orson stood to his right with his hands around the sheriff's white hair.

These two made tangible the impossible news Woodside had brought. The sheriff's attendants took a half step back and beckoned John Willford to his father's side.

Deputy John Willford Simms looked at the star pinned to his father's vest. In twenty-nine years, he had never held it. When Brigham made Luke Willford the sheriff, he told him he could have a star if he wanted to buy one. No money for it otherwise. Luke Willford, the cooper, knew many hoopers. He had this star made. To John Willford it was not the sheriff's star, it was the family star. He reached and took it in his hand and held it, now his. He pinned on his star.

Deputy Orson broke the still silence when he lifted his right hand and pointed to John Willford's chest. "You want to make that official, you're gonna need the mayor to say an oath."

"Go find him. I'm not in the mood to listen to any words, but I'll let him swear me in."

Sheriff John Willford Simms had on his star and, with his first act, he pulled his father's suit coat over the bloody chest and buttoned two of the buttons. The effect of the wound showed around the edge of the lapel. Sheriff Simms turned to Seth Parker.

"Does my mother know?" A question to take up time while he figured out how to be Sheriff Simms.

"Of course she does," said Seth Parker. "Everybody in town knows and not because of me. It happened right there in broad daylight. Ten o'clock this morning. She was sitting right next to him before he ran to the door."

Parker's mention reminded John Willford that he had carried his father's request to Elizabeth Jensen that she sit next to him. First, he would take care of his mother, and then he would check on his wife.

"He sent me away because the marshals wanted to arrest me. I couldn't be here to help."

"Don't blame yourself. It was your father's decision," said Deputy Orson.

John Willford glared at the older man. "So, I'm the reason for a decision that killed him. What good is that?"

"When you're sheriff, you need deputies who do what they're told." Deputy Orson showed his normal calm. "He told you to go to Wanship."

Age and temperament let nothing upset Clive Orson. The same age as John Willford's father and having emigrated from England at the same time though on a different ship, Clive Orson reminded the new sheriff that now was the time to show his mettle.

He had pinned on the family star; now he had things to do. John Willford turned to Seth Parker. "Have you talked to my mother?"

"Not yet. I can't see as how she'll want to use the livery as a funeral home," said Seth. "And I'm guessing she'll want to bury him before Sunday."

"Don't guess—ask her," said Sheriff Simms. He gauged the hour with a look into the bright yellow sun on the verge of its drop behind the sage covered hills. "Take him to our place. She'll want him there. She'll decide when to bury him."

★ ★ ★ ★ ★

II: Fugitive Sheriff

★ ★ ★ ★ ★

CHAPTER 4:
JULY 21, 1883

Sheriff Luke Willford Simms ran a hand through his thick, white hair and clucked his tongue at the puffed-up banty rooster standing over his desk. He dropped his eyes and finished signing the papers before him. Tightening the lid of his ink bottle, he placed his dip pen in the tray and gazed at the mayor. After a moment of silence, he unfolded his lodgepole pine frame and stood, angling his head and neck as he rose to hold the mayor's eyes despite the eight-inch difference in their height. Fully erect, he lifted his eyes to the ceiling. He pointed to the cells. "A jail is for prisoners, not celebrations. Something will happen. Someone will get hurt."

Deputy Sheriff John Willford Simms felt a chill when he heard the sheriff's last word on the subject. He hoped the mayor had the good sense to trust the sheriff's judgment. Authority should always have good sense. He hoped in vain. The sheriff could not stand bombast. His father respected authority. The sheriff would stand up for what was right. Authority and bombast would win.

"I *am* the mayor of Coalville," Eldridge bounced up to his tiptoes with his declaration of authority at the same time he backed up. Deputy Simms looked to see the other two deputies smile at the sight. "We must resume this celebration to preserve our heritage."

With a long, slow turn, the sheriff fixed on the eyes of his tormentor. "Yes, sir. You are the mayor."

"That's right," the mayor snapped. He let his heels down,

and his chest swelled. "It falls on me to look out for the health and spirit of our community."

"Don't know about the health . . ." The sheriff stepped around his desk. "Best I can tell, the bishop does a respectable job with the spirit."

"For sure he agrees with me." Mayor Eldridge dropped back another step. He planted his feet and waited for a response. When he received none, he took back the step given and resumed his official voice. "A jail must be dedicated to its public purpose. You would have a modest little ceremony. I see an opportunity for a much-needed celebration. That's why I am the mayor; I have vision. The territory did precious little to celebrate Pioneer Day last year. We did less. A Pioneer Day celebration is a religious responsibility. You know that."

Deputy John Willford Simms could not remember a time when telling Sheriff Luke Willford Simms what he did and did not know had led to the desired result. In town some fourteen years, the mayor should have known that by now.

Sheriff Simms had a large voice and the confidence it would be available when he needed it, yet when he looked down on the mayor, he adopted a quiet and emphatic tone in the clipped cadence of his accent. "The celebrations have been subdued because that is wise. Our people are under siege. Summit County should follow the leadership and not call attention to its citizens."

"Luke," said the mayor, his official voice now changed to that of an intimate and confidential friend, along with the presumption to use Luke Willford's first name, "the leadership has good reason to stay hidden, but your worries are for your son. You must not be influenced by personal considerations in your official capacity."

Deputy Simms felt uncomfortable with the mayor thrusting him into the middle of his dispute with the sheriff. His father raised a hand to stay John Willford's muffled attempt to protest. The sheriff paused at the door a moment before he opened it. Then he held it ajar and said, "Coalville may be the county seat, but the county jail is not the province of the city's Pioneer Day."

"So much the better. Remember, I am a county commissioner. It shall be the county's Pioneer Day." The mayor beamed.

Mountain air and desert sun had made the sheriff's face permanently red. It grew darker as he yielded to authority without a word and ushered the mayor out with the signal of his hand.

Mayor Eldridge paused at the door and turned to deliver a big smile with his goodbye. "What better way to break our melancholy? I assure you all the county commissioners want our county jail dedicated in a proper manner. I am here to tell you it is right, fit, and proper to have a celebration on Pioneer Day, and there is going to be one."

Deputy Simms had seen that glare on his father's face before. He wondered if he could defuse an explosion by volunteering to play his organ. A commotion on Main Street disrupted what may have happened next.

A racing one-horse buggy announced its noisy arrival.

"Sheriff," the driver yelled as he pulled to a rattling stop in front of the jail, "they robbed the express!"

Deputy Simms felt no need to look at the wide main street to see the cause of this disturbance. He knew Rabbi Sol to be the only man in the county who chose a one-horse buggy over one horse. He had known Rabbi Sol a little over a year. Upon their first meeting, Sol explained he rode all the way from Brooklyn in a buggy instead of the train in search of a community where he could practice his trade as a lawyer. His village cart had served him well in his need to push farther and farther west. When Denver turned out to be hostile to him, he gave up on finding a home in the vast space between the coasts. Trusting his village cart to carry him to California, he climbed over the mountains and found this mountain desert valley where the people called *him* a Gentile. That was the place to settle.

Deputy Simms had smiled and asked if Sol had ever heard of what Brigham Young said. Rabbi Sol denied all knowledge of Brigham Young, save that the great man had died five years previous. He did all this telling and denying with a face devoid of expression.

In their year of growing friendship, Deputy Simms also learned that Sol appeared to live life delivered without visible excitement. He made that observation to his new friend, and Sol told him rabbis never get excited. From that exchange, John Willford called him Rabbi Sol, despite Sol's repeated protests that he was a lawyer, not a rabbi. Lawyer or rabbi, the man standing reins in hand at the front of his village cart had yelled.

Deputy Simms raced around the sheriff, past the gaping mayor, and down the steps before he heard the instructions he expected from his father but did not need. "John Willford, go steady Rabbi Sol's horse. Both the rabbi and the horse seem upset."

Taking hold of the reins, Deputy Simms inched his hand to the horse's chin, whispered in his ear, and stroked his nose. He watched Sheriff Simms take the steps, unhurried, to the street and let the mood outside the jail quiet down some.

"Good morning, Rabbi Sol." Sheriff Simms stood next to the village cart and offered his hand. "Who robbed the express?"

Sol paused. "Good question." He reached for the sheriff's hand before he continued. "Harding told me three men stole twenty thousand dollars and took out in all directions."

Mayor Eldridge had stepped next to the sheriff at the first commotion and now leaned in and said, "Quite a sum. That express office holds freight and packages for the train. Twenty thousand dollars? Something of a surprise."

"Most secrets are," Sheriff Simms said.

People hurried up the wide main street toward the jail, attracted by the village cart's noise and the growing crowd. Deputy Simms edged forward with the reins in hand and whispered to Sol, "Dramatic. And on a Saturday."

Sol frowned and whispered in reply, "I had no choice. He rode in hard from Echo. It's not a life at stake, but he thought he was killing his horse."

Mayor Eldridge faced the assembly as it grew and with a heave of his chest sucked in air to power his words out over the eight or ten people surrounding them. "You know someone robbed that office before I came, back when it was a labor camp. You figure it's the same men?"

The sheriff shrugged. "Doubt it."

"How would you know?" The mayor continued to face his newfound audience as he responded. "Those robbers hauled lickety-split down the canyon, long gone by the time you made it to Echo."

"A labor camp," Sheriff Simms said. "About fifteen years ago."

The mayor sucked in more air to address his growing audience, and Deputy Simms growled to Rabbi Sol, "You sure know how to draw a crowd."

"You give me too much credit." Rabbi Sol spoke over his shoulder to the deputy. "I grant you, it's good for my law business, but I agree with the sheriff. The perpetrators are not the same three men. For sure, this gang did not go down the canyon. The sheriff made his point. That first robbery occurred before the railroad. Today a posse could ride the train and catch anyone who took off down that narrow canyon. It has only one way out. Harding said the three took out in all directions. The smart choice is to go up the canyon. Up there it's wide and

Edward Massey

opens out onto the high plain. They'll look to connect with each
other and find their way into the mountains."

"Too smart!" John Willford said in a raised voice so the mayor
would hear. "Trying to escape my pa in the high mountains is a
sure way to come back in handcuffs."

"No doubt," Rabbi Sol said. He could not keep his expres-
sionless face as he signaled John Willford to let go of the reins.
"Your pa's good for my business."

Rabbi Sol guided his village cart through the crowd now grown
to fifty or so, handing cards to anyone who shot a look at him.
John Willford lingered a moment to watch men, women, and
children circle around the sheriff with questions, trying to latch
onto a reason to delay going back to their Saturday chores.

The sheriff mounted the steps leaving questions unanswered,
and John Willford joined his father at the top.

"I told you not to call me pa," Sheriff Simms said without
looking at his deputy as he reached to grasp the door handle.
John Willford couldn't remember what comment had provoked
this running rebuke. Sheriff Simms opened the door and called
to Rabbi Sol at the beginning of his slow progress. "Thanks. I
don't know much about your spiritual business, driving here on
a Saturday. I hope it'll be okay. Rest assured, I'll do what I can
to help your law business."

The sheriff opened the door and signaled Deputy Woodside
and his son to enter in front of him. He backed in to close the
door. "Damn them!" Sheriff Simms said first thing inside. "How
many shiftless no-goods in this county? Maybe three."

"Oh, plenty more than that," said John Willford.

Clive Orson sat at the desk he had not left with the onset of
all the commotion. "For twenty thousand dollars, you could at-
tract someone from outside the county."

Woodside stood inside the door next to Sheriff Simms. "I agree."

"Maybe," Sheriff Simms answered his deputies, "but even that blowhard mayor called it right. It was a pretty good secret. Who might catch wind of it and try something like that? One of our good-for-nothings recruited some help. He picked a Saturday because he had a smart-aleck thought that hauling their ass in here on a Sunday'd make a difference to me? It wouldn't."

His father's withering words brought a smile to John Willford.

"Maybe it should," said Deputy Simms. "Go to church tomorrow, observe the Sabbath, and go after them Monday. Clive would be the only one around on Tuesday. That'd put the mayor off his celebration, or he can have his celebration alone. We'll be busy doing our work."

"You can't wait that long," Deputy Orson said, speaking to the sheriff with the ease of long acquaintance. "Whoever did it'll make it to Wyoming."

Deputy Woodside pointed at the wall-hung railroad clock. "If anybody went to Wyoming, they're already there."

"Nobody's going to Wyoming," Sheriff Simms said with assurance. He smiled. "If I'm wrong, they'll come back."

Deputy Simms laughed. "Meaning, you'll bring 'em back?"

"You sound like you know who did this," Deputy Woodside said.

"It's best to know the people in your county," Sheriff Simms said as he stepped to the gun rack. "Not even five thousand souls in our county . . . half are men, and two-thirds of the men are boys, maybe little more. Adds up to a thousand men, and all but a few are married. Not a dozen bad eggs in the whole county. That makes it easier. We'll track 'em all down, but my first bet is Lester McCormick. He's the only ruffian in my county who thinks he's big enough to try a shenanigan like this."

"You mean Charlie's boy?" asked Clive Orson. "He's not but eighteen or nineteen."

"I count him in with the men, even if he is still living with his father," Sheriff Simms answered. Next to his rifle stood the oversized walking stick he had carved from a barrel stave. With his cooper's love for wood, he wrapped his gnarled hand around the walking stick. He turned to his three deputies. "Charlie has a shack on Porcupine Mountain."

"Do you think he's the brains behind this?" asked Woodside.

"Charlie has good sense. I can't imagine he'll be happy about this." Sheriff Simms tapped his walking stick on the pine board floor. "Lester lives with his father. Don't know how long he'll stay, but that's where he'll go."

Deputy Simms heard his father's teaching, *take care to know your people.*

The sheriff looked at each of his deputies. He slammed his walking stick down hard enough to create a dent in the new floor. The loud rap caught their attention. "We'll start there."

Chapter 5:
July 21, 1883

U.S. Marshal Jacob J. Eire stepped before the mirror inside the federal district courthouse. Appointed eleventh U.S. marshal of Utah Territory two weeks after the Edmunds Act became law fifteen months before, he looked in that mirror each time he visited the courthouse. Never once had he bothered to wonder who put it three feet inside the door and why. He adjusted his coat and hat and affirmed the crisp figure of authority he saw in the glass.

Eire followed the corridor between the two judges' chambers to his office. U.S. marshals executed all lawful warrants issued by the federal courts under the authority of the United States. Marshals held the authority to appoint deputy marshals. President Arthur appointed Eire, who clerked for him in the customhouse in New York City.

The U.S. President told the U.S. marshal that the U.S. Congress had finally passed a law with teeth in their battle against polygamy. President Arthur used all the references to the authority of the United States he could muster. He assured Eire the Edmunds Act provided the tools to break the back of those pesky Mormons out in Salt Lake City and the mountains that surrounded it. Right away, U.S. Marshal Eire appointed six deputy marshals and undertook to bring the Mormons to heel.

The Edmunds Act created authority to bring a wife before the grand jury to answer questions designed to lead to her husband's arrest. Annie Gallifant and Belle Harris refused to so testify, and Eire administered the sentence levied on both. The entire United States government stood behind the anti-Mormons, a blanket of rectitude in which to wrap the decision to imprison both women, the pregnant Annie and Belle along with her infant son.

Eire soon discovered that, even armed with the extensive powers of the Edmunds Act, he and his small army of deputy marshals could not arrest a single polygamist. He had agreed to take up the leadership of the crusade for the good of the country and his personal profit. In his fifteen months, he had succeeded in duplicating the record of the ten U.S. marshals for the Utah Territory appointed prior to him by the president of the United States, the last nine being as ambitious and non-Mormon as he. Zero arrests for polygamy.

Eire had sneered when his predecessor, Shaughnessy, predicted the Edmunds Act would do no good because "90 percent of Utah Territory practices Mormonism, and 10 percent of the Mormons practice polygamy." Now he took that warning to heart. Eire knew the president of the Mormon Church to be an adamant and defiant polygamist, the living prophet for one hundred thirty-six thousand souls in the territory. He could not even find the man.

Marshal Jacob J. Eire looked at a man in the mirror who had no stomach for continued failure. Success in his position demanded arrests, as well did his fortune, with a daily stipend dependent upon the number of prisoners in the penitentiary. First, he determined to appoint no more deputy marshals from outside the territory. He saw the wisdom in the policy that all deputy marshals be non-Mormon, but if a man wanted the job, he had to qualify as a local hire. Let him show he had come out here on his own and made his way in the community. He decided not to worry too much about deputy marshals, anyway. He planned to use his power to appoint special deputies in every judicial district, county, and community. He thrilled to the warning that only Mormons called apostates and Jack Mormons would take the job. "That means raised as Mormons," he laughed. "Perfect, because their income depends entirely upon their effort."

As he approached his office, Marshal Eire looked forward to meeting the two special deputies he had recruited for Judicial District Six. The judicial district mattered less to him than the fact these boys were from Summit County.

Right away after he launched his campaign to hire special deputies, two Mormon brothers, not brothers the way the Mormons called each other but true brothers, Enoch and Enos Williams, found him. Marshal Eire had expected the smell of money to draw special deputies to him from cities like Salt Lake and Ogden, even from all the towns up and down the valley, but he considered himself lucky to find these two in a mountain county made up entirely of communities well-versed in protecting their own. He assumed, but did not yet know for sure, that these brothers shared the industriousness of the Mormons they lived among. Of more concern, even fortified by the rationalization that Mormons were not Christian, his Catholic childhood raised in him doubts about how much to trust a pair who were willing to make money by leading the authorities to their own people. He might have to watch closely when it came to a matter of his own pocket.

It was all a matter of pocket. Being a thoughtful and deliberate man, Marshal Eire found himself in the position where he could not gain lawful warrants handed down by a grand jury to arrest named polygamists. Most polygamists were wealthy men or in high positions or both. That described the leadership of the LDS church, and all were easy to find in Salt Lake. Arresting them should have amounted to nothing special. To date it amounted to nothing.

The requirement of going to the grand jury to secure a warrant had led to no crusade, no arrests, no fines, no daily stipend for prisoners, no money for the marshal.

The entrepreneur in Marshal Eire paired up with the thoughtful. The solution lay in the stroke of the Edmunds Act that created a misdemeanor for unlawful cohabitation. All the Mormons had boodles of children, and Marshal Eire chuckled at the cleverness of the people who wrote the law. One thing for certain: if you were going to have a second woman, wife or not, you were going to cohabitate with her. Cohabs could be profitable.

Marshal Eire and his special deputies could arrest for a misdemeanor on sight, needing no lawful warrant to detain the cohab. Hearsay gathered from anyone in the street held up in court. Convictions flowed from arrests. Neither J. J. Eire, nor anybody else, cared about the prison term, up to six months. The certain conviction meant a three-hundred-dollar fine—half of it to the arresting officers to split as agreed with the special deputies. At half, thirty-seven dollars and fifty cents a head promised lucrative employment hunting cohabs for the Williams brothers.

U.S. Marshal Jacob J. Eire had earned the right to collect his seventy-five dollars a cohab. He wanted to make proud the man he had worked for as custom house clerk. He had done what he had been told to do. He had kept his head down, followed orders for more than a year after his appointment, and led the crusade. Judged by the results, what he had done failed. None to blame, he had the authority, and now he figured he had a better strategy. Now it was time to make some money. On second thought, that cohab prison term could net him twenty cents a day on his daily stipend. He chided himself. Thirty-six bucks clear profit per cohab was not to sneeze at.

Marshal Eire paused in the door of his office and watched

the Williams brothers looking out the window at the garden of grass and trees, green among the tan and brown surfaces of the July landscape. One tall and slim, the other short and thick, the brothers looked so dissimilar that upon first meeting Marshal Eire wondered aloud whether their father had been a polygamist.

"You been sworn in?" he called to their backs.

"Yep." Enoch Williams, the taller and older brother, turned around and pointed at his badge. "Went to see the judge first thing, like you told us."

"Who was it?"

"Nameplate said Justice Hunter."

"Hmm, the chief justice himself," said Eire. "Did he say anything to you?"

"He told us we were working in the tradition of legendary lawmen."

"That'd be me." Eire laughed. "Anything else?"

"He asked if we had a warrant," Enos answered. He continued to look out the window and made no effort to face his boss. "I told him what you told us. We're going after cohabitators. We don't need a warrant for cohabs. He congratulated you for knowing your law and asked if we knew where we're going." Now Enos stepped into the center of the room and tilted his eyes up to speak to Eire. "I told him you was the boss, but we sort of expected you to send us up to Summit County, where we're from. We told him we know about a hundred polygs and cohabs up there. One's even a deputy." Enos jerked his chin for emphasis. "Same's we told you."

"It don't matter to Judge Hunter how much you exaggerate," said Marshal Eire. "Did he ask how you know the deputy's a cohab?"

"He seemed to know the sheriff's son was a deputy," said Enoch. "I don't think he knew the sheriff's son's a polyg."

"All the polygs are cohabs. That's why they do it." Enos gave a provocative pump of his hips. "This one's had kids, so you know for sure. All dead now, but he produced 'em."

"Two houses and kids on both women," said Enoch. "Judge agreed. It was enough."

"Good," said Eire. "If he abandoned one woman, no house, no support, no fornication, that might save him being a cohab. He'd still be a polyg, till he divorced one of 'em, but it wouldn't be worth going after him, not high enough in the church. Too damn much work."

Deputy Enoch Williams shook his head *no*. "No fear 'o that. Not this deputy. He's not the type to shed one of his wives. Best to think he's set in his ways."

"I don't want him to do anything about his wives," said Marshal Eire. "I want you to arrest him for being a cohab."

"Don't make sense," interrupted Enos, "treating polygs different from cohabs."

"Don't look a gift horse in the mouth." Marshal Eire shook his finger. "That's what the U.S. is paying you for. Reforming his lecherous ways is not the job of a U.S. marshal." Eire took a breath but gave no pause to allow his special deputy to interrupt him again. "Now, tell me about this sheriff."

"Been there since the beginning," said Enos. "People say Brigham Young himself told Bishop Wilde to name him sheriff when they settled Wanship."

"Is the sheriff a cohab?" asked Marshal Eire.

"One wife, one kid. The deputy," said Enoch.

"The judge knows about the sheriff," said Enos, "but he said the news about the deputy might be hearsay. Said we should bring him in, and if the deputy gave the judge first-hand information, he'd try him right then."

Enoch stepped up behind his brother and said, "Judge told us to warn you. We're bitin' off a pretty big chunk, going after

44

the sheriff's son."

"We're not going after him. We're sending the sheriff."

July 22, 1883

Marshal Eire left Salt Lake City on Sunday for the Summit County seat, a long trip, and he looked forward to a good room and a beer in Park City to break it up. He and his special deputies made it to the Kawley Hotel and Saloon by dinner time. With luck, he thought he could snag some leads and find some local cohabs.

Althus Kawley, the cadaverous, well-dressed owner of the hotel, answered the marshal's inquiry after he finished writing in the register. "The papers come up here. You're leading the crusade against polygamists, but I doubt you'll find any up here. Nothing but gentiles. I'm about the only Latter-day Saint in town. A few, like my pa, found their way up here to farm before the soldiers discovered the silver."

"I'm looking for cohabs," said Eire.

"Don't see much difference," said Kawley. He noted three names in the register and closed it. "Lot o' men slide their snake in another man's cave. Outside Utah Territory, too. It's more convenient for it to be your own."

"Inside Utah Territory," said Eire, "Mormons are preaching marriage so they can do it."

"Slim pickings." Kawley leaned toward his guests and after a moment resumed. "I'll wager you won't find none in Park City. In the whole county, you'd be lucky to find five thousand people and half a hundred polygamists."

Without hesitation, Eire said, "If I catch them cohabiting . . ."

"Catch them?" Kawley interrupted with a good laugh.

". . . I mean bring in half a hundred for cohabiting, I'd be doing a good job."

"How much money'd we make?" asked Enos Williams.

"Sssh," said Enoch Williams.

Althus Kawley eyed Enos before he turned to Marshal Eire with a smile. "Here's all gentiles. Over to Coalville, you might find one gentile, the Jew. Town's smaller than Park City, but over there's the place to find cohabs. And other towns, like Wanship. My guess is you know about the bishop in Wanship. What'd I make if I helped you catch that deputy in Coalville?"

"We're staying here," Marshal Eire said. He pointed to the glasses behind the bar. "We'll be buying your beer. You're already making money."

"Yeah, because I turned my pa's house into a hotel." Kawley took two room keys. He dangled the keys by his fingers and studied each key as he talked. "Mind you, Sheriff Simms and me are on good terms. No grudge there. He always played me straight, even when he hauled drunks outta here. I own the rooms you rent, like I own the information. It ought to be worth something. Something like a commission? Five percent'd be fair."

"How could your information be worth that much?" Eire reached for the keys.

Kawley closed his hand and smiled again. "I won't ask for anything in advance. I'd trust you to pay me after you collect."

"We know he's a cohab. We know he's a deputy. We know he's the sheriff's son. Nothing more we need to know," said Eire.

"Maybe, maybe not." Kawley left outstretched his bony hand. "This here's a trust problem. You're looking to trust I have valuable information before you commit to pay. I'm needing to trust you'll be competent . . ."

"That's a pretty big word," Enos interrupted. Eire signaled him to be quiet by patting the air in a downward motion.

". . . meaning you'll be able to see how valuable my information is and be able to put it to use, seeing as how hard it's been for you so far." Kawley continued to smile.

Eire ignored the reminder that the crusade had produced very little. He said, "I'll know when you tell us."

"So you say. You could tell me first if you think it'd be valuable to know where and when to nab him. Me, I think it'd be worth three hundred bucks. To you, that is."

"Could be." Eire waggled his fingers, beckoning the keys.

"Okay. That's enough for me to trust you." Kawley opened his palm. "You know we got a thing called Pioneer Day, and it's on Tuesday? Right?"

"I been here more'n a year." Eire sniffed as he took the keys. He pointed to the Williams brothers. "And these two boys are Mormons. They know all about that stuff."

"I know who they are," said Kawley. "Kamas is not so far away. What I don't know is if their pa knows what they're doing. I make it that's why you're here on a Sunday night."

"We're here looking for cohabs," said Marshal Eire, "on the way to Coalville to see the sheriff tomorrow morning."

"I don't know that I'd do that." Kawley closed his empty hand and walked toward the stairs. "What you don't know that's worth fifteen bucks . . ."

"We get half," interrupted Eire. "Five percent of our share is seven-fifty."

"Agreed." Kawley said. He continued to the foot of the stairs and stopped. "These boys may have told you there's a new jailhouse, but do you know there's a dedication ceremony for the new jailhouse at ten in the morning on Pioneer Day."

Eire wheeled to face his two special deputies. "Why didn't you know that?"

Enoch dropped his glance to the floor in front of rounded shoulders in his silence. Enos puffed up and took two forceful strides to stand in front of Kawley on the stairs. He said, "Hell, whole county knows. That ain't worth seven-fifty."

Kawley stepped around the shorter brother to wave Marshal Eire up the stairs. "I don't think you should listen to your young man, or he'd 'a told you already. The word went out yesterday. The mayor asked the bishop and the relief society to spread a breakfast at eight."

"And you think the sheriff's son will be at the dedication?" asked Eire.

"Wouldn't you be at your father's shindig? Besides, John Willford plays the organ and sings." Kawley broke into a big smile. "Not if you waltz in there and warn him."

Marshal Eire looked at the room key, at the proprietor at the foot of the stairs, and over at the bar lined with empty beer glasses. He congratulated himself on staying overnight in Park City. The town had no value in cohabs, but this information could put one in his hands.

"Can't be helped. I'm obliged to tell him I'm working in his county. It's our bad luck the cohab is his son." Eire paused and thought a moment. "Give me a beer and draw me a map of Coalville." He reached in his pocket. "I'll give you two bits for the map."

Kawley walked into the kitchen and returned with a piece of butcher paper. Marshal Eire watched over his shoulder, and the town's north, east, and south exits appeared on the paper, with none to the west. Eire called his deputies to the counter.

"We don't need no map," said Enos.

"Good," said Marshal Eire. He tapped the map. "Then go guard the bridge that crosses Chalk Creek. You'll know all the places to the east the cohab can go in or out." Eire pointed to Enoch. "You watch the north end of town. I'll ride in from the south."

Eire finished the beer from Kawley's pitcher and folded the

map. "Damn bad luck I have to tell that sheriff we're in town looking for cohabs. He'll tell his son to hide or send him away."

"Same's he'd do for anyone," said Kawley. "Son or no."

"Won't work." Marshal Eire held up the map and looked over it to Kawley. "Let the sheriff send his cohab son away. When he returns, he'll meet a U.S. marshal."

CHAPTER 6:
JULY 22, 1883

After Sunday's first meeting of the day, Deputy Woodside walked the long block and half to fetch Deputy Simms from nailing siding on the little yellow house. He carried instructions to meet the sheriff at the jail and plan to be away all day.

"I'm happy enough for any excuse to skip Sunday school," said Deputy Simms upon arrival, "but I thought you decided not to go after McCormick until tomorrow, so you could miss the mayor's celebration."

"That would please me. That mayor tests my soul," said Sheriff Simms, mounted and waiting for his son. "I was thinking. The only thing I am sure of is where Lester went, not how long he'll stay there. I have a duty, and I best be true to it."

Deputy Simms wiggled in his saddle to test the cinch under his blue roan. "I guess you thought this out in priesthood meeting. Did you even change your clothes?"

"No need to," Sheriff Simms said.

"Evidently," said Deputy Simms, completing the test of his saddle. "Woodside told me not to bother with a bedroll when he told me to plan for a day. What's up?"

"Nothing special," Sheriff Simms said. "A long day, but only a day."

"Uh-huh," said Deputy Simms. "You seem pretty certain. What if things don't go the way you'd like."

"Can't see why," said the sheriff. "Even if it doesn't work out the way I see it, we'll be back here for Eldridge's damned celebration."

Deputy Simms chuckled at how his father acknowledged authority.

Sheriff and deputy rode side by side to join Deputy Woodside at the Chalk Creek bridge. From there, the sheriff set a pace meant to preserve the horses through the afternoon heat and to cover the twenty-three miles to Porcupine Mountain in good time. The posse climbed the smooth flatland as it sloped higher and higher away from the cool embrace of the deep morning shade. An occasional sand sage crossed the endless dirt, almost barren of desert needle grass. Here and there a lone mountain ash struggled to survive, the only interruption in the line of sight for miles.

About when John Willford began to think they were an easy target, he saw the smoke rising from the shack's unseen chimney. Someone cooking up a storm without a care in the world. No other reason for a fire in the shack on a July afternoon.

He nudged his horse closer to the sheriff. "Figure it's our boy?"

Sheriff Simms nodded recognition of the smoke. "Judging from that, he has company."

"Why so reckless?" asked John Willford.

"Their plan's working out," said Sheriff Simms. "The gang split in all directions. They're back together now. They don't think it's reckless."

Deputy Woodside leaned in and whispered, "Figure Charlie's in there, too?"

"No," answered the sheriff. "I don't think Charlie knew Lester was up to this. I doubt he's anywhere around."

The posse crossed the creek and continued into a clump of cottonwoods growing about three hundred feet from the shack. They dismounted and hobbled their horses, and the two deputies bent forward to catch the instructions from Sheriff Simms.

"John Willford, hie to the front and wait for my signal. Set up a ruckus. No one'll use the front. After you make a lot of noise, run around the back. Don't fire any shots."

The sheriff turned to Woodside. "This'll be tricky. I'll take care of Lester. There are two more in there. They're apt to make after you. If they're shooting, let them go. No matter what. I don't want either one of you hurt. I don't even want them hurt."

Sheriff Simms reached for the black hickory walking stick in its scabbard next to his rifle. The sheriff shook a *no* with his chin. He left both stick and rifle on his horse. He found a good branch in the creek with a diameter about the size of his wrist. He cleared off the few twiggy growths and made a new stick longer than his arm, much thicker than his walking stick. Finished, he looked to see his deputies watching. He waved his stick.

Deputy Simms smiled at the sheriff's impatient shoo-ing motion with the club. He felt a thrill of pride. *Lester McCormick is about to deal with my pa.*

The harsh and inhospitable desert landscape of Porcupine Mountain had made for an advantage in seeing the smoke. Now, Deputy Simms thought the ones who made that smoke would see him when he tried to cross a hundred feet of the same landscape. He needed a plan that took advantage of their exposure. He reached to take the rope from his saddle and carried it to the biggest clump of sagebrush he could find. Before he tied the rope to the roots of the sagebrush, he watched Woodside stuff rocks in his pockets on his way to the back corner of the shack. Then, with steady strength, he pulled the bush loose from its mooring in the sand. He dragged it along to his spot of cover at the corner of the shack.

Deputy Simms signaled his readiness and could see Woodside had reached his designated place. A small caution, like the flicker of fear, fluttered in the back of his mind. No windows in this side of the shack—and he had no view of the back—but he expected an opening back there. He hoped Woodside would follow his father's order to sneak in as close as possible without exposing himself. With July heat and cooking going on, the wooden shutter in the back would be open for certain.

The sheriff started toward the shack, standing straight and walking across the dusty desert, taking enough care not to make too much noise. He arrived at John Willford's corner and flattened against it, edging forward next to the one window near the door. Sheriff Simms leaned away from the wall and could have looked in had he chosen. Instead he jerked his stick twice.

John Willford paid no attention to his father's instruction to stay hidden. At the signal, he began to drag the lashed sagebrush behind him, all the time running, hooting, and howling. By the time he crossed the angle of the shack where he could be seen from inside, he and his sage brush had created a dust cloud that kept growing. With no wind, the dust cloud floated as high as John Willford's speed energized it and returned to the ground with a slow grace. He crossed from his corner of the shack to the other. A thick fog of desert sand hung in the air as he prepared to make the return trip.

Before he took his first step, the deputy saw a rifle barrel poke out the front window, pause, and with hesitation snake out again. He watched the sheriff grab it and pull. His father's pull brought McCormick's head and shoulders behind the rifle.

Sheriff Simms swung the water-soaked stick hard with one hand. McCormick's movement coming through the window gave his shoulder to the blow. That one blow did not neutralize him. The sheriff let go of the rifle barrel and, with both hands, swung again, four inches further out. The second blow did the trick—it hit the young man behind the left ear.

Gunshots from the back interrupted the deputy's delight

with the sheriff's police methods. Leaving their leader to check on the commotion, the two gang members raced for the back window. No telling if any of Woodside's rocks flew in the shack's opening, but for sure, McCormick's gang had tumbled out the back window, shooting.

John Willford dropped his sagebrush and aborted his return trip. He had to run the long way around the other side of the shack. He could see the sheriff, running around the corner, stick in hand.

Out the back window, the two men had gained their feet to run to their horses in the little corral in the back. Woodside chased them, gaining.

The men passed through the gate and mounted their horses. Woodside scrambled to the top of the fence and lunged. He grabbed one. The man Woodside held stood in his saddle and swung the butt of his gun on the top of Woodside's skull.

Deputy Simms arrived at the gate and tried to lock the two gang members in the corral. Both men and horses brushed past him and out.

With a kick at the endless sand, Sheriff Simms turned on his heel. His intention to thump them with the same stick he used on their leader dwindled to naught, replaced by his concern for Woodside. "Lester will wait," he said to himself as much as to his deputies.

"I'll live," said Woodside. "It was my own damn fault. Too cautious. I should have gone all the way to the corral before I threw any rocks. No matter how relaxed that gang looked, you had to figure someone had been careful, leaving the horses saddled and the reins loose on the fence. To top it off, when the shooting started, I hesitated. That gave them the jump."

"No," Sheriff Simms said. He separated Woodside's hair to look at the wound. "That was my doing. I didn't want you at that corral for the very reason you said. Shooting. At least, we cut the head off the snake. We'll take in McCormick . . . if I haven't kilt him."

"That welt'll be tender for a while," said John Willford. He chuckled as he signaled the sheriff to give him the stick. "But he'll live."

Deputy Simms helped Lester into the saddle on the horse in the corral, then lashed his feet to the sheriff's stick he threaded below the girth.

"Take him straight to jail," said Sheriff Simms. He looked at his prisoner. "I will admit, it's something of a thrill to say that."

Taking McCormick straight to jail posed no problem. The full moon past but two days, Porcupine Mountain's barren landscape reflected the light off sand and rock. Even the sage brush with its silvery foliage seemed to add to the light.

"Thank you, boys," Sheriff Simms said when the posse arrived at the new jailhouse after midnight, into Monday. "It made for a long day."

"No one's complaining," Deputy Woodside said.

As he reached up to pull McCormick down from his horse, Deputy Simms said, "No one, except Lester here. You gave up your buddies Elsemore and Hopt easy enough, but that won't change how long you're going to be behind bars."

"Didn't give 'em up," McCormick said and shrugged. "All I said was Elsemore and Hopt was better'n me. They got away."

"It will go better for you, if you help us catch those two," Sheriff Simms said. He started to climb the steps. "Albert Hopt's not from around here, and Leonard Elsemore's not from my county. It won't go as quick as it did with you, even if you help."

Deputy Simms guided Lester McCormick up the steps and into his cell. With more than twenty-four hours left before the mayor's celebration, he chuckled and said, "Your partners will soon join you. I'm guessing my pa wished he could take out right now."

CHAPTER 7:
JULY 23, 1883

Albert Hopt rode his horse across the Weber River onto the grassy mountainside and looked up the slope of parallel limestone ridges to the summit. He had ridden all night after his escape at Porcupine Mountain to reach Devil's Slide.

Hopt spotted a perfect hiding place in the space between the two breathtaking blades protruding from the earth, an even twenty feet apart. The three had agreed to meet here if separated by their escape, being across the Summit County line into Morgan County, beyond the reach of Sheriff Simms. Hopt knew the reputation of Sheriff Simms and doubted the sheriff saw it that way. Nevertheless, Elsemore had chosen well. The loose, jagged shale between the walls made climbing difficult. It made hiding easy.

Hopt had no idea when to expect Elsemore. He let his horse drink in the river, and he led him to shade at the base of the chute. The horse found plenty to eat in the wild flowers and clinging vines that blanketed the fallen shale. Hopt liked the feel of the protective walls. He stretched out against the steep mountain and slept, cuddling his pistol to his chest.

A rock clattered near him on the shale.

"Hopt? You there?" Elsemore, standing at the river's edge, peered into the dark shadows of the chute. A moment passed.

Hopt followed his pistol out of the chute. His steps set off a slide of shale that preceded him as he emerged from the shadows.

"Where in Hell do you think I am?"

"Couldn't see you. I ain't taking no chances."

"What took you so long, anyway?"

"Brought you some food."

Hopt holstered his pistol. He considered the sun straight up over the limestone slabs and decided it was about noon. He sat in the bed of shale and stuck out his hand.

"My wife made you Denver sandwiches," said Elsemore, handing Hopt one. "The eggs are from her chickens and the peppers from my garden." Hopt offered no reply, unwrapped it, and ripped off half of it with his teeth. "She'll be pleased you liked her cooking."

Hopt finished the first and unwrapped the second.

"First thing, we need to pull McCormick out o' that jail," said Elsemore.

"Yeah," said Hopt, finishing the second sandwich. "And find the money."

"I thought you had it," said Elsemore.

"How could I have it?"

"How? Lester told me you had it. Said you was bringing it to his pa's shack. You sure you ain't already buried it?"

"I dived out the window with you," said Hopt.

"Yeah, you did, but who took the saddlebag?" Elsemore scratched behind his ear. "You coulda took it. Or you buried it. I don't remember you asking where it was."

"Didn't need to. McCormick's the one took it when we left the express office."

Elsemore tried to look Hopt in the eyes, but that took edging up closer than he wanted. He gave up. "Anyways, we still need to know how we're gonna take McCormick away from Sheriff Simms."

"We'll just go do it."

"Like that?" Elsemore put his hat back on. "It ain't gonna be that easy. Lester's locked up in that new county jail."

"Then we'll bust him out."

"Can't." Elsemore shook an emphatic *no*. "Not unless we do it today. Everybody will be at the dedication tomorrow."

"Dedication? That's the best time. Lots of people to get in the way. We'll break him out."

"Rodeo starts at noon," said Elsemore. "I figure the dedication'll be finished by then."

"How far's Coalville from here?" asked Hopt.

"Three, four hours."

"Then we'll leave at sunup."

Elsemore swung his leg over the saddle and settled in, ready to go back home for the night. "You sure you're telling me the truth? Lester told me you had the money."

"He's your friend, not mine," said Hopt. "Why would I break him out of jail if I had it?"

Chapter 8:
July 23, 1883

U.S. Marshal J. J. Eire heeled his horse into a walk up the center of Coalville's main street, sitting tall and in charge. His peripheral vision told him he held the eyes of everyone who stood on the wooden sidewalks in front of the five buildings that lined the two sides of the wide street. To his mind their attention and careful observation of his every move amounted to adulation. He wasted no effort looking to see if his two special deputies followed.

His gaze fixed on the sixth building, the new, stone jailhouse. A tall, lean man stepped out and took a stance on the top step. Like everyone else in town, he stared down the street watching the marshal's progress. The marshal continued to the hitching rail in front of the man; his two special deputies drew up on either side to flank him. For a few moments, each man regarded the other; both stayed silent, and neither moved.

"We're looking for the sheriff around here. Do you know him?" asked the stocky man sitting on the center horse who looked like something of a businessman.

"I know everyone in the county," said Sheriff Simms. "By face, by name, and by character. Those two boys either side of you be the Williams brothers, live over in Kamas. They'd do well to work as hard as their father."

"Do you know who I am?" asked the marshal.

Sheriff Simms pointed down Main Street to all the people still standing in front of the buildings. "They do, too, Marshal

Eire. We had a robbery here on Saturday, but we didn't know you and your deputies were coming today."

"We're not here about a robbery; we're here about your deputy."

"Which one?"

"The one's a polygamist."

"Meaning my son?"

"We're trying to keep it professional. We're trying to make it easier for you to do your duty and arrest him."

"Why should the Summit County sheriff arrest my son?"

"Because he's breaking the law."

"Not in this county," said Sheriff Simms.

"Federal law," said Marshal Eire.

"Have a warrant?" asked Sheriff Simms.

"Don't need one. Knowledge is enough for a misdemeanor."

"What misdemeanor?"

"Don't play games with me," said Marshal Eire shaking his finger like a schoolmaster. "I told you we're trying to keep this professional. You know the Edmunds Act passed last year; at least you should if you're doing your job. It says you Mormons are committing a felony because you're polygamists, and you're committing a misdemeanor because you're cohabiting. He's cohabiting. Don't try to pretend you don't know what it is. Cohabitation is a misdemeanor."

"Have an indictment?"

"Don't need one. Produce him, and we'll take him for the judge. He's had kids on two women; that's enough. If you were doing your duty, you'd arrest him. It don't matter a damn he's your son."

"No, it doesn't. I wouldn't agree to arrest any man in my county for polygamy, certainly not if you don't have a legal warrant." Sheriff Simms set his chin. With a wave of his walking stick pointing back down Main Street, the sheriff's tone changed. His words rolled out in a pleasant voice, carrying his English accent. "You can go back home to Salt Lake and never think another thought about it. I'll arrest all the men need arresting in my county, and that includes my son, if ever I think it's my duty."

"You're sandbagging," Eire said. "You know all I need to do is tell you I'm here. I have the authority to arrest whom I please, and I can set up a dedicated watch with these two deputies at the jail and at his houses. We'll get him."

"I am aware of the powers of a U.S. marshal," responded Sheriff Simms with energy in his voice. He stepped to one side and pointed toward the door. "But I forgot my hospitality. We even have coffee, though my deputy, Clive Orson, doesn't really approve. It's not my place to tell a U.S. marshal how to do his business—you can start your watch at the jail right now. And then, again, you might find a dedicated watch will make it easy for the people around here to tell John Willford exactly where you are."

The sheriff's eyes flickered across Eire's shoulders to take in the dust kicked up by a man hurrying across the street.

The man stepped forward and held out his hand. "Mayor Eldridge. Who might you be?"

"U.S. Marshal Jacob J. Eire."

"I'm Enoch Williams," said the tall brother, leaning down to offer a hand to the mayor. He jerked a thumb at the squat deputy on the other side of the marshal. "Enos is my brother."

"Of course, you are. You were appointed more than a year ago. Not until now do we see you here, and tomorrow is Pioneer Day. Is that a coincidence?" asked Mayor Eldridge.

"No coincidence," said Sheriff Simms. "Here for your celebration."

"Is that right?" The mayor beamed and turned to Marshal Eire. "Make sure to enjoy our pancake breakfast. The feast begins promptly at eight."

"Thanks," said Enoch Williams. "We will."

Marshal Eire glared at him. "We'll be on the job."

"There's not much about the mayor's celebration I agree with," said the sheriff, "but eating's a fine idea. I told you we had a robbery on Saturday. With a couple of no goods on the loose, you could be a help."

Marshal Eire looked at the mayor and at the sheriff before he spoke. "Is that a trade?"

"Nope," said Sheriff Simms.

"Out of our jurisdiction," said Marshal Eire.

Chapter 9:
July 24, 1883

Deputy John Willford Simms squinted into the sun at the sheriff atop the steps of the jailhouse. His father's face soaked up the warmth of the day from the sun full bright an hour. The lodgepole pine smiled at the sturdy oak.

"I saw you walk down the hill. All's well with Elizabeth Jensen?" The sheriff's question made a statement that did not seek an answer. "Please tell her I want her to sit at my side during the mayor's dedication today."

"And Elizabeth Tonsil?" asked John Willford.

"She'd best help you. About time you finished that little yellow house." Sheriff Simms continued to look toward the sun and talk into the sky. "You've been working on it three years."

"Yeah, right," John Willford said. The sheriff beckoned him up the steps. His father never played favorites, and he meant something by everything he said. Until John Willford knew what that might be, best say little.

Deputy Simms followed Sheriff Simms into the single room fronting the cells. The sheriff pretended he had routine work to do, settling into his chair and turning his attention to papers Deputy Clive Orson brought to him. John Willford thought, *Nothing routine about today.*

He stepped in front of his father's desk. The sheriff did not look at him—confusing behavior. Blunt honesty had been the bedrock teaching from father to son. "You don't fool me. You're making me scarce."

Now Sheriff Simms looked up from his paperwork. "I decided to give you some time to finish the siding before the snow flies." He delivered the words with a voice loud enough for all to hear and with a flick of the hand to wave his deputy through the door.

"Pa . . ." John Willford began.

"Don't call me Pa." John Willford could see his father's cheek muscles working hard to keep the smile from the corners of his mouth. His next words came as no surprise. "You know I don't like it. Sheriff or Father or Dad will do fine."

John Willford laughed. His father emigrated to this country and crossed the plains to this territory at twenty-two, bringing his wife, Mary Ann Opshaw, and John Willford, five. His father had not been old enough to be set in his ways when he arrived, yet he showed little willingness to accept the manners or the language overtaking the mountain county where he was the law.

"Whatever I call you, Father"—John Willford elongated the word into a full breath—"the truth is you don't want me at the dedication. Snow won't start for three months. I know those U.S. marshals came here yesterday. You're afraid they'll show at the mayor's dedication." He suffered a moment of concern at his words. Blunt honesty served talk between father and son, talking back did not.

"Not afraid at all." The sheriff's tone continued light, but in charge. "I allowed as how you would know their every move, even before they made it. You have a point, though. Those U.S. marshals might snoop around for you at this shindig."

John Willford grinned and nodded. He knew not to butt up against his father's will.

"It's the mayor's doing," Sheriff Simms continued. "He insists. We'll have to go along. Nobody's going to do much work, so it's not like giving you time off from county work. You could at least tell me you appreciate it."

John Willford's suspicions collapsed. He saw the second smile of the morning from a man who measured his smiles. He stepped to the window and pointed to the crowd gathering for the pancake breakfast. "To show I appreciate it, I'm going out to tell anyone who asks that you are a generous man, even to your own son."

The deputy could see each had a side. The dedication of this new jailhouse *could* make a better Pioneer Day than any of the last three. Of course, a celebration caused distraction, and, Pioneer Day or not, Sheriff Simms didn't want Elsemore and Hopt on the loose, even one day. That seemed like reason enough to try once more to win his way with his father.

"Let's take a serious look at this. McCormick's in jail right now. You don't know where the money is. My bet is Hopt doesn't, either. That's what makes him your worry. He's gonna want McCormick, and you're gonna need help. Don't let the U.S. marshals back you into a decision that'll cause problems."

"We're covered." The sheriff's tone showed he accepted his son's concern. "Clive's inside and Woodside with me at breakfast."

"That breakfast will draw a crowd. Woodside and Orson are not enough hands to take care of things if there's trouble."

Sheriff Simms lifted his long frame from his desk and stepped next to his son. He pointed out the window at the husbands setting up the tables below the steps and the Relief Society sisters covering every other one with food.

"That U.S. marshal doesn't care about Pioneer Day. Mark my words: he'll know you play the organ and want to be at the dedication. You'll make more distraction and make it worse for me." The sheriff shooed his son toward the door with both hands. "Go to your carpentry. Make sure and tell people you'll be here. Learn not to be where he is. No harm in being cautious."

Deputy Simms had talked back to the sheriff as much as a son dared. He backed out the door, crossed Main Street, and followed Lumber Lane to load siding into the yard's wagon. If he had to accept his father's banishment, he might as well see it as a blessing.

John Willford took three years to finish adding all the rooms. Those new rooms were no use in winter until he nailed up all the siding. He wondered at the sheriff's invisible calculations. The sheriff never explained much about what he did or said. He took every opportunity to teach, and he left it up to a person to think about what he was being taught. The space of this one day sized up to be about how much time John Willford needed to finish the job before snow flew. With the marshals now shown up, he had to take care not to work too regular and create an easy chance to nab him. This extra day translated into twelve or more calendar days of work.

John Willford emerged from Lumber Lane, crossed Main Street, jogged to the left, and drove up State Street. He climbed the hill to the house he lived in with Elizabeth Jensen to deliver his father's message. The sheriff had not given him an explanation why he wanted Elizabeth Jensen at the dedication, but he understood. The sheriff wanted the U.S. marshals to see his first wife there and only his first wife.

Elizabeth Jensen walked across the porch to meet him at the top step. She extended her hand, bent at the wrist. He took it and squeezed it. She accepted this sign of affection, then withdrew her hand.

"Your father has sent word," she said. "I am to bring a cake and sit next to him."

"He didn't tell me about the cake."

"I believe he wants to display me."

John Willford almost said the sheriff showed good taste in

wanting to display her, but he held his tongue. An attractive woman and aware of it, Elizabeth Jensen would think the comment out of place. At least, that is what she would say.

"The seat of honor," said John Willford. "Along with Mother, on the other side."

"You know what I mean," said Elizabeth Jensen, opening the front door.

"I wanted to see if you need for anything. I have this siding to deliver and return the wagon. While you're at the celebration, I'll go over and work on it."

"Yes," said Elizabeth Jensen. She passed through the door and closed it, leaving John Willford on the porch.

After her dismissal, he clucked his tongue, considered a moment, opened the screen door, and stepped into the foyer. He called to her in the kitchen. "Like I said, I came by to see if you need for anything before you go to the ceremony."

"No," her voice rolled down the hall, a pause separating the words, "you didn't."

He waited to hear more and quelled the urge to ask the question again.

"You've taken to not staying here . . ."

"Wise choice. Now I hear the U.S. marshal has visited Pa." John Willford interrupted, but he knew talking over her made no difference. "I'm not staying there, neither."

". . . Once you finish those bedrooms, are you going to sleep over there?"

"I never have," he said. "What are you trying to ask me?"

"Well, you've been building on that house for three years. Are you going to have more children?" she said, back to him and words carrying over her shoulder. "With her, I mean."

John Willford considered reminding Elizabeth Jensen that he thought Elizabeth Tonsil too old to consider having another child. He held his tongue. That veered too close to expressing an opinion about one wife to the other. He said, "That's not my plan."

CHAPTER 10:
JUNE 1869

The moment Deputy John Willford Simms set his horse to the watering trough, Bishop Barber grabbed a hot towel and wrapped it around the face of the customer in the chair. Deputy Simms saw the bishop race across the street pulling on his coat. The title conferred authority on Bishop Barber. He had no need for that coat in the June sun. Sheriff Simms had honed his son's survival instinct to a fine edge by insisting that his deputy size up people and make a judgment. Sheriff or deputy in a county three years old, in a territory not yet a state, served as police, judge, jury, and executioner at any one time, even at the same time.

"Trust your judgment." The sheriff's English accent rang in his son's ears. "You have to get used to being right."

Deputy Simms had long since judged this person now standing in the doorway, bishop or not, to be a blowhard.

"Brother Simms, I must talk to you." The bishop took a stance that blocked the exit and folded his hands across his stomach in a stolid, reverential posture. Consistent with his pose, he spoke in his deep, official voice. "We have a problem here in town, and we need your help. Elizabeth Tonsil needs marrying."

Deputy Simms had a wife and a family, four years now. He kept his silence, and he kept his face blank.

The official voice continued. "She arrived in May in that company of sick Saints."

Deputy John Willford had been the one to meet the wagon train. No need to tell the man and interrupt him while he was listening to himself talk.

"Her mother died two weeks after the company arrived," continued the bishop. "Her father died a week later. An orphan, alone, with no money. Don't mistake me—she's twenty-two, in her prime—but she's still an orphan. She's living under my roof, and we're not even kin. To be sure, Brother Simms, it's all virtuous. I'm doing the bishop's responsibility. And, today, it's the bishop's duty to find a husband to take responsibility."

"Send her to find a job," John Willford said. "Best way to meet a man."

"Now, Brother Simms," the official voice continued, heavy with authority, arms held at his side, shoulders pulled back, and coat opened across his chest. "This little English and Scots settlement is a haven for Saints who crossed an ocean and walked to this valley, like the Tonsils.

"We protect our own, especially our orphans and our women.

"You are to become one of the leaders in this county, a man above all the rest, a man like Elder Simms."

John Willford had never known an Elder Simms before, even if the bishop meant his father. The words put John Willford on his guard. His father was lean with praise. By his example, he had trained John Willford to know flattery for what it was: a signal somebody wanted something.

"For Elizabeth Tonsil to be married is best for her. You are a born leader, and you should have a second wife. The doctrine of plural marriage is a divine obligation."

Deputy John Willford Simms stood and looked at the bishop. The man wanted so much to be what he thought a bishop should be, he had memorized his life.

"It's God's will," the bishop continued.

Well, now, that made all the difference.

"And, to boot, she's a good-looking girl." The bishop smiled and nodded toward John Willford. "You'd like that about her."

Damn the man. Deputy Simms knew young Elizabeth Tonsil was attractive. No feelings attended his knowledge; he knew she was attractive because he knew the names and faces of every person in the county.

"Marrying Elizabeth Tonsil won't do no good," said John Willford. "I already have a regular marriage, to Elizabeth Jensen. Two Elizabeths is too many. It'd be confusing. Not to mention, while it might work for the leaders of the church, two wives is too many for me."

"Are you saying no to me?" asked the bishop.

"Finding a way to say no to a bishop is hard," said Deputy Simms. "But, dammit, I have a wife and kids two and four and one on the way. It already takes two jobs to support my family."

"Brother Simms, the reason it is hard to say no to the bishop is that, when the bishop tells you you have a calling, you have a calling."

"I got no inclination to stray any, church sanctioned or not," said John Willford. "There's nothing in it but obligation and responsibility . . . and more work. No good comes of it. I want none of it."

"Sunday, after church," Bishop Barber said with not the slightest recognition of John Willford's words, "I will take you to my home to meet Elizabeth Tonsil."

This buffoon of a bishop had skills John Willford did not have. He did not want to meet this woman. Nothing against her . . . there just wasn't any reason to make her acquaintance. He had an English-born wife, baptized at home, and brought by English parents here to Zion. Nobody expected intimacy or passion in this hard land. He accepted the job to work together and make a family and knew Elizabeth had said nothing about their marriage to the bishop.

The bishop had decided he was to marry Elizabeth Tonsil based on the fact he was the son of Elder Simms, Sheriff Simms to everyone else in the county. To make sure the deputy did his bidding, the bishop made the one request the deputy could not deny. He invited the deputy to his home.

The next Sunday the bishop arrived at the deputy's doorway to carry out his invitation. John Willford's certainty that he wanted no more responsibility fought with the bishop's will until the moment the bishop introduced him to Elizabeth Tonsil.

He stood before her in the parlor, saying nothing. He knew her story down to the detail that of two hundred new arrivals in the county, her mother and father became the eleventh and twelfth bodies buried in the town cemetery.

Tall and fresh-faced, with a slight ruddiness that created a shine on her cheeks, Elizabeth Tonsil's look was as open as the mountains that surrounded their valley. She offered her hand; he shifted his hat, took her hand, and shook it. The force that ran between them, joined them. He stopped shaking her hand, but he did not let go.

She smiled and broke the silence with a directness that startled him.

"The bishop tells me you are to be my husband."

"Told me the same thing."

"And how about that?"

He tried to concentrate on her accent, closer to the sheriff's than to his. Concentration did not work. He thought about something else. Married four years to Elizabeth Jensen, the intimacies between husband and first wife were scarce, on the way to becoming rare.

"Ma'am, that's not for me to say."

It was not for him to think, let alone to say. He dared not suggest the thought that appeared from its formless state. Those shapeless clothes of awkward materials in homespun and muslin lay on her body like a single extra skin. He could feel this beautiful June day and . . . a glow. He swallowed hard and a second swallow, to give him time, as he realized he had gone from not wanting to marry her to yearning to peel off that single extra skin. *Where did those thoughts come from?*

"Well, the English aren't very romantic, either." She did not even smile.

When next he saw her, the following Saturday at the church, pretty much the whole town was there. He had invited no one to the wedding, but this town existed because of the church, and everyone viewed marriage as public, like Sunday school. She offered her hand. Once again, he took it and held it and did not let it go. Everyone noticed, including Elizabeth Jensen.

Elizabeth Jensen never mentioned her feelings when asked and expected to give her first wife's consent to the marriage. The bishop asked her; she gave her consent.

Dedicated to carving a life in that mountain desert, prudent stock married four years before but not yet sealed, she and her husband travelled with Elizabeth Tonsil to Settlement House, where the ordinances sealed all three in eternal marriage on June 29, 1869. Upon returning, John Willford guided the buggy to his house with Elizabeth Jensen and walked her up the stairs, across the porch, to the front door.

He then drove the buggy and Elizabeth Tonsil to the one-room house built by his hand and church members rallied to the task from the pulpit of the good Bishop Barber. Deputy Simms carried his new wife and her satchel of possessions through the door.

John Willford dropped the satchel before he set Elizabeth in the brass frame bed brought in the wagon by her parents. He held her tight, and she quivered. He touched. She touched. Neither spoke.

After man and woman became husband and wife, he found a pillow to put under her head. He lay close to her, connected, in her aura. She held him, as taken by him as he by her.

That day began a life. John Willford refused to burden his first wife with the tradition of sharing her home with his second wife, and he never moved into his second wife's house.

In the eyes of God, He married one man and two women on the same day. Who was to say there was a second wife?

Well, Elizabeth Jensen Simms, for one. She tolerated the obligation of the second wife and the three daughters who survived birth in the first nine years. She knew her role, and she had given her consent. She knew these actions fulfilled the doctrine of the church preached by the leadership, alternately to keep their society together and to partake of celestial marriage. In the usual manner of deciding without any discussion, she expected, and John Willford accepted, it proper for her husband to continue living in her house with his first family. She never accepted the second family as family. Elizabeth Tonsil may have become her husband's second wife, but she had been an orphan, a ward of the ward. Elizabeth Jensen made certain no one forgot that.

The one-room house became the little yellow house and a sanctuary for Elizabeth Tonsil Simms and John Willford. They were with each other almost every time he visited the house. She never asked. She never said no.

"We shouldn't," he said the day she told him of the expected first baby.

Over that still-born first baby, neither spoke a word of their feared guilt.

"We have been blessed again," Elizabeth told her husband one Wednesday afternoon.

He kissed her on the nose and left. John Willford's love for her had created life a second time, and he feared it threatened life. He could take care of that threat by his own action. People would have to deal with what he did. Those who wanted to know how he felt . . . well, that was none of their damn business.

John Willford banished himself three times. Their family complete with three beautiful little girls, ages eight, six, and two, all born healthy as could be, the little cabin at the corner of 50 E. and 100 N. glowed as bright as Elizabeth Tonsil Simms.

1879

Diphtheria arrived in the valley the first week of March 1879. Its unseen waves of disease and death bounced off the low foothills blocking the entrance to the north and back to the Wasatch Mountains in the south. It caromed off the Uintas in the east, looking for an outlet to the west down to the Great Salt Lake. Thought to be offspring to unsanitary conditions, it could not be—not in this community of careful, hardworking, clean-living souls. All death and disease is unfair, and the most unfair is the disease that targets children more than their parents. Few knew that contact was its source, and yet they knew not to expose others. Freezing weather and winter's deep snow piled high kept families huddled together, and quarantine kept them apart. The diphtheria trapped in the little valley stayed there, until it, like its victims, died.

Elizabeth Tonsil met John Willford at the door, home from his duties with this growing scourge. "We can't go out. If you come in, you can't go out."

"What are you doing for medicine?"

"There isn't any medicine I can make that will take this fever away," Elizabeth answered, her voice made firm by truth and fear.

"I'll find a doctor."

"Where?" The question was like setting a challenge to her husband, and when she saw his reaction, she shook her head to retract her question. "A doctor can't come in, either. Besides, he has nothing for us. I've been boiling ragweed and bitterroot."

John Willford knew her words were true; he had the job of enforcing the quarantine. By her blocking the door, he knew his daughters were sick. He knew the symptoms. Their throats swelled. They could not breathe. Their hearts raced.

He was helpless, and a helpless man was useless. This worthless badge gave him no power to stop the sickness and death, not for his family and not for the other settlers living a black end to ten years of hard struggle in a dry, hot, cold place.

"If I can't go in my own house to comfort you and our daughters," said John Willford, "then I'll stay here till it breaks."

Elizabeth smiled at her headstrong husband, his passions always spelled out in action, and asked, "You plan to camp there in front of the house?"

"What house? It's nothing but a little cabin with broken chink and drafty walls that surround one small room. I might have been proud of it once, but now all I see is a box for three daughters dying in the same bed. Make's what I do pretty useless."

For nine days he camped in the yard, blessed that the children of his first family had not been exposed. Those children he now protected by his daily efforts to ensure the town observed the quarantine. As to this dear family that seemed unable to survive his loving touch, all he could do was speak to his wife through the window each morning.

When he arose and spoke to his wife on the tenth day, God's will brought John Willford more important work to do than enforcing the quarantine. He had a responsibility greater than the county could confer. He opened the door and walked to the bed in the one room. Each daughter had died in her own time.

One on the third, one on the fourth, and the last on the ninth. Man and wife talked to each other through the window, never discussed the details of the first death or the second, and decided to wait to bury all three together.

He stood before the bed, ready to embrace his daughters, one by one, real duty.

"I've made each of our girls a white dress," said Elizabeth. "And I'll wrap each one in a clean sheet."

She handed him the little white bundle that was their two year old.

He held the bundle in his arms and carried it to the window. He opened the window and handed the two year old through the opening to the sexton who collected bodies for the town. He closed the window. Again. For the six year old. And again. For the eight year old.

The sexton laid each girl in a little pine box and positioned a fitted plank to the top.

"Stop," John Willford called out the window. He stepped through the door and took the hammer from the sexton. "I'll do it."

He nailed each box shut.

All the life created by Elizabeth Tonsil and John Willford Simms had been given up. Suffocated. Elizabeth watched, herself burdened by shallow breaths, as committed to shielding her grief from view as her husband was to hide his love.

John Willford stepped back into the house to his wife. He bent toward her to kiss her before he left. She shook her head, saying nothing. His hands holding her arms below the shoulders felt skin that was warm and damp and told him through the thin fabric that close quarters with a disease rarely fatal to adults had infected her.

Father buried daughters with a prayer, no Bishop Barber to perform the ceremony. He laid each sealed pine box in the family plot next to Grandma and Grandpa, the pioneers who had brought their mother to this merciless land.

Elizabeth Tonsil passed her thirty-third birthday, mother of four children, all buried. Work every day and five years of sickness shrouded the glow of this bright spirited woman. Her low fever became no fever, and the quarantine lifted. She had only him, and she let him into the house. Ever mindful of her weakness and of the grief she never spoke, he held her. She held him. Their lovemaking became very careful, most times holding, locked together almost motionless. Often, he would leave before the holding became intimate. She never asked. She never said no.

He feared the risk taken with each coupling. He feared that his dear family could not survive his loving touch. This, too, John Willford and Elizabeth Tonsil never discussed.

CHAPTER 11:
JULY 24, 1883

Indigo had carried John Willford to Wanship as faithfully as he followed his father's command. She returned him to the new jailhouse as urgently as his fear required. From his father's body, Deputy John Willford Simms had pinned on the family star and became Sheriff Simms.

He had ordered Deputy Orson to find Mayor Eldridge to say an oath, but already he heard someone on the steps. It could have been Woodside back from Wanship. Caution told Sheriff Simms to move into the afternoon shadows against the wall. Orson and Seth Parker formed up behind the light streaming through the window over his father's body. All three waited.

Mayor Eldridge stepped through the door and to the body opposite Orson and Parker. He looked down. Orson and Parker said nothing, and John Willford stepped from the shadows to his father's side. Mayor Eldridge jumped. When he settled, he saw the star on John Willford's chest. Tinged with terror, he screamed, "What're you doing with that on?"

"I'm sending my father with Seth so Mother can bury him. I have work to do."

"A son's work, perhaps, for a dead father, but take off that star," said the mayor. "You know the Edmunds Act don't allow you to hold public office."

"That's my pa, and this is his star," said John Willford. "He doesn't like me to call him Pa, and he doesn't like me to swear. So, I won't tell you what to do with that Edmunds Act."

"Easy now . . . have you read it?" asked Eldridge. "You know it had your father worried."

"No, I haven't read the damn thing," said Sheriff Simms. "It'd be a waste of time, but I could. What I have read is enough to know the government can't pass an ex post facto law. I married my Elizabeths in 1869. That's a long time before last March."

"Not last March, March of '82," Mayor Eldridge corrected. "Those folks in Washington claim the Edmunds Acts dates back to perfect a law passed in 1862, but the Civil War got in the way. Not figuring to rely on that, so they wrote right into the law no punishment for past action. The act punishes a man or even a woman for practicing polygamy, or a man for cohabiting, from the date of the passage of the bill and after. If you stop, you won't be punished for what you did before. So, I know you, and you're not going to abandon one of those two families, but here's where you have a problem. If you continue your ways as a polygamist or cohabiter, you no longer have the right to vote or be elected or hold office."

Sheriff Simms looked at Mayor Eldridge, no longer seeing a banty rooster, seeing only a small man. He took the star by the point in his thumb and forefinger. "This star allows me to hold public office. At least until the election. Now give me the oath."

"It won't do no good," said Mayor Eldridge. "I'm the mayor of this town. Sheriff's a county office."

"Don't give me that bull-pucky. You told my father on Saturday to remember you are a county commissioner. I heard you."

Mayor Eldridge shrugged, threw up his hands. "Aw, hell, I'm a county commissioner, too," he said.

Sheriff Simms cocked his head, trying to understand this behavior. "My father's the sheriff twenty-nine years, the founding sheriff, and you're setting up a problem about me stepping in when he's murdered?"

"Don't get me wrong, John Willford. I've had to deal with a Simms sheriff since I arrived here fourteen years ago. It won't be much different dealing with you. That law says you got no authority unless you stop being a polygamist as of March 23, 1882."

"You mean all I need to do is forget the wife and children. Pick one, and let the rest take the hindmost." He stood over the mayor and quivered. Finally, he raised one hand and pointed at his tormentor. "Two families depend upon me today by virtue of a promise made before God, and no one, you nor anybody else, has a right to ignore that."

The mayor fidgeted and tried to find his words. "I'll swear you in." He stepped far enough away to regain his strength, and then he stamped his foot. "But I'm telling you: you're going to be a fugitive sheriff."

Chapter 12:
July 24, 1883

Sheriff John Willford Simms touched the Simms star. It belonged to the sheriff of Summit County. With slow deliberation, he took a moment to consider the late afternoon sun and turned back around to a full stop in front of the mayor. He bent in close and studied the man's face. "Am I going to have problems with you?"

"Why?" answered the mayor, shoving his chin out. "Because I told you the truth?"

"The truth is my father's dead because of your damned celebration."

"Don't put this on me. This town needed a celebration. Yet, Luke Willford opposed it." Mayor Eldridge stepped up to Sheriff Simms and jutted out his chin. "Because he knew the U.S. marshals were looking for you."

"Are you saying my father put his family before his county? He opposed your damn celebration for selfish reasons?"

"Those are your words. They got the law, and they want to arrest you."

"You'd do to remember that Brigham asked my father to be constable because he wanted somebody he could trust."

"Makes no difference. Brigham could trust you; you still can't be sheriff."

"I am sheriff." John Willford made his proclamation with no physical gestures, an oak of a man, rooted in place.

"Look, John Willford, I'm Latter-day Saint, too. We all are, but it's time we all looked to become American. I know you'll do the right thing. Same as your pa. They're trying to take church property. Even the church will want someone who can look the other way."

"I'll do what's right."

"Sure you will," said the mayor, cooing now. "But that's not the problem. With you arrested, the Utah Commission is apt to produce a U.S. man."

"Damn you, Eldridge." John Willford had watched the mayor try to manipulate his father. He knew the mayor thought he could win his argument by preying on the Simms commitment to do what's right. "That's not where we're going right now. We're going after my father's killer. After all these years and all he's done for this county, that ought to be your first concern."

"You're the one who's talking about doing what's right." Mayor Eldridge sniffed.

"Let them send me to prison, and you leave my father's killer to people who don't care and won't pursue him. Not to mention, you deprive my family of a father. My wives will do fine, but taking away a father is a terrible thing. I know; I had mine murdered. I'll go to jail, and his killer will go free. Is that what you want—to be the one who makes that a fact?"

Mayor Eldridge folded his arms and continued his prim posture. "All I'm saying is go underground. Go to Mexico for all I care, and I'll find a new sheriff."

Sheriff Simms glared at the little man and answered in a whisper. "All I'm saying is we need to bring in Hopt. He killed my father. If your ambition blinds you to what needs to be done, let me spell it out: he needs to atone for it."

Eldridge took a step back and gasped.

"Now, you're talking blood atonement!" Breathless notes of accusation carried his first words. When he caught his breath, Eldridge yelled, "You're gonna kill him!"

"Brigham believed in blood atonement."

"You're planning to be the instrument of blood atonement." The mayor was practically panting at Sheriff Simms. "Even the church doesn't believe in it anymore." He looked around the room—two desks, a bench, and three men. He twisted to place his back to the other two lawmen. He leaned in to Simms and said, "You don't have to be sheriff to do that."

"Sort of depends on you," said John Willford, loud enough for all to hear. "If you swear me in, I'll have to bring him back. Thanks to the man shot because of you, I know what my duty is. You don't swear me in, I'll still have the duty of blood atonement." The sheriff leaned in toward the mayor. "Either way depends on you."

"What about the Edmunds Act?"

"What about it? It has nothing to do with hunting my father's killer."

"The feds'll arrest you. If I try to help you, the Utah Commission will send somebody in to take over. The town won't have a voice in it," said Mayor Eldridge.

John Willford recognized some truth in the mayor's words. That he could no longer vote, be elected, or hold office amounted to little consequence. What with the Utah Commission, it was a rigged deal, anyway. The Edmunds Act allowed a vote for the people picked by the five appointed—not elected—commissioners. The Edmunds Act disenfranchised every past and future voter and current elected official.

He did not like wasting his time. Let the big people back East in Washington, D.C., think there was no sheriff in Summit County. Fact is, they were not thinking about him at all. Except for Park City, there was not enough money in Summit County to command the attention of the commission. No money to be made.

The law denied Sheriff Simms either his calling or his family, and he had no alternative but to ignore it.

"They won't arrest me if you don't get in my way. I'll be so busy bringing in McCormick and Hopt, they'll play Billy Hell finding me. When that's done, we'll deal with it."

"The marshals'll be hunting you all the time, like they're hunting you now."

"To the same result," the sheriff said. "With the good people in this county, I'll be okay."

"If you're counting on legal help from Sol, forget it. What help he can give you won't keep you from going to prison. Best you should bury your pa and do what I said. Go with the Saints who are resettling in Mexico."

Sheriff Simms fingered his star. "Not while I wear this star. It says a Simms is sheriff." He took his watch from his vest pocket and looked at it—three hours to dark. He snapped it shut. "Are you going to swear me in or not? I need to round up the whole gang by the end of October. We're losing sunlight."

"It's not but the end of July. What does sunlight have to do with October?"

"Nothing, if you stop talking before the snow flies."

Sheriff John Willford Simms stepped to the front of the desk where his father lay. Sheriff Luke Willford's hand had fallen to his side. His son took it and held it for a moment before he put it across his father's chest. He opened the top drawer of the desk bearing the dead sheriff and found a Bible. He handed it to Mayor Eldridge.

"My, My," said Mayor Eldridge. "A Bible in his desk. I knew Luke Willford was an elder, but I didn't know he was that religious."

"Get on with it," Sheriff Simms said. His father never discussed his faith with anyone. "One thing's sure—he didn't believe in wasting time."

"Where's the paperwork?" asked Eldridge. "We're gonna need

paperwork."

"I'll sign a blank piece of paper for the county clerk to take care of."

"That's not the way it should be done," said the mayor.

Both men still held the Bible. John Willford shoved it in Eldridge's hands and let go, daring him to drop it.

"Stop wasting time," said the sheriff.

Mayor Eldridge cleared his throat and held the Bible for John Willford's hand.

"I do."

Leaving Eldridge to choke on the unspoken words of the oath, the now sworn-in sheriff turned to his deputies. "Witness my signature. Clive, you take the paper to Rabbi Sol. He'll take it to the clerk."

"Don't you trust me to make it official?" asked the mayor.

Sheriff Simms looked at the mayor and smiled. "Sure do. It's too much running around for a busy man like the mayor."

John Willford took the Bible from Mayor Eldridge and opened the drawer to put it back. He noticed a piece of paper at the bottom and paused to read it. After a moment, he placed the Bible on top of the paper and closed the drawer.

"Best you go back to Mrs. Eldridge, now," he said to the mayor. "Thanks for your good work, but it's done here. It'll be dinner time soon. I'm sure she wants you at home."

"I'm not so sure," said Eldridge. Deputy Orson tittered, and the mayor hastened to add, "I mean, my work's not done—not till I know if you are going to bring him back alive."

The sheriff began to understand why his father was a respecter of authority. He considered telling the mayor where to go, but it turned out best to do the work and be done with it. "Which one?"

"All three," said Eldridge.

"Not for me to decide. I'll bring all three back alive, if they'll let me."

The sheriff turned from the mayor to Seth Parker. Seth's close attention to the swearing-in ceremony would feed gossip the next day at his livery, but Seth's gossip mattered little compared to what they trusted him to do.

"Do you know what my mother wants?"

"Yes, sir, I sure do."

"Then go to it," said John Willford.

"She wants him in the parlor, tonight," said Seth Parker.

"Do it; don't tell me about it." Sheriff Simms watched Parker and Woodside lift the table bearing the sheriff off the desk and carry him to Seth's wagon. His mind played out how to catch the sheriff's murderers and also be around for his father's funeral. He could not do both. He could not let a misstep allow the marshals to deprive him of capturing his father's killers.

First things first. Let the bastards have their start. He would catch them. Let the U.S. marshals stare him in the face. He would get away from them. He would be there at his mother's side to bury his father.

CHAPTER 13:
JULY 24, 1883

Sheriff Simms watched Seth Parker wave the boy aside on the plank seat of the wagon and climb up to take the reins. The wide street seemed barren, few people standing still, no one busy moving from building to building, like any other day. Considering the body of his father lay in the back of the livery's freight wagon on the afternoon of Pioneer Day, he had no idea what he expected to see. He struggled to make sense of it. Parker's hand moved to pull back the reins and he called, "Hold up."

The sheriff turned to his deputies. "You two can lock up. No need staying overnight in an empty jail. I best be with Mother when she receives his body."

"I'm coming with you," said Deputy Woodside.

"I'll sleep here," said Deputy Orson. "I won't be fit company to Mary Beth tonight."

The sheriff and the deputy mounted their horses. Sheriff Simms nodded and Seth Parker began to roll the wagon up Center Street. Deputy Woodside spurred his horse into the lead. Sheriff Simms held Indigo back a moment and slid in behind.

Mary Ann Simms, guided by her own sense, stepped onto the front steps as the bearers approached the family home, built behind the shack that had served her husband's profession, whether cooper or sheriff, until today. She watched the cortege make its stately way up Center Street to a halt in front of her gate at 100 E. She nodded a silent greeting to Seth Parker.

John Willford saw his mother's life pass in review. She had given birth to Luke Willford's child at twenty-one. Not five years later, she followed—in truth, led—his father from a snug cottage in New Mills, Lancashire, to this merciless land. After a year alone in Great Salt Lake City she brought her son to join her husband in the calling Brigham had set upon him. Now sixty, she waited for her Luke, Summit County's Sheriff Luke Willford Simms, to complete his final journey.

Seth motioned John Willford to his side and whispered in his ear. The sheriff nodded. He swung his leg over Indigo's back and stepped through the gate onto the concrete walk his father had poured. He climbed the steps and kissed his mother on the cheek.

"Seth suggests we take the door off in the parlor. He'll use it to bring in Pa and give him a place to rest till he can bring the casket over here."

Dry-eyed, firm chin held above the broad shoulders that gave her son his oaken look, she gave her response in a silent nod.

Woodside and the boy removed the door and carried it outside to transfer the body. Once Seth decided he had Sheriff Luke Willford laid out to his liking, he turned to Mary Ann and said, "I'm sorry, but there are some things I need to know . . ." She stood in her black dress and embroidered white shawl, chin still firm, jaw still clenched. He waited another moment and then resumed. "Would you rather I go to the Bishop? He can plan the funeral."

"No," John Willford answered. He took his mother's hand. "We can make the decisions."

Deputy Woodside whispered in the sheriff's ear. "If you're thinking of going to a funeral, the marshals are gonna know you want to be there."

Sheriff Simms looked at his young deputy. He had already

decided to discard that concern, and the young boy had stepped in to tell him to think about it. Again, Woodside had shown him he kept a mind on what was best for the sheriff.

"Those marshals aren't going to scare me off," Sheriff Simms said. He heard his voice a little too loud and wondered if he alone might have been his intended audience. "They better damn fear for their skin if they try anything at Pa's funeral."

Mary Ann patted her son's hand. She looked and smiled at Deputy Woodside.

"Young man, don't you listen to his bluster," she said. "They're after him, and they'll do what they can."

"Mother," the sheriff protested.

She raised her patting hand and put a finger across his lips.

"I know you think you have to stand up in the face of those marshals bearing down on you," she said. She took the finger from his lips and held his hand in both of hers. "You have a higher obligation. You have your children to consider, and you need to catch the man who killed your father."

"Are you saying I should make myself scarce until I bring in Hopt?"

"Listen to Deputy Woodside." She smiled again, no mirth, cold calm. "We'll have a funeral the marshals can attend. Seth and the Bishop will decide what to do. He'll want it at the Ward, eleven o'clock. I imagine he has already told the Relief Society to set up a meal over here after church. That'll take care of everybody."

She dropped her son's hand and looked at each face around the circle surrounding her husband in the twilight. "These are men we can trust to honor your father's life. Meet us about sun-up at the cemetery. We will bury your father."

Marshal Eire stared into the dusk around eight o'clock. No one had passed through since he took his post after leaving the jail and the dead sheriff. He had been sure someone had found a way to tell the sheriff's son. Eire concluded his target had ridden in from one of the other entrances. Marshal Eire rode his horse over to the east entrance to collect Special Deputy Enos Williams. The two rode to the north entrance.

"Good you're here," said Enoch Williams. The special deputy waved his arm in the direction of the fairground. "Don't figure. Nobody much showed up for the rodeo. I can't understand it. No sign of Deputy Simms."

"Somebody shot the sheriff," said Marshal Eire. "They cancelled everything."

"You told us to stay put. How'd you find out?" asked Enoch.

Eire craned a studied look west of him, all flat and dry with no known trail leading into town. "I thought Deputy Simms would come back through one of us. Appears he didn't. For sure he's in town. Now we have to find him."

"We got to find a place to stay," said Enos. "Too far to go home."

"Right here's as good a place as any," said Enoch. "We could hole up in the stalls."

"Too cold outside, even in July," said Enos. "How about the jail? Those cots may not be the best, but Deputy Simms is bound to go back there."

"Not a bad idea," Marshal Eire said. He spurred his horse into a studied pace and motioned his two special deputies, one on either side, to follow him into town. He saw no one on the street all the way to the jail. The evening's darkness almost complete, Marshal Eire contented himself with the conviction that he had shown a determined U.S. presence to those behind the curtained windows.

"We want to stay here tonight," announced Marshal Eire upon opening the jail door.

Deputy Orson had sat bathed in the light of an oil lamp at

his desk for ten minutes after a young boy brought him word, watching the door for the arrival of the U.S. Marshals. He stayed seated as the two deputies followed the U.S. Marshal into the empty jail. "No, sir."

The marshal settled his feet a little wider than his shoulders. Deputy Orson reached his hands out to each end of the desk and settled into a firm grip.

"Then where'll we stay?" Enoch interrupted the stare-off.

"Go home," said Deputy Orson.

"Four hours?" asked Enos. "Are you nuts?"

"Brother Williams," Deputy Orson's tone and words amounted to a full sentence. His eyes did not leave Marshal Eire. "You're from here. Shame on you. You shouldn't be here."

"Is there a hotel in this town?" asked Marshal Eire. "I'd rather have a bed, anyway."

"The Cluff Hotel," said Orson.

"What do you know about the funeral?" asked Marshal Eire.

"Don't know nothing. Ask the Bishop."

★ ★ ★ ★ ★

III: Hunter

★ ★ ★ ★ ★

Chapter 14:
July 25, 1883

Sheriff Simms peered through the slats in the stall at the empty fairgrounds in the pre-dawn twilight. The wide-open fairgrounds in the north end of town gave the advantage he could hear every approach and see anyone before they saw him. He could be gone, even if someone knew he slept there, before they arrived. He saw no one and little evidence remained of the lunch the Relief Society sisters had piled in to feed the whole county in response to the mayor's plea to create a feast for the all-day celebration. The sisters packed the food on the serving tables at the end of the day and took it to his mother and his two Elizabeths. When he stopped by the night before to say his goodbyes and not-to-worries, he collected provisions enough to last for days. He mentioned nothing about his mother's plan and gave both wives a promise to show up in good health.

"Why can't you stay in this house?" asked Elizabeth Jensen. "You're meant to sleep here. The marshals can prove nothing upon finding you in the house of your first wife."

He felt the sliver of flesh taken, and her clever logic impressed him. "If the marshal took hold of me, it would play mayhem with what I have to do." Sheriff Simms accepted the basket. He leaned in to kiss her. "It's not wise to tell anyone, even you, where I plan to sleep."

"Why not? We're your family. We've a right to know where you sleep," Elizabeth Jensen said, a deep breath raising her shoulders as she turned away. "No matter where it is."

Sheriff Simms took a long moment to respond, then lifted the saddlebag stuffed with food and said, "This'll help me catch Hopt. Kiss the girls."

Sheriff Simms rode Indigo from the fairgrounds into the hills above the town cemetery. He hobbled her, though he had concerns that anyone looking could see her. That the best he could do might not be good enough had never entered his mind before. As he squatted among the juniper and sage and watched civil twilight spread from the foothills behind him into the cemetery, he knew the marshal and his special deputies would now follow every step.

Seth Parker guided his mule through the gate. Man and mule worked together to pull the livery wagon bearing the casket and two boys to the edge of the Simms family plot. Sheriff Simms first met Elizabeth Tonsil's mother and father when, as deputy, he oversaw their burial soon after their arrival. When they met their grandchildren in death, one stillborn and three girls given up to diphtheria, it became the family plot. Now John Willford would escort his father to his place in it. Sheriff Simms prayed it would be twenty years before his mother joined the man she loved and then married in England.

Seth Parker directed the boys to dig the grave in the upper right-hand corner. Digging a hole is hard work, harder when the hole is a grave. The boys showed wet with sweat in the chill dawn mountain air by the time Mary Ann Opshaw Simms arrived.

She had walked up the lane that led from her house out the east end of town to the little canyon where the cemetery nestled. John Willford appeared from the dim of his early morning vigil and reached to take her hand.

"How you doing, Mother?"

She pulled the embroidered white shawl tighter over her black dress and looked at him for a moment. She replied in a voice both quiet and strong, "I had him longer than a lot of women who came here."

Mother and son stood next to the wagon in silence. Seth's boys finished opening the grave. At sunrise, Seth Parker nodded to the sheriff. He stepped away from his mother's side and bent to Seth's whisper. John Willford returned to his mother and took her by the elbow. He guided her to the east end of the grave, where his father's head would lie.

"It's time to lower the casket," he said.

"I want to say a prayer, first," she said.

John Willford waited for her to say her prayer and noticed her head bowed, her hands clasped—a silent prayer. He followed her example. Seth and the two boys stood, heads bowed, at the west end of the grave.

"Do you have any words you want to say?" she asked.

Sheriff John Willford Simms looked away from his mother and squinted into the rising sun, unhappy he had not thought to bring a Bible, because he did not have any words. His father was too big a man, too big a subject, to do justice with but a few words over his grave. "I don't have the words. Maybe someone down the line will be able to do it."

He could see his mother thought a son had to do more. He had to find words.

"Pa always favored the book of Matthew. 'Judge not, that ye be not judged.' He quoted that, and he lived by it. I am going to find it hard to live by that. When he sent me to Wanship yesterday, he told me he knew it was the right thing to do. He quoted Matthew. 'Think not that I am come to destroy the law, . . . I am not come to destroy, but to fulfill.' He even gave me chapter and verse. He wanted to protect my chance to do my job as sheriff. He did that with his life. So, I aim to wear this star for as long as I breathe. And I'm going to find Hopt. It may not be in Matthew, but he'll atone for his deed."

John Willford's mother reached up and kissed him on the cheek. Seth signaled the boys to lower the casket.

Mary Ann Simms took a handful of dirt from the mound of grave diggings and pitched it on the box holding her husband, Sheriff Luke Willford Simms.

"Goodbye, Luke, until we meet again."

Her son, Sheriff John Willford Simms, took a handful of dirt and threw it on the lowered box. He had no more words to say. Mother and son watched the boys close the grave. He turned to his mother. "What are you going to do when the marshals show up this morning to find he's all buried?"

"The marshals?" she asked, mesmerized by the boys making permanent her husband's resting place. Then she turned to her son with full concentration. "I'll tell them the ceremony is for the county. I decided I wanted to bury my husband alone."

No surprise, those words cheered him. The tough pioneer woman who brought him here and nurtured him with her will never surprised him. She would be all right. Sheriff Simms turned and walked away. His mother stayed to oversee the final task—to set the headstone.

Luke Willford Simms

Derbyshire, England, June 16, 1827

Coalville, Utah Territory, July 24, 1883

Cautious in the growing sunlight, Sheriff Simms rode Indigo back to the fairgrounds and left her in the stall. He walked a circuitous mile and half to his jail. The thought, *his jail,* jolted him. He had his star and his jail and not yet sheriff twenty-four hours. He found the door open at his jail. He could smell coffee.

"Clive?" he called, staying out of the line of sight through the door.

"Alone," said the oldest deputy. "But take care, they were here last night."

Sheriff Simms looked behind him; up and down the empty street, only dust eddies blew in swirls, some rising to the height of the buildings, but no people. He stepped through the door and closed it. "Having you around will be a constant reminder of my father."

"Ought to," said Deputy Orson. "With my gray hair and England our common mother."

"Aside from that," said Sheriff Simms, "I was thinking about the coffee. You and Pa both kept the church close, at about arm's length."

"I'm a little closer, but he was close enough for Brigham to make him constable, and he followed the prophet's own teaching on the Word of Wisdom, 'a commandment of God, but the following of it is left, to an extent, with the people.' "

"My attitude," Sheriff Simms nodded toward the pot, "when it comes to hot drinks."

"This coffee's special for you." Deputy Orson pointed to his glass. "My drink is milk. Not sure I know how to make the stuff, but I watched often enough."

Sheriff Simms laughed and poured coffee in a mug. Woodside bounded up the steps and through the door.

"Even with the door closed, I can hear you laughing and smell the coffee halfway down the street," Woodside said. "Don't you know the marshals stayed at the Cluff Hotel last night?"

"How'd you know?" Deputy Orson asked. "I sent 'em there late last night."

"Cluff sent a boy, late," Deputy Woodside said, "to tell me."

"W.W.'s a good man," Sheriff Simms said. "We best set to work, now you're here."

"Ann Cluff said to tell you there'll be a pink curtain in the window when she hears the marshals're about," said Woodside.

He pulled his hat firmer down. "And it ain't but seven."

Sheriff John Willford Simms waved away the unnecessary protest. The young deputy joined Orson and him. The entire police force of Summit County, legacy of his father, stood around the desk in the little office that fronted the three empty cells.

Sheriff Simms put down his coffee mug and opened the drawer. He held up a single sheet of parchment-like paper he had spotted the night before. The printing looked official and ancient at the same time. "Like you said, Clive, Brigham made him constable, but when he sent my father up here to settle the mission, he meant him to be a cooper. With the Walker War, he needed a man he could trust. Pa was twenty-six and didn't know anything about being constable. My guess is he looked to London for guidance. He needed to figure out what to do."

"Coulda done," said Clive Orson. "Nobody'd know. I joined him here right after the legislature made it a county and he became sheriff. Whatever he said was law. It amazed me. It flowed straight out of him, like it was all bottled up, and no end to it."

"At home, too," said John Willford. "His law. Some set of principles seemed to guide him, all the time. I don't know what was the church, what was the Englishman, or what he figured out for himself. He didn't explain much. Turns out he had this in his desk, right under the Bible." The sheriff tacked the piece of paper to the wall. He stepped back with his deputies.

Sir Robert Peel's
Principles of Law Enforcement
1829

"Take your time. I found it. He never mentioned it to me. We don't need to mention it to anybody, neither. Those that visit us here will see what's hanging on the wall."

Sheriff Simms stepped back. Woodside removed the defiant hat and stepped forward to look at the paper. He pointed at one of the principles. "Look at this one."

"You latched onto the same one that caught my eye," said Sheriff Simms.

PRINCIPLE 7: Police, at all times, should maintain a relationship with the public that gives reality to the historic tradition that the police are the public and the public are the police; the police being only members of the public who are paid to give full-time attention to duties which are incumbent on every citizen in the intent of community welfare and existence.

"Might seem like a lot of words," the sheriff said. "But that's what my father believed. The police are the public and the public are the police. All men like us."

Chapter 15:
July 25, 1883

Clatter from the street interrupted. No need to look out the window. "Rabbi Sol, your carriage announced you," Sheriff Simms said from the front door.

"Sol will do," said Rabbi Sol as he made his determined way up the steps.

"Is that proper?" asked Sheriff Simms, holding the door by way of welcome. He recognized purpose in the rabbi's stride.

"The synagogue in Salt Lake will be finished in a couple of months, but it's not mine. I don't have a following," said Sol. He paused at the door, peered through the door frame, then took one more deliberate step inside the jail. "Except for the one I want to talk to you about."

Sheriff Simms thought Rabbi Sol's formal dress, including coat and tie, however rumpled, nothing unusual. He always looked ready to sign a client.

"This an official visit?"

"Can't say." Even in his briefest comments Rabbi Sol sounded hurried and important.

"That sounds official," said Sheriff Simms.

"Not yet. I don't know if I have a client. Not yet. I can't say for sure I have a reason for an official visit . . . Not yet." Sol bit his lip. John Willford bent to close some of the difference in their height. He could see Sol thinking. The sheriff waited to see if the lawyer or the rabbi would speak. "No, when I parse it through that way, I guess I know I don't have any real reason to be here. So, no, it's not an official visit."

Deputy Woodside turned to Deputy Orson and said under his breath, "Parse it through?"

"No. I'm sure of it," Rabbi Sol announced. "My presence here is to try to assist you."

"Assist me? Interesting," said Sheriff Simms. He nodded and made a point of scratching his beardless chin. Simms had plenty of experience not understanding Rabbi Sol, and he felt quite sure that others did, too. "Good that you want to be of help. I was thinking of coming to see if I could spend a night or two in the barn or carriage house or whatever you call it where you keep that cart."

"A man with two houses asks?" Sol answered without hesitation in his style of an ironic question. He smiled at his implied reference. He seemed not sure what to say next and that pause gave him the attention of the three men in the room. "You know, my ancestors knew a lot about how to hide out in the woods. Now don't tell me where you are staying. Don't even tell me when you're coming. Don't take this as an invitation. Don't take this as permission. If you do show up, go in without asking. Should you decide to come and go as you please, you don't need to let me know. Best you didn't, in fact."

Trying to understand that little speech held its audience until Deputy Woodside broke the spell. "Rabbi, would you like some coffee?"

"Thanks, but I remind you, you need not call me rabbi."

"Yes, I do," said Woodside. "I can't call you Sol. I'm not but eighteen, and when I try to pronounce your last name, I'm thinking it sounds like I'm being disrespectful."

"What's disrespectful about calling me Mr. Slonik?"

"There ain't many names like that around here. I'm afraid people will think . . ." Woodside's voice trailed lower, and his words arrived spaced further apart.

". . . You're calling me 'Slow Nick.' That's all right deputy. I've been 'Slow Nick' for as long as I've been Slonik."

"Now that's all taken care of," broke in Sheriff Simms, "I have these deputies to organize. We have somebody to catch."

"That's why I'm here," said Mr. Slonik.

"No doubt!" The sheriff's voice barked in frustration. "Took the long way 'round."

"Not the name, the nature." Sol's face brightened, and his energy reflected moves in known territory. "Wouldn't be a rabbi if I took a straight line."

"But I thought you . . ." Deputy Orson said.

"Never mind, Clive." Sheriff Simms turned to Sol. "Would you mind making your point? We can't spend all morning chatting with you. Woodside and I have a trail to pick up."

"My point exactly. I think your main guy left me a note." Sol paused, appeared to go back inside himself, and then returned. "Or maybe he sent it. Well, doesn't matter. It was under a rock on my doorstep this morning."

"You mean Hopt?" asked Sheriff Simms.

"No, McCormick. He's the one you had in jail."

"Doesn't make him my main guy. He's not the one killed my father."

"Good to know he's not your main guy," said lawyer Sol. "Maybe you should still pursue him first."

"What'd the note say," asked Sheriff Simms.

"That note might have made McCormick my client. I can't divulge what it said."

"Divulge?" whispered Woodside to Orson, loud enough for all to hear. Rabbi-lawyer Sol looked over at the young deputy and half shrugged before he continued.

"If it did make him my client, then what's best for him is for you to apprehend him right away. If it didn't, make him my client that is, then what it says may help you find him and do what you need to do."

Deputy Woodside walked over and lifted the coffee pot off the stove. He muttered, "Apprehend," under his breath and took it to refill the lawyer's mug.

"Rabbi, Sol," he said. "McCormick's some more than a year older'n me, and I know him. It don't surprise me none that he's in a tough spot." The deputy stepped back to the stove, and the lawyer's eyes followed him. "I don't know that it's right he can have somebody like you help him. Don't seem fair. Someday I hope to have a son, and I want him to go to law school. I never heard anybody talk like you talk."

"He does use a lot of words," chuckled Sheriff Simms. "If you listen close, you can hear him telling us without saying it, that note says where McCormick's hiding. Sol also said 'he left it' or 'he sent it.' That means Charlie's involved. My guess is the note says McCormick's at his pa's place again, back on Porcupine Mountain."

Lawyer Sol smiled and adjusted his tie. He even buttoned his coat. Sheriff Simms took all his fidgeting as a sign of wanting to talk. "It's best we tell him Charlie's place was at the top of our list. It's logical."

"Sheriff," protested Deputy Woodside, "ain't it more logical to expect that a body on the run would steer clear of the very place we caught him?"

"There is that." Sheriff Simms nodded in agreement. "Still, you don't want the lawyer in Rabbi Sol to think we went there because of something he told us. It's best to check there first."

"Where's the money?" asked Deputy Orson. "What with the mayor's celebration, Sheriff Simms—I mean your father—never had a chance to hunt for the twenty thousand dollars."

"There's those who say I'm new to this, and finding the money's more important to being sheriff than finding the killer. And there's those who say it's revenge I'm after 'cause it was my pa he killed." Sheriff Simms paused, opened his mouth to talk, stopped before the first words formed, and after another moment said, "Those that don't know what's important won't understand it's Hopt I'm after."

"With all three in custody," said Sol, "one might tell you where the money is. First, apprehend the leader."

Woodside shook his head in a slow back and forth and repeated, "Apprehend?"

The sheriff touched his deputy's arm. "I'll bring McCormick in. He'll know where the money is, but it's Hopt I'm after. That's what sheriff means: hunting down the killer means seeing that justice is served. Those who think I'm only interested in wearing my father's star and taking revenge'll never understand what we were about here, anyway."

Sheriff Simms spotted no one on the street as he watched Rabbi Sol return to his cart. He needed to get the hell out of there before the marshals started sneaking around again. He knew the marshals would grab any Mormon they could charge with cohabiting. And, for sure, the marshals would not admit to sneaking around. But the marshals weren't there to track down a killer, even a sheriff's killer. No money in it.

"Vernon." The sheriff sensed Deputy Woodside arrive next to him as he continued to watch. He talked into the emptiness of the streets as he spoke to his deputy at his side. "It's gonna be hotter'n the hosts of Hell today. Those marshals'll make a bee line right here to the jail, like last night. If they're industrious, they'll make it here soon. If not, they'll show up after the beginning of the heat."

"And you'll be long gone?" The deputy's question carried the tone of a suggestion.

"For sure. That's why you'll need to help and make sure they don't hurt themselves in this dry mountain air."

"What?"

"If you need more information, all you have to do is to ask," Sheriff Simms said with a straight face.

"Ho, boy," said Deputy Woodside. "I worked for your father a month and a day for you, long enough working for a Simms to know not to ask."

"It's good to figure things out for yourself." This time he smiled. "And it's good to know when to ask."

Deputy and sheriff began to turn away from the empty streets, and both spotted the village cart before the noise announced its return trip up Main Street. It clattered to a stop at the foot of the steps.

Sol pressed his foot to the brake lever, the seat moved back across its worm drive, and the leaf springs moved the cart up on its shaft. He had their attention.

"I meant to tell you," called Sol from the bench seat, "but I forgot when I told you about that note. I talked to your father, and I know your troubles. You might say your troubles make it complicated for me. What I can say and what I can't say."

"It's always a lesson to listen to you," said Sheriff Simms. "Lucky the Cluff Hotel's south o' here with all your clatter, but I'm listening."

The lawyer gave the sheriff a quizzical look. "I guess I can tell you what I told your father. Those marshals are acting on their own. Polygamy's a felony. The Fifth Amendment says criminal prosecution must begin by indictment. The marshals have no warrant."

The import of Rabbi Sol's words dawned on Sheriff Simms. "Did my pa know that?"

"He asked. I told him. No grand jury, no warrant." Sheriff Simms made to ask a question, but Rabbi Sol held up a hand and waggled a finger. He took a deep breath. "There's more to it. There's more I told him. The Edmunds Act made cohabita-

109

tion illegal, and it's a misdemeanor. You know what cohabitation is, don't you?"

Sheriff Simms nodded, and Woodside said, "I'm married, and I ain't delicate."

"Wanted to make sure you're following with me," said Sol. "Those marshals can arrest you without an indictment or a warrant for a misdemeanor. It carries a three-hundred-dollar fine. Our law enforcement officers are working for fines."

"You mean the U.S. marshals are bounty hunters?" asked Sheriff Simms.

"That don't seem right," said Deputy Woodside.

"The whole damn thing isn't right, making money that way," said Rabbi Sol, every angle in his face slanted downward. His normal serious look gave way to a frown. "And that's coming from a Jew."

"Fair don't touch it," said Sheriff Simms. His chin jutted out as he repeated his understanding. "My pa knew all of that when he sent me to Wanship?"

"Must have," said Sol. "He asked me about the warrant Monday. To be sure I covered everything, I drove in before the breakfast to tell him even if you're doing nothing but providing support for your wife, a marshal can nab you for cohabitation."

"Nailing a few shingles," muttered Simms. "First, he sent me to work on the house. Then he sent me to Wanship. That explains it."

"May have been my fault. I told him you'd best stay clear," said Sol, nodding in agreement. "Your best bet's not to get too chummy with the marshals."

"No worry about that," said Sheriff Simms. He took a step through the door of the jail and turned around for one last comment. "Because those bounty hunters caused him to send me away, those sons-'o-bitches made it possible for Hopt to kill my father. They best damn well worry I'm gonna go after them."

He noticed Rabbi Sol made a studied effort to roll his eyes. "I know, Pa warned me to stay away. I know that's the sensible bet. I told Woodside to treat 'em with kindness. That way he'll keep good track of them."

Rabbi Sol took a moment to regain his normal unreadable look. "It was in my self-interest to tell you, because I can't afford to let anyone nab you." The tone in his voice gave away what his face meant to hide. He tried to match his tone to his mask. "Fact is, the whole county wants to keep you from being nabbed."

"Not everyone," Woodside said. "Not if they're making money from it."

Rabbi Sol released the lever, and the cart settled. Deputy Woodside and Sheriff Simms watched him maneuver around to the direction out of town, same as ten minutes before.

"Like your father, you'll keep me in business. See you don't end up as my client."

Rabbi Sol's cart receded once again, message delivered. Deputy Woodside opened his mouth to speak. Sheriff Simms shook his head, *no*. He kept the village cart in sight all the way until it followed the slight curve around the bluffs at the north end of town.

"Those two special deputies is from around here," said Woodside upon the sheriff's signal he could speak. "They ought to know how to take care of themselves."

"Don't matter." The sheriff turned back into his jail.

"Kill 'em with kindness." Woodside nodded.

"The more you help, the more they do what you say," said Sheriff Simms. "Besides, he needs your help. That U.S. marshal's from back East somewhere."

"Makes sense he signed two Kamas boys as special deputies," Woodside said. He looked down and scuffed the floor. "It ain't right. Fixin' to make trouble for one o' your own."

"People got to work." Sheriff Simms shrugged. He took off his tan felt hat and wiped the sweat band. "Already too hot. I best move along. Make sure they're taken care of."

"That could have more than one meaning."

"Like I said, there's times when you need to know for yourself. And there's times when you need to ask. Use your good judgment. They might've found a place already, but offer Seth's livery. He'll keep their horses, and he'll talk their ears off for an hour. Also, remind Marshal Eire to stay out of the sun. You can walk him back to sit in the cool of the jailhouse with Orson. 'Course, you don't want to let all this hospitality interfere none in the way of your duties."

Woodside laughed and replied with a touch of his hat.

Simms turned to Deputy Orson. "Clive, no matter how bad you make it, you offer the marshals coffee. Make yourself amenable, but them being U.S., you'd be in the right to tell them not to conduct their business out of our office. Short of that, offer all the cooperation you can. Offer to help when they plan to return. Don't press 'em. Eire might want to keep everything a secret. For the sake of good hospitality, make sure he knows he's invited to the funeral."

"I told him last night to ask the bishop," said Deputy Orson.

"Good man," Sheriff Simms said. "When he shows this morning, be neighborly and tell him you asked the bishop. Let him know the time."

"Yes, sir, I will," said Orson.

"Don't ask too many questions, but listen good to what he wants to tell you." The sheriff walked past Woodside to the gun rack and took hold of his Winchester '73. "He's gonna ask what I'm doing. Tell him I'm catching my pa's killers."

"Oh, I will," Orson said, his anger showing through again.

"And invite him to help," Sheriff Simms said, smiling and

patting the deputy's arm.

"Boss," said Woodside, "don't you think it'd be better to let the marshals visit with Orson and leave me to go with you to bring in McCormick?"

The sheriff picked up shells to load his rifle and answered with eyes held to the front. "Things move fast. Never been called boss before." He continued to press cartridges into his magazine and stopped with five. He put five more in his pocket and left the rest of the box at the base of the gun rack. After all this deliberate motion, he looked to his deputy.

"I think I'll go on out to Porcupine Mountain. You stay here. I think Luke Willford judged you're going to be a real good deputy. He worked awful hard to teach me people judgment, and it looks that way to me. Eire'll figure out you're on the way to being my top deputy. It's good he knows I take him serious."

Sheriff Simms called to Deputy Orson. "Clive, you won't need to stay over tonight. Tomorrow night, neither. Go home to your wife."

"Well, if you want the marshals to help, why don't I bring them to McCormick's?" asked Deputy Woodside, unable to conceal a slight smile.

Sheriff Simms let out a whoop. "Hell, Deputy, you're cheekier than I thought." He laughed a little more at this delicious idea. "Maybe there is something short of that you can find for them to do. Something in town. They won't do it, mind you. Catching the killers doesn't add a penny to their pockets, but it's a good idea to offer."

Sheriff Simms made a move for the door and stopped at the threshold. His settled face showed his certainty. He passed one last word to Woodside. "This ain't Hopt out there. No need to worry about McCormick. You heard Rabbi Sol: there won't be any problems out at Porcupine Mountain. My problem's the marshals. Your best help will be to shake them and meet me at the swimming hole. Then make a big show. Make sure you're seen when you bring him in."

Chapter 16:
July 25, 1883

About eight o'clock, Sheriff Simms crossed Main and dropped in behind the mercantile before he edged around the building to catch a glimpse of the Cluff Hotel, inching his way up until he could see the closed front door and the pink curtain. He told himself to take caution with the conclusion the marshals had not yet emerged. He made his hidden way behind each of the four buildings on Main until he arrived at the last cross street at the north end of town. Seeing no one about, he walked the west side of the road for the last quarter mile to the fairgrounds. Indigo stood in the stall, saddled, and saddlebags filled with the food from the Relief Society sisters.

The sheriff took his own advice. He considered his blue roan in practical terms. He had no choice but to ride her through the heat of the day to do the work of finding McCormick and returning with him. A living being demanded some care, and Indigo had been the gift of his father for his twenty-first birthday. He had more concern for making it back safely with her than with McCormick. Simms followed Chalk Creek, and whenever he found a bit of shade from a decent copse of trees along the side of the creek, he stopped to let Indigo drink.

Turning at Sage Hollow could have saved some few miles, but that would bring him in from west to east. He remembered from Sunday, McCormick's cabin pointed west. He kept going to Turner Hollow and followed it until his senses told him he was less than a mile from the cabin. He pulled the pocket watch from his vest; it was after half past five. He figured he had been about nine hours or more under way, about as fast as walking. Even with a lot of it uphill, he and Indigo had plenty left.

Well below Porcupine Mountain's 12,900-foot peak, he sat on Indigo in the harsh desert, more desert than most of the rest of his county, and thought about time and distance and what to do next. He did not yet feel the chill, but temperatures fall fast in the desert mountain air, not to freezing in July, yet low enough for a fire to be a good companion. He could not see the cabin. That didn't mean the cabin couldn't see a fire. No need to think about the marshals. Tonight, the McCormick boy alone concerned him. If he saw the fire, even if he guessed it to be the sheriff, he was not looking for trouble. He'd be more apt to clear out overnight than to confront Sheriff Simms. That was the problem. Sheriff Simms discarded the idea of a warm fire. He opened some of the food packed by his mother and his two Elizabeths and spread a meal.

Before letting the food lull him to sleep in his warm bedroll as dusk sneaked in, Sheriff Simms thought about the note that had sent him here. Rabbi Sol implied it suggested Lester McCormick hid at his father's cabin. No mention who might be with him, and neither the sheriff nor the deputy had asked. He had assumed he would find McCormick alone, but he didn't know. He believed the gang had scattered with the wind, like before, and not yet found their way back together. Walking in on McCormick would be a lot more dangerous if he had holed up there with his gang. If Charlie sent that note and was at the cabin, things would go a lot smoother.

Sheriff Simms drew the blanket around his neck, his Winchester resting at his side. *Well, I'll find out in the morning.*

Twilight woke Sheriff Simms before dawn broke over the summits that gave his county its name. He tended to Indigo's food and water. The food from his saddlebags, even squashed and cold, tasted good, especially the chocolate cake. He untied Indigo's reins from the sage brush and took a few steps to tie her to the last tree at the edge of a long field. He looked over it. Nothing grew higher than his knees.

There was no sneaking across that field to reach the back of the cabin without being seen. Sheriff Simms knew eyes watched him. He walked standing straight and tall, carrying his rifle in his right hand. Like his father, he didn't like pistols and didn't wear one.

He could smell the chimney smoke. He could hear an axe cutting wood. That answered at least one question, two people were there. As soon as he had his answer, he began to doubt it. Maybe not two; maybe one or more than two?

Simms knelt in the middle of the sage brush. Yonder he saw a larger bush, almost a tree. Mesquite. Not much cover. He knew he was big by way of the average among men, and what covered the ground did not offer enough to cover him. As certain as he knew no trouble faced him, he still knew that catching his father's killers meant following the man's teaching. *No reason to take chances.*

He needed to make his way to the front of the house. He needed to see who was chopping wood. He figured he had one more need: he needed not to be seen.

Charlie McCormick, builder of the cabin, father of Lester, walked around the corner of the house with an axe in his hand. He peered across the expanse of sage brush. Twice. He didn't appear to see what he looked for. Then with his free hand and a noticeable smile, he waved in his unseen visitor. "C'mon in, John Willford, coffee's about ready."

Sheriff Simms put his Winchester to his cheek. He thought he might crawl a little closer. That wasn't any better idea than crawling all the way around to the front of the house. He jumped to his feet, rifle aimed.

"Charlie, drop that axe, and tell Lester I want him out here. Up with your hands, too."

Charlie dropped his axe and raised his hands. He didn't move. "Oh, he'll be out, Deputy."

"Sheriff."

"Of course," said Charlie.

"Thanks to your boy," said Sheriff Simms.

"Now, that's what we want to talk about," said Charlie McCormick. He twisted around to call over his shoulder. "Lester, get on out here. You keep a comin', Sheriff. Like I said, we cooked coffee for you. There ain't gonna be no trouble."

Sheriff Simms began to walk, his Winchester '73 level aimed at Charlie McCormick. With his head locked face front, his eyes roamed as he looked for Lester McCormick. The man who appeared around the side of the house, hands in the air, a boy nineteen years old, stood nose-to-chin taller than his father.

"Nice rifle," said Charlie. "County buy you that?"

"Bought it myself," said Sheriff Simms.

"I heard tell, most any man who can save twenty dollars, can buy one," said Charlie. "Me, I couldn't."

"That why you put your boy to robbing the express?"

Sheriff Simms stood in front of the two men, his rifle still at his shoulder.

"Wasn't my idea," said Charlie. "Now he's done it, he's got to pay for it."

His father's words, *take great care in your people judgment,* rang in John Willford's ears. Something about this might be wrong. He could feel Charlie watching him.

"No trick, Sheriff," said the senior McCormick. "It's a simple matter of my son going to the penitentiary at Sugar House for armed robbery. Don't know how long the judge'll give him, but it beats gettin' shot or hung."

Now it all made sense. Sheriff Simms lowered his rifle from his cheek to his waist, still aimed at the two McCormicks. He wondered if Charlie noticed he breathed some relief.

"You the one put the note on Rabbi Sol's doorstep?"

"Lester's idea. I want you to know that. He reasoned it out for himself. Once he had the idea, I knew the Jew would know what to do. All's I did was leave the note on his stoop."

Caution still called in John Willford's thoughts. He didn't believe it was Lester's idea, and it didn't make much sense to take the son and leave the father here to maraud around.

"I'm gonna take you both in," said Sheriff Simms.

"Too bad about your pa," said Charlie. "He was an Englishman, but damn I liked the way he caught the boy the first time. With a tree stump. Can you beat that?"

"Got him killed," said Sheriff John Willford Simms.

"Wasn't my Lester's doing. That's why he's giving himself up to you without any fight or problem." McCormick was wearing overalls, and his posture exaggerated his farmer act. "Hell, if he'd 'a knowed Hopt was going to shoot your pa, he wouldn't 'a left the jail in the first place."

"He never left it till after they shot my father."

Charlie McCormick took a while, appearing to concentrate on Sheriff Simms's words. He answered in a rush. "My meaning, exactly. Same difference. 'Cept there's no 'they' to it."

"Where's the money?"

"Don't know."

Sheriff Simms turned to Lester.

"Where's the money?"

He shrugged. "Dunno. Out there, somewhere."

"Where's Hopt?"

"Dunno." Lester shrugged again. "Out there, somewhere. I didn't go with him."

Sheriff Simms handcuffed Lester. He looked at Charlie. Some

instinct told him he had put himself in a situation he shouldn't trust all too much.

"Am I going to have problems with you?" Sheriff Simms asked it from the trained-in caution his father had taught, but, once out of his mouth, he knew it changed nothing. He had no handcuffs for Charlie, and Charlie had one available answer, *no.*

"Nope," said Charlie. "Like I said, I'm a whole lot more interested in my boy going away for armed robbery than I am in having him escape to the firing squad."

Sheriff Luke Willford believed that; but, not to take any chances, he pointed his rifle at Charlie and then swung it back toward his horse in the trees.

"Prove it. Go fetch Indigo for me and give me the rope that's on her."

"What for?" asked Charlie.

"Like I said, I'm taking you in."

"What for?" asked Charlie.

"For safety's sake." Sheriff Simms looked around outside the cabin—no rope, not much of anything. "I'll let you go once Lester's behind bars again."

"It ain't respectful to tie a man," Charlie said. "There's no need 'o that."

"Like I said, for safety's sake. Last time your boy was in jail, it got my father killed. I don't aim to see that happen to me."

"Naw, naw. Twarn't no need 'o that, neither," Charlie insisted. "You'll have my boy back in jail tonight. He'll be in state prison in August. Even if the judge gives him twelve years, he'll be back in three, worst, four years to spend Christmas with me."

Sheriff Simms and the two McCormicks in front of him rode to the edge of the gully where East Chalk Creek Road crosses the Chalk Creek on the way into Coalville. A stand of trees around an eddy in the creek created a shady spot around a pool, a nice place to spend a hot July afternoon. The heat of a July day had not brought any of the town's lovebirds for a late-afternoon swim. Empty and not five hours till sunset, no one would wander in for a picnic or a swim now. Today's worst heat had passed. Sheriff Simms waved the McCormicks along the path into the shade of the trees. He had picked it as a safe enough place to wait for Deputy Woodside—lovebirds were not what he looked to avoid.

"Untie me," said Charlie, holding his wrists toward the sheriff. "I'll fetch the food."

Sheriff Simms took his rifle from its scabbard. "It's a good enough idea if I can do it with one hand."

When Woodside arrived, he found Sheriff Simms, rifle in one hand, a biscuit in the other, sitting with the two McCormicks on the little sand beach next to the pool.

"Lucky for us nobody was in a spoonin' mood," said Sheriff Simms, looking up at his deputy. "Unless you cleaned up here earlier."

"I did," said Woodside.

"Thought that might be. Too pretty a day for young people to let pass. Too bad you needed to do that. How's everything in town?"

"Haven't seen the marshals since yesterday." Woodside dismounted and accepted Charlie's silent offer of a sandwich. "Seth told Eire the funeral was at eleven. The Relief Society sisters invited him to lunch after. The mayor insisted all three attend both funeral and lunch."

"He would," Sheriff Simms said. "When you return, put Lester in a cell. Then go find those marshals. Tell Eire you brought him in."

"He didn't track me here, but he ain't stupid," Woodside said. "Even if I didn't see him today, I told you I saw him yesterday."

"That's the right attitude. So far, the marshals have been people other people stay clear of." Sheriff Simms caught himself and laughed. "You can trust for sure Eire's on a quest to make a name for himself. Well, you're taking Lester in, aren't you? So, it's true. For good measure, tell Marshal Eire the whole truth. You found him at the swimming hole. Make sure you listen to what Eire says and tell me."

"Okay. What about the other one?" Woodside pointed at the self-designated host. "Never met him, but that's Lester's Pa, ain't it?"

"Sure is." Sheriff Simms stood. "Charlie, meet Deputy Woodside. He's a year younger than your boy, but a whole lot smarter. He's smart enough not to be the one in the cell when he's sleeping in the jail tonight."

"Good, I'm happy to have a smart one watchin' over my boy."

"That's a start on half your problem," said Woodside. "Need help on the other half?"

Sheriff Simms waved the back of his hand on his way to Indigo. He needed no help to keep secret his plans concerning the marshals.

CHAPTER 17:
JULY 27, 1883

U.S. Marshal J. J. Eire took a problem to bed Thursday in the Cluff Hotel, and it worked on him all night until it woke him Friday morning. He had a territory the size of New England, and he planned to arrest two thousand polygamists. He had been told there were thousands, but he had been a businessman, the owner of his own light fixture store, before his appointment, and he knew numbers as well as nonsense. By his own calculation there were two to four thousand. Maybe that qualified as thousands, but he suspected the estimate of *thousands* served well the political arguments. He was a practical man, and he did not need to inflame anyone. He needed to make money. His cut amounted to seventy-five dollars in fines and a dollar a day maintenance cost for each man in the penitentiary. He knew he could keep men for twenty cents. No need to be greedy; call it two hundred bucks a head. For that kind of money, he had to be shrewd in how he used his time. More than half of the territory's population lived in Salt Lake and the counties surrounding it in the valley. Most polygamists were wealthy or high up in the church or both. All told, Eire calculated more than three-fourths of his potential income lived down there.

Up here, he had a county the size of Rhode Island and maybe a hundred polygamists. Of course, down there or up here, he wasn't going to be arresting any polygamists. Without a warrant, he couldn't earn a cent—a waste of time. Let the U.S. attorney hand him a warrant. For damn sure he'd make the arrest and be happy for the larger fine. Polygamists interested him for one reason—an arrest for cohabiting. It mattered not that men married to one woman, or even single, were doing the same thing. He knew that no judge would levy a fine on a man for enjoying a little extra on the side.

Marshal Eire sat down on the edge of the bed to put on his boots. How to manage this wonderful opportunity in this vast territory? Think of it—four hundred thousand dollars. Lucky that the government had picked a U.S. marshal who could see the business opportunity, and how to solve the sales problem. Create the territories and assign the salesmen. He had hired the Williams brothers into his phalanx of special deputies. He had told the deputy marshals not to be so damn greedy and expand their reach by hiring special deputies, but deputy marshals had done nothing. Eire hired the Williams brothers directly. They lived far away from Salt Lake City, and now he understood how to build a network that covered the entire territory.

Marshal Eire felt convinced his acumen would enable him to organize special deputies to catch a hundred cohabs. *Hundred times three hundred* had a nice ring to it.

That the deputy sheriff target had become the new sheriff bent on hunting down his father's killer complicated matters for the marshal. There were those who thought a U.S. marshal would go after the killer. Lucky that those romantic types did not have any influence on the U.S. attorney who told him what to do. He had his orders: five counties with fifteen hundred polygamists and eighteen with five hundred. Those were his numbers . . . could be double. It suited him fine that some people said there were three times, or even five times, that many. His job was to hire special deputies, and he could hire as many special deputies as he could convince there was money to make from the fines collected. Even if the special deputy had only one arrest, it meant seventy-five dollars and eighty cents a day for six months to Eire. The crux of the matter amounted to finding people who would spy on their neighbors and arrest their brethren for money.

He walked to the door vowing to visit each county every four months to work with his special deputies. He had worked it all out. He stepped back to go over to the mirror above the dresser. Good. He looked like a U.S. marshal. Now, to breakfast and set those Williams brothers to their job so he could go back to Salt Lake.

The Williams brothers sat at the table he had picked on Wednesday, at the window in the northeast corner of the dining room. Marshal Eire checked his watch—seven on the dot. "Best table. We can see the back of the jail from here."

"What do you expect to see?" Enoch asked. "Woodside brought McCormick in last night, and you know the sheriff is out looking for Hopt."

"Maybe," Marshal Eire said while he poured a cup of coffee. "Maybe what Deputy Orson told us about the sheriff wanting him to help us is a bunch of hooey. Like that funeral at eleven on Wednesday. That wasn't no funeral. Just a bunch of unpleasantness with the sheriff's widow. And then Deputy Woodside shows up last night to tell us McCormick's in jail."

"He did say we should keep an eye out in case Hopt tries to break him out again," ventured Enos.

"He knows that's not why we're here," said Eire, pouring coffee into his saucer and blowing it. He put the saucer down and waved Mrs. Cluff to the table.

Enoch sipped hot coffee from his cup and asked, "So what do you want us to do today?"

"I must go back to Salt Lake. I have eighty-five special deputies to worry about." He turned to the waiting Cluff. "Steak, fried eggs, and some of those skillet potatoes you had for dinner last night."

"Same," said Enos.

Enoch watched Eire and, seeing no objection, said, "If the government's paying, me, too."

Marshal Eire resumed. "Tell me what you're going to do so I can return to supervising the rest of Utah Territory."

"You mean about Sheriff Simms," Enoch asked.

"Him and the rest of the county, too. You got another hundred up here, all worth thirty-seven fifty to you. That's three thousand seven hundred fifty bucks you stand to make. Five year's wages. And you can make it in a year, if you're a mind to."

When the food arrived, Enos picked up his knife and cut through the yolk into the steak in front of him. "Something tells me this may be all we'll ever make. A meal off your government allowance."

"Not mine," Eire said. "You're going to have to fill out your own expense report."

"Same difference," Enos said. "How many have you arrested so far? Anybody?"

"That's gonna change." Eire stuffed potato in his mouth and could not talk until he chewed a while. "The deputy marshals didn't know anyone. That's why I decided to hire you special deputies."

"Uh-huh," Enos said while he chewed.

"And we're happy for that," Enoch said.

"So, what's your plan?" Eire asked.

"I'm thinking it doesn't make any sense to watch the jail," Enoch answered. He had cut everything on his plate—eggs, meat, potatoes—with care and had not yet taken a bite. "There's two of us. We'll watch his houses."

"Yeah, great," Enos said, his mouth clear of food. "And let

the other hundred go their own way." He took another forkful of breakfast and chewed it.

Before he could speak again, Marshal Eire repeated, "So, what's your plan?"

"Don't rightly know," Enos said. "But there's two things I do know: we best go after the cohabs that ain't movin' around. That bishop down in Wanship. Everyone knows he's a polygamist. My pa knows of a farmer in Kamas, and I heard tell of a rancher up in Upton. Those are the ones we want." He put more food in his mouth and resumed chewing again.

"We want them all," Eire said as he continued to eat his breakfast. Then he looked up to say, "You said two things."

"I did," Enos answered, and he piled his fork high, then looked at it while he continued. "Wives. Even men tied down are not tied down as much as their wives."

Eire looked at Enos, and his eyes opened. "That's smart. You're something of a snake, but that's smart. That's what the Edmunds Act made possible."

Marshal Eire swallowed and aimed a fork at Enos. "So, how many you figure you can round up by the time I'm back here in three or four months?"

"Don't know," Enos answered. "Even the one's tied down are gonna hide when they see us coming. You'll know as soon as we catch one."

"Might as well start right now," said Enoch. "We can visit both the sheriff's wives before you leave town."

Up at dawn Friday, Sheriff Simms figured he could sneak in an hour in the back of the little yellow house before anyone looked for him, and he could work without fear of anyone coming upon him from behind. Standing high on his ladder, he spotted Mayor Eldridge walk up 50 N long before the mayor arrived at the front of the house.

"John Willford, you there?" he called. "I thought I could hear the hammer."

The sheriff doubted that. He had not swung his hammer since spotting the mayor, but he took it as a caution. This might not be something he should be doing. The sheriff climbed down the ladder. He looked toward his rifle propped at the corner of the house and wondered if he needed it. He left it there and walked around to the front, nodding a silent greeting to the mayor.

"Good work bringing in McCormick," said the mayor. "Where's the money?"

"Woodside brought him in."

"You looking for it?"

"We're looking for Elsemore and Hopt."

Not yet seven and already hot, the mayor loosened his tie. The sheriff, hammer in hand, stood tall and oaken in his overalls. He watched the town mayor, round and soft, fidget in the July sun in his three-piece suit.

"Want to know why I'm here to see you?"

"Aren't we talking about it?"

The mayor thought for a moment. "No . . . well, maybe. You need to know there's some in this town think you're gonna be too interested in tracking down Hopt."

"How can I be too interested in catching my father's killer?"

"Everyone knows you talked blood atonement."

The sheriff considered this little man. In general, his father had taught him to say less rather than more. How did that work with someone who was going to make up what he wanted to, anyway? "If you think catching my father's killer is revenge, then the county's lucky you're not the sheriff." He stopped, but he could not stay stopped. "And blood atonement is what you're talking. Not me."

The mayor opened the lapels of his coat, then flapped them,

and wiped his face with his handkerchief. "Folks don't think you're gonna pay enough attention to recovering the money."

Sheriff Simms made a show of looking up and down his street. "Don't see many folks," he said. "I told you: first, people, then money."

"Well, I don't think you should sneeze at twenty thousand dollars."

"You think I should find the money? And let the killer walk loose until I do? Is that the express company talking?"

"Don't matter." The mayor gave an upward jerk of his nose. "Folks."

"Folks?" From the day his father swore him in as deputy to the moment he pinned on his father's star, John Willford had never had a single thought about being unprepared to be sheriff. "I don't need you to stand up for me. Folks complain, bring 'em on over. I'll hear 'em out." He had also never had a single thought about dealing with Mayor Eldridge. "Been on the job four days, one's already in jail."

Sheriff Simms caught his breath and halted. It would not do to sound boastful. Worse, he was on the verge of explaining himself. "We'll catch all three. Then we'll deal with the money."

"Others don't think it'll do for us to have a sheriff disenfranchised by the U.S. Congress."

"Which camp you in?"

"I want what's best for the town."

"Do you think it best to let those folks in Washington, never been here, tell the county who it should have for sheriff?"

"John Willford, be reasonable. I ain't saying that. I'm saying the law is the law."

"I'm not so sure of that. I need to talk to Rabbi Sol about that."

"What's a Jew got to do with it? You know the Christian thing is to observe the law."

"What I know is Bishop Barber asked me to marry Elizabeth Tonsil . . . fourteen years ago. That Edmunds Act passed last year."

"Don't give me that sanctimonious excuse. I go to priesthood meeting. I know what the president of the church says, and I don't have two wives." With the energy of his righteousness, Mayor Eldridge stretched himself as tall as he could and almost shrieked. "It was lust, pure lust."

Sheriff Simms smiled, with distrust, not with amusement.

"I'm not saying Bishop Barber railroaded me. I admit I fell in love with her."

"And you continue to cohabitate with her."

Sheriff Simms noticed that Mayor Eldridge's sneering emphasis on *cohabitate* meant *fornicate*. He never talked about that with Elizabeth Tonsil. He for damn sure was not going to talk about that with Mayor Eldridge.

The sheriff watched the mayor mistake his silence for victory. Eldridge pulled at his coattails and straightened his tie. Finished, the mayor stood official and resplendent and stared with the full authority of his office at the sheriff.

"Well, you tell those folks not to think too much," Sheriff Simms said in a low, soft voice. He waved the hand that held the hammer around to the right, to point to the house. The mayor ducked. "My father thought it was a fool's errand to build on to this house. He had one kid. I've had eleven, all four with Elizabeth Tonsil dead in their graves. I grant him I doubt I'll ever have any more kids." The sheriff stopped and took a step forward. He stood tall above the mayor, and he leaned lower to bring their eyes closer. "But, gone or not, it's for damn sure, I'm not turning my back. I'd no more deny my dead daughters than I'd deny my calling. I'm the sheriff. I have two families to take care of. I have a killer to catch. I have to do both."

The mayor stepped back. He stretched as if trying to stand as tall as the sheriff. Coming up short, he shrugged. "I'm the mayor, here to do the people's bidding. I can't fire you, and I won't ask the county commissioners to do it, but the federals don't respect your authority."

"Uh-huh," said Sheriff Simms. "The federals get a lot wrong, don't they?"

"Don't be so sure," Mayor Eldridge said, shaking an emphatic *no*. "People around here are apt to see it's best to cooperate with the government. You're gonna be a fugitive sheriff, and it ain't gonna be easy."

John Willford considered the source and his warning and took a deep breath before he spoke. "I didn't ask for easy."

Marshal Eire and his two special deputies finished breakfast and made their way up Main Street, past the jail, and up the hill to visit Elizabeth Jensen Simms in her home.

Long the daughter-in-law of a sheriff and the wife of a deputy, now sheriff, she understood well why her husband had chosen to build their house where he had. She saw the marshals before their horses finished a second step up the hill.

She summoned Anna, their thirteen-year-old daughter, and told her to find her father at the yellow house and tell him the marshals were at her house.

Before the marshals arrived at the steps below her broad front porch, she took to her mirror and made sure she was presentable.

She stood at the top of the steps and waited for the U.S. marshal and his special deputies.

Two hours after the marshals left, Sheriff Simms walked down out of the hills, across the plateau that gave a wide field of vision centered by his house, and into the back door that entered on the kitchen. Elizabeth Jensen Simms, still as combed and tidy as she had made herself for the marshals, stood at her stove.

"I have taken sick." Elizabeth Jensen's words started when the screen door opened and ended before it had closed. "I will confine myself to bed on Sunday."

Tough, even a little unfriendly, John Willford's wife surprised him. "Why? Pa never considered you as close to him as he wanted."

"I have told the children while we waited for you."

"Thanks for sending Anna," John Willford said. "I know the marshals were here."

'Yes," Elizabeth Jensen said into space. "Marshal Eire was the one who had Annie Gallifant in prison."

"Did they threaten you?"

"He told me he let Annie go after one day, and she had the baby four days later," Elizabeth Jensen said. "He also told me he still had Belle Harris in custody, since May."

"Is that why you're sick?" asked Sheriff Simms.

She looked at him, steady and attractive, and disregarded his interruption. "He plans to release her, as soon as he gets back to Salt Lake." She paused. "After he finishes with you."

"So, that's why?" he said with a question, still not understanding.

"Nervous prostration," answered Elizabeth Jensen.

Sheriff Simms had no idea what the words meant or how she knew them. He looked at his wife for an explanation that she left him to find on his own.

Sheriff Simms returned to the yellow house from Elizabeth Jensen's house about noon with a lot of thinking to do. Elizabeth Tonsil opened the kitchen door.

First thing, after registering surprise that she was not at the mercantile, he noticed her light-yellow dress, a reflection of the summer sun itself. The dress contrasted with the workmanlike attitude she displayed as she set a platter of chicken and bread-dough rolls in the shade at the corner of the house. Task completed, she glanced at him watching her and smiled. Without a word, she disappeared back into the house. He picked up the hammer, bent on doing some work. He heard the screen door again. He turned back to see her appear with a pitcher of milk and two glasses. She surveyed everything and raised a finger, as if discovering a thought. Once more, she disappeared through the door. This time she reappeared with a quilt she had made—white background, green trees, and a blue stream.

"Looks like a picnic," he called. "All set with our own stream and shady trees."

"Come here and find out," she challenged him. When she lifted her eyes up to him, he could not help but notice the dress fit snug over her breasts and ribs and waist. She said, "Best I recall, you like fried chicken and bread-dough rolls."

"Dangerous offerings." He turned away from his work and kissed her in the hair. "Better watch out, things could get a bit frisky."

"And men think they're in control," she said.

She bent to spread the picnic next to the stream she had brought. Now he could not help but notice the top two buttons of her yellow dress open and exposing a V of neck and chest.

"You take off work?" he asked, pointing at her dress, trying to find some way to create distance from the warmth she and that dress radiated.

"Lunch break." She showed no hint of the moment being unusual as she settled on the quilt. She took his hand and tugged him into sitting. He complied. "I guess you haven't noticed. I'm a whole lot stronger."

He took a piece of chicken and concentrated on biting into

it. He ate a bread roll and a second piece of chicken and kept trying to think of a subject that would send her off in another direction. He found the subjects of their life all too raw: their dead children or his dead father or what would happen with the marshals or how dangerous it was for him to bring in Hopt. He hit upon one, and his eyes brightened.

"How're things at the co-op?"

She looked at him, her face showing some puzzlement. "You never asked anything about that before."

"I haven't?" he asked, trying best as he could to make light of it. "Well, now I have."

"The mercantile is a co-op, but the members of the co-op don't like each other. Co-op members don't really cooperate very much."

"How so?" he asked. "Isn't everyone trying to save money?"

"Supposed to be," she said. "But it's more like a top-op than a co-op. Everybody's trying to end up on top."

John Willford laughed at her story and her made-up word. She leaned over and bent so her cheek rested in his lap. He ate one more roll and drank the rest of his milk and stroked her hair. Stroking progressed no further than stroking, and after a few minutes, she rose and kissed him. It was a good, deep kiss— one not shared in four years. He made no effort to stop it and stayed with her as long as both took pleasure.

When their kiss ended, he stood. He had noticed before, and he knew now, she was stronger. He recognized her determination to take on anything they faced. Still, the risk of what their love might bring came too early and with too many complications, one of which could be a surprise from the marshals at the moment he least expected it. Determined to take responsibility and hide his concerns, he said, "I better put the ladder away.

Can't trust those Williams boys, and, like I told the mayor this morning, I have a job to do."

Sheriff Simms beat it down to Main Street as fast as he could. He took a careful look and saw no one for more than a mile in either direction, then he hurried down the street and through the screen door of the jailhouse. Deputy Woodside sat at his desk.

"Surprised to see you here." The sheriff's exclamation claimed the tone of criticism.

"Can't leave the place alone." Woodside's wave encompassed the room and the cells before he pointed to the round wall clock. "What's keeping Orson? It's after one o'clock."

"Closer to one thirty." Sheriff Simms had not meant to correct his deputy. He had seen his father look at his pocket watch and correct a person. His mother had pressed the watch into his hand at the graveside. When Woodside called out the time, he looked at his watch. It said different, so he corrected his deputy. "Not that it matters. We can make good use of our time."

"So, what we going to do?" Deputy Woodside showed no awareness of the sheriff's correcting him. Having a Sheriff Simms correct him about time amounted to nothing more than order in the way of things.

"We're going our separate ways. Clive will sit here with the prisoner and the jail. You go after Elsemore."

It never occurred to Simms to ask the deputy if he could do that. If he asked the question, the deputy had to say he could do it. Any other answer, and he could not be the deputy.

"You sending Clive to the judge Wednesday?" asked Woodside.

"Yep. Charlie McCormick figured it out for his boy. The judge rides through on Wednesdays. This year, the first Wednesday happens to be the first of August."

"Sounds like Clive could leave it to Charlie," said Woodside.

"Right down to helping if that crazy Hopt tries to break Lester out again."

"You think he's that crazy?"

"No telling." Sheriff Simms took off his hat and looked deep into it. Not finding the answer there, he hung it and sat behind his desk. He looked full on at his deputy. "Hopt won't matter to the marshals. Anybody thinks a U.S. marshal is going after someone who murdered a Mormon don't know U.S. marshals in Utah Territory. And the marshals won't matter to Hopt. It'd be a surprise to me if he tries it again. If he does, the marshals won't matter to me, neither."

CHAPTER 18:
JULY 29, 1883

"Bring back Elsemore" amounted to explicit direction. As to instruction on how to catch him, Sheriff Simms left it to Deputy Woodside to decide. One thing for sure, it took a lot of legwork and talking and very little riding horses and waving guns. "I'm goin' down to Elsemore's place in Morgan. No need for him to stew about if we're coming after him," Woodside told Simms.

On Sunday morning, the waning moon gave Sheriff Simms little light and sure cover. He risked the direct route down Main Street from the fairgrounds to the jailhouse at five a.m. No way in hell those Williams boys would bestir themselves at this hour. The night's cloudless sky had let all the desert heat escape in that high mountain air, and the temperature dropped to forty. He looked forward to his first cup of coffee. He walked his brisk pace until a glow in the window surprised him as he approached the jail. He peeked in the window.

"You must have been up with the chickens," Deputy Woodside said when Sheriff Simms stepped through the door.

"Me?" Sheriff Simms rejoined. "Where'd you sleep last night?"

"Elsemore flew the coop," replied Woodside. "I came in during the night and told Clive to go home. I think I know where he's gone to."

"Should do," said Sheriff Simms. "That's why you went out there." He lit the kindling in the stove and put the coffee pot on the cast-iron top. He turned from his completed task and faced his deputy. After a moment, he said, "Do you need an invitation?"

"Huh? Uh, n-no," stammered Woodside. "I'm trying to figure out where to begin." Woodside searched another moment to find his starting point. "After I left you Friday, I went home and kissed Angeline and told her I'd be gone a while. I headed down to Elsemore's farm so I could show up first thing Saturday morning. Sure enough, two boys out there hoeing. Six in the morning, doing the work, like McCormick said. The boys petted my horse, and we visited until Mrs. Elsemore shouted them in the house.

"I tried to calm her down. Told her all I'd asked was if their pa was Leonard Elsemore. She went berserk. 'The nerve of you. Who in Sam Hill do you think their pa is?' she screamed."

Woodside, half-nervous, half-laughing, said, "I told her I didn't mean it that way. Well, she stepped right up to my horse and used her broom to scoot those boys. Then she turned to me and said, 'He's out collecting wood, but he'll be back anytime.'

"She acted for all the world like she thought I might try something. That made me wonder why she shushed the two boys. Truth is, I think she's stacking up to be a little smarter than her husband.

"I told her I was glad he'd be back soon and I'd wait. 'Wait all you want,' she said, 'but Leonard had to go way down the canyon. There's no telling when he'll be back with his load.'

"That downright confused me, but I didn't say anything. I told her I'd heard he was a church goer, and I'd be back Sunday. She said, 'I can't promise he'll be here.'

"She didn't need to say that. She knew I knew he wouldn't be there. Well, I didn't want to be, so I left, and I spent the rest of the morning talking to anybody I could. I found two sheepherders. You know Basques run sheep on about sixty thousand acres way back in the hills, above Morgan?"

"Pa knew 'em, the Etcheverrys," said Simms. "How'd the Etcheverrys know Elsemore?"

"They didn't, leastwise, not until they fed him a meal Friday night. He told 'em he'd spent the day collecting wood, and now he had to push on, south, maybe Frisco, the mining town, maybe even further south. He didn't spend the night.

"The sheepherders' story lined up with what McCormick said. Mrs. Elsemore played her role good. She never asked me who I was nor why I was looking for her husband. I decided to talk to her again. This time, she sent the boys to meet me and take me and the bay up to the front door. I couldn't see her anywhere, so I called through the screen. 'The boys tell me Leonard's not at home. But I know he's not down the canyon collecting wood.'

"Mrs. Elsemore spoke through the screen. 'Never was. I didn't trust you. Still don't. But he's gone. To Santa Clara. Told me we have better prospects there. We'll be moving.' "

Sheriff Simms took two gulps of hot coffee and thought about what he had learned. "Clive can take care of the jail. Someone needs to take care of county business. If you go after Elsemore, I can't go after Hopt till you're back. I don't want to wait. Trouble is, McCormick didn't offer any help. My best idea is to cut down where he ain't."

"That'll be the same whenever you start. Leonard might offer some help. He's the one knew Hopt." Woodside took a sip of his coffee. The sheriff sat at his desk, feet up, the emerging light of Sunday morning streaming through the windows, showing him to the street outside. The deputy asked, "Ain't this a little risky, boss?"

"It's okay—long as it turns out. Eldridge's not gonna let the county commissioners pay for another deputy, not as long as I'm sheriff. And we can't leave Orson here alone."

"I'm meaning us sitting here at the jail," said Woodside. "You being the sheriff, it seems logical to look for you here."

Sheriff Simms looked at his surroundings as if it were the first time he noticed he sat in the jail. "Other people told me they don't understand why I can wander about with those marshals looking for me. Fact is, I'm not wandering around. The marshals're never off my mind. I do everything I can to avoid them. And folks around here help me a lot. That what worries you so much?" He pointed to the window. "Not much risk being in front of that window on a Sunday, at six o'clock."

"Being's even the special deputies work for the government, they take their days off." Woodside laughed. Then he sobered and said, "They could surprise you."

"They're not incompetent, not even totally lazy," Sheriff Simms said. "Somebody'll conjure up the idea to surprise someone. Since they're working for fines, it'd be worth working every day, but, like you said, those Williams boys are working for the federal government. The hearing on Wednesday'll bring them, and none of that bunch is around today. We best move things along."

Woodside picked up on the sheriff's direction. "I don't lay much store in Leonard's going to Santa Clara." He rolled his eyes. "She'd not tell a stranger the truth about where he's going. I'm not too good on geography, but the Basques told me south, to Frisco, maybe even further south."

Sheriff Simms walked to the wood stove and put his cup on the hook. "I make your point. You think the Basques would 'a said west."

"That's what I think. South is Frisco, the mining town, down in southern Utah."

Sheriff Simms sat and thought. Woodside had an idea where to look for Elsemore. That had to be better than having no idea at all about where Hopt had gone. Thousands of square miles, and each day Hopt could put more distance between him and justice.

"It'll take a month or more for you to go south and bring Elsemore back." Sheriff Simms heard the lack of energy in his voice. He stopped, took a couple of breaths, and sat still until he resumed with renewed resolve. "If Hopt's in my county, I'll catch him within a month. If he's not, I'll need to go out to catch him. You be back in a month."

"Might be a little short." Woodside put his mug on the wood stove and cleared his throat. "And that means you might catch Hopt before I get back . . . Boss, there's one more thing . . . It's more important than when I get back."

"I'm not sure anything could be more important than when I catch Hopt." Sheriff Simms noticed Woodside settle into a determined stance. It reminded him of how he worked up courage to speak his mind to his father. He nodded and waved his hand, keep going.

"You need to buy a pistol."

"Not something I expected," responded the startled sheriff in an instant. "Who gave you that idea?"

"Your father did. When I woke up this morning."

"I don't know. I'm as fast from my hip with my rifle as I'll ever be with a pistol. And a better shot. Doesn't seem necessary. Pa never had one."

"Not even the day Hopt shot him with one," said Woodside.

"You got me." Damn, he liked the boy. The sheriff nodded his chin up and down in affirmation. He took Woodside by the elbow and walked him out on the front steps to mount his horse. "Go kiss Angeline good-bye." The next time Sheriff Simms expected to see his deputy, he expected to see Elsemore in hand. Only the question of when remained. The sheriff had told Woodside to bring back Elsemore within the month, and both knew that order was a wish. The same as his wish that Hopt had stayed in his county.

Sheriff Simms left the jail and climbed into the hills behind the Jensen house to survey it and the surroundings. The Williams brothers possibly held the same watch, but, confident he could see any threat in time to flee, he crept down the back approach to the house. He gained the porch and inched around to the front. From that high perch he looked down at the jailhouse. If he kept a lookout, no one could surprise him there.

"Mother is in bed." Anna's greeting crushed his hope that Marshal Eire's having left town on Friday would cheer Elizabeth Jensen into changing her decision. "I am now the woman of the house."

"So, she put you in charge?" said Sheriff Simms. "No surprise; she's true to her word. Did she even leave her bed today?"

"Yes, Papa, she dressed and went to Sunday school. Then she went to bed. We didn't see you there."

"Couldn't go. Had work to do."

"On Sunday?"

John Willford heard as much reproach as question in Anna's voice. He paused and decided to respond to neither. "How long's she been back in bed?"

"An hour or so."

Simms felt like he needed permission to see his own wife in his own home in their own bed. That would not do. "Well, fix lunch. I'll go see your mother."

"Oh, I already did. We ate. It's after twelve thirty."

Propped up by pillows, an unopened book next to her, curtains drawn against the bright July day, Elizabeth Jensen offered no greeting when her husband stepped through the door.

"How are you?" he asked.

Her eyes followed him as he approached the bed, but she said nothing.

"Have you taken to silence, as well as to your bed?"

She shook her head, *no.*

"Well, then say something. I wanted to see how you are before I leave."

"No need. It's all done."

"What's all done?"

"Everything."

"That's a help." He waited for more, then asked, "Did you talk to the marshals?"

"When?"

He thought that a curious response. "Again?"

"No."

"Did you talk to Mother?"

"No."

"She'll visit you, I know. Will you talk to her?"

"Yes."

He looked at her. High cheekbones and silken hair, seeming still to have energy and color, after seven children, Elizabeth Jensen remained a very attractive woman. He did not know what to say.

"I have to go after Albert Hopt."

"Yes."

"Are you concerned about him shooting me, too?"

She looked at him and offered no answer, no sign.

"Are you concerned the marshals will catch me?"

Same look, same response.

"Are you concerned the judge will make you testify?"

Same response.

"I can't let the marshals stand in my way."

"Yes."

He stood at the end of her bed, twirling his hat in his hand.

He felt certain he should know some way to discover what ailed her.

"I'll be going now. To take care of that."

"Yes."

Simms wanted to look out the window to spot if anyone approached the house, but the curtains were drawn. He turned to Elizabeth Jensen in the dark shadows and kissed her forehead. "I'll make my own lunch. The girls have eaten."

"Whatever you want to do." Elizabeth Jensen gave her unrequested permission.

Missing her normal, more direct tone in telling him what to do, he wondered if she wanted something from him. "What if I fix you lunch?"

"Whatever you want to do."

"Should I tell the girls to help you?"

"No need for you to ask."

That sounded like a rebuke. Not certain, he said, "I'm not sure what we're talking about."

"We're not talking about anything. Why should we?"

"You want to talk? We'll talk all you want to."

"I'm tired," she said without looking at him. He wondered where she was looking.

"You're tired?"

"I'm tired."

"Haven't you been sleeping?"

"I'm tired of . . ." Silent moments passed until she waved her hand. ". . . all this."

Not sure how all this amounted to more than they had already faced, he felt even less sure what he could do about it. "Well, it'll get better."

"Nervous prostration won't get better," she said.

"We'll go to Salt Lake to a doctor."

"I'll have to get better to go to a doctor."

John Willford suspected he could do nothing to take care of her. He wondered should he be the one to go to the southern end of the state in search of Elsemore. He wondered if rest alone would bring her recovery. If she rested and did not have to think about his dead father and the U.S. marshals and all the work it took to be his wife, would she recover? He kissed her on the same spot and left the bedroom. He couldn't find James and found Anna with the rest of the girls in the kitchen.

"I'll fix my own lunch," he said. "How you faring since your mother took to her bed?"

"We'll take care of her."

Anna said what he expected her to say. She knew the role of the oldest of his five remaining daughters. He approved.

"I'll stop by, best as I can, probably Saturdays," said Simms. "You can always go to the jail and tell Clive, Deputy Orson. He'll find me."

"Word's out about Mama," said Anna. "We know the marshals watch our house. It don't matter much to us. Go catch the man who killed Grandpa. Poke your head in from time to time."

CHAPTER 19:
JULY 30, 1883

Sheriff John Willford Simms felt the need to look over his shoulder, and he felt the need to speed up the hunt for his father's killer. Six days into his calling, and how would he ever measure up to his father—never confused or uncertain about what to do next. He searched his mind for anything to help him find Hopt. And he had a new worry about Elizabeth Jensen. He cast about for what to do. Uncertainty bred confusion, a state he never remembered seeing in his father.

Woodside's message refused his efforts to put it aside. The boy was right. It might even help Elizabeth Jensen if part of her problem arose from concern for him. He doubted that. He could not deny that taking to bed cast her in a bad light in his eyes. He could not deny that he never asked how much of her problem had been his fault.

As the sheriff grappled with the wisdom of his young deputy's plea, he didn't want to shoot anybody, but maybe he should stop at the Coalville Cooperative Mercantile Institution.

Elizabeth Tonsil Simms had barely unlocked the door when she saw him coming. "You've never stopped to see me at work before." She stepped in close next to him. Neither mentioned Sunday's picnic. Both knew she felt a whole lot better. She punched him. "How about lunch today. I'll fix you something you'll like."

Her smile told him what she planned to fix for lunch. He smiled at the thought. It could cause some more confusion, and, worse still, he could do something that might bring risk to her health, not even four years after the diphtheria, not at her age, not while he had his mind set on bringing in Hopt.

"I don't aim to be a sitting duck in case those marshals take it in their mind to look for me at noon," he said. He leaned in and whispered into her hair, "There'll be time."

"The lord works in mysterious ways," she said, holding his hand tight.

"Is Trueman around?" asked John Willford.

"Can I help you?" she asked.

"No," he answered.

She looked at him like he was not telling her everything. After a moment's silence, she shrugged her shoulders and called, "Michael, there's a man here to see you." She stuck out her tongue at John Willford and disappeared behind the counter stacked high with bolts of cloth.

Michael Trueman, owner and butcher, emerged from behind the meat counter, wiping his hands on his apron.

"Well, it's the new sheriff. It's been more'n a week, and I haven't seen you yet. Consolations and congratulations. Hard to know what's the right thing to say, seein's the circumstances about your job, but it is a promotion, so to speak." He paused for a moment. Simms could see he did not want to overstep any bounds, but he was such a good-hearted man, he could not hold back. "I expect that means congratulations are in order."

"No need to say anything," said Sheriff Simms.

"Well, you didn't grace my establishment for nothing. Are you wanting to talk about feeding the jail, prisoners and such, the job your father asked me about before . . . uh, before it opened?"

"First I heard of it. I didn't know anything about that," said Sheriff Simms. "I think I'll leave that to you and Clive. I'm here because my deputy thinks I should buy a pistol. I don't know how to do that, but it can't be too much different from buying a rifle."

"Best pistol to buy right now is that Schofield-Smith and Wesson. Selling like hotcakes. And for cheap since Schofield committed suicide last December. Might could find you one." Michael Trueman shot a look at the Winchester 1873 the sheriff carried. "Otherwise, I have one pistol in stock. A revolver called the Frontier Six Shooter. It's chambered for a .44-40, like that Winchester. You'd have both the same."

"Don't much like the name," said Sheriff Simms. "It would be practical to have it chambered the same as my rifle. How much?"

"Well, it's not been out but since 1878, and I'm not selling you a used one. So, it ain't cheap like the Schofield-Smith and Wesson."

"How much?"

"County paying?"

"Never thought about that. Never thought to ask. Better think I'm paying. How much?"

"Twenty bucks."

"Twenty bucks?" said Sheriff Simms. "That's twice what a pistol ought to cost."

"Don't know about that," said Trueman. "When you get right down to it, it's the same as your rifle, but a pistol. I'll give you the same terms, too."

Sheriff Simms studied the owner of the cooperative and thought about the pistol and the price and the proposition. He wanted to buy the damn thing and think nothing more about it, but he always had the reality of two families to consider. He would be paying off for ten months, and he didn't have a very good handle on how a storekeeper calculated prices. He thought Trueman would be collecting profit for eight of those months, five for sure. He did not begrudge him his profit none. Still, that was a long time, and he had some dangerous and powerful people against him. He had two wives to consider. One saying she was sick, and he wasn't so sure of. One saying she was well, and he wasn't so sure of. If anything happened to him, his debt to Trueman could not go back to his wives.

"I won't bargain your price," said John Willford. "On one condition."

Trueman held up his hand. "If anything happens, one of your wives can bring your pistol back to me, and we're even."

Simms thought again. The man would have five months of profit or even more. If anything happened, it'd be earlier rather than later. Maybe that squared it. He could not figure all the combinations—too complicated. He had never thought about owning a mercantile. Now he was glad of that.

"Depends," said Sheriff Simms. "Maybe best off to sell it."

"Maybe," said Trueman. "You could trust your Elizabeth Tonsil to decide."

"You're right there." Sherriff Simms shook Trueman's hand on the deal. "I'd be gone."

One job squared away before he could leave to hunt for Hopt, two left to do. Sheriff Simms walked to the stone schoolhouse and edged part way through the door.

"Miss Lorimer?" he called.

"How unexpected," she answered, her voice full of delight, as she stood up from her desk. "I didn't think you'd be speaking to me."

Her greeting took him by surprise. "Why's that?"

"Well, in a way, I'm responsible for your father's death."

He stood at the open door and puzzled at her meaning. Understanding kicked in.

"No, no, don't think that, at all. My father always wanted a proper jailhouse; tried for ten years. He liked the one the town fathers dug in the ground over in Parley's Park, but he wanted a proper one for the county."

"It wasn't charitable of me. I put up such a ruckus, him using my schoolhouse as a jail."

"Yes, you did. He might not have seen it so clear from your side, but there's no call to think you're the reason crazy Hopt shot him."

"That is kind of you." Miss Lorimer's response melted into a growing silence as the two looked at each other. She motioned to beckon him all the way in. "I assume you have not come to tell me that."

Sheriff Simms looked around the room. "I'm wondering if you have a dictionary."

"You're wondering if a schoolhouse has a dictionary?" He saw her smile and heard the *Tsk, tsk.* in her voice. "Why, Sheriff, we may be far out in a high mountain desert, but Webster's *American Dictionary of the English Language* rode out with us."

"Can I use it?"

"May I," Miss Lorimer corrected, and she laughed. "For once, I approve of the way my school is used by the sheriff." She pulled a book from a row on the wall behind her desk. "Even better. It's G. & C. Merriam Co.'s edition, *Corrected and Enlarged.*" She pointed to her desk chair and stepped aside. The sheriff flipped the pages until he found "nervous prostration."

In medicine, a latent, not an exhausted, state of the vital energies; great oppression of natural strength and vigor. Prostration is different and distinct from exhaustion; it is analogous to the state of a spring lying under such a weight that it is incapable of action; while exhaustion is analogous to the state of a spring deprived of its elastic powers.

Sheriff Simms turned the book around and beckoned Miss

Lorimer to read it. She finished and looked at him. Hesitating, she said, "I assume this is for Elizabeth Jensen?"

He nodded.

"You might understand more if you talked to her. Better than a dictionary."

"I tried," Sheriff Simms said. He waited a polite moment for Miss Lorimer to say more, then added. "It says it's not as bad as nervous exhaustion. Meaning it could get worse?"

"I think we might know more about this now than we did in . . . let's see." Miss Lorimer looked at the frontispiece of the dictionary. "Oh, 1841. I think, nowadays, doctors may be more apt to call this neurasthenia. If I'm right, it covers many symptoms. It might also include fears, even fear of the future."

"Sounds like nowhere to turn." Sheriff Simms still needed to find some way to deal with this situation, some action he could take. "Is it a real thing?"

"All I know is what I read. I can't answer your questions. Some people consider it a physical illness, even claiming actual loss of strength. Some people believe the nerves have a natural electrical charge of energy which could run down, like the voltaic pile."

"The what?"

"Never mind." Miss Lorimer smiled. "I may have gone a little too far trying to answer whether it's a real thing."

Sheriff Simms stood, shifted his hat to his left hand, and shook Miss Lorimer's hand.

"Thank you." He gave an involuntary shake and frowned. "If you don't mind, now that I know what the book says, I don't know a damn thing."

The sheriff backed out the door and left. He was not sick at heart like he had been when he and Elizabeth Tonsil faced the diphtheria, but he recognized that helpless feeling.

He never forgot those marshals were after him. He tried not

to underestimate anyone. He would never underestimate them, but the marshals posed no more problem than to force him to take a detour when a straight line would do. He planned to have his hands around Hopt's neck, either before Woodside's return with Elsemore or soon thereafter. Time alone measured his certainty. Certainty marked John Willford's view of life, including the certainty he could do nothing to help Elizabeth Jensen.

Sheriff's pay never supported a family, much less two, and now it had to pay for a pistol. An extra job, odd jobs, and sheriff's pay added up to enough for the sheriff's families so long as everyone remembered how to do without. Childless now with Elizabeth Tonsil and her having a job, that family needed no money except for the little he spent rebuilding the yellow house. Some judge would agree with the U.S. marshal. That small amount proved he cohabited. In the sheriff's mind, he spent the money he earned taking care of his first family, Elizabeth Jensen and their six children. Elizabeth Jensen Simms had never worked. When he counted the dollars and cents, her taking to bed needed no extra money. Still, the burden of it felt like the need had grown. The odd jobs he snared from time to time helped, but the silver freight made it possible to meet his family obligations. Steady job and steady pay, the fifteenth of the month, every month, even when the fifteenth fell on a Sunday. Mr. Parley owned the silver freight, and he liked having *Deputy* Simms work for him. He tolerated the interruptions in the shipping schedule caused by the deputy's job. His father's murder and his need to go underground had taken place since the last fifteenth of the month. John Willford had yet to ask if Mr. Parley liked having *Sheriff* Simms work for him.

Sheriff Simms worried some about collecting his pay in the future. Even those Williams boys were good enough to discover he needed this second job. He had no doubt Marshal Eire could sniff it out when he visited town, however infrequent. He shook his shoulders and arms to shiver the worry out of him. He could trust Mr. Parley to handle his pay so he could live up to his bargain with Trueman.

Mr. Parley's hand signal answered John Willford's knock on the open door and beckoned him into the office. No words passed. Parley assumed he knew why Simms was there, and he bent over his stand-up desk to take out a metal box. He made to hand over cash and said, "You know, John Willford, I don't know how much longer this is going to last."

"Whoa," Sheriff Simms said, holding his hands out to stave off the words and the receipt of the cash. "You don't owe me anything. Are you worried I'm going to be more unreliable now that I'm sheriff? Or about something the marshals'll do?"

"Nah." Mr. Parley laughed at the thought, though a little forced. "That ain't it. Who better to drive my freight than the sheriff? Trouble is, railroads should be doing it. That's what the spur line's for. Their greed's the reason we're still hauling up to Echo in a wagon."

"Been going on quite a few years now."

"True, but we still try," Mr. Parley continued, a little tired, half dejected, half apologetic. He looked at the cash in his hand. "Are we up to date?"

Simms nodded.

"I might need you to take some different routes. Maybe that ain't so bad, but, you know, it might end altogether."

Sheriff Simms looked at Mr. Parley, a man coming on close to his father's age. He held steady a moment, then bobbed his chin to show he understood. He pointed to the cash in Mr. Parley's hand.

"When my pay's due, take two dollars over to Trueman at the mercantile. Tell him you'll bring two dollars on the fifteenth, regular. That's what I told him." Sheriff Simms reached to shake. "Do it every payday until you tell me it ends."

Deputy Simms spent his days as deputy walking the streets or riding his blue roan to another town in his county . . . and walking those streets. He counted all the people in his county as friends, and he counted all as help. Now, as sheriff, he needed to know where to find Hopt. He needed friends, and he needed help.

Simms did not even know Hopt's origins. That didn't sit right. It meant Hopt grew up in somebody else's county. He'd as soon the bastard had remained somebody else's problem.

Before he lit out to canvass his county, Sheriff Simms judged his best source of information sat in his own jail. Monday night after dusk had turned to dark, he returned to question Lester McCormick. He sent Clive to round up Charlie. Once more he expected the father to stand over his son and remind him to co-operate, save his life, and take his punishment.

"I'm grateful to your pa for his guidance, here," Sheriff Simms told Lester. "If your pa's expecting something taken off your sentence, you're going to have to tell me more than just that you don't know much."

"I don't, I swear. Hopt told me about the money being there the day I met him, about a week before we did the express office."

"D'ya ever think you'd be alive today for the sole and simple reason Sheriff Simms caught you?" asked Charlie. Simms knew very well the practiced technique of making a statement with a question. The lucky boy had his father around to keep him alive.

"How d'ya figure that?" asked young McCormick, his tone not sounding as cooperative as he was making out to be.

"Hopt might 'a shot you for the money," said Charlie.

"Did he have it?" asked Sheriff Simms.

"Well, I don't," said McCormick. "I'm here, as you can see."

"Sure, he has it," said Charlie, alert to add a further note of cooperation. "He hid it, and he'll stick around to watch over it."

"He'll stick around if he thinks you got it," Sheriff Simms. "That's why he'll stick around. Do you?"

Once again, McCormick shrugged.

"Now I'm thinking he's somewhere around because of you. And you know."

"That sure would be nice," said Charlie, "but he don't know. We're doing the best my boy can do."

Sheriff Simms looked at Charlie McCormick, dressed in overalls and a flannel shirt. As simple as could be. The fact his son sat in that cell proved his cunning. The sheriff turned to the son. "I'd call for some lenience if you gave me Hopt."

Sheriff Simms stopped and called Clive from his desk to the cells. In his loud voice, he told his deputy, "Clive, tell the judge to give him extra because he's hid the money." With a stern look and a hand held up to silence his prisoner's father, he said to Lester, "You can be sure, when you get out, I'll be there to watch you dig it up."

CHAPTER 20:
JULY 31, 1883

Sheriff Simms awoke with the dawn to start scouring his county for his father's murderer. He rode to Summit Park and planned to work his way back talking to people. By the end of Wednesday, he had heard enough of the same answer to believe it. People told him nobody ever heard of Albert Hopt. He told himself he had made progress in narrowing down the vast territory where Hopt could hide. Thursday, he admitted he had taken that long ride to avoid the marshals. He knew the marshals would not look for him out in the county. With that thought, he chided himself for letting the Williams brothers achieve such an influence on his actions. He could have made as much progress in his own jail while he sat and reasoned it out in his mind.

He turned toward home and reasoned while he rode. If Hopt had left the county, he had left somewhere through the northeast end. That ruled out Duchesne and Wasatch Counties. He slept Thursday night against the back wall of Samuel P. Hoyt's grist mill. Before he mounted to leave Hoytsville Friday morning, he thought again that for all the use it did him, he should as well have stayed put. His mind would be wherever he was, and he'd be best off thinking straight. He recalled McCormick's conversation. Now he realized it told him Hopt had stuck around, distant enough to be out of Simms's county, but not far. He trusted Woodside would soon bring Elsemore in to question. If Hopt had hidden in Morgan County, or somewhere else farther away, Elsemore would be a better bet to know than any of these farmers who struggled every day to make a life in the high meadows of Summit County.

Sheriff Simms stood with one hand on Indigo's pommel and marveled at what he had done. So much for standing up to the marshals. He was running like everyone else. Worse still, the marshals he ran from amounted to two hooligans who lived off their father.

On his way into Coalville, he decided to have lunch at the house he shared with Elizabeth Jensen. Four days' work to collect no information amounted to a waste of time caused by the marshals. He realized the lunch decision might be of the same sort. He had to think straight and work at it until he had an answer. Defiance could wait.

Hopt's logic had to be to stay out of the county but close enough to make it back quick. It seemed too far to go north to Idaho Territory, but it didn't take too many smarts to skip out of Summit County into Wyoming Territory. He could keep going east into Uinta County, on to Colorado, already a state.

There was an idea that made sense. A known loner, Hopt had been smart enough to create a contradiction. One rumor had told of Hopt bragging about how he planned to join the Hole-in-the-Wall gang. Putting on airs, boasting, and, like all boasters, trying to make himself bigger than he was, Hopt wanted to deflect attention from a place in the direction of Colorado, Brown's Hole, that had garnered some reputation.

Sheriff Simms had answered the riddle. He stopped looking for any other escape routes. He trusted his instinct, but he did not stop thinking. In fact, now Simms had the advantage. The rustlers and thieves in Brown's Park, as it was now called, had a code—a code that allowed all sorts of outlaw deeds, except one. They drew the line at murder.

The vast, wild terrain of Brown's Park made it a safe place to hide, but Hopt would receive no welcome. He could find many places to hide alone in a lot of territory, and nobody in Brown's Park would raise a hand to help the sheriff, but that was as safe as Hopt had the prospect to be.

Simms second-guessed his certainty. He wanted tangible evidence to make the rumor real. What with maneuvering the marshals, catching McCormick, and sending Woodside to bring in Elsemore, he couldn't deny Hopt's trail had gone cold. He knew someone would look over his shoulder and say, *Catch the killer, and leave McCormick and Elsemore for later.*

Simms thought on it again. He knew the least about Hopt, except for his unpredictable and crazy behavior. McCormick had fallen in his lap because of his father's conviction that life after thirty amounted to a better deal than death at nineteen. Sending Woodside to round up Elsemore added up to his best bet on how to corral Hopt. He had picked up Hopt's trail. He smiled at those who thought tracking meant looking for signs of horses' hooves in the dirt. Tracking meant thinking. He thought he'd done the best he could. Now he was going to find out.

Sheriff Simms made his way from Hoytsville insisting he saw everything clearer in his mind yet knowing the marshals out there hunting him might be warping his judgment some. He had to trust. Nothing about catching Hopt worried him. He needed to know where to go, nothing more. Nothing about eluding the marshals worried him. Be alert. Stay cautious. Keep moving. He had one worry, and she lay in bed.

Sheriff Simms put Indigo in her stall at the fairgrounds and walked down the gully created by the river on the west side of town to the mercantile. Before setting out, he looked at his pocket watch to consider the small chance the marshals would be around town looking for him or anyone else on a Friday afternoon. For a moment, he considered what would happen if those two young boys happened upon him, face to face. He chuckled; near on to three o'clock, those hard-working Williams boys were on their way home.

"I'm here to make sure you're comfortable with the Parley arrangement," Simms said when he found Trueman behind the meat counter.

"Nobody needs to worry about Mr. Parley's credit," said Trueman.

"Parley ain't the one you gave credit to." Sheriff Simms awaited a response, heard none, and considered he had his answer. "In that case, I'll say goodbye to my Elizabeth." He made it a point to tell Elizabeth he would not see her that evening. He promised he would stop by the yellow house next morning.

He stepped onto the wooden sidewalk and breathed in the hot, dry air of an August afternoon. The walk to the little yellow house felt good after days of riding. He had no doubt he could do what needed doing and be gone before Elizabeth Tonsil returned.

To finish this four-year project looked like two hours' work, giving him an easy hour to spare before Elizabeth's return from work. He felt the afternoon cool off. He had been travelling and sleeping outdoors all week, and it made for a pleasant feeling on his skin. Taking advantage of the extra time, he stepped in the house to sit a spell on the sofa and stretched out.

Elizabeth Tonsil found him asleep when she returned from the mercantile. She did not disturb him. Twilight had already brought the cool evening, making for good sleeping weather. She took a quilt from the chest and drew it over them both as she lay down to snuggle next to him. He moved a little but did not wake up. She whispered in his ear, "It's been four years, and I'm stronger again."

CHAPTER 21:
AUGUST 11, 1883

Sheriff Simms chafed against his urgent desire for action. He did not know for sure where Hopt had gone, and he believed Elsemore had valuable information. Sensible enough reason for staying put, but it proved a constant challenge to stay on Hopt's trail in the face of those damn marshals. Every day he woke up and thought it through and made the same decision: take no risks. Last Saturday he skipped hauling the silver freight. Today the obligation to catch up on two weeks of hauling for Mr. Parley demanded action. For certain those Williams boys would not be working on Saturday. He chose not to ask how much of that certainty amounted to wanting to believe.

While sitting on the wagon's bench traveling the scarred trail, Sheriff Simms calculated he could handle all his loads on a Saturday. Once a week he could go twenty-four hours without sleep. He could keep an eye on the marshals, and he had a warning system. The townspeople would tell him. He would not be taking too much of a risk. The trouble with that plan was trouble. Unlike the Williams brothers, it did not take Saturday off. Ask the McCormick gang.

The sheriff finished the load on the silver freight after two o'clock in the afternoon, and, on his return to the mine, he paused at the north end of town. He decided to take the risk to drive the empty wagon the length of Main Street and park it at the jail. Clive Orson jumped when he saw the sheriff walk in the door. He ran to him and shook his hand.

"Whoa," said Sheriff Simms. "What's this all about?"

"You're doing it—everything—and I haven't told anybody about it yet, because you're the sheriff, and you need to be the judge of who to tell what when, but I do think it's all right for me to tell you how well it is all working."

"I think I'm going to have to say it again: what's this all about?"

"Here." Orson pressed a telegram in the sheriff's hands.

Frisco, Utah, August 9, 1883.
Apprehended Elsemore, Johnson's Fort, Monday.
Frisco nearest telegraph.
Home in a week.

"Apprehended, huh? Smart aleck." Sheriff Simms put the telegram on the desk and his hat on the peg. He stepped to the little cupboard that held the basin and began to wash his face. He looked up to smile at Orson. "This'll prove old Charlie McCormick right. The judge gave his boy twelve years because he didn't run. He'll give Elsemore more, wife and kids or no. If Hopt's not in hand before the trial, maybe the judge'll agree to hang Elsemore."

"He can't do that." Orson's startled voice mirrored the look on his face.

The sheriff held tight not to laugh. "Right, of course. The condemned gets to choose."

"No, not that," said Orson with unusual energy for him. "He didn't kill the sheriff."

"I wasn't there," said Sheriff Simms. "Maybe he did."

Deputy Orson screwed up his face in confusion. He made to ask a question, and Sheriff Simms met him with a wet hand held in the air.

" 'Course, I won't be there to testify. I think I'll go out and learn if you can put an accessory before the firing squad, being's

161

the actual killer hasn't been caught."

Orson calmed. Sheriff Simms dried his hands and put his hat on. Visit over.

Four hours later, Sheriff Simms stopped the loaded silver freight at Rabbi Sol's gate. The sheriff walked to the barn and found the village cart. He returned to knock on the front door.

Sol opened the door dressed in a coat and a tie.

"I have a question." Sheriff Simms noticed Rabbi Sol's attire for a late Saturday afternoon; no surprise, no reason to comment. "I'd like a quick answer."

"Good afternoon to you, too." Sol looked at his watch and stepped out onto his porch. "None of your questions have quick answers." He looked over the sheriff's shoulder at the full wagon covered with canvas tied down all around. "Make it fast. In about forty-five minutes, I'm leaving for Salt Lake."

"Why you doing that?" Simms turned around to look at the horizon. "It's almost sundown. You'll be travelling in the dark. Go tomorrow."

"Can't. Tomorrow is the rehearsal for dedicating our first permanent home."

"Home?"

"Shul. Synagogue. Not words I'd expect you to understand. You understand congregation? The Congregation B'nai Israel. The rehearsal's tomorrow, because in a month or so it'll be Rosh Hashanah, and we haven't yet settled on the actual day for the dedication."

Sheriff Simms didn't know which part of what he did not understand to inquire about. He said, "Rosh Hashanah?"

"Jewish New Year," said Sol with a shrug.

"New Year . . . oh, well, I understand that. Why didn't you go today?" asked Sheriff Simms. "You could have spent New Year's Eve celebrating. A beautiful day. Nice day to travel."

Sheriff Simms thought he could see a look flicker across Sol's face. Before he could ask, Sol shot him a wry smile. "Because I wouldn't have been here to answer your question."

"Oh, that's right, my question. We're bringing Elsemore in, meaning Woodside has him, and he'll be here in about a week. If he goes to trial before we catch Hopt, can we ask the county prosecutor to try him for the murder?"

"You ask me that question knowing he's apt to be my client?"

"He's not your client yet, so what's wrong with answering my question?"

"Because if you tried to hurry his trial so you can try him for murder, you know I'd have to oppose that, even if it was your father who was the victim."

"That doesn't surprise me." Sheriff Simms nodded in understanding. "Everybody has a calling. Leastwise, some people. But if we don't have Hopt yet, it's not a matter of hurrying up Elsemore's trial. Without Hopt, we could try Elsemore for murder. Is that about right?"

"That's the main reason I'd have to oppose it. If you had Hopt in custody, you couldn't try my client, assuming Elsemore were my client, for anything more than armed robbery, accessory to murder at most. Worst he'd have to face is fifteen years. Now, I'm out of time."

Sheriff Simms touched his hat in salute and stepped backward off the porch. He walked to the freight wagon, climbed in, and released the brake. He held his foot on the lever to keep the wheel from rolling. He called to Rabbi Sol, still standing in his doorway.

"Best I can tell, you used all those words to say if we have Hopt, we can't try Elsemore for murder. If we don't, we can. Make sure you tell Elsemore that. If he helps me find Hopt, I might have him in custody before Elsemore's tried. That might be in time to save his hide."

CHAPTER 22:
AUGUST 17, 1883

Sheriff Simms decided to make a picnic lunch for Elizabeth Jensen to cheer her up. He could use a little cheering up, too. Waiting weighed heavy since Woodside's telegram. He trusted Erik down at the telegraph office, about the only Scandinavian in the county, and a good LDS convert. Still, somebody might find out. That he expected Woodside to bring in Elsemore was worth money to the marshals.

Despite the risk he took on a Friday, the sheriff made his way up the hill to the house. As he climbed, he thought about how this whole deal with the polygamists amounted to a money circle. The church had money somebody wanted. Somebody— whoever that was—offered money to church members to betray their brethren. A circle . . . and he was in the middle.

Like every day when he returned to his home with Elizabeth Jensen, he stopped to take advantage of the view. He could see the six streets north to south and the four streets east to west that marked off Coalville in its rectangles. Right below him, at the corner of Main and Center, he had a clear view of the jailhouse. When he brought his survey of every house and street to its usual conclusion, he saw two horses in front of the jail. He recognized Woodside's bay. A moment's relief surged. No one ever knew where he was, coming from or going to, and Elizabeth Jensen did not expect him. He promised himself he would tend to her bedside and fix her that picnic later. He scrambled down the hill to the jail.

Woodside, Orson, and Elsemore in his cell all shared the lunch Clive's wife had sent with him. Clive's wife believed her calling in life had been to look after the deputy and his sheriff, first Clive's countryman, Luke Willford, and now the son, Sheriff John Willford.

"Sheriff," called Deputy Orson. "I been expecting young Vernon here for the past two days, so there's plenty of sandwiches. Elsemore took his pick and still enough to feed you."

Orson lifted a platter with three sandwiches left.

"That's a lot of sandwiches," said Simms.

"Not much . . . a little venison, moistened a bit from the bottle of drippings Mary Beth keeps on her stove."

"Well, Mary Beth's bread is always good," said the sheriff. He remembered he had abandoned Elizabeth Jensen's picnic. It made him feel disloyal to Elizabeth Jensen in her bed. "I'm sure it lasts well."

The sheriff walked to Elsemore's cell and chuckled at the two sandwiches piled on the tin plate, one more than half gone. "You're eating better than you have in a long time," he said. "Make the best of it. Vernon'll have you in front of the judge, Wednesday. You'll be eating the territory's food for a long time, maybe until you die."

Confusion played across Elsemore's face. He finished his first sandwich and began to make decent work of the second. Simms stared at him the whole time.

"He asked to see that lawyer, Slonik," said Deputy Orson, mouth half full, stepping up behind the sheriff.

"I imagine he did," said Sheriff Simms, not moving, staring at his prisoner.

Simms held the tension a moment longer and then returned to the front room. He took a venison sandwich, bit into it, and motioned Deputy Orson to his desk.

"Word'll spread Woodside brought him in. You best take care of the jail this afternoon, while I make myself scarce. I'll be back to talk to him in the morning, and I'll watch over the jail." He finished and wiped his hands on his vest. "That way, you can go see Rabbi Sol."

"Does that mean lawyer? Rabbi?" asked Deputy Orson.

"I don't rightly know," said the sheriff. "I thought it meant bishop, but you might have it better. It could mean lawyer or lawgiver, something like that."

"I've seen him around," said Deputy Orson. "But tomorrow's Saturday. Do you think he'll be home?"

"Oh, he'll be home," said Sheriff Simms with a chuckle. "Tell him Elsemore wants to see him, and he'll be along, first thing he can."

CHAPTER 23:
AUGUST 18, 1883

No hardship oppressed Sheriff John Willford Simms. Sleeping in the stall at the fairgrounds or on the ground somewhere in his county posed no burden. He felt the soft, warm air and arose remembering his father taught him the coldest hour of the day greets the sun in its rise. He walked in the bare light before dawn from his stall to the trough to let Indigo drink and to wash his face. It would warm up to a mighty hot day.

Sheriff Simms rode Indigo to the jail a little past six, and, sure enough, Mary Beth Orson had sent over breakfast sandwiches—fried eggs over easy between two pancakes. Deputy Orson offered a glass of milk. "We're going to have to do something about paying Mary Beth," said the sheriff. "Trueman tells me my father was working an arrangement to pay the co-op to take care of the food here."

"Oh, my sakes," said Deputy Orson. "He can't cook. I'd rather eat nothing for free than pay him for something I can't eat. You ever had one of his trail sandwiches?"

The sheriff took a moment to figure out the logic of that sentence and gave up with a chuckle. "Can't say as I have. Like you, my wife's a good cook. If we're going to keep eating your wife's cooking, we're going to have to find a way to pay her."

"You go right ahead and do that, Sheriff, but we're not complaining. All she's doing is feeding me and sometimes you and Woodside."

"If he's not here soon, he'll go hungry." Sheriff Simms took a second fried egg and pancake sandwich.

"Plenty—two left," said Orson. "Elsemore's fed, and I'm finished. When do you want me to go tell Slonik there's a man here wants to talk with him?"

"Anytime you like. He'll be there all day."

"It shouldn't take all that long. I'll be back with lunch."

"No rush." Sheriff Simms smiled at his father's deputy. He turned to call into the area of the cells. "Brother Elsemore. I'm glad to see you here."

"You being funny?"

Simms gave Elsemore an appraising look. Not from the sheriff's county, looked a little soft, his reputation for being lazy seemed right. "Not in my nature. I hear you're a good Latter-day Saint. I figured I best call you by your brotherly name."

"You got something up your sleeve." Elsemore startled as he looked over the sheriff's shoulder and saw Orson leave the jail, closing the door behind him.

"Nothing but my arm," said Simms. "My fists aren't up my sleeve."

"You fixin' to give me a beating?"

"Do I need to?"

"Say, you talk funny. You one of them Saints here from England?"

"Not like the one you shot."

"I didn't shoot him," said Elsemore. "That was Hopt."

Simms waved at the other two cells. "As you can see, he isn't here. You're the killer we've caught."

"I'm no killer. Ask McCormick. You caught him. He'll back me."

"You're right there." Simms could see Elsemore's body relax. "At least about the fact we caught him. He's already at the territorial prison. His Pa thinks he can reduce his sentence if he gives the right evidence."

"Lester wouldn't lie," said Elsemore.

"Steal, but not lie." Sheriff Simms shook his head in his simple disbelief. "Ain't that the thing with LDS outlaws? I wouldn't ask him to lie. He's already said what we know, anyway. He was sitting in jail when you shot the sheriff. As a fact, it was either you or Hopt. Look around—empty cells, either side; we don't have Hopt."

"Look, I told you before, I didn't shoot your—" Elsemore's snarling reply stopped and, after a moment, resumed. ". . . the sheriff. No matter how fancy you say it."

Sheriff Simms nodded, the picture of understanding. He delivered his next words low and agreeable. "So, where're you from, Brother Elsemore?"

"Right here. I was born in Weber City."

"Not my county; that's good," said Simms. "You know, good people live in my county. I wish you hadn't wandered over here and brought your bad deeds."

Elsemore opened and closed his mouth and said nothing. Simms smiled at the certainty his prisoner had not understood what he heard.

"Still, Morgan County's right next door. It's good for the soul to die in the place where you're born. I guess next door's next best."

"I never heard that," said Elsemore. "You fixing to kill me?"

"Yer damn tootin'," snorted Sheriff Simms. "We'll be sure and do it with the firing squad. In case you didn't know, Brother Elsemore, the law in this territory brings you right back here to be executed in the county where you committed your murder. Deputy Woodside—that'd be Brother Woodside to you—will take you to the judge on Wednesday. It's all according to the church. You know the church prescribes blood atonement for what you did."

"But I didn't do nothing. I didn't shoot nobody. That was Hopt."

"Nobody?" repeated Simms with concentration, "Hmmm. The judge can't be sure of that without Hopt before him."

"Well, do your damn job—go catch him!" screamed Elsemore.

"Thanks for the instruction." Sheriff Simms spoke in a voice as soft as his prisoner's was agitated. "I'm of a mind to do that. Whether I do or I don't, I don't care who's shot for shooting my pa. Same as you didn't care." Simms leaned in close to the bar and gave one decisive nod.

"But I did care. I didn't want Hopt to shoot nobody."

"So you say," said Simms. "If I don't catch him before you're sentenced, we're not going to know if you did it or you told him to do it or anything. Fact is, I wasn't even there. All I know is McCormick wasn't there, either, and he says it was you or Hopt. Like I said. Look around. No Hopt. I don't even know where the man is. He didn't go tell any sheepherders where he was going. 'Course, we'll keep looking for him, even after the firing squad takes care of you."

"Well, he told me where he was going," yelled Elsemore.

Sheriff Simms stepped away from the cell and walked to the door of the jail. He opened it and looked up and down the street and walked back to the cell to stand in front of Elsemore.

"I wish Deputy Woodside was here. One of us needs a witness."

"What do you mean by that?"

"You're going to tell me where Hopt said he was going, and I will believe you. Fair enough. But we have a problem. There's no way I can catch him and bring him back by Wednesday unless you tell me he's holed up in Echo at the express office you robbed. If you told me that, I wouldn't believe you, anyway. We're right back where we started."

"Give me a piece of paper," said Elsemore. "I'll write it down, and you can sign that I told you. That'll do it."

"Might at that." Simms stroked his chin with the thought. "That's the first smart thing I ever heard you say. You know, you're right. If we never find Hopt, we can always send you back to the judge. He can give the order to shoot you then."

"Shoot?"

"Blood atonement, Brother Elsemore. Weren't you listening? I told you three separate times. What did you think I was talking about?"

Elsemore faced the sheriff, motionless, his jaws not working to form words.

"Funny," said Simms. "That prospect is thought to concentrate the mind."

"Don't seem right," said Elsemore.

"Neither does murder." Simms could see his prisoner hold onto the bars with each hand and shrink under his gaze. "I'll give you one more idea. You tell me where Hopt is, and you tell me where you hid the money. I'll go find the money and bring it back in time for Brother Woodside to take along with you to the judge."

"I can't." Elsemore's weak voice carried across the cells, near to weeping.

"You can't what?" asked Woodside, joining them at the cell.

"Glad to see you, Deputy," said Sheriff Simms. "Brother Elsemore was saying he can tell us where Hopt is, but he can't tell us where the money is."

"Well, where is he?" asked Woodside. "I'll go get him."

"No, no, that I'm going to do," said Simms. "But that is the question I've been asking."

"You didn't ask me that," said Elsemore.

"I didn't? Are you sure, Brother Elsemore?"

Elsemore took a breath and pulled himself up to a little bigger with his grip on the bars.

"So, where is he?" asked Sheriff Simms.

"We had it all planned to go in opposite directions. He wouldn't say where he was going except he said he had a fancy to go to Flaming Gorge. Hell, he must 'a thought I was stupid. The only thing over there is Brown's Hole."

"It's called Brown's Park nowadays," said Woodside.

"Well, it's the same place," said Elsemore. "And that's where he said he was going."

"Best way to Brown's Park is through Wyoming," said Woodside. "Up to Rock Springs and drop down. Hopt might 'a stayed in Wyoming."

Sheriff Simms nodded and stepped to the cell. He drew in close to his prisoner's face. "Brother Elsemore, you might have saved your hide. My Uncle over to Rock Springs will be a help. Woodside can go with you and tell the judge to hold your execution till I return. If my Uncle Frank and I bring Hopt back here, we'll let the judge decide which one or both of you to shoot. If we can't bring him back, we can shoot you then."

Twenty-five days after the murder of his father, Sheriff Simms had two of the gang in jail and the certain knowledge where to catch Hopt. He spent no more time second-guessing himself. Judging how efficient he had been fell to those who made a business of such judgments but did not make a business of catching killers.

Simms looked at the railroad clock on the wall. "Okay, you know what to do," he said to Woodside. "Hold it down here until Clive returns. Take care of the county while I'm gone. Make sure Elsemore goes before the judge. If I'm back by then, you can take Hopt with him."

With all his urgency to hit the trail, Sheriff Simms had one stop to make. Expectations and loving support were two sides of the same coin, but he wanted his son, James, to know face to face that he trusted the boy to handle his responsibilities.

"Of course, I'm bearing up, Pa," said James. "It was good of you to stop by, but you got better things to do than worry about us."

"All my worries are about you," Sheriff Simms said.

James gave him a funny look that held for a moment. "Well, nothing to worry about." James gave an unexpected laugh. "If you're out of town, not even about the marshals."

James's comment reassured him. Elizabeth Jensen may declare she could not deal with it all. She had that luxury. John Willford had to go after Hopt. Fifteen-year-old James had to take care of his mother. The whole family had to put up with the marshals.

Again, in a moment when he couldn't do it, he remembered he wanted to spend more time with James. Of the seven children with Elizabeth Jensen, he hardly counted two sons, not since John left home. John had decided to make his father dead before his time. Hopt took John Willford's father from him when he was thirty-nine—too young. John Willford still wanted a father around. At fourteen, John had decided to banish him. Something in John Willford's mind demanded that he respect his son's act, if respecting it meant allowing his son to make the wrong decision and go his separate way.

Those thoughts were for another time. Sheriff Simms hurried from the Jensen house to the yellow house in the afternoon. He put his tools away, and, ready to leave, he walked into the kitchen for a drink of water. On the table, he found half a rhubarb pie in its tin, sandwiches, and the other half of the pie wrapped in butcher paper. He smiled. She knew he would not risk seeing her again that day.

Several hours of daylight remained, even more if he pushed on through the twilight. He created a rough map in his mind's eye and followed it to Echo, traced the railroad to Evanston, and imagined the trail to Rock Springs. He had never traveled farther east than Evanston, and he fussed with the thought of what he would find on the way to Rock Springs. He liked to know where he was going before he left. He did know where he was going, but not the trail to follow. He banished doubts from his mind. Fact is, having an uncle there meant he could make it.

Sheriff Simms cleared the north end of town earlier than he expected, time enough to stop in and talk to Rabbi Sol.

"Aren't you the tricky one?" Sol's greeting floated out the open front door before the sheriff's knock.

"Me?"

"Saw your deputy this morning. Told me he'd had Elsemore in your jail since yesterday. Seems Elsemore even asked for me. Of course, your deputy had something to do so he couldn't leave until this morning to tell me."

"Orson's a good man," said Simms. "He makes good judgments that way."

"Right." Sol rolled a nodding assent. "I told him I'd be over to see my client right after sundown. Now you show up. Is that a coincidence, too?"

"In fact, it is," said John Willford. "I'm out to bring in Hopt. Thought I'd ask a question."

"Careful, now," said Sol. "He's apt to be my client, too, you know."

"Yeah, that's always the answer, and that's the question. Can Elsemore and Hopt both be your client?"

"Of course."

"I mean at the same time?"

Slonik stood on his porch and looked at the sheriff and began to smile.

"Oh, I see. You're thinking both can't be tried for murder."

"Not at all. I'm thinking the territory can try both for murder. If it does, can you defend both at the same time?"

"Won't happen. Not if Elsemore's already been sentenced."

"Is that right?" Sheriff Simms looked up and stared into the cloudless, clear blue sky. "Well, let's say give me five or six days to find Hopt and about the same back. I can have him before the judge same time you're trying to get Elsemore off."

"Well, I'm glad to hear you don't plan to shoot him out there . . ."

"That'll be his decision," interrupted Simms.

". . . but what's this about getting Elsemore off? The judge'll give him fifteen years for armed robbery. That's not 'off.' "

"It is to somebody who's going to be dead." Simms brought his look out of the sky and concentrated on Rabbi Sol. "Straight out, is Hopt gonna have reason for all sorts of delays—or worse still, go scot freebecause you traded him to save Elsemore?"

"Well, that's not an argument I'm going to make! For sure," sputtered the lawyer.

"Like I said, I want to know straight out. If you play it so Elsemore beats the firing squad, is that going to help Hopt?"

"I want to do my job," said Slonik. "It's what I promised myself."

"And I want to do mine," said Simms. "I want Hopt shot."

"Making that decision is not your job," said Slonik.

"Depends."

"On what?" Rabbi Sol's voice told Sheriff Simms that the rabbi enjoyed this contentious back and forth much more than the sheriff.

"If it hadn't been for the goddamn U.S. marshals, I would have been there. It would have been in my right to shoot him before he killed my father. And if I didn't shoot him then, for damn sure, I could have shot him as soon as I had him in my sights after he shot my father."

"Maybe." Slonik's voice soothed. "I admit, I would have defended you in that, but now it's different. It's your job to bring him in to let the jury decide and the judge to sentence."

"That's why I want to know what you're going to do with Elsemore. I'd be better off shooting Hopt when he tries to escape, if he's going to find a way to wiggle out of this."

"John Willford, I'm going to do my job." Rabbi Sol did not pose a hard and chiseled counter to the sheriff, but his conviction firmed him up solid. "And you must do your job. If you shoot him unjustly, it'll be a stain on your life, forever."

"If he doesn't face the firing squad," said Sheriff Simms, "that'll be a stain on my life."

Never a man to doubt himself, Sheriff Simms had no doubt about that, either. He thanked his father's way of dealing with him: direct and positive, face up, and move forward. He had tried to do that with his sons. It had half worked. The one who left home over a disagreement never faced up to him to tell him, and, now gone, John would not speak to him. John Willford expected he would never have a son with Elizabeth Tonsil, but he would raise him the same way. You are not a man if you do not face things.

Sheriff Simms rode his certainty five miles and more from Rabbi Sol's house to the old church in Echo that had been a school for three years. Simms trusted Indigo. Like life, she kept going. He expected the old church to be open. Folks did not lock their houses; it seemed foolish to spend money putting locks on schoolhouses. With a good night's rest in shelter, he and Indigo could make the steep grade, the one that needed pusher locomotives, to Wahsatch and then on to Evanston, all in one day.

But no use to lose six good hours of sunshine. He ate some of Elizabeth's pie and rode to the loading dock to find some hay for Indigo and some water to fill his canteen. He would follow Echo Creek for a while. Somewhere up there he would find Aspen Creek and Brown Creek. Indigo would have plenty of water along the way.

Twenty-three miles from Echo to Wahsatch. "Damn near a full one-percent grade all the way," Emma Wilde Carruth had told him. "Twenty percent higher, think 'o that." Now he did. With luck, he might could make it all the way to Wahsatch that night.

He had not been over to see Emma in a while. Damn, that would not do. If Emma Wilde had not been at work, grading the railroad and living in that camp at Wahsatch, Elizabeth Tonsil would not be alive. He aimed never to let his family forget that young girl who saved the Saints foundering in Hilliard. Except he had no family to remind. With his wife thirty-seven, going on thirty-eight, he did not know what to do about that. He wondered if he had already done it. He couldn't think about that and Hopt, too. Emma had given birth to her baby girl last year, and he had not been over to see her but the once. He told himself to go see her after he brought in Hopt.

By dusk, Indigo and Simms made it to Wahsatch. Thank God for dry mountain air that plummets in temperature when the sun starts its downward arc. When every single step is uphill, air that grows cooler as the climb continues is a blessed gift.

On his approach to the water tower and pens, Sheriff Simms spotted Justin Twomley loading his sheep. The sheriff had never paid much attention to sheep. He knew shearing took place in the spring, to give the sheep a little relief during the summer and a little warmth during the winter, but he did not know for sure the best time to sell sheep. The season was coming onto Fall. Seemed like Twomley'd give up some of the wool, but otherwise as good a time as any.

"Hey, Deputy," called Twomley. "Good to see ya. We finished

eating, but we have food. We always have food for you."

"Sheriff, I'm sad to say," Simms said from his saddle on Indigo.

"What happened?" asked Twomley.

"They shot the sheriff," Sheriff Simms said.

"When's that?" asked Twomley. "We been out all summer."

"Pioneer Day."

"Who? The federals?" asked Twomley. "One o' the reasons we stayed out. It's been rough around here on Pioneer Day."

"No, not the federals," said Simms. "A guy named Hopt."

"Albert. He's crazy."

"You're right there. Seen him around?"

"Oh, hell, John Willford," laughed Twomley, "we ain't seen nobody around in a long time. Except you, now that you showed up. How about that food? It's mutton, but it eats good."

"I'm pushing to Evanston tonight," Sheriff Simms said.

"No call to do that. It'll be dark soon." Twomley waved his hands at the twilight that brought the hills right up close. "It ain't but three hours, maybe a little more. Have somethin' good to eat. Get a little sleep. If you're up early, you'll make it there. Plenty of time."

"Sounds mighty tempting. I had nothing but pie so far today; some meat would do good."

"There you go." Twomley reached in his pack, and the look of concentration on his face opened into bright recognition. "You know, Sheriff, we found two lambs killed and butchered right around that time. Maybe three weeks ago. I never thought about Pioneer Day. Could 'a been Bert. He's a hunter. I know everybody around here's supposed to be a hunter, but the one butchered those lambs knew his stuff, right down to their wool and their hooves. Don't know how he carried all he took, if it was him. But the signs didn't look like two had been at it. Whatever way he did it, he has meat for a good long time. In fact, if he ain't done it by now, he's gonna have to find some place to dry it out to keep it all good."

By the time Sheriff Simms set out to find his own place to sleep, he had mutton wrapped in his saddlebag and grain for Indigo. On top of having food enough to see him through to his uncle in Rock Springs, he had the first confirmation he was on the right trail.

Hopt, crazy enough to kill the sheriff in the middle of Pioneer Day breakfast, had the skills to butcher the lambs he killed, and by taking away more than he could eat, appeared to have the confidence he could find somewhere to dry the meat.

Crazy Bert Hopt had a normal streak, and Sheriff Simms knew he would find him.

The sheriff awoke refreshed. Twomley had called it right. Though every direction in those high mountain plains looked uphill, Simms could feel with each step Indigo took what his eyes refused to tell: Wahsatch to Evanston took a downward slope. Horse and man made it to Evanston by eight o'clock, long before the heat.

Sheriff Simms had no business in Evanston, save getting on to the next day's goal, Lyman, further east. Twomley's mutton saved Sheriff Simms the need to shoot, dress, and cook jack rabbits. With the saved time, he hatched a plan to spend but two nights exposed to the cold of an evening in the high plains and the heat of a dry day. With this first stop a little beyond Lyman, he planned to make camp the next night in James Town or Green River and make it to his uncle's house Wednesday, by noon.

"You here about my brother?" Sheriff Simms heard the call a hundred yards out, before he saw anyone. Frank Dewey Simms had stepped onto the front porch and watched the rider approach. Uncle Frank recognized his nephew. Displaying a Simms family trait, he found no need for extra words in his greeting.

"Yes, I am." Sheriff Simms spoke as well as possible, reminded by his uncle's accent that, like his father, Frank still spoke the careful English learned as a boy, not accepting the mountain patois that had overwhelmed the region after the Civil War.

"Do you need help?"

Another family trait. If you needed something, you had to ask for it. Sheriff Simms made a point of stretching tall in his saddle and looking around him. He noticed the neat yard and grass and bushes and trees. Another family trait.

"Do all this alone?" He waved an arm in appreciation over the oasis carved from the dusty high plains.

Uncle Frank considered his nephew for a moment. The sheriff waited and wondered how long since he'd last seen his uncle. Ever since he'd become deputy, twenty-one years now. His uncle would move on to deciding whether his brother had done a good job.

"Had some help. A hand never hurts."

"Could do it alone." Sheriff Simms remained sitting in the saddle of his blue roan, feeling almost like he was talking to his father. "A hand wouldn't hurt."

"Time for lunch?" asked Frank.

"We're going to Brown's Park. You know better than me. What do you think?"

"I think if we leave after lunch, we can be there Friday afternoon."

CHAPTER 24:
AUGUST 22, 1883

Uncle Frank set the course and the pace. Sheriff Simms fell in line behind him. Every Simms family had a Frank Simms. Every Frank Simms knew what he was doing. First thing, Uncle Frank told John Willford he had overshot by coming to Rock Springs.

"Not to join up with you," John Willford said. "You're in Rock Springs."

The younger version of his father held him in his gaze. He disliked contradiction, even when wrong. The tension felt familiar.

"We'll go back about seven or eight miles to a section of Sweetwater County called Purple Sage," Uncle Frank said. "There we'll join the trail and follow it south to Brown's Park, about sixty miles or so." He paused, considered his nephew another moment, and then asked, "Do you know where you're going?"

"Give me Brown's Park, and I'll find the bastard."

"Not so long ago, this part of Utah Territory still belonged to the Utes," said Uncle Frank. " 'Course the Shoshoni might have disagreed. Both had trails leading into Brown's Park, the same trails the white man took. The white men around here were all mountain men until the railroad. We'll take the Wagon Road south; no need to go all the way back to Green River."

Uncle Frank led the way to Little Bitter Creek and turned south, down in his words, but it was up, up to the top of Miller Mountain. Once up there, down Miller Mountain to Sage

Creek. Uncle and nephew travelled in trusting silence, concentrated on the up and down until clear of it.

"We'll be there tomorrow," said Uncle Frank when they set up camp Thursday at dusk. He threw down his bedroll and turned to face his nephew. "You still haven't answered my question. Do you know where you're going?"

"Yes, sir, I did. I'm going where I'll find the bastard who killed my pa."

Close upon his man, the excitement troubled the sheriff's sleep Thursday night over to Friday morning. Sheriff Simms rousted Uncle Frank early. They followed the Green River downstream from Flaming Gorge until their trail opened into a wide basin. Sheriff Simms felt the valley's isolation. "No wonder," he said, "it looks . . ."

An osprey interrupted. It flew in at shoulder height over the water and followed at their pace until it dropped out of the sky into the water and back up with a fish struggling in its talons.

"I was about to say Brown's Park looks brown enough to have earned its name, but that was beautiful. With that river everything should be green, like its name." Sheriff Simms and Indigo continued toward the vast meadow covered with summer brown mountain grass.

Uncle Frank pulled his horse up and held still. "I'd be careful about stepping out there." He pointed. "It's called the Crook Campground."

"Don't look like there's been a crook around for a couple of days or more," Sheriff Simms said. He pointed. "Look at that old homestead over there. Maybe there's someone there."

"It's primitive, I grant you, but that's the Maxon Ranch," said Uncle Frank. He turned around to face his nephew, considered a moment, and gave a slow shake of his head. "Best not poke in at that ranch. And I know you're proud of that star, being my brother's, but out here it might be wise to tuck it away in your pocket."

Sheriff Simms took off his star and pinned it inside his jacket, and the two avoided Maxon Ranch. The trail crossed the stream and rose back up the flanks of Little Mountain among the trees. John Willford followed Uncle Frank through the bristlecone pines, the limber pines over the eastern flank of the mountain, and under the soaring red hoodoos continuing down into the Red Creek Badlands.

True to Uncle Frank's plan, they rode into Brown's Park Friday afternoon with plenty of daylight left. Uncle Frank stopped in a stand of bristlecone pines and pointed.

"The trail follows Red Creek through Richards Gap and then down the canyon. The people around here, being of an original nature, call all that sandstone Red Creek Canyon. It goes right into Brown's Park. Your man did not go any farther than the Red Creek area. To go any farther south, he would have to go without a trail."

Uncle Frank's observation made sense for most of the men Sheriff Simms had brought in as deputy. Most men who found themselves in trouble were somehow lost, shiftless, and often a little lazy. Taking a trail, they stopped when it stopped. Hopt was older, and he had good skills. John Willford also knew Hopt's crazy streak made for the type who would arrive at the end of this barren trail and keep going.

"Over there." Sheriff Simms pulled up and pointed. "Where's that fork go?"

"Being a fork, it goes its separate ways," Uncle Frank said without any change of expression. After a beat, he added, "Both would be in Jesse Ewing Canyon. One fork goes west to Jarvie's Ferry. The other fork goes southeast to Taylor Ranch, maybe further."

At the mouth of the fork, bright yellow evening primrose

grew in the red dirt. The sheriff looked down at the colorful display and said, "Funny thing about a fork, most times it makes some difference which trail you follow." Now he looked at his uncle. "I see four shacks. We'll have to ask."

"You mean to go to each one of those shacks and ask people if they know Albert Hopt?" A Simms for sure, Uncle Frank used a question to make a statement when he disapproved.

"I sure do. Maybe not that way, but if he's around here, somebody would 'a seen him."

"Well, someone might have." Uncle Frank paused, and the correction registered on his nephew. After a moment, he resumed, his tone of voice almost laughing. "Go on, show me how it's done."

John Willford walked to the first shack, holding his hands in front of him. Ten feet from the door, he stopped and called.

"Hey!" Nothing. "Hey." Again nothing. John Willford tried again. "Can you give me some help. I'm lost."

The door of the shack opened, and the barrel of a Henry rifle inched out its full length followed by a man about Uncle Frank's age, his face hidden by a beard that must have grown without interruption since the year he first acquired his Henry rifle.

"Git. Yer lyin'." He waved the rifle in a shooing motion.

"How d'ya make that?" asked John Willford.

"There's two of ya." The man waved his Henry rifle toward Uncle Frank. "And yer too clean." He had nothing more to say. He backed his way into his shack and closed the door.

No better luck followed John Willford at any of the four shacks. Uncle Frank watched and after the last one said, "You must have been a missionary."

"You know better than that," said John Willford. "Been a deputy since I was eighteen."

"Well, you should have been," Uncle Frank laughed. "What now?"

"Nothing to do but pick one of those forks."

Uncle Frank nodded and said, "Like you said, that's the thing about life." He ticked a look toward the forks. "Which one?"

"You said the one goes to the Taylor Ranch. Any of the others lead to people?"

"I don't know for sure. If there's another ranch around, it would surely have a name." Uncle Frank sat in his saddle and looked down each fork as if he could see what lay at the end. "I haven't been here in a while. It might be different."

Slow and in single file, the two rode into the Taylor Ranch. Two hands worked outside taking the harness off a team of horses. This time John Willford took the direct approach.

"Hey, we're looking for somebody. Seen anyone you don't know around here?"

"We don't know much of anybody around here," answered one of the hands.

"What he means," added the other, "is we run the Southern Stage Lines from Green River to Ashley Valley, and we're not from around here."

"Could 'a seen anyone in the past month we been running this line," said the first hand.

Sheriff Simms wondered what had made this fellow so antagonistic.

"There's someone over in Sears Canyon," said the second hand. "Nobody much asks questions around here, so don't mind my partner."

"No offense," said Sheriff Simms. "Tell me more about who's in Sears Canyon."

"He probably ain't your man. He can't be hiding out. That'd be crazy with a big fire. That's how I know he's there. He's either dryin' up somethin' he shot or he's meetin' someone."

"Jesus, Marvin!" exclaimed the first hand.

"I don't wish him no harm," answered Marvin, calm and quiet. "I'm wanting no trouble when we go through there."

Sheriff Simms checked the light, soft, almost blue. Their search had lasted into the last hour of dusk. He asked, "Are you resting the horses so you can make it through, tonight? Or you finished?"

"No need to push," said the first hand. "No passengers. The freight we're hauling makes it there when we do. The Taylors let us bunk here and feed us good in the morning."

"Sounds comfortable," said Uncle Frank.

"That's a family's real good to strangers," said Marvin. "You could stay here if you need a place to stay."

"Thanks for offering the Taylors' hospitality," Sheriff Simms said. "This here's my Uncle Frank. We're on a little hunting trip. We don't so much need a place to stay as we need to know where to find our game. I figure we'll camp in Sears Canyon."

Uncle Frank led the way in the direction of Sears Canyon. Baptiste Brown discovered a good wintering spot and named it Brown's Hole. The explorer who travelled the Green River down to Grand Canyon changed its name to Brown's Park. Sixty-two hundred feet in the midst of massive mountains amounted to a hole. Even that high on the third Friday in August counted as far from winter. Chilly but not cold. No reason for a big fire. On top of that, it had been the better part of three weeks since Twomley had discovered the sheep slaughtered. Sheriff Simms did not expect to see the big fire promised by the stage hand.

Uncle Frank touched his sleeve and pointing out a glow in the distant gloom. "That's more than a mile. He's making one hell of a batch of coals or, like the hand said . . ."

". . . Never heard he knew anyone," interrupted Sheriff Simms, " 'cept Elsemore."

Riding almost to the glow, Uncle Frank reached over and

took Indigo's bridle. He led John Willford to a stand of old bristlecone pine. The reddish-brown bark formed a trunk that rose to twice the height of the two tall Simms men before it gave way to live branches. Not much cover, but, in the dark hours, Uncle Frank gauged it time to secure the horses and take to foot.

"I'd as soon be up here hunting, like you said, or even fishing," Uncle Frank whispered. "Since we're not, I'll take care of this."

"No, you won't." John Willford had a vision of losing his uncle to the man who shot his father. Each stood his ground; each faced the other in silence. Frank made to speak, and John Willford held up his hand. "I'm the sheriff, and he shot my father."

"My brother," Uncle Frank said. "You are not the sheriff in this county. This is Uinta. It won't do to shoot him. I know you're thinking blood atonement, but you already have U.S. marshals after you."

"How do you know that?" asked Sheriff Simms.

"Good God, Nephew," exclaimed Uncle Frank, a little too loud for the risk of discovery. "I know what's going on in my church and in my own family."

The sheriff nodded, then said, "You may know what I'm thinking, but you don't know what he's thinking. And Brigham'd approve."

"Well, you can't know that. What you can know is your father would not approve."

"Now how can you know that?"

"I imagine your father talked to you about Peel's Principles?"

John Willford strained in the gathering dark to see his uncle's face, to read what he knew about that sheet of paper he had discovered when he searched through his father's desk.

"Well, no, he didn't. I found a piece of paper after he died."

"He might not have told you, but he taught you. When Brigham called him, he wanted to do the best job he could. He couldn't apprentice like he had as a cooper, but he tried to learn what he could. It turned out the man who had been asked to do the same job in London came from his hometown, Bury. Your father believed in Peel's ethical force. He would approve of how you found this Hopt. He would not approve of shooting him."

Uncle Frank dropped the bridle of John Willford's blue roan and chortled. "He might handle him a bit rough, I admit. Even if he took him in broken up a bit, he'd still take him in alive for the judge."

John Willford recognized Uncle Frank had given him free rein when he dropped his hold on the bridle. He sat for a moment. Damn it, talking back to Uncle Frank felt like talking back to Luke Willford himself. After a moment, John Willford said, "It depends on Hopt."

"Some, maybe, but not all," said Frank. "I tell you what: I'll bring him in."

"Whoa," said Sheriff Simms. "No, sir."

"He won't shoot me," said Uncle Frank. "He may be crazy enough to try, but he got the drop on your father, or he would not have been able to shoot him."

"I don't want to take that chance," insisted Sheriff Simms.

"I don't even want your gun in your hand." Uncle Frank hissed his whispered command. He shooed his nephew away with both hands. "You go around behind him. That'll put my mind to ease. I know you wouldn't shoot a man in the back."

John Willford judged he needed to sneak about two hundred feet around behind Hopt. Now upon him, after three weeks figuring out where to find him, three days tracking him down, and doing everything under the noses of the marshals, capturing him seemed like something of a letdown. His prey sat feeding small sticks to his fire. John Willford moved in closer, cutting the distance in half, straining to see something of his uncle.

Uncle Frank appeared two steps out of the darkness to the right of Hopt's fire. He announced his presence by touching the muzzle of his repeating rifle to Hopt's temple. It surprised John Willford as much as it surprised Hopt.

Even as he felt something of a letdown in capturing this small man, Sheriff Simms realized he didn't know Hopt. He had never met him before and neither had his uncle. Surrounding and taking prisoner a stranger in Brown's Park, who seemed to be drying meat for winter, required concluding the man who killed Sheriff Simms had killed the lambs and found a cave to keep them cool these last three weeks. Maybe not enough information, maybe wrong, and some people might judge him after the fact, but it all added up to enough information for Sheriff Simms to target this man as his father's killer.

He had made only one promise: to let him live. Sheriff Simms grasped his rifle and began to run, closing the thirty feet with no care for silence. While he ran, he edged his hands from the stock of his Winchester until he held the rifle by its barrel. He angled to arrive at Hopt's left and stopped. His running and his stop added momentum to his swing. He crashed the side of the rifle butt into Hopt's ear.

Chapter 25:
August 26, 1883

Uncle Frank and Sheriff Simms and their hostage started early morning and travelled two full days with one short night to arrive at the turn-off, Rock Springs to the right and Coalville, three days' ride, to the left.

"Will you be okay with this bloke by yourself?" asked Uncle Frank.

"Sure. He don't bother me." Sheriff John Willford looked at Albert Hopt, not tall enough to reach Luke Willford's shoulder or Uncle Frank's chin. "He's a puny little thing, except when he's shooting a pistol at an unarmed man."

"You'll make sure he doesn't escape?" said Uncle Frank, question-statement.

"Don't worry. He won't."

"That is my worry." Uncle Frank turned away from his nephew and spoke to Hopt. "This is not too complicated. You got a knot on your head, but you're not dead. That's good. Where you're going, they'll either shoot you or hang you. That's bad. If you go back without trying to get away, you'll get there alive. That's good. If you try to get away, you'll get there dead. That's bad." He paused for a moment and leaned in close. "Get my drift?"

Hopt nodded. He understood. Uncle Frank had posed the limits of the sheriff's restraint and, at the same time, had given his permission.

Sheriff Simms kept Hopt in handcuffs, and, at night, he set a twist hobble on Hopt's feet. Having but one length of rope, he tied Hopt's horse to it as well. Two birds with one stone, how Daedalus got the feathers. *Where did that thought come from?* His mother, teaching him to read. He made a mental note to visit her with news of Hopt's capture.

Sheriff Simms and his prisoner arrived at the fairgrounds about lunchtime. He had to find Woodside to take Hopt to the jail, and Uncle Frank's warning would mean nothing to Hopt if left alone. Simms looked around the fairgrounds for an idea. He took Hopt into a stall and tied the length of rope to one ankle, around two of the posts, and back down to the other ankle. With his hands cuffed behind him, if Hopt was smart, he could take his comfort in the hay.

"You ain't gonna leave me like this, for Christ's sake," said Hopt.

"You're right." Sheriff Simms took a bandanna from his hip pocket and tied it around Hopt's mouth.

The sheriff mounted Indigo. Before he left, he surveyed the fairgrounds. He could see Hopt's horse in one stall, nothing else. For the moment, Hopt lay still, and the sheriff could hear nothing. *A bad risk to take.* One more precaution—take the horse. The sheriff attached the reins to a rigging dee on his saddle. Taking the route up east of town allowed him to avoid Main Street. The detour took ten minutes to ride to the jail instead of five. It added to the risk with Hopt, but Simms recognized he had returned to his life of choosing between the risks of the hunted and tasks of the hunter. He had been gone two weeks. He couldn't see Ann Cluff's window, and he needed information on the whereabouts of the marshals before he allowed himself to be seen.

The sheriff arrived at the jail and pulled the door closed behind him before he stepped to Woodside's desk. "Go straight to the fairgrounds. Hopt's been there alone about ten minutes.

Fifteen, by the time you make it there. He's tied up and handcuffed, but there's still no telling how much mischief he can get into in fifteen minutes."

"Do you want me to babysit him? Or bring him in?"

"Oh, bring him in, for sure, but make it after dark. I don't want anybody to see him." Sheriff Simms paused for a minute and chuckled. "I'll tell Rabbi Sol I did it for his client's protection. And it'll be true."

Though Sheriff Simms continued to think of them as the Williams boys, he knew their badge and their money interest made the special deputies dangerous to him. He didn't know where they were, and he had things to do. He left Indigo to serve as a decoy at the jail and walked the back way up onto the plateau behind Elizabeth Jensen's house. He completed his detour down out of the hills to find James had done a respectable job and his mother still in bed. Neither a surprise. James had made it clear he would never be the sheriff. He wanted to find some security, even go to Salt Lake. That was all right by John Willford. James had done a respectable job taking care of his mother, and that was enough to ask.

Before he left the Jensen house, Simms surveyed all the streets below. Finding all clear, he walked down the hill, across Main Street, and behind the buildings to the mercantile. He waited until Elizabeth Tonsil emerged at the end of her workday. He called to her from behind and walked her home. After their meal, after dark, in the crisp August evening, he left over her protests. Her pleading was so insistent and so beguiling, he broke a rule and told her he needed to stop by the jail before he slept tonight.

Late of a Friday evening, Sheriff Simms had no worries about the industriousness of the Williams brothers and walked down Main Street to his jail. He continued through the front door, leaving it open against the heat of the evening and against the potential for surprise, to a position in front of Hopt's cell. He stood and looked at the man who had shot his father. Silence and his feelings were enough. He had no desire to speak to someone he planned to shoot.

Uncle Frank had kept him from shooting Hopt twice, once at the campfire and the second time by making Hopt understand his life depended on not trying to escape. Now he had the man behind bars. Being a sheriff in Utah Territory, he had the job to mete out the justice Hopt deserved. He looked forward to that job. He thanked Uncle Frank for making sure he had kept it in his hands. He hoped the bastard would be man enough to choose the firing squad.

Sheriff Simms rose after dawn and walked from his fairgrounds' stall the short distance to Rabbi Sol's house on the outskirts of town at the north end. He opened Sol's gate about seven o'clock.

"There's more business for you, down at the jail," Simms said when the front door opened to his knock.

"Something funny about your jail," said Sol. "Nobody ever seems to end up there except on a Friday night. Your father's jail never seemed to have that problem."

"Well, it's Friday morning, and, more to the point, nobody ever ended up in my father's jail . . . but once."

"You know what I mean," said Sol. "Are you here to tell me you have Hopt in custody?"

"I do."

"Where'd you find him?"

"Brown's Park."

"Brown's Park," repeated Sol. "I haven't been out here as long as you, but I don't think that's in Summit County."

"Uinta County."

"Show me the paperwork," said Sol.

"Hot pursuit."

"It's going on two months," said Sol.

"Hot pursuit," repeated Sheriff Simms. "And barely past a month."

"That won't work," said Sol. "It pains me to tell you this, but he'll walk out of the courthouse on Wednesday."

"Onto the streets of Coalville." Sheriff Simms let his words hang a moment before he continued, with no emphasis. "The county seat of Summit County."

The two adversaries let the silence drag for a few moments. Each knew the first who spoke, lost. Sheriff Simms shrugged, considering both had won their point.

"When should I tell your client you're coming."

Sol laughed. "Well, for once, it'll be today."

CHAPTER 26:
SEPTEMBER 5, 1883

At dusk, Woodside walked his bay through the gate into the center of the rodeo ground. He held his horse still and waited. The sheriff came out through one of the chutes behind him.

"Boss, you caught Hopt with those marshals bearing down on you, and that's a blessing, but they're still bearing down on you," Woodside said without looking around. "You pretty much made this home since Pioneer Day. It ain't like folks don't know where you sleep."

"I've been considering that," said Sheriff Simms. He scuffed his boots in the turf as he walked around the deputy to stand in front of him and his horse. "The more people know where I sleep, the more it takes relying on them. That includes some best not relied on."

"You can stay with me. Weren't for your pa, Angeline and me never could 'a married. Everybody thought we was too young. Sheriff Simms gave me a job, and that way we could be married. She'd be happy to accommodate you."

"I remember that happy event," said Sheriff Simms. "You married that little Thomas girl, not a week after he made you deputy."

"Like I said."

Sheriff Simms raised his eyes in doubt. "Folks'd catch wind of that, too."

"The problem ain't folks knowing where you sleep." Woodside leaned toward the sheriff and gestured with his hands.

196

"Problem's with folks knowing when you sleep there. Your houses, the fairgrounds, and now me: take your pick of four places. Don't tell anybody, not even me, not even when you stay with Angeline and me. That would afford you some protection. And, I don't mind saying, give me some peace of mind."

The deputy seemed larger, and the dusk made him seem closer. Thoughts about his father flooded the sheriff's mind. Luke Willford had done the boy a favor, yet Woodside had not made the offer as repayment of a favor. The boy had no more qualifications to be deputy than he needed a job so he could marry his sweetheart. His father saw a young man who could think through a serious problem and arrive at a solution that worked.

"That's a fine idea, Deputy," said Sheriff Simms. "I'll sleep over at your house, tonight. Thank you. Don't know when I'll sleep with you again, but when I do, I'll let you know. Maybe I best give you a day's notice for Angeline? I don't want to burden her."

"Best not," said Woodside. "Be more of a burden her taking care not to say anything."

"Good," said the sheriff. "Now, what happened today with the judge?"

"You were right about Elsemore. The judge gave him fifteen years, three more than McCormick. He didn't even notice. He was so happy to see Hopt there. Rabbi Sol told the judge it was fortunate to hold Elsemore's hearing over until today. Don't know what *fortunate* meant, but nobody talked about the death sentence for Elsemore."

The sheriff hooked his thumbs in his denims and kicked the turf again and said "Uh-huh." He left the sitting deputy and when he returned with Indigo, he asked, "Did the judge let Rabbi Sol do the lawyering for both Elsemore and Hopt?"

"We had more than plenty to do with that. 'Ceptin' it wasn't the judge." Woodside answered with his excitement at the day's events. He steadied his bay, waiting until Simms mounted Indigo. "It ain't like there's a whole lot of other lawyers in the county."

The two pulled together and exited through the gates toward Woodside's house. The deputy closed the gate and said, "On second thought, that might've been what it was all about."

Sheriff Simms pulled Indigo's reins to stop. "You don't know how to tell a story at all. What 'what was all about'?"

"Like I was telling you, Hopt didn't talk right to Rabbi Sol. The rabbi don't like me to call him rabbi, but I can't call him anything other because he's older 'n me, and Mr. Slonik don't sound right because he's got so damn much learnin'."

"Vernon, you weren't telling me that," said Sheriff Simms. "You don't need to call him anything to tell me what happened. What happened?"

"I was leading up to that. Don't be so impatient."

Simms laughed out loud. Woodside paused, a question in the look he gave the sheriff. Simms chuckled again and waved him to go on. Damn, it was different when your deputy was not your son. He would never have said that to his father.

"Hopt seemed to treat him poor two times in the jail. I was there Friday and then again Monday. Today, he stands there and tells the judge he don't want no Jew lawyer. Hopt says he don't know nothing about Jews, but he's sure they're's bad as Mormons. Said he wants a Christian lawyer."

"I would have thought Hopt himself was LDS. If he said that, maybe not."

"Whatever he is, he don't seem to think Latter-day Saints are Christians," said Woodside.

"So, what happened?"

"The judge sent him to the territorial prison. Said he might as well sit there until they find him a lawyer in Salt Lake City."

"This doesn't smell right to me," said Sheriff Simms. "The judge is going to find him a lawyer in Salt Lake City who's a Gentile, but not a Jew?"

"The judge didn't say that. But I take it to be his meaning."

"Who's going to do the looking?" Sheriff Simms asked. "That'll use up a lot of time. And, who's going to pay for it?"

"Don't know," said Woodside. "Nobody mentioned the money today. 'Course, Mayor Eldridge still says people are asking where that money is."

"Money seems to hold the attention of people who don't know what's important," mused Sheriff Simms. "What'd the prosecuting attorney say about that?"

Woodside gave a sharp look at the sheriff, and the pair rode further. Woodside said nothing. Sheriff Simms did not understand his deputy's silence but let the question go when he spotted the pens behind Woodside's house.

"I'm guessing you never been down to court with your father?" said Woodside in his own use of the question-statement.

"There was a murder back in sixty-five," Sheriff Simms said as he urged Indigo into the pen. Once inside, he looked at his deputy and said, "That would have been about when you were born, but otherwise I can't remember having the need. I guess he took care of everything, or we didn't have much to take care of."

"You sent Orson with McCormick and me with Elsemore for evident reasons."

"True," said Sheriff Simms. "What's that have to do with Hopt?"

Woodside swung one foot over, stepped down from his bay, and talked over its back while he took off the saddle. "And I'm guessing the judge sent Hopt to the territorial prison because the mayor don't want him in Coalville, even if he is in jail." He stopped talking to concentrate on the belly strap.

"Like I said, you can't tell a good story. What's all this guessing about? Makes me think you're beatin' around the bush."

Woodside threw his saddle over the rail for the night. "I'm guessing you don't know the prosecuting attorney is Elmo Eldridge."

"What? Mayor? County commissioner? Prosecuting attorney?" The questions brought to a halt the sheriff's effort to remove the saddle and blanket from Indigo.

"All three. And he's going to throw all three in the creek. He's wanting to be elected probate judge next month." Woodside tried to hide a grin and gave up. "He was himself today. Full of speeches, campaigning at every turn, and not too sure which job he was working."

"So, now I have to worry about how Hopt's date with the firing squad fits into Eldridge's political ambitions?"

"Maybe not." Woodside chuckled and took the saddle out of the sheriff's hands. "You'd 'a liked him today. He told the judge he didn't care where the judge put Hopt, so long as he knew where to go find him for his appointment with the firing squad."

"Hmm," said Simms. "Don't know what to think when I agree with a man I don't trust."

Chapter 27:
September 29, 1883

Mr. Parley arrived Saturday at seven o'clock in the morning to find Sheriff Simms sitting on the wooden step at his door.

"Here to collect your pay?" asked Parley.

"Not if you gave Trueman his due." Sheriff Simms looked up, barely noticing that the tall, lean man wore a suit and a white shirt and a tie. His appearance seemed part of him.

"That I did," said Mr. Parley.

"Well, then, I'm here to make amends." Simms grinned and unfolded to stand up.

"No amends necessary," Parley smiled. "Since you put Hopt in your jail, I noticed you show up at night or of a Saturday and take out the freight." He offered his hand to the sheriff. "Where'd you find him? He wasn't from around here. Somebody had to tell him the high Uintas belong to you and your father."

"Maybe," said Sheriff Simms nodding in understanding. "I'd've gone up there and squeezed on him as long as it took. It turned out to be Brown's Park."

"Hah," laughed Mr. Parley. "He did me a favor. When you're up in those mountains, you lose all track of time. But, that's not why you're here. What happened?"

"Nothing. I'm here to make amends for so many disruptions to your business."

Mr. Parley stood on the steps and laughed out his disagreement. "Nothing of the kind." He sorted out his keys until he pointed the right one out of his key ring and unlocked his office door. "The balance of your pay is still owing."

Simms followed Mr. Parley into his office. He noticed the *Deseret News* propped on the slant top of a reading stand. A stacked headline across three columns in the upper right caught his attention:

PROSECUTING POLYGAMY: WHAT THE UTAH COMMISSION HAS BEEN DOING. MORMONS DISENFRANCHISED BY THE THOUSAND UNDER RIGID ENFORCEMENT OF THE EDMUNDS ACT.

Parley took the newspaper off the stand and handed it to Simms. "Might be some exaggeration there, unless 'by the thousand' means three or four, but you made the paper. Made us famous."

"How so?"

"Marshal Eire brought along a reporter. He already knew how hard it would be to find you. He must've figured publicity would help. Dumb as posts. Those Williams boys may be Jack Mormons, but they were dealing with the *Deseret News*." Parley touched his finger to a section of the front page. "Look right here; those marshals show up here with the misguided hope people will help find you, and the *Deseret News* writes:

'The people of Coalville are just good honest souls building a little at a time to that which they already have. There is solidity that betokens absolute security.' "

"The paper's right," said Simms. The sheriff put the paper back on its stand. "The Williams brothers don't mean the people here aren't good and solid. Even Hopt. He's not the people. He's a lunatic with a gun. Lucky for me, we don't have a territorial insane asylum to put him in. I'd rather see him shot."

"Blood atonement?" asked Mr. Parley with a raised eyebrow.

The question caught Sheriff Simms up short. He looked at Mr. Parley. True, Coalville had good people, but it took just one. He remembered his father's lessons: *No need to take chances. Make your people judgments. Trust your judgment.* He considered Mr. Parley another moment and judged him solid, asking a sincere question. He gave a little snort. "No, not at all. With the federals already holding the two families against me, I'll leave the question of Hopt's execution to the territory."

Mr. Parley uttered one slow, drawn-out word. "Good."

Sheriff Simms reached out his hands and grabbed Parley by both shoulders. "I'll be careful." He laughed. "And I won't miss any loads."

Parley nodded. He took hold of the sheriff's elbow. "I'm not worried about when you're going to take the wagon." He pointed at the sheriff's hip. "And I'm glad to see you wearing that pistol. Your man's in jail, and you're wanting the judge to send him back here for the firing squad. Prepare yourself to give that up." He handed the sheriff his pay envelope. "Eire's going to want to use that against you. If I know that, so will some sharp Salt Lake City lawyer. Eire hasn't produced one arrest. None have, back to Haywood, the last LDS appointed U.S. marshal. That's nine, Eire's the tenth, who can't put anybody in the penitentiary except two women. They kept Belle Harris five months, released her soon after you brought in Hopt. Now they're calling it *The Crusade*, and they're going to find a way to keep from executing Hopt until they have you."

Sheriff Simms nodded his understanding and put on his hat. "I appreciate your warning. Like my pa telling me not to take any chances I don't have to. Hopt's going to wiggle every way he can. I'll keep my eyes open . . . and focused on getting Hopt before the firing squad."

" 'Course that'll be Hopt's choice," reminded Mr. Parley. "I'm following you, but I'm not sure you're seeing my point.

The pressure's going to get worse on you. Those marshals have to arrest someone to satisfy all the wolves."

Sheriff Simms opened the door. He held it open, standing half in, half out, and responded to Mr. Parley. "They didn't help me get Hopt, and they didn't get me. I hear you. They won't help me with justice for Hopt, and they'll keep trying to grab me—I'm telling you. They won't."

★ ★ ★ ★ ★

IV: HUNTED

★ ★ ★ ★ ★

CHAPTER 28:
NOVEMBER 1, 1883

U.S. Marshal Jacob J. Eire could not see the street when he looked out the window of the Cluff Hotel. Bright, gray light made every contour near to invisible, and the cloak of snow made every surface flat.

Marshal Eire had ridden to Coalville for the third time since July to make progress in catching any of these cohabs, especially the sheriff who seemed able to conduct his business in the open with little interruption. Eire's one success this trip had been to find a new informant in town. It all cost money, but he planned to deduct the five dollars from the Williams brothers' fee if they ever earned one. This informant had told him to forget trying anything else and stay close to the sheriff's second house. Everyone knew John Willford had been trying to finish the outside work for Elizabeth Tonsil before the snows came. Well, last night the snows came.

President Arthur appointed Marshal Eire because he was conscientious and a good businessman, not to mention he had worked for Arthur in the New York Custom House. Everyone involved, including Jacob J. Eire, expected those characteristics to turn him into a wealthy man from the arrest of polygamists. Now fifteen months on the job, he had concluded that the political types, the U.S. attorney, and the governor should spend their time securing grand jury indictments and warrants—which he would serve and arrest polygamists. Left to his own strategy, the profit lay in arresting cohabs. He lived on his salary. The profit from those arrests amounted to the money he planned to lay aside. He aimed to create a fund and one day go back East again to find a wife and go into business for himself. So far, he had accumulated one hundred thirteen dollars from keeping a woman in the penitentiary apartment next to his. His first cohab arrest would amount to more than that. If he could make enough arrests, he would make some real money. He did not give a damn about polygamy or polygamists, except that polygamists were cohabs and counted as valuable lawbreakers.

Marshal Eire peered into the snowy gray morning and judged one thing for sure: there were more cohabs in Salt Lake County than in Summit County. This snow decided it for him. Coming up and down mountains and valleys to chase cohabs in the snow cost him way too much compared to what he could make by simply taking care of his duties in Salt Lake. More than the snow, the truth prompted a chill. He had reasons beyond his own income to make arrests in 1884. There were people looking over his shoulder.

Marshal Eire finished dressing and pulled on his boots. He planned to meet his special deputy U.S. marshals at nine. He trusted they would be punctual. Snow or no, and despite their willingness to profit from it, the Williams brothers were Mormons.

Eire left for the breakfast room thinking the U.S. government had adopted its pay-for-betrayal policy straight out of the Bible. Cohabs broke the law laid down by the Edmunds Act, and that made the payment a sanctified reward for the capture of a criminal. He was an agent of the courts of the U.S. government. U.S. Marshal Eire knew the U.S. government was in the right. The government had an obligation not to waste public money. It made sense to pay only if he caught cohabs.

Snow or no Eire repeated to himself when he saw the Williams brothers, already arrived and before nine o'clock. Such industry impressed the U.S. marshal. He rewarded the brothers with breakfast before he launched into the task at hand.

"My job is to do what is efficient for the U.S. government." Marshal Eire paused while Mrs. Huff served each of his special deputies a bowl of mush and a glass of milk. "I promised you a good opportunity, if you could handle it." The marshal continued his preamble while Mrs. Huff brought him a plate of pancakes, fried eggs, steak, and bacon. "Now it is time for me to make a decision. I will go back to Salt Lake, and you will be responsible for this whole county."

"Thanks," Enos's tone sounded a lot like a contradiction. "I thought we were."

"In a manner of speaking," Eire replied. "Under close supervision. Now you will report to me in Salt Lake, and I expect results."

"What kind of results?" Enos asked. "This county's no hotbed of polygamy. Mostly farmers who couldn't afford to follow the general authorities."

"Enough did." Marshal Eire waved away his deputy's demurral with a forkful of fried egg. "The bishop gives 'em license for lust, plain lust. Few men turn that down."

"Even so, not three in a hundred take another wife," said Enos. "You want the sheriff. Enoch'll take the jail and his first house, and I'll take the other one. Like I told you before, it'll be easier to catch the ones tied down. But I'm telling you, we'd all do better going to Salt Lake."

"I have been given the responsibility for those decisions." Marshal Eire's tone brooked no response. He paused for effect, then lifted the piece of steak speared by his fork. He pointed it at Enos. "It won't do you no good to put on a dedicated watch for him. Everybody's watching you watching him. Like you said, I've entrusted you with this entire county. If three in a hundred signed on to ride two mares in the herd, that means

six in this town alone, thirty all to yourself in the whole county."
Marshal Eire resumed chewing. After he finished his steak, he
speared the air with his empty fork. "In the totality of it all, my
responsibility is to take care of all the counties and organize
things for the coming winter. The thirty that lives in the county
is a goodly number, worth more'n two thousand dollars to you.
I'll give you more when you show you can handle it, but right
now show me you can handle what you have, a county the size
of the whole of Rhode Island, all to yourself."

"You leavin' all thirty to us?" asked Enos.

"Of course, under my supervision, and on the terms we set
out."

Enoch Williams finished his mush. "We appreciate what
you're doing for us, Marshal. Not many folks has jobs, except
for the ones want to work in the mines. And we'll do our best
for you, but it'll be hard. Most of the polygs all married before
the railroad. Even the sheriff you're after took his second wife
right about Promontory."

"Don't go after 'em because they're polygs. With this Edmunds Act they're all cohabs worth seventy-five bucks to you
and your brother."

"So far, nobody's caught none"—Enos's voice firmed—"and
this one cohab we been after has been damned hard to nab."

U.S. Marshal Eire continued pouring syrup on his pancakes
and reflected on his mistake in giving the special deputy some
latitude to speak his mind. Noticing the syrup almost overflowing the plate, he put the pitcher back on the table and waved
away Enos's concern. "He's been chasing his father's killer.
Stands to reason. You didn't know where to look for him. Now,
he'll be around. Might be he's the hardest one, being the sheriff.
We ought to be paid more for him, but the rest still add up to
more than two thousand dollars for the two of you. Do you
know how much that is?"

"About half of what you make off 'em," Enos muttered in a muffled voice.

Eire sucked the syrupy pancakes off his fork and left his mouth in its sweet pucker for a deliberate moment. "Only if my supervision makes you do your job." Once again, he pointed his fork at Enos. "Don't test me again. Your brother's right. I could have two more like you by noon, even in this snow." Eire looked at the brothers. Enoch dropped his eyes. Enos held his gaze.

Eire stood up and pointed his finger at Enos. "As it is, I'll let you prove yourself. I have to go to Salt Lake."

"Me," Enos said, "I'd stay here. Go to Salt Lake tomorrow."

"Tomorrow is Friday. I have a weekly report to make. I have to leave today."

"Today, tomorrow, don't matter. You make Salt Lake by Sunday," said Enoch.

"I couldn't make my weekly report until Monday," Marshal Eire said. "My God, I can't afford that. I have to be responsible to the burden of my duties."

Chapter 29:
November 29, 1883

U.S. marshals proved useless to John Willford's father in the jailbreak. Useless to catch Hopt. Useless to catch John Willford. He did not consider them incompetent. He considered them good for nothing, useless. He had to evade the marshals, catch Hopt, and finish nailing the siding before the snows stormed in with the end of October. And, by God, he had.

Damned few blessings came when the heavy snows arrived, save one. The snows showed up, and the marshals did not, leastwise not U.S. Marshal Eire. The pink curtain hung with less frequency, and no one sought out Sheriff Simms with warnings of Marshal Eire. He gave thanks for that blessing, but he never forgot the Williams brothers posed the real danger. Not seeing them gave no comfort. He had to make sure they did not see him.

The crusade led by the marshal and his horde of deputy marshals and special deputies had built to the point that going underground now meant more than hiding. President Taylor counseled hiding and followed his own counsel, lamenting he could not follow the many who moved their multiple families to Mexico. Amidst this growing pursuit of polygamous families, the governor declared November 29 a day of "Thanksgiving and Praise." Sheriff Simms planned to split the day between the houses of his two wives.

Acting Governor Arthur L. Thomas supplied the flowery proclamation, and John Wilford's five daughters prepared the food. James presided as the man of the house, and, with six of their seven children present, the sheriff shared a somber meal in Elizabeth Jensen's bedroom.

The sheriff left his first family late in the afternoon to go to the little yellow house. In the spirit of "Thanksgiving and Praise," guarding against the spirit of comparison, he looked forward to a late afternoon and evening spent with Elizabeth Tonsil Simms.

Elizabeth Tonsil opened the front door the minute she saw Sheriff Simms at the gate. She ran down the concrete walkway and threw her arms around him. She nestled her nose against his neck and nibbled his ear. Caution called, underscored by her recent news about the result of his moment of weakness in July, but this promised to be a hard evening to stay cautious.

"Best put Indigo out back," she whispered in his ear between nibbles. She pulled his arm in between her breasts and turned him back toward the gate where he had tied his blue roan.

"What the . . ." A bubble of laughter expanded from the center of his protest.

"I can't wait till we're in the house for a proper kiss," Elizabeth Tonsil said as she grabbed his chin with her hand and pointed his face toward her. Then she moved her mouth back to her nibbles on his ear. "Don't try to spot them."

He counted his Elizabeth Tonsil a smart woman, a tough woman, and she knew he wanted even more to call them out. He also trusted her.

She let go of his hand while he untied Indigo and then took it again to lead him to the back of the house. She took the reins. Too loud for any necessary reason, she said, "Why don't you put him on the feedbag. You're not going anywhere. Let him eat while we're eating."

"Good thinking." He took her cue to a big voice. "But I couldn't eat another thing."

"Better yet," she said, her voice almost in song, and punched him in the ribs.

He finished setting Indigo to eat at the back door. In the house, he found the dinner table arranged in its full Thanksgiving setting. What he said about eating did not matter one whit to Elizabeth Tonsil. He paused in wonder at the table covered with formal dinnerware.

She asked in a teasing voice, "It takes you fourteen years of marriage to notice we set this table twice a year?"

Elizabeth Tonsil scurried past the dining room table to the kitchen, where she busied herself working at the counter. She sliced turkey and bread and pie and wrapped food along with preparing dessert. It looked like she packed a picnic.

"Full or not, we can sit at the table and have some dessert." This time she kissed him for real. "You like my dessert."

"Yes, I do. And I have the feeling you best keep dessert to pie today."

"We could always shock the marshals," she teased again, and she took him by the hand to the formal dining room table in its Thanksgiving array.

He watched each window as she led him. She placed him at the end of the table nearest the kitchen, facing the front door— opposite his normal chair.

She cut a piece of pie and put it on his plate and sat at the corner of the table, next to him.

"So," he said between bites, "you think somebody's out there."

"You don't fool me, John Willford. I know who the Williams brothers are."

He finished his pie and both waited in silence. Maybe no one was coming. He said no to her offer of a second piece. As she ignored him and put it on his plate, the knock on the door launched her into action. She grabbed his hand and pulled him into the kitchen, where she thrust a flour-sack picnic against his chest and held open the back door.

After she closed it, Elizabeth Tonsil straightened her dress and her hair, tied her apron, and walked to the front door.

"Is Sheriff Simms here?" asked Enoch Williams. Both brothers stood on her porch in the waning daylight.

"Oh, you poor dears, all the way here from Kamas on your Thanksgiving. It must be a trial to your parents, you having the job you do." She let the words hang in the air for a moment before she resumed. "And what it requires you to do. Even leave your parents Thanksgiving dinner table to visit with the sheriff."

"It don't burden them," said Enos. "They know we have to work. Ma put dinner on the table at noon for the whole family."

"She's a good mother." Elizabeth nodded and smiled at the boys. "I imagine you help support her from what you earn?"

The brothers shifted and exchanged glances with each other.

"Is the sheriff here?" asked Enoch Williams.

"Oh, my sakes. You missed him. He had to leave."

"Official duties?" asked Enos.

"He never tells me."

"Where'd he go?" asked Enoch.

"Like I said, he never tells me." Comfortable with an honest statement of fact, her face remained open, supported by the reality that John Willford never told her what he was doing or where he was going. "I packed him some food. I'd have nothing more than a guess. If you want my guess, well, you know, he is a Simms. You might try the high Uintas."

U.S. Marshal Eire planned to weather the snows in Salt Lake. Sheriff Simms knew the special deputies were not up to facing him on the street, even from the back. They could roust themselves to attempt something again at Christmas. He calculated the Williams brothers were good learners, good enough not to try the little yellow house again so soon. That left only the one move, and it made no sense to try to trap him over at the Jensen house. Who could make a cohab case out of a man sleeping in the house of his first wife?

Sheriff Simms felt confident enough to undertake the carpentry work he needed to finish inside the yellow house as the holiday season wore on. The judge had sent Hopt off to the territorial prison, and the sheriff's suspicions proved true. Nothing happened. By Christmas Eve, Hopt's maneuverings around a lawyer who was neither Mormon nor Jew had taken on more importance than what needed doing—stand him up against a wall and give the order to fire.

John Willford left an early dinner with Elizabeth Tonsil to go read " 'Twas the Night Before Christmas" with his daughters around Elizabeth Jensen's bed. Despite his protest that the story had been written to be read to a daughter, his daughters insisted on doing the reading.

Christmas begs thinking, and Sheriff Simms thought about the season of clemency. It sent a chill up his spine. Those who thought him crazy because of his single-minded pursuit of putting his father's killer to the territory's justice did not think Hopt crazy for trying to worm his way out of a sentence to die.

With a calm that felt like the blessings of the season, Sheriff Simms realized Hopt's success had given him an unexpected gift. He feared most Hopt's inclusion in the governor's Christmas amnesty. The governor pardons the convicted. Hopt's delaying meant no trial, no conviction, no pardon.

CHAPTER 30:
JANUARY 2, 1884

Sheriff Simms had hunted Hopt, and the U.S. marshals had hunted him every day since he became sheriff. His mission had been to avoid the marshals so he could stand Hopt before the firing squad. Today Hopt stood before the judge and jury at trial. January snows brought some relief but called for no less caution, and the nights proved a cold proposition. Upon arising, he had in mind refuge in the warm jail to wait for word of the Hopt decision, read the Edmunds Act, and thaw out.

The glow in the window against the pre-dawn gloom warned the sheriff. He opened the door to an empty front room and looked to the cells before stepping all the way in. He puzzled at alert in the doorway until he saw Woodside standing in front of two female prisoners in separate cells. U.S. marshals had arrested women, but he had never seen a woman in a jail, much less two young girls. He took a startled second look and recognized Alvin Hooper's twin daughters.

"Can't say as I expected this," Sheriff Simms said. "Aren't you in Salt Lake?"

"There's been a complaint." Woodside tried to hold back a smile.

"That don't tell me much. What's so funny?"

"Nothing funny, boss," Woodside said. "Serious, in fact. These twins been accused of sexual assault."

"By who?"

"And torture," Woodside said, now allowing a chuckle.

"Deputy, I can see you're having some fun with this, but I'm wondering about the trial in Salt Lake, and I'm damned uncomfortable standing in front of two young girls talking about sexual assault and torture. Why did you bring 'em here?"

"Leander Pulsipher stormed up to my house last night and insisted I go arrest the Hooper girls. I thought it'd be best to bring them here."

"Insisted? And you let him?"

"Well, he says they tortured Ben, and the way I figured it, I best get them out of the way of harm from him. I planned to wait the night until Clive showed up so I could go find you. You beat me to it."

Sheriff Simms stayed in the front room, outside the cell area. "Ben Pulsipher's a good-sized teenage boy. Those two girls could never overcome him. The other way around maybe. He's the only boy in the county we ever had on an actual charge of rape."

Sheriff Simms believed in teenage boys. Most started out a little weak, too much under the influence of their mother. Those who weren't sometimes acted a little unruly, thinking to be a man meant to ignore good manners and small kindnesses. Still, Simms believed most boys grew into fine men if someone took them by the hair and tugged up straight a little bit. This Ben Pulsipher landed in the very small group of boys the sheriff didn't like, but he still thought he could straighten him out with some hard work and a good firm hand.

Sheriff Simms believed his firm hand could change any boy's attitude, but he harbored some doubt he could overcome the permanent damage done to Ben Pulsipher by the jury. They had let the boy go. His lawyer used a big word—consensual. The night of the incident, Sheriff Simms had seen a big boy and a battered girl, and the only consent he saw existed in the instinct to preserve life. Indeed, the boy had not killed her, and

Sheriff Simms wondered if the jury needed her death to prove she had said, *No!*

After that trial two other mothers found Sheriff Simms, at the time a deputy. In both cases he concluded the mothers told him true versions of events. His father approved, and he planned to arrest Ben once again, only to have the mothers decide not to let the sheriff interview their daughters. It would always be the girl's word against the boy's. Once again, it made him angry when he thought about it. Rape was a form of sexual intercourse that the anti-Mormon laws proclaimed to be a fixture of polygamous marriage. Indeed, the boy said *how could I do it if she didn't want me to,* and someone on the jury took that for consent.

Leander hid behind the jury's decision and defended the boy from any measure Sheriff Simms wanted Leander to impose. Sheriff Simms, father and son, wondered how the boy would ever learn if his father refused to teach him.

Now that same father had sworn out a complaint against these two girls.

Sheriff Simms didn't like it. He didn't like the Pulsiphers, and he didn't like having these two young women in his jail. Their presence weighed on him; he tried hard not to look at them—identical twins, standing on long legs in blue denims so threadbare and tight they must have been worn since the girls were ten. Their plain brown shirts appeared frayed and ready to burst. To his great relief, the shirts had all the buttons properly buttoned. The clothes, tight and frayed and clean, proved what Sheriff Simms already knew: the Hooper twins came from one of the poorest and proudest families in the county.

As with all the souls in his county, Sheriff Simms knew their father. Mr. Hooper kept to himself and struggled with a small farm out in Peoa, mostly rocks, and a one-room shack. Simms remembered having one conversation with him. Hooper had talked about how raising animals for their fur would be better than trapping. New Hoopers seemed to arrive regularly every fall. The sheriff knew Christmas brought cold sleeping. He chided himself for that thought.

"How old are you?" he asked, not too sure which one, so he considered it both.

"Seventeen, last September," said Elisa. He couldn't tell much between them, though there seemed to be something a little softer about this one. He continued to try to ignore the two girls and keep his eyes on Woodside. Had God made Hooper the gift of these two beautiful daughters to bestow riches on a poor man or to test him more?

He gave up in frustration and barked, "Oh, hell." Elisa and Esther jumped, and Woodside chuckled. "There's nothing to do here but deal with it. Woodside, are you telling me that Leander Pulsipher made a complaint against these two girls?"

Woodside nodded.

"And he said they assaulted . . ."

"Sexually assaulted," corrected Woodside.

". . . oh. All right, assaulted and tortured his boy, a man bigger than the two of them put together." The sheriff finished his statement and stood glowering at his deputy. He asked, "Is that it? What does he claim they did?"

Woodside looked down at his shoes; he looked at the girls. With as much composure as he could muster, he looked at Sheriff Simms.

"They stuck a twig up his whatsis."

Simms twitched before he succeeded in freezing his face in a blank. He bent over and made a point of looking at the twins' feet clad in heavy shoes.

"And did you ask them if they did it?" asked Sheriff Simms, now studying if those were shoelaces and if they were tied.

"Oh, they did it, and like I said, I figured it'd be safer here."

"You mean you went all the way down to Peoa to bring them

in here?" He had never doubted Woodside's judgment. "You already had a job to do. Did you think these girls were going to live a life of fugitives, and they'd be disappeared after the trial?"

"Seemed safest," Woodside said in a quiet but firm voice. "Leander brought Ben to my house last evening and made the complaint. He said if you didn't take care of it, he was going out to the Hoopers' and take care of these girls, personally."

"That boy comes by his attitude from his father." Simms thought the shoelaces looked like baling twine. Finished studying their shoes, taking a deep breath, for the second time he bucked up his determination to deal with this. "Was the boy injured?"

"His father says he's pissing blood."

"I hope he is," said Esther. She stepped to the bars and grabbed one. "Serves him right."

Simms looked at the young girl. Her buttoned shirt bulged, and it did not help that the top button of her tight denims had no button. Somebody should tell her, but not him. He took another deep breath. In fact, he was simply going to make it through this.

"So, you did what he said?" asked Simms.

"No," said Esther, holding her ground, eyes flashing. "Not a twig. A pine needle."

"Piñon pine," said Elisa.

"I don't need the details," said Simms.

Simms normally tracked down all the unanswered questions. He still did not know where all this happened. After that last piece of information, he didn't know how many questions he wanted answered.

You must have had a good reason is what he wanted to say, and he realized his instincts and his calling conflicted. He could not simply dismiss such a violent act. There was no way around more questions. "Why?"

"Because he tried to stick his—" said Esther, then she turned to her sister in the next cell. "What did Vernon call it?"

"His whatsis," said Elisa.

"He tried to stick his whatsis up my rear end," said Esther.

"Did he?" Simms stammered out the question in his amazement without realizing it might be taken to have two meanings.

"Do you mean did he really try to?" snapped Esther at Simms. Before he could explain, she said, "Well he had me spread, and he damn near tore me up with his poking, but maybe that wasn't what he was trying to do!"

The anger he felt coming from Esther reminded him of the jury, and he was not all that sure he even wanted her to answer the question he meant to ask.

"Did he do anything else?" asked Simms, more in hopes of moving on to another subject than wanting to learn anything more.

"He made me . . ." started Elisa.

"He made my sister play with his whatsis," said Esther.

Now that raised questions again, and again Simms was not all that sure he wanted to know the details. "How did he make you . . . ?"

Elisa touched a deep-blue bruise high on her left cheekbone spreading up aside her eye.

Woodside interrupted. ". . . you're gonna hafta know everything. He'll claim Esther sashayed up to him with no bottoms on."

"He had my sister, and he was forcing her to use her hand. I told him he wasn't half a man if all he wanted was some girl to pull his . . ." Esther looked at her sister then at Woodside ". . . whatsis. *I* couldn't stop him, but I figured that would. Besides, I had my underpants on."

"Ben said they tied him up," said Woodside quietly.

"Did you?" asked Simms.

"Of course I did," said Esther. "After he took me down and tried—"

". . . that's when I smashed him one because he was trying to—" said Elisa.

"I understand," said Sheriff Simms. Then he corrected himself. "No, I don't. How did you tie him up?"

"Elisa is stronger'n me," said Esther. "She laid him out good. Then we tied him up."

"How? With what?"

"Laid him out?" asked Elisa. "Or tied him up?"

"Or d'ya mean," said Esther, her voice defiant, "did we take a rope over to the church aiming to do this all along?"

"It does raise a question," said Woodside. "Why were you alone with him in the church?"

"No, it doesn't," said Simms. "All I need to know is what you tied him up with."

Both girls laughed. Elisa pointed to her shoes and said, "String. Like we use for hay."

"Do you need to tell me more?" asked the sheriff.

"Maybe not," said Woodside. "Do you want to know what they did next?"

"I think I already know," said Simms. He turned to the two girls. "Besides forcing you to . . . ah, play . . . er, do something you didn't want to do, did he do anything else to you?"

"You mean did he stick it in me?" said Esther, not a real question.

Elisa stopped her by interrupting. "No, sir. We was taking down the tree from the dance. We never told him we were gonna be there. He might 'a known they asked us because he surprised us. Like we said, he forced me to do bad things, and he tried to do bad things to Esther. We fixed him, and then we let him go. He didn't do what he was trying to do."

"You let him go?" asked Simms. "I thought you tied him up.

Why didn't he kill you?"

"I mean we let him go; we didn't bedevil him anymore," said Elisa. "We tried to take his clothes off, but we had him tied up, and we couldn't. We left him there, under the tree."

Esther laughed. "We knew someone was coming to pick up the decorations. So, we left him, like a present, all decorated."

A lot of what he heard, from the girls and from Woodside, didn't make all that much sense to Sheriff Simms. He had fought intense embarrassment from the moment he entered the jail, and now he discovered he needed to solve the problem of the Hooper twins without laughing.

By God, those twins took care of Ben Pulsipher better than his poor powers as sheriff could. He guessed how they did that nasty part with the pine needle, but he did not ask to know the details. He could hear a lawyer argue they did it in self defense. Leaving Ben tied down in the recreation hall of the church, which had held the New Year's Eve dance, seemed benign but effective. Girls, yes, but not backing down, each one stared Sheriff Simms in the face when they told him what they had done. He didn't want them to stare him in the face at all, but he couldn't look away, and he couldn't laugh. He had no idea how to solve the problem.

Sheriff Simms could not keep the Hooper twins in his jail. Seeming to have very long legs for girls of normal height, wearing denims not dresses, not to mention being fully formed with soft features and flawless skin had nothing to do with it. The jail lacked the facilities for taking care of a woman. Worse, Sheriff Simms didn't trust Ben and Leander. Those two would not try anything in his jail, but they would run their mouths. The sheriff figured that was why Leander swore out the complaint. If he put the girls in jail, Ben and Leander would have something bigger to talk about than Ben being tied up with a bow under the Christmas tree.

Sheriff Luke Willford had taught him people judgment amounted to the most part of doing a respectable job as a sheriff. Ben and Leander were not going to volunteer talk about the pine needle incident when the county teased Ben. If Sheriff Simms put the twins in his jail, even without a charge, it gave Ben and Leander something to talk about. Simms had no desire to levy any charge nor to give the Pulsiphers anything to talk about. Leander might show up and holler at him, even call him a name or two, but he'd do it in private.

A little before seven, Deputy Orson opened the door and walked in with his sack full of breakfast. Before John Willford became a deputy, Orson and Mary Beth already had three boys. Simms remembered one of the boys had since married. He had the idea there should be room in the Orson home.

"Clive, the Hooper twins need a home for a while. They could live with you while we figure this out."

"No, I don't think so," said Clive. He made no effort to move toward the cells and perhaps did not even see the girls. "Take 'em with you. You built that place with plenty of rooms. Put them up for the winter and help your Elizabeth while the baby's coming. Elizabeth has to work, don't she?"

"That's an idea, Clive," said Simms. "I'll talk to Elizabeth about it. If she wants to give them a place to live for a while, I'll talk to their pa."

"You know, with this Hoar amendment," said Woodside, "Pulsipher could go after you. I wouldn't want that."

Simms appreciated Woodside. Not yet nineteen, he worked hard and he kept track. Even with the isolation of the winter, he kept a watchful eye out for the marshals. Somewhere along the line he appeared to have done his studying, too. He knew the governor had used the Hoar amendment to bypass legitimate elections and shove non-Mormons into positions now vacated by the Edmunds Act.

"Vernon, I been careful these seven months, and I appreciate your warning," said Simms. "I'm sorry you had to miss Hopt's trial for this, but it sure wouldn't do to lose my job over something that involved the likes of Ben Pulsipher. I'm thinking we'll sit down and talk about it, Leander and me."

He turned back to the Hooper twins and their crime. "You're coming to my house," he said, again more between them than to them.

"Are we in trouble?" asked Esther.

Now he looked right at her. The question startled him some. He knew they were poor. He thought pretty sure they no longer attended school. Still those facts could not connect for him with the naivete of the question.

"Well, I don't know," Sheriff Simms said at first. Then he changed his course. "Well, yes, I do know. You can't go off and maim a boy . . ."

"We didn't maim him."

". . . without being in some kind of trouble." He continued his thought despite Esther's interruption. He stopped again and stared at the two girls. He didn't like the feel of all the femaleness that floated in their presence. With a shudder, as if he tried to shake it off him, he said, "No, I guess you didn't." Simms paused and struggled to find words for a subject he had never discussed in front of a woman.

"He can still use it," Esther said.

Esther looked straight at him, didn't budge, and he wondered if she meant to register his shock. Elisa looked away into some vacant corner. "When you conked him, you might could argue you were defending yourself, even though a lawyer's going to argue it was Esther was in danger, not Elisa. When you tied him up, you could argue that was so's you could get away. That other you did, though, even if he did try to bugger you, you can't call that defending yourself. I don't know what you can call it, but you can't do that without having some kind of trouble. My question is what I'm going to do about it."

Sheriff Simms noticed Esther fixing to speak up. He held up his hand to silence her.

Elisa no longer looked away; both waited for his judgment. "I am going to take you over to Elizabeth Tonsil. That should 'a been where I went before I got tangled up in this mess."

Everything about the Hooper twins disconcerted Sheriff Simms: their looks, their presence, and, most of all, their story. Their problem had completely derailed his plan for the day. Standing in front of the three cells, he remembered he had not performed his daily inspection. Those marshals were the reason Sheriff Simms took up the habit of inspecting first thing. He could only visit his jail from time to time, and first thing he had to make sure no marshals lurked hiding in the cells. Leaving Esther's cell, he marched past Elisa in her cell, past the empty cell, and turned around to return to his deputy.

"Woodside, you tell Pulsipher the girls are in custody, and he better stay clear."

Still twilight at seven-thirty on the second day of January, no one struggled with the new year and the snowy streets. The sheriff doubted anyone behind their curtains raised an eyebrow when he marched the two girls out the door and straight to the yellow house. To see Sheriff Luke Willford Simms marching one or two teenagers down the street on the way to their parents had been a common sight. Nothing had changed with Sheriff John Willford Simms making the same march, regardless of the hovering presence of the marshals. Probably no one marked that the Hooper twins lived in Peoa. He was glad they wore heavy boots, and he took advantage to march them six feet in front of him every step of the way.

"Well, what do we have here?" asked Elizabeth Tonsil upon their arrival.

"This is Esther," said Simms. "And the quiet one is Elisa. They're Hooper girls, and they're twins. I thought maybe they could help you."

Elizabeth smiled. John Willford trusted her not to talk up too much until she knew what was what. She put her hand out, one to each girl. "He's meaning there's a baby coming." She took them into her kitchen where she put them to work preparing hot water and milk.

"Is there more you want to tell me?" asked Elizabeth upon her return. "We can't afford help, and I won't take advantage of them."

"We have extra bedrooms. I thought they could work for room and board."

"That serious?" asked Elizabeth.

"Don't know, for sure. It's that Pulsipher boy. They did him some harm."

"What harm could they do to such a big boy?"

Sheriff Simms held up both hands and laughed, not an easy laugh. He said, "You could be a help to me. Me repeating what they did won't do any good. I doubt I'd get it right, anyway. You could talk to them and write it down. Then we'd have it all down in black and white."

"And you just had this idea, did you?"

"Right," said Simms, and he kissed his wife on the forehead. "I admit I don't feel all that fulsome talking about it, but we don't know where this is all going. It'd be best to set their accounts down."

"Does it need doing today?" she asked. "You know I have to go to the mercantile."

"I respect you have your job, but it's best to get it done," said Sheriff Simms "That's not saying you should disrupt your work.

Talk to the twins off and on, while you're in the kitchen and such."

CHAPTER 31:
JANUARY 3, 1884

Elizabeth Tonsil opened the door to meet Sheriff Simms before he reached for the handle in the still-dark morning. Upon her invitation to tarry for breakfast, he delivered a refusal she appeared to expect.

"You best have some breakfast," she said. She pulled him down to deliver today's kiss and slipped a school notebook in his vest pocket. With it, she whispered, "I don't envy you."

The Hooper twins served him toasted bread and eggs, and, upon his compliment, Elizabeth Tonsil swore she had nothing to do with it. They had done all the cooking right down to baking the bread. He left the house wondering if he should believe his wife.

Having no knowledge or warning of where the special deputies might be, Sheriff Simms rode Indigo to the sagebrush bench on the south of Coalville where the Shoshoni had made their camping ground on their passage through town for the past twenty years. This year brought not the train of hundreds and hundreds like had trekked through after helping the U.S. cavalry to defeat the Sioux but a decent size traveling company for Chief Washakie. Sheriff Simms made his way to Washakie's wickiup.

"Chief," Sheriff Simms said after the ritual of greeting each other had been finished, "I have need of a warm place to sit and read. May I sit here."

"Government still hunt you?" asked Washakie.

Sheriff Simms knew it was important to show nothing. He guarded his face, looked around, saw no braves, and took a moment to collect his thoughts before he answered.

"Have no fear," said Washakie. "I work for the white man's army when they fight my enemies. I am not a police man."

"You probably have a few wives of your own," said Sheriff Simms, an effort at humor that brought no smile.

"I joined your church," said Chief Washakie, "but that is not why."

"That's right," said Sheriff Simms. "Three years ago, or so. I'd heard that."

"I knew Brigham Young. Visited him often," said Chief Washakie. "But that is not why." He invited Sheriff Simms into his wickiup. "You may stay here as long as you have need of a place. I will go see President Cluff."

Sheriff Simms thought that was interesting. He debated with himself and decided it was not for him to ask.

"At his hotel," volunteered Chief Washakie. "The Episcopal church has assigned John Roberts to me on the reservation. I want to know what the Latter-day Saints are offering."

"Well, he'd be the man to ask," affirmed Sheriff Simms, surprised at every single word he had heard, but not knowing what else to say. "I'll sit here and read."

The sagebrush bench served as campground, not reservation, and the Williams brothers could surprise him. Still astonished by Washakie's expected negotiation with President W. W. Cluff, the chief's wickiup amounted to the safest haven Sheriff Simms could find. He settled on a blanket to read the notebook in his pocket.

Elizabeth's fine clear handwriting set down the facts as he remembered hearing them. He hoped the account written so near the event protected the girls against a future that held some twisting and turning.

He read through the story he knew, leaving Ben Pulsipher tied up. Simms read, "They wanted the bishop or somebody to find him. No one said it, but I agree with them. I believe humiliation will be his only punishment." He liked Elizabeth's summing up. He turned the page, expecting to find it blank.

Instead, Elizabeth's fine hand took up a whole new story. "Upon hearing the end of their account of rough justice toward Ben Pulsipher, I thanked them. Esther Hooper asked, 'Do you want to know why we did it?'

'I thought that was what you told me.'

'Why we left him for everyone to see?'

'Is there a reason that's not obvious?'

'I don't know what that means,' said Esther. 'We tried to do what he did to Elisa.'

'You mean he left her tied up?'

'Not tied up. He's strong. We needed to tie him up; he didn't need to tie her up.'

'What do you mean?'

'It's why we don't go to school anymore,' said Esther. Elisa sat there silent.

'I thought their father, like so many fool men, simply did not see the utility in educating a girl. Of course, it wouldn't do to bring that up.

'What is the reason you don't go to school anymore?'

'Ben grabbed Elisa on our sixteenth birthday. She had on a new dress.'

'Our first dress,' said Elisa.

'Right,' said Esther. 'No way was I going to wear mine to school, but cow eyes, here, did. All it got her is ripped off her.'

'Ben Pulsipher ripped your dress?' I asked Elisa.

'More'n that,' said Esther. Elisa continued to say nothing. 'He ripped her dress. I guess he liked that, so he ripped her dress off, and I guess he liked that, so he ripped off everything.

Then he held her down.'

'Needless to say, I was shocked. All I could do was repeat, "He held her down?" '

'Yes. He held her arms above her head, and he sat on her legs. He took his time and looked her over.'

'What'd he do then? Did he let her go?'

'Not until he called all his friends over and told them it was her birthday, and she was his present to them.'

'Did the boys rape her? You know what rape means, don't you?'

'Yes, we do. They got their full of looking at her. A couple of them ran away; a couple of them touched her. One of them poked her.'

'"Did not." Elisa at once interrupted, but I don't think I believe her.'

'When they finished,' Esther resumed her story without arguing with her sister, 'Ben got up off her legs and left her lying there. He told her nothing had happened. He told her all she had to do was put her dress back on and go home.'

'Esther stopped talking and looked at me. I guess she expected me to say something about how could she put a ripped dress back on. I said, "So, you took his clothes off?" '

'We tried to. We tried to do the same thing, except accounting for how strong he is, we had to tie him up, and then we couldn't take his clothes off. We did what we could, and we had to get out of there before he came untied. We took his pants with us, but you can be sure we told him all he had to do was get up and go home.' "

Elizabeth left a page empty. On the last page she wrote, "That was the end of their story, but I fear it is not the end of their ordeal. I'm afraid those girls are in for a lot of trouble."

Sheriff Simms knew what he had to do. He pulled on his heavy coat against the January cold and left Chief Washakie's wickiup. In his concentration, he almost bumped into the chief coming in.

"Good," said Washakie. "You are still here. The president's wife sent you a message."

Sheriff Simms assumed she had sent a warning, but when he accepted the folded piece of paper he recognized it as a telegram.

"Guilty. Six mo stay. Sol."

So many thoughts flew into his mind at the same time, he needed to stand still for a moment to fight the dizziness.

"Bad?" asked Chief Washakie. "You need to sit again?"

"Bad?" repeated Sheriff Simms trying to sort out the thoughts. "No," he said in a slow monotone to himself. He saw the snow falling again and brightened. "It looks like what we call half-a-loaf."

"Bread?" asked Washakie.

"Result," laughed the sheriff. He reached for the chief's hand. He talked as though to himself. "I was thinking this morning about my calling. I need to work on the other half." He caught his self-conscious moment and asked, "Did your meeting with W.W. work out the way you wanted?"

"Half-a-loaf."

From the moment he finished reading Elizabeth's notebook, he knew he would visit Leander Pulsipher when he returned home from his hardware store. That left Sheriff Simms the bulk of the day to ride to Wanship and turn the tables on the U.S. marshal. He did not know Bishop Roundy all that well, and, being a bishop, Roundy undoubtedly knew the U.S. attorney would be looking to the grand jury to indict him for polygamy, for taking a second wife, Nellie White, in December. Sheriff Simms warned the bishop that he faced more danger being nabbed for cohabitation. Simms felt blessed to have received so much help;

he wanted to give some back. He warned Roundy to stay on the lookout for the Williams brothers, since the bishop lived on the way from Kamas to Coalville. For good measure, he added those special deputies would be apt to squeeze Nellie White since, so far, the special deputies had arrested no one.

Returned from Wanship, he looked out the window of his jail at the cold gray twilight and felt an unexpected sense of satisfaction preparing for this mission. Sheriff Simms pulled his Winchester 1873 from its place next to his father's walking stick in the gun rack. He inspected his Frontier Six and thought how much he would like to use that walking stick on both the Pulsiphers. He didn't expect the special deputies to surprise him, but, if they did, he would deal with them, too.

Sheriff Simms looked from the gun rack to Woodside. The boy knew enough about this case. There were particulars he didn't need to know. Simms looked up at the clock on the wall. He had done what he could to help Bishop Roundy with his troubles, and he turned his thoughts to getting out to the Pulsipher house by about seven. Only his wife and deputies knew the Hooper twins' story and where he hid them. He had no idea how many knew by now about Ben under the Christmas tree. He smiled at that image, and a notion of admiration for the twins flicked through his mind. He chided himself for that. He needed to make sure he took care of things before that image spread.

The sheriff rode Indigo at a walk up Main Street to the expansive entrance Leander Pulsipher had given his house, one of the few houses with grass. Simms knew the risk, but the notebook and the afternoon at Bishop Roundy's had made him determined to fulfill his sheriff's calling, regardless of the U.S. government and its bounty hunting marshals. He tied his blue roan at the hitching post and walked rifle in hand up the long sidewalk to the front door.

Leander answered his knock.

"I'm here to see you," said Sheriff Simms.

"It's a good thing," said Leander. "I rousted your deputy on Tuesday and went to your jail yesterday to talk to him again. I still have not heard a thing."

"Correct that," said Sheriff Simms. "I'm here to see you and Ben,"

"No need to see Ben," said Leander. "I'm the one made the complaint."

"And for good reason," Sheriff Simms nodded in the affirmative. "You and Ben."

Leander looked at him. Simms knew Leander was among the people in the county who thought himself a special person. He was considering a test of wills. It seemed like a waste to Sheriff Simms, but not his call. He stood and waited.

The pause continued a little while longer until, finally, "Come in."

"Do you drink coffee?" asked Leander, hesitating between living room and kitchen.

"I do," said Sheriff Simms.

Leander led them into the kitchen. Ben sat at a round table in the center of the large room. Simms noticed Mrs. Pulsipher at the stove. It wasn't his place to dictate what they did in their own home, but he did not want to discuss this subject in front of a woman. He took off his hat and waited for Leander to deal with it.

Mrs. Pulsipher turned around and noticed the rifle in Simms's hand. "Sheriff, I was fixing Ben's dinner. Have you been out hunting? You can eat with us."

"No, thank you," said Sheriff Simms.

"Well, sit down and have coffee." Mrs. Pulsipher pulled a chair away from the table.

Sheriff Simms sat, rifle upright between his legs. When Leander made no effort to spare Mrs. Pulsipher what was coming, the sheriff considered he had no choice. "Leander, what we have to discuss may not be fit for a woman to hear."

"His mother knows what those girls did to Ben," said Leander.

Simms considered Pulsipher's tone. He took a moment to make his studied decision. He took care to modulate his outdoor voice into one strong, steady tone. "Does she know what he did to them?"

Silence followed, and Simms waited.

"Maisy," said Leander, "best you leave this piece of business to us."

After Mrs. Pulsipher poured the sheriff's coffee, she left the kitchen, all three sets of eyes trailing her. Leander Pulsipher took a seat at the table and turned to Sheriff Simms.

"What are you going to do about those girls?"

"You know, Utah Territory is fixing to do something about the problems it's having with rowdies," said Sheriff Simms. "The territory is calling them delinquents."

He had the Pulsiphers' attention for sure.

"What's that to do with what those girls done to Ben?" asked Leander.

"And they're even talking about a special place to send them, called a reform school." Sheriff Simms sipped his coffee and looked first at Ben then at Leander.

Ben and Leander did their best to stare back at him.

" 'Course maybe I got it wrong. Since schools are so expensive, the ones who want it to be a pen to reform the rowdies might win out."

"Will they send the girls there, Sheriff?" asked Leander. The sheriff considered him, about the same height but massive beyond the sheriff's oaken frame. He had to go two hundred fifty pounds. Sheriff Simms considered that bulk and stubbornness contributed much to the source of his success down at the hardware store.

"I thought you'd like to know about how some people see what needs to be done with rowdies. Now they could be rowdy girls, but most folks think of rowdies as rowdy boys. Of course, like in all things, there's more to it. Worse things, you might say, in store. There's always that possibility, you know. If you don't like the judgment, there's always the chance of worse things in store."

The three sat there, saying nothing, and Simms could see Leander preparing to undertake his test of wills. Simms turned away from the father and spoke directly to the boy.

"Like I said, I was talking about how some people see things right. Ben, do you know what your father wants me to do?"

"Arrest those Hooper twins for what they did to me?"

"Kind of just retribution, right? You been arrested once for what you did to a girl. That give you the idea?"

"Didn't do it," said Ben. "I told my side of the story; the jury let me off."

"Uh, huh," said Sheriff Simms. "You know they have a school down in Salt Lake you can live at. A bit fancy for my tastes, but it probably beats the reform school they're planning."

"That costs money," said Leander.

"It does," said Sheriff Simms. "And it won't do to wait for them until the reform school's going. I imagine things are doing pretty well down at the hardware store."

"What's that to do with what those Hooper girls done?"

Sheriff Simms looked at Leander for a long moment and shrugged. "You know, Leander, that's the second time you asked that same question. They tell me they got students down there trying to get ready to go to the university. Preparing is what I hear they call it. I'm betting you could have your choice. To my eye, it'd be a good thing to graduate from there and maybe even go on to college."

"So, answer my question," insisted Leander.

Simms raised and dropped his shoulders in another shrug, paused again, and resumed. "Remember that last trial?"

"Yes, two kids got all hot and bothered. The girl tried to convince her father Ben forced her. Of course, no boy could force a girl."

Sheriff Simms looked around the kitchen. It was the first time he had been in it. He realized he had not been in very many kitchens in his county. He noticed how much space spread in all directions beyond the round table and how something covered every surface and all the walls. He thought about these details to take his mind off his impulse to knock Leander up the side of the head.

"I take that to mean you know both sides of the story will come out." Simms could see Leander puffing up to talk again and held up his hand. "Ben, I'm wondering if you told your father what you tried to do to that Esther Hooper?" The sheriff looked at the boy as if expecting an answer. Silence. He nodded. "Didn't think so. I'm guessing you also never told him what you did do to that Elisa Hooper at school?"

Ben continued to eat, but he watched his father over his plate.

"It's a hard question," said Sheriff Simms. He pulled the school notebook filled with Elizabeth's Tonsil's record of Ben's treatment of the Hooper twins and held it between his two fingers. "I can make it easier for you. We have a record here. You can call it their testimony. Of course, that isn't the church meaning of testimony. Your pa can read it."

"It'd be their word against mine," said Ben.

"True, if we knew what your word was," said Sheriff Simms. "You want to tell us what you did to those Hooper girls."

Ben looked at the sheriff and said, "Nothing."

The sheriff's head snapped back, his eyes lit up, and he laughed. He turned his full attention on Ben's father.

"Leander. You're one of the lucky ones who has a good business, and my bet is you want it to stay that way. You have one wife, and you're one of the Mormons trying to persuade your brethren to drop the People's Party and join up with the Republican Party. You probably have visions where we're going the next five or ten years, and you have plans of your own."

Simms placed the school notebook in front of Leander at the kitchen table. He liked the solution. It felt like his father had spoken it into his ear. He considered himself in a line of men in the business of seeing things clearly, and, when he thought about how to protect the Hooper twins—even if it protected Ben's reputation—he saw how to help this boy and his county. Ben watched every move. Simms sat back, and Ben and Sheriff Simms both watched while Leander read the notebook. His face grew red, then ashen by the time he finished.

"This true?" he asked his son.

"Don't know what it says," Ben said.

"Don't play games with me," said Leander. "I want a yes or no answer."

"No."

Sheriff Simms made a slow turn of his head to the right and then to the left and back to center. He took the notebook out of Leander's hands and put it in his vest pocket, tucking it so the top showed. He looked at son and father and, with one more slow turn, stood up.

"Wednesday's the day the territorial court sits at our courthouse," Simms said looking down at Leander, "being delayed this month because of New Year's. The judge is one of those trying to solve the problem with rowdies. He's more into the reform than the school, but that doesn't matter, 'cause there's no school. He's free to pass whatever sentence he wants for reform. He might not, of course. Then again, maybe we could persuade him based on these facts. And, consider this: for him to hear these facts, somebody'd have to speak them in open court. How many people know about Ben under the Christmas tree? Hell, the whole county'll know those two girls did it to get back at him for what he did to Elisa. They'll know he tried to bugger Esther. People might pass over rape in these parts, but they don't look kindly on sodomites. It'd save me some work, and you a lot of business, if you arranged with that Salt Lake preparatory school before Wednesday."

"Might be a difficulty getting him down there and getting back to you by Tuesday night," said Leander.

"I think you can do it," said Simms. He clapped Ben's father on the shoulder. He made his way toward the front door. "You know, we got the telegraph now."

CHAPTER 32:
APRIL 1, 1884

Sheriff Simms read through the winter, and, by the end, he had learned something he already knew. He would see this through to the firing squad for Albert Hopt only if he avoided the marshals. He never trusted the thought he could outsmart them. It mattered little that those Williams boys thought they were smarter than him. He did trust he could avoid them.

On the last day of March, Sheriff Simms and Deputy Woodside loosely tied their horses to the column on the back porch, left their rifles at the door, and wore their pistols in the house. They ignored the burden of one more day hiding and sneaking and celebrated the deputy's nineteenth birthday at his home with his wife.

Simms had not enjoyed the feeling of family since his father died. If he took to the court to divorce, the U.S. government would no longer hunt him. It would let him honor his financial obligations, so long as he disavowed his emotional and familial ties to one of his past marriages. Upon leaving next morning, he thanked Woodside for that feeling of family.

Sheriff Simms shivered and waited for the stove to banish the cold of April 1st from the jail. The stove boiled the water before it warmed the room. He looked forward to the coffee and to Clive's arrival with breakfast. When Clive arrived, he brought a surprise, Bishop Roundy.

"Jared," exclaimed Sheriff Simms holding coffee pot in left hand and mug in right, "you were up early in Wanship."

"Yesterday to be sure," answered Bishop Roundy. "Today I rose with Clive." Deputy Orson handed out sandwiches of waffle, eggs, and venison. The sheriff drank coffee with his, and Orson handed milk to the bishop before he settled with his breakfast at his desk. "You rode down to warn me, so I thought maybe you could help," continued Bishop Roundy. "Marshal Eire is fixing to arrest Nellie, or at least take her to court. They can't prove we are married, but I am told that Edmunds Act you mentioned lets the judge force her to testify against me."

"They've had a couple of those already," said Sheriff Simms. "Eire told my wife the same thing."

"When your father emigrated here, like Clive and me, but one ship apart, to live as a Latter-day Saint," Bishop Roundy said, "Mormon had yet to become the derogatory term we now know. We were Mormon in a community of Mormons. We followed what the authorities told us about being Mormon. We know the faithful should follow the word of President Taylor:

'I understand the law of celestial marriage to mean that every man in this Church, who has the ability to obey and practice it in righteousness and will not, shall be damned.' "

How could Bishop Roundy remember word for word? It reminded Sheriff Simms of Bishop Barber's memorized lines nine years before President Taylor gave his sermon.

"Bishop, the little warning I gave you in January is about as much help as I can give."

"George Reynolds is but two years older than you," said Bishop Roundy. "Already he has taken leadership on behalf of the church and our God-given right to practice celestial marriage."

"My good heavens, don't put me up there with him," protested Sheriff Simms. "I've done nothing. You might say what he did got him nowhere but in prison. He volunteered to be a test case, and it got him four years of hard labor. He trusted in the Supreme Court. All the court did was say, 'prison's okay, but hard labor's a mite too much.' They retrieved a letter from Thomas Jefferson to argue that the government can legislate religious practices. The leaders of the church can preach it's God's belief. God's belief is a right. We can accept the teaching, and we have a right to believe. What the government has the right to stop is the practice, not the belief."

"Well, that don't mean Nellie should testify in court."

"Now the law says different," said Sheriff Simms. "I married my Elizabeths thirteen years before that law was passed, and now the government tells me I have to abandon one. Which one? The one taken to bed with nervous prostration who can't take care of her six children? Or the one without children, whose children were burned alive in the fever of diphtheria? I'm no bishop, but my conscience won't let me divorce the sick one. Honesty doesn't let me divorce the healthy one. I'm not going to divorce anyone.

"I try to be a good sheriff for this county. If the law said from this point forward, *no*, I could enforce that. It says past marriages have to be disfavored. All I need do is tell the healthy wife to take care of herself. Of all women, she can do that. Like I said, it isn't even the support. If I divorced her but still loved her, those little Williams boys'd still have me, them without wives, families, or responsibilities."

"John Willford, we may be on different sides," said Bishop Roundy. "Even I understand that Edmunds law passed before I took Nellie to wife in December."

"You don't have to worry about me," said Sheriff Simms. "I'm not a federal officer, and I can't do what's right and do that law." He stood up from his desk and put his arm around the bishop. "Truth is, Jared, I don't think there's anything you, or we, can do. So far the U.S. marshal and his deputies have succeeded in putting away two or three wives and a man who volunteered. Eire is hiring more and more Jack Mormons, but what are they gonna do? Arrest four or five of us this year? A hundred next year? And keep going until one year, a thousand? It's valuable business. They'll keep at it, but that won't stop us from supporting the families we already have. We'd stop practicing the belief in the future, under the law, but they want to eliminate the church itself."

Sheriff Simms lingered with his arm around the older man. Orson busied himself at his desk. Woodside took a seat on the bench. The door opened to break the moment. A man filled the frame, silhouetted against the sun.

"I'm Special Deputy U.S. Marshal Samuel Grange," he announced. "And I'm looking for Sheriff John Simms."

"How did you get here?" Deputy Woodside blurted, standing up. Sheriff Simms stopped him with a firm grip on Woodside's arm and rolled Bishop Roundy to Deputy Orson.

"I'm the man you're looking for." Sheriff Simms stuck out his right hand, causing the special deputy to shift an official looking sheaf of folded papers from his right hand to his left. He pulled the deputy toward him in a deliberate gesture of friendship. Deputy Orson guided the bishop out the door, edging past the man who shook the sheriff's hand.

The special deputy ranged about the same size as Sheriff Simms. Hands locked, each took the measure of the other, surveying everything from a tense, ready stance.

"I have an order here . . ." The special deputy U. S. marshal stayed at the spot where he gave way to the sheriff's pull and held up the official looking papers.

"Would you mind stepping in and closing the door?" Deputy Orson said behind him from outside, his tone a deliberate effort to remind the special deputy of his manners.

". . . and I need to give it to you." The special deputy continued as he dropped the handshake and shifted the papers back to his right hand. He ignored the deputy who rebuked him. After a brief pause, the special deputy stepped in. Orson followed and closed the door.

"What is it?" asked Sheriff Simms.

"I can't serve it," said the special deputy.

Sheriff Simms flicked his eyes, not appearing to understand the marshal's words. "Feel free." To show no physical opposition, he reached his left hand forward. "Serve it."

"The sheriff of the county has to serve it," said the special deputy. "It's an order to take possession of the coal mines up here owned by the church."

Sheriff Simms had held his hand out expecting the subpoena. He continued to the stove and the coffee pot. He held the pot in front of him. "Coffee?"

"Nope. I accept the teaching. No hot drinks."

"This has to be an April Fool's joke," said Sheriff Simms. "Who put you up to this?"

"No joke," said the U.S. marshal. "I was told to instruct you to go out to the mines and serve this order."

Sheriff Simms looked at the special deputy. He looked at the clock, well before noon.

"You don't sound English; are you?"

"New England," said the U.S. marshal. "So what?"

"You come here before noon to send me on a fool's errand." Sheriff Simms waved at the clock. "My father told me all about April 1st and All Fools Day."

"No, Brother, I don't even want to be here. I mean this morning. I signed on as a special deputy some years ago because the pay was good. Jobs haven't been easy to find, not for ten years. Then my boss resigned last year. I should've gone with him. Believe me; I don't want to be here. This is no joke."

Sheriff Simms remained wary. True words can look the same and sound the same as words of deception. "So, why are you here?"

"Like I said, I should have resigned with my boss. I'm Latter-day Saint, like all of us, here for the church. I know there's no promotion for me." The special deputy paused, then words poured out in a rush. "I'm blessed. I never inherited the detail going after our brethren. What I mean is, I didn't have to do it. Best I can tell, no LDS on that detail, but I never asked."

"Some." Woodside shifted sideways in his chair so his hand would rest on his pistol. "Not the deputies, but best I can tell, all you special deputies hail from LDS families. You could still arrest a cohab if you was a mind to."

"I'm not a mind to." His voice pleasant, Marshal Grange nodded toward Woodside's hand to leave no mistake that he saw it. "Delivering these papers upsets me enough."

Sheriff Simms began to believe the man had no plan to trick him. Judging from the hour, he must have stayed somewhere in town, or near town, the night before. That counted for something, though it would also have been necessary for the April fool's joke.

"You could still resign," said Sheriff Simms. "It's a Tuesday. Resign as of yesterday."

"You're right, Brother. You read my mind." Staying a little inside the closed door, the special deputy gestured with the official papers. "I took these papers over to the bishop and asked him what I should do. You know, we're good citizens as a rule. There's nothing personal in this for me. I'm not a polygamist, but I'm not so sure I should be a party to taking property from the church."

"I'd never do it." Deputy Orson's voice continued to carry the tone of an older man teaching a boy his manners. "You're here. I guess I don't agree with your bishop."

"Oh, I ain't doing it," said the special deputy U. S. marshal. "The U.S. attorney told me, repeated it, and then asked me if I understood that I could not serve the papers; I had to find the sheriff to do that. When I told the bishop that, he allowed as I was just doing my job."

"He would," said Deputy Orson.

"Lucky for the bishop," said Deputy Woodside.

"And you're here giving me the papers to serve on the church?" asked Sheriff Simms. "Are you asking or telling?"

"I'm doing what the bishop counseled. I'm doing my job." Marshal Grange looked at each of the three men. He returned his focus to Sheriff Simms. "I'm giving you the papers. I think the U.S. government is telling."

"Do you know anything about me?"

"You told me you're the man I need. The sheriff of Summit County."

"I am that." Sheriff Simms replaced the coffee pot. He resumed the position and posture of accepting formal papers. The U.S. marshal raised the papers from his side in a quiet motion to place in the sheriff's palm.

Simms opened the folded sheaf and read the first page. After a moment's pause, he folded it again in its tri-fold and said, "Clive, give this man a glass of milk. It's going to take me a while to read all these papers." He poured the coffee from his mug back in the pot, poured another mug full, and placed it next to the papers.

The special deputy moved to take a position in front of the sheriff's desk.

"So's I know I've done my job, do you accept those papers?"

"Oh, I accept them." Sheriff Simms smiled.

Deputy Orson stepped in behind the U.S. marshal and tapped him on the shoulder. "Here's your milk. I brought it from home this morning."

The special deputy turned to the senior deputy, "Thank you, Brother, but I'll be leaving. I figured if I could put these papers in the sheriff's hands and be out of here by ten, I could make it home with no more than an hour or so of darkness. And that on the other side of the summit."

"You're not wanting me to read these before you leave?" asked Sheriff Simms.

"No need. They're yours to carry out."

Sheriff Simms stuck out his hand. "I'm not meaning to send you on your way, but, from what you said, home must mean you're going back to Salt Lake. You best be going. I won't detain you any."

"Bountiful." The special deputy extended his hand to the sheriff. "Almost the same."

Sheriff Simms saw the special deputy through the door. While still standing there, he re-opened the sheaf of papers.

". . . The Congress of the United States acting within its power and beholden to its duty hereby declares the coal lands in the County of Summit, Territory of Utah, to have been acquired by the Church of Jesus Christ of Latter-day Saints after 1862.

". . . said lands are hereby forfeit.

". . . said lands upon the Service of this Notice of Forfeiture by the duly elected Sheriff of the County of Summit, Territory of Utah, shall be restored to the United States of America."

Sheriff Simms put the document back on his desk and thought for a minute.

First, he would have to consider that declaration of fact. Had the church bought those coal lands after 1862? He was not at all sure how to do that. He could go to Miss Lorimer tomorrow and ask if one of her students could do it. And there was the question of how the church had acquired those coal lands. Something bought and paid for, the church viewed to be permanent. He would have to inquire whether the Congress did, too.

For service to be perfected, everything had to be right. He found it convenient to roll over in his mind the question of whether he was the sheriff of Summit County, duly elected or not. He had spent the whole winter reading the Edmunds Act. Section 8 would not let him be the sheriff anymore. Section 9 said he was not the sheriff now. With questions like that in the air, how could service ever be perfected?

He opened the center drawer of his desk, refolded the sheaf of papers, and laid the tri-fold in before he closed it. An awful lot needed to be sorted out before he served these papers.

Three days later, Sheriff Simms approached the jail from the hills above, watching for any sign of the Williams brothers. The lack of a pink curtain told him they had not slept the night in town, but caution told him they could try to surprise him on a Friday by getting up early. He spotted the two Relief Society sisters standing on the steps.

Meant to be a source of calm befitting their name, relief society, those two women in their long dresses of dark fabric looked formal and stark and filled him with alarm. Elizabeth Tonsil's first birth in the five years since the diphtheria may have brought joy to her, but he was the one responsible. It brought risk and danger, and he convinced himself those sisters stood there waiting to tell him something bad had happened.

They stood at the base of the steps, waiting, saying nothing; both seemed unwilling to tell him the news. Radiating purpose, Emma Bullock stepped forward.

"You have a new baby. A girl."

Joyful news, but why so stern looking? He waited.

"Both are fine," said Sister Wilson.

"You may visit her, if you like," said Sister Bullock.

The sisters looked over his shoulder, up and down the street and, without a further word, left in their purposeful strides. He noticed the sisters did not walk toward the yellow house.

Sheriff Simms called his thanks to their backs for the good news. Their behavior spoke concern. He wondered why. He had no doubt the marshals' spies had reported Elizabeth Tonsil's pregnancy. What better proof that he was a cohabiter. Perhaps the marshals were not at the jail but at the yellow house?

Still, habits were habits. If the Williams brothers looked for him on a Friday and heard about the baby girl, when they went to the yellow house, they would go to the front door and knock. Sure, he could be surprised, but not too much to worry about. He'd have to be alert, but he could see his wife and new daughter on the day of her birth.

Elizabeth Tonsil handed him his new daughter. "I'd like to name her Clara."

"Of course," he said, beaming at his wife with baby Clara in his arms. "I should have kept my mouth shut."

"What are you talking about?" asked Elizabeth.

He bent over, cradling baby Clara. "I told you I noticed you were stronger."

"And I caught you napping." She pulled him down for a kiss and released him. He stood straight up. She laughed at his awkward shuffling around as if he had never held a baby. "I'm sorry your father's not here to see her."

Simms looked at Clara. "I guess he's in on it." He looked at Elizabeth. "I might 'a let myself get too cozy after a few days out looking for Hopt. You comfort me, and now look what that brought."

"What that brought, John Willford," said Elizabeth Tonsil, "is a beautiful new daughter. Life is wonderful. It forces its will on us."

CHAPTER 33:
JUNE 13, 1884

On April 24, after a winter and spring stalking cohabs and polygs in Salt Lake City, U.S. Marshal Jacob J. Eire took Rudger Clawson in hand on his first ever arrest and charge of cohabitation. The attorney general placed Clawson under a $3,000 bond. The strategy he cooked up with the marshal sought to bring the young man before the court using the cohabitation charge to subpoena and examine his suspected wife, Lydia Spencer. In their plan, she would answer questions proving she was Clawson's wife, and the grand jury would have evidence to indict him for polygamy. Eire's strategy impressed his special deputies in Summit County.

The Williams brothers, like all the special deputies hired by Eire, starved for lack of arrests, convictions, and—their goal—fines. At their boss's urging to greater motivation, they decided to try Eire's strategy on Bishop Roundy in Wanship. Although not yet knowing her name, they saw Nellie White go in and out of his home with Lovisa. That amounted to evidence adequate to charge Bishop Roundy with cohabiting. The six or seven months Eire stalked Clawson seemed a total waste to Enos Williams. The brothers convinced the attorney general to subpoena Nellie White, whom they then served and escorted to the courthouse in Salt Lake City.

When Albert Hopt showed up in the territorial penitentiary last September, he counted for a dollar a day less subsistence cost and a renewed opportunity to ensnare Sheriff Simms.

Hopt's January trial, conviction, and stay of execution till June barely registered with Marshal Eire. Fractious women plagued his major opportunities and demanded all his attention. He had not enjoyed the two and half months he held Belle Harris and her little boy in the apartment next to his. He arranged to have Rudger Clawson's trial held over to October so he would not have to face the prospect of housing Lydia Spencer at the same time he held Bishop Roundy's Nellie White for as long as she refused to testify or until the judge gave up. Defending his gentlemanly treatment of the twenty-year-old music teacher to the small, but rabid, group who wanted her pressured, if not tortured, into testifying occupied his attention without a moment to think about Hopt until he awoke Friday, June 13, and looked out the window.

"Penitentiary in danger. Mob congregated. Send U.S. Army for protection. Authorize hire thirty special deputies for pay. Danger in court delay Hopt execution date. Letter to detail."

Following his telegram, Eire dispatched a guard with his hastily written letter. An idea gave him one other hope to avert the lynch mob—the man he had raised no hand to help and had hunted for eleven months, Sheriff John Willford Simms.

As soon as Woodside understood Sheriff Turner's message from Marshal Eire he sent four boys in four directions to find Sheriff Simms.

"You stay right here and enjoy a scone," the deputy told the Salt Lake County sheriff. "I ain't about to let him walk in on anyone who associates with the U.S. marshal."

"Understood," said Sheriff Turner. "I been on the trail six and half hours from Sugar House; it'll do me fine to rest up."

The deputy left him to go check with Ann Cluff, the woman

who seemed to know the whereabouts of everyone without even inquiring. One of his four scouts caught him on the steps of the Cluff Hotel.

"Meet Sheriff Simms up on the sage bench," the panting boy breathed out. "You said urgent. He said right now."

Deputy Woodside spied Sheriff Simms in the middle of the sage bench beyond two Utes mounted at the front edge toward town. He rode his horse at a slow, deliberate pace.

"I see the Utes have moved in now the Shoshoni are on to Wyoming," Deputy Woodside said, pulling up to the sheriff, between the Utes.

"Like every year," Sheriff Simms said. "Good place. Washakie watches out for me, and I watch out for them. I notice you didn't tell the boy to fetch me to the jail."

"Sheriff Turner's there, up from Salt Lake . . . well, Sugar House," Woodside said. "Eire sent him. He says there's a mob upset at Hopt's stay of execution by the Utah Supreme Court. The penitentiary's in danger of a mob. He wants you to help prevent a riot."

"Whoa," Sheriff Simms said. "I'm on the mob's side. The court's supposed to set his execution date."

"Well, I guess the judge stayed it," Woodside said. "Turner didn't say that, though. Maybe the mob thinks he's going to. Anyway, Eire thinks it's a lynch mob."

"It's a trick." Sheriff Simms took a while before he said anything more. "And it's a damn good one. He's has to know I don't want Hopt lynched." He paused again to look west, gauging the four or five hours of daylight left. "What's he want me to do?"

"Turner wouldn't tell me," Deputy Woodside said. "He says he has to talk to you personally. That could be part of the trick, but I don't know that a county sheriff can arrest you if you don't want him to."

"Never met Turner," Sheriff Simms said. "Don't even know if he's LDS. Don't know if he was elected or Utah Commission. Don't know what to think."

"Boss, I don't want you to take any chances. I could tell Clive to put him in a cell before you'll show up to talk to him."

"There's an idea," Sheriff Simms chuckled. "Let's hold that one in reserve. What you might do is tell him to check his guns with Clive if he wears any."

Sheriff Simms told Woodside he'd be along and sent him on his way. He descended from the bench through the high hills, so he could see all Coalville beneath him. Careful to look up and down each street, no need to take the risk those Williams boys were in on the trick, he saw no sign or any horse he did not recognize. When he walked through the door, Sheriff Turner sat at his desk eating a scone and drinking milk.

"Well, that answers one question," Sheriff Simms noted, trying to gauge who Turner was.

"Not so much. The summer is upon us." Sheriff Turner held out his right hand. "And, may I simply say, my wife and I are aware that more than half the United States Congress has two families and three-quarters of those esteemed Congressmen cohabit with two women."

Simms laughed as he reached to shake Sheriff Turner's extended hand. "That answers the second question."

"I'm sure your deputy's told you"—Sheriff Turner moved from behind Sheriff Simms's desk—"there's a lot of excitement down there. Marshal Eire's concerned about mob violence."

"I already told my deputy. I line up with the people. Hopt's been convicted and sentenced; now the Utah Supreme Court gives him another stay." Sheriff Simms tried to gauge Turner, make a good people judgment. "I don't know where you stand, but that court is all the product of the Utah Commission, all non-Mormon, and—"

"I'm not so sure of that," interrupted Sheriff Turner in an amiable enough tone.

". . . well, maybe I'm not, either, for a fact, but the whole bunch knows a murderer has to be executed, and they're using him for advantage."

"That may be," agreed Turner. "It's not the court making this decision, it's the governor. Eire's trying to stop a lynching, and he's asked for extra deputies and the U.S. Army. You must believe he's really worried if he's sent me up here to ask for your help."

"Or he's cooked up a good trick," Simms said despite hearing the urgency in Turner's words. He stood behind his desk trying to decide whether to trust the sense of protection he felt in Turner's presence. It could have been pre-arranged, and the Williams brothers were now coming into town. He left his desk to grab a scone and returned to sit down and chew on it, hoping to mask his thoughts.

"The U.S. marshal has to have a grand jury indict you. Then he has to arrest you. Then the judge has to convict you. All of that to make a polygamy felony stick," Sheriff Turner said. "I'm told you're called a fugitive sheriff, but you're still called Sheriff Simms. All you have had to do is keep from being nabbed as a cohab."

Sheriff Simms watched Turner finish his scone, leaving the room in silence.

"Did you ever meet my pa?" he asked, brushing crumbs from his vest.

"Yes, I did," Sheriff Turner said. "He told me to get my people judgments right, first."

"Where are the special deputies?" Sheriff Simms asked.

"Don't know. Don't even know them," Sheriff Turned answered. "But we must move fast. There's a meeting at the Walker Opera House tomorrow noon to protest the stay of execution recommended by the supreme court."

"So what's Eire want me to do?"

"He wants you to talk to the mob, calm down the mob spirit, maybe make a committee to go see the governor," said Sheriff Turner. "He'll protect you. I believe him."

"Desperate measures," muttered Sheriff Simms.

"What's that?" Sheriff Turner asked.

Simms waved his hand at the question. "The marshal has promises out to a hundred special deputies who ain't made a dime yet off his promises. I'd best not trust one of his promises, neither." Sheriff Simms nodded toward his deputy. "Woodside can go speak for me. If you leave by five, you'll have four or five hours before dark, and you can let your horse rest overnight. You'll make it there by eight in the morning. Will your horse make it?"

"He's a good animal," Sheriff Turner answered. "And I know how to take care of him."

Sheriff Simms stepped around his desk to shake hands again with Sheriff Turner. "I don't want him lynched. I want him sent back to me, like the law says."

Woodside found a group of citizens interested in honor and the integrity of the law assembled at the Walker Opera House, no mob. He spoke and joined two other men in a committee of three to go to the governor, who said he refused to make a decision. With that decision, the governor postponed the execution until the supreme court met in October. Marshal Eire received authorization for thirty temporary guards at the penitentiary. In the afternoon of June 14th, he and Sheriff Turner rode out to the prison and found all was quiet. Upon their return to Salt Lake, Eire sent another telegram to the attorney general.

"Danger to penitentiary I think now past."

CHAPTER 34:
JULY 4, 1884

The three boys who planned the rodeo asked Sheriff Simms to open the festivities with a song. He considered the risk. The special deputies posed the threat. Marshal Eire would go to the celebration in Salt Lake for the nation's birthday. The whole county knew Deputy Simms carried his organ around on his back and accepted all invitations to sing. He had not sung once nor played his organ in public since he became Sheriff Simms last Pioneer Day. The three boys promised to keep a lookout, and,trusting their word, he now shivered his right shoulder out of the strap, twisted a bit, and slid his left shoulder out to leave his hand holding the strap. He set the organ on the reviewing stand and remembered Mayor Eldridge, of all people, had decided it for him.

That Saturday when he sent Woodside down to the Walker Opera House, Simms spotted the mayor emerging from the courthouse. By Eldridge's purposeful stride, he could tell the man had in mind to see him in the jail. Against his will, he knew he would have to talk to the mayor.

"I am here to tell you," Mayor Eldridge spoke with his first step through the door, and he kept talking and walking to the sheriff's desk without invitation or preamble, "it's my responsibility as the mayor and a county commissioner to be concerned about all the polygs and cohabs in town."

The sheriff said nothing, knowing the mayor's intended focus was not all the polygs and cohabs in town.

"I don't mind telling you that you are bringing undue attention."

"Undue attention?" repeated Sheriff Simms.

"Because of you, Saints who abide by the law of celestial marriage live in danger."

"Because of me?" repeated Sheriff Simms.

"More danger," Mayor Eldridge said. He held up a hand to forestall any further interruption. "Don't tell me you're not the only polygamist, and, if you weren't sheriff, the marshals would still be hunting polygs and cohabs. The truth is, they would not be hunting them here! We are not one percent of this whole territory. That you bring down on us."

Sheriff Simms sat at his desk facing the mayor. Respect for the office and contempt for the man fueled his stare. There was something to what the man said. "You think I'm the reason they took Nellie White to the penitentiary."

"Yes, I do," Mayor Eldridge answered and shook his whole body at the same time. "Those shiftless Williams boys would not even have been hired as special deputies if it wasn't for you."

The kernel of truth in the mayor's words stopped an immediate objection from the sheriff. He could only think that he would not consider handing over his job until he had fulfilled the county sheriff's responsibility with Hopt's firing squad. "You want to stop that, turn Hopt's stay into a real date."

The mayor found calm for his reply. "I'm not here to discuss that. I'm here to tell you I don't believe the marshals will be around on the Fourth. Last year they came on Pioneer Day only to find you. Logical enough given the dedication of your father's new jailhouse."

Sheriff Simms bit his lip. It didn't matter that because of him the marshals invaded an event the mayor insisted upon and his father did not want. All that mattered was the catastrophe that ensued from the mayor's self-centered creation. "You don't know that." Simms could hear his defensive words.

"Marshal Eire doesn't give a damn about Brigham Young saying, 'This is the Place,' but he does think Pioneer Day is more important to Latter-day Saints than Independence Day," continued the mayor. "He's not LDS."

"None are," muttered Sheriff Simms.

"To the good for our plans," continued Mayor Eldridge. "He'll be in Salt Lake with the rest of the federals celebrating the Fourth to prove the United States is more important than the church. It wouldn't surprise me if he demands the Williams brothers go down there to prove their loyalties are in the right place."

For the second time Sheriff Simms heard something he liked from a man he didn't trust. Still, it calmed him some that the boys would keep an eye out for the marshals. He decided he could relax his constant vigilance and sleep overnight in the Jensen house. Sleeping Thursday night in the fairgrounds wouldn't do, anyway. People started bringing their horses and rodeo stock the day before.

Sheriff Simms finished setting up the legs of his organ. One of the boys who had planned the rodeo, a sturdy young man but not as tall as the sheriff, climbed the steps to the reviewing stand and asked, "Do you have music?"

"Some," said Sheriff Simms. "I don't play much these days."

"Any popular music? Any new stuff?"

"Figured you'd ask. Young people want all the new things." Sheriff Simms lifted the top of his organ and looked at sheet music. "Not much here. You know Rabbi Sol?"

The boy shook, *no.*

"You wouldn't have any reason to know him." Sheriff Simms looked at the young man a moment. "You're a Pike, aren't you?

261

Your father was the trail captain, James Pike. Right?"

"Yes, sir. I'm Frank Pike."

"Of course." Sheriff Simms paused and it gave way to a question. "Say, don't you have a brother named Franklin?"

"Yes, sir, I do," said Frank Pike. "But we call him Dewey to keep things straight."

"Makes sense to me," said Sheriff Simms. "A bunch of Franks in our family, too. Anyway, I heard someone sing this new song a while back—'My Darling Clementine.' I asked Rabbi Sol to bring it to me. It's kind of funny."

"You got it?"

"Not yet. He was down to Salt Lake and should have made it back last night. I brought some hymns. 'The Battle Hymn of the Republic' ought to be a good one for the rodeo."

"You know that's a Yankee tune?" Young Pike leaned in close, like he was trying to see if he should say more and said, "Was that deliberate?"

"Nah, just a rousing song for the Fourth."

"I had the same idea. Only different."

"That makes sense." The sheriff laughed. He liked this young man's direct talk, a good family trait. "If you have something you want me to play, I'd be obliged. It's your rodeo."

"I was thinking 'The Star-Spangled Banner.' We had to learn it in school. It's not easy. Think you could pick it up?"

The sheriff saw nothing in the boy's hands.

"I'd need some music, but I'll give it a try."

"I have the music." Frank pulled the sheet music from a hind pocket and handed it to the sheriff. "People are playing it more and more on July Fourth."

Frank's grin made Sheriff Simms suspicious. It seemed all out of proportion to the simple subject of picking a tune to play before the rodeo starts. He decided it best to ask. He thought this boy would give him a straight answer.

"Am I missing something?"

"You were thinking a battle song, and you said it was rousing. Mine has rockets and bombs and even the gloom of the grave."

"The gloom of the grave?" repeated Simms. "Quite a phrase. Doesn't seem so funny. Why are you smiling like that?"

"Sheriff," the young man paused and hemmed and hawed. "Maybe I ought not to be suggesting you play it."

"Spit it out."

"It's a taunt. *See that flag still flying, the one you tried to capture? Well, I'm still here!*"

"Taunt the British? You think it'd upset me because my father's from England? Hell, I was born there."

"No. You!" Frank paused and looked to the sheriff for encouragement. Simms nodded. "You're the flag. See me, the one you tried to capture. Well, I'm still here!"

Sheriff Simms smiled and clapped the boy on the back.

"My pa agrees."

"You talked to the trail captain about this?"

"He thinks you're hard done by."

Sheriff Simms took a half step back in the rising temperature of the July morning. "Not hard done by"—he smiled his disagreement—"but the trail captain has a point. A rodeo's like a battlefield. Seems we both picked a song hatched in a war. Kind of an anthem before you go and give your all."

"Like saying, 'I'm gonna win.'" Frank studied the sheriff's face for any disapproval. "For the U.S. marshals to hear. Not that we want any marshals around today."

"A good day to play it, I agree, and let's hope the marshals're not here to hear it." Sheriff Simms laughed. He looked again at the young man, sizing him up. "Say, how old are you?"

"Eighteen."

"You know my father made Woodside a deputy last year when

he was eighteen."

"I know Vernon. He's a good bareback rider."

"I have an Uncle Frank. He's a good man. I'm always on the lookout for a good man."

"My ma and my pa both think we ought to leave the sheriff's job to the Simms family," said Frank Pike. "My ma says it's no kinda job to ask a woman to put up with. The last thing she'd want is for a daughter to marry a sheriff. I imagine she thinks the same for a son. Not that I can't think for myself, but I do believe she's right."

Ten a.m., July 4, 1884, Sheriff John Willford Simms played and sang "The Star-Spangled Banner."

Frank had called it right, a tricky piece. It surprised the sheriff to discover he felt nervous. No one had ever played to such a crowd in his county. His father had taught him he needed to be good at estimating crowds. The two stands had long since filled, and the overflow lined the fences. It looked like one out of every five in the county—had to be a thousand people.

Of one thing Sheriff Simms could be sure: nobody in his audience had more experience with "The Star-Spangled Banner" than he had. Even knowing the government had sent agents to hunt him for bounty, his excitement grew as he played and sang and thrilled to each new line, losing all sense of audience. He hit the last crashing note and lifted his finger off the key.

Dead silence.

A full five seconds followed before Mayor Eldridge recognized the opportunity to be the inspiration for a thousand souls. He leapt with his megaphone and shouted, "Let's rodeo!"

The parade's first flag walked through the gates, and Sheriff Simms broke down the organ. As he readied it to sling on his back, Rabbi Sol arrived at the foot of the reviewing stand.

"Inspiring." He held a printed sheet of music. "I guess you

don't need this."

"Young Pike's idea," said Simms. "Lucky. Where were you?"

"I might have set out a little late."

"Avoiding me?" Simms remained in a good mood from his performance, continuing to mount the organ on his back and now ready to go.

"No," said Sol. "Well, not a deliberate effort. You won't be happy."

"What'd you do?"

"Not me. I don't represent him, anymore. He doesn't trust Jews. Nor Mormons. Somebody, the judge maybe, asked Baskin to represent him."

Sheriff Simms felt sure he did not know all the implications of this news, but there was something familiar with the name.

"Isn't he the one behind those laws and the Edmunds Act?"

"He might have been in the business of drafting legislation," said Sol. "He's a Protestant, and I hear he's Harvard trained. So Hopt seems to have what he wants."

"A lawyer like that'd cost money, big money. Where'd it come from?"

"He might be useful to some people," Rabbi Sol answered. "Or the government."

"It don't matter." Sheriff Simms felt the full spirit of the anthem in him. "He'll still face the firing squad. You can't shoot a man in full view of everyone and go free."

"You may be right about that," said Sol. "The question's when? Baskin won him a stay."

"This the one to October?" asked Simms.

"You know?" asked Sol in surprise. "Do you know there's been a whole lot of changing with the judges. Seems Hopt has been assigned one who wants to cite your Apostle Penrose."

"I didn't even know we had an Apostle Penrose," said Sheriff Simms.

"Well, you do. Charles W. Penrose. He wrote an article for the *Deseret News* last July Fourth. He said in some cases murder might be forgiven, but only after the guilty party atones for the murder by the shedding of blood."

"I don't want to forgive the son-of-a-bitch. That's not why I want the judge to follow the territory's law." Sheriff Simms pumped once with his knees to hoist the organ higher on his back and walked off. For a moment Rabbi Sol did not realize Simms had left him behind. With two hurried steps he caught up.

"I have my cart," he said. "I'll give you a ride."

"No, walking will do me good." Simms did not stop walking. He did not look over his shoulder. "Thanks." He took the path south into town and turned on 100 N. A sheriff with an organ slung on his back walked to the yellow house.

He had guessed right about Marshal Eire and the Fourth of July. One more day free, now to think about tomorrow, though he didn't expect the Williams brothers to be working on a Saturday. He put his organ in the parlor and lifted the top to put away the new piece of sheet music. A country that spawned "The Star-Spangled Banner" did not deserve the laws—nor the marshals—that hounded him. Hound him but, like the anthem, never take him.

Chapter 35:
October 26, 1884

Samuel Carruth walked through the door straight to the sheriff's desk, oblivious to the conversation he interrupted.

"Sam." Sheriff Simms clapped him on the back. The interruption by such a polite man surprised the sheriff as much as the visit. "Meet Deputy Woodside. He and I were talking about the judge putting Lydia Spencer in the penitentiary." The blank look he received signaled no knowledge of the current controversy. Sheriff Simms motioned Deputy Woodside to give him some private space with Sam Carruth. "How's Emma? Seeing you reminds me; I haven't been to see her regular, or the baby. You have to tell her I'm sorry."

"The baby's three, and Emma understands," said Sam. "She knows the reason why. Your Elizabeth's baby is already six months old. The women talk."

The bond cast when Emma saved Elizabeth in the snows of Hilliard remained, though Luke Willford's death and John Willford's need to avoid regular habits created tributaries to the river of time that carved greater distance between the two families.

"Still, my troubles don't excuse me." The sheriff looked at his wall clock. He knew Sam Carruth left his house at five every morning, except Sunday, to make the trip to his mill. The big hand had not yet crossed ten o'clock. That about made for turning around and coming right back. "I'm pretty sure you're not here about my manners."

"Maybe mine." With a tone that carried a note of self-criticism, Sam looked and sounded dejected. "I may have talked too much. Every single thing about that mill was personal." In the month Emma Wilde made daily trips with food and medicine to save the Saints in Hilliard, Sam set out from Coalville and followed the railroad track down Weber Canyon on the lookout for a spot where he could build his mill. About five miles away, and about five miles east of Henefer, at the shoulder of the free-flowing Weber River, he found it. "After it took me four years to build, I've made a lot of flour these last eleven years, even when some years didn't yield but thirty bushels an acre. Now, we have a good year, and I guess I talked too much. I'm here to deal with the consequences."

"Sounds bad." Sheriff Simms watched Sam for a sign, but he had no idea what problem he faced. "Here, take a seat."

"It is bad." Sam looked at the chair, looked at Woodside, and sat. "I was a boy in Cheshire, England, and I wanted to be one of the men who made the flour. Not to be rich; it's a position of trust. Now, look what I've done."

"What have you done?" Sheriff Simms waved Woodside back to his desk.

"In poor years, people try to save a little grain. The church encourages that. We've had a good harvest this year. I'm not the only one's been talking about that.

"We had rain this year. That sandy soil soaked up the rain like a sponge. It doesn't sound like much, but it made this one of the years when there's extra. Three good harvests piled up thousands of sacks of grain in my mill. Every day I had more sacks of grain than I could turn into flour. You know, it's raised with a hoist to the top of the mill house and emptied into a hopper that runs the grain through a sieve, cleans out the chaff and the stone, and . . ."

"That all sounds good, Sam. What's the problem in that?"

Rude or not, Sheriff Simms had to interrupt, or he'd never learn what brought Sam to his jailhouse.

"Well, the wheel rolls over the stone to grind the flour, and, for once, everyone had extra. I offered all my customers to sell the extra flour, no charge for that service. I'd already received my miller's toll. When someone wanted to use it to pay their tithing, I gave it to the Church's welfare program."

Sheriff Simms guessed he might be at the beginning of the thread. "Did something happen to the Church's wheat?"

"Oh, no." Sam stood up and swung a firm back and forth, *no.* "The Church picks up their flour the day after I send the boy with word. Even one sack. No, the Church's flour has already long since been gone. This is the first chance we've had to sell flour. I tried to talk it up for the good of the farmers, and I might have caused the problem all by myself."

Sam seemed so upset by what had happened that he was going to beat around the bush all morning and never say what brought him to the jail. The sheriff tried once again to guess. "What problem? You showed up this morning after a day off, and some of the flour is gone?"

"Some?" sputtered Sam, his question an answer. "I found a spot where I could build a sluice gate and use a water wheel to drive the wallower to grind the grain, and that's where I built my mill, and I built a siding. I had to pay for the siding myself. The Zion's mercantile started collecting grain and flour to sell way back in '79. That didn't matter. Until this year, that siding of mine was nothing but a waste of money in the service of grand ambition. Now with some flour stored up and some flour to sell, the railroad gave me a freight car to fill. UP promised to hook it up and take it to Ogden for me."

Sheriff Simms now guessed Sam had unveiled the truth of the problem. "Someone stole your freight car? Where'd they round up a locomotive?"

"No, thank God," Sam said. His words seemed to weigh on him until he slumped back into the chair. "If they stole that, too, I'd have to pay the Union Pacific for the freight car. They took the flour. Broke the door, and I'll already have to pay for that damage. But it's all those poor people who are out. It's not my money; I never bought the flour. I was doing a favor with what's extra. Farmers could order finer or coarser flour, and I'd raise and lower the stone to produce what I was told."

Sheriff Simms could hear another explanation of milling about to delay the important message. "How much are we talking about?"

"A lot of money."

"How much?"

"We've been milling six days a week for two weeks, taking the flour and . . ." Carruth stopped talking, and his eyes flew wide open. "Oh, my God!"

"What now?"

"I never checked the grain sacks; maybe it's worse. Some farmers bring me corn, and I gave back corn meal. Most of the corn grown up here goes straight into silos and feeds the animals; half the wheat, hard red wheat, too. By the time the grain's sent to me, most've already fed their livestock. The flour feeds their family. Few families ever had extra; that's why this year was so special. I told you that only the families who had extra were hurt—"

"No you didn't," corrected Sheriff Simms.

". . . I didn't? . . . of course, I did. That's where the flour comes from, the extra, but . . . oh, anyway, if someone cleared out the grain sacks, too, some of that grain wasn't extra. A lot of families can't afford to lose much, if anything."

"How much?"

Sam Carruth fidgeted a little and hesitated. A pained expression crossed his face with whatever he was thinking. "The box car was near to full of milled flour. Milled flour gives grain a higher value, you know, so I had the box car locked. The grain was there, like always, some in the mill, some outside. It still needed to be worked, and you need a mill to work on it, so I never gave a thought to locking it up."

"How much?"

"I don't know, Sheriff. The door to the boxcar was open. I looked in; I didn't go in. Like I said, I didn't even check the grain. I climbed on my horse and rode straight to you. A boxcar's worth of whole wheat flour would go five, six hundred dollars. For the white flour, maybe a thousand, maybe a little more. It was all finely milled white flour. Damn. I made it easy. I had sacked it all in English sacks, two hundred eighty pounds each, trying to be ready for export."

"That is a lot," said Simms. He let a moment pass, calculating in silence, then he opened his desk drawer and pulled out a school notebook and a pencil. He made his calculations on paper. "I didn't mean the money. All that grain and flour must weigh a ton."

"Thirty, to be exact," said Sam. "Thirty tons. Thirty-ton carload."

"How'd anyone move all of that?" asked Woodside.

"See why I feel bad about it," said Sam, not a question. "I can't tell you how many families. Last year's crop was so bad, farmers could have done as well to burn it for fuel. I didn't do it, but I feel responsible. I can't make up that money."

Sam Carruth kept talking. Simms continued to make his calculations and did not look up from his school notebook. Deputy Clive Orson watched the one talk and the other calculate. Deputy Woodside stepped closer to the desk, looking to interrupt.

Sheriff Simms waved his deputy away and stood. He stepped over to his gun rack and took his Winchester. Rifle in hand, he moved closer to Sam and put a hand on his forearm. "Sam, we best go take a look. I don't see how someone made it away with all that. Best I can make out, two men working midnight to midnight might've been able to move a third of the flour. Even that's doing a lot."

"Easy," Sam said. "Bring more than two men."

"What they'd need," said Simms, "is more wagons—at least three. That's a lot of wagons. And most men aren't up to working twenty-four hours."

"I gave everyone off, Saturday. I gave 'em more time . . . made it worse." Sam paused. He didn't need a school notebook to do his calculations. "Even so. A third of a boxcar of flour works out to more than four months' railroad pay. Maybe twice that in two days. It'd be worth it. Most men don't have jobs these days, let alone make railroad pay."

"We'll go together and look." Simms laid his hand on Sam's arm, and it became a grip. He pulled until Sam followed his arm and stood.

"You've calmed me down some." Sam smiled.

"How're they going to make it pay?"

"Sell the flour."

"Well, you know that means whoever you're up against has to be awful smart," said Simms. "Like you, Sam. You have to know a lot to know you can sell flour."

"It doesn't take too much in the way of brains to know you can sell flour."

"Not so sure about that, Sam . . . not a thought I've ever had. Fact is, to sell that flour means getting it down to Ogden. Even if they move it piecemeal, there're lots of barns and sheds along the way, all with enough room to store a couple of hundred sacks of flour. I don't want you to think I'll be able to bring that flour back."

"Emma and I'll be plain satisfied if you can catch the ones

who took it," said Sam.

"Maybe not." Woodside stepped up next to the sheriff and tried to make his voice so only Simms could hear. He tugged at the sheriff's sleeve and guided him back into the barred area that separated the three cells from the front room. In a whisper, he continued. "What you said about how much it took to steal that flour, remember what we were talking about when Mr. Carruth interrupted?"

"Deputies invading Rudger Clawson's house? What's that to do with Sam?"

"Six deputies to chase down the kids dressed up as women." Woodside continued to speak as low as he could. "The government's the only organization can do a job that big."

"Government?" The sheriff's voice blurted full-force in his surprise at the deputy's suggestion. "You mean the U.S. Army?"

"Don't need to be the army." Woodside worked around so he was between the sheriff and Sam. "Lots of people work for the government for money. Like Enos Williams, for one."

"That's some theory." Even with his trust in the young man's judgment, Sheriff Simms could not accept this idea at its first mention. "You can't be thinking U.S. marshals are stealing flour to make money?"

"Those particular U.S. marshals are trying to arrest their brethren to make money. I'm thinking this make's icing on the cake." Deputy Woodside looked back over his shoulder at Sam. He returned to his answer in his quiet voice. "The whole county knows what Emma did. Those boys could know she's special to your wife."

The sheriff's eyes opened in an involuntary reaction, and now he spoke in a low voice. "You think Eire figures he can smoke me out? Because I'll want to help Sam?"

"I'm sayin', be careful."

"I don't know." Sheriff Simms shook his head, partly in

disagreement, partly to clear it. "Eire had a pretty big day on Saturday putting Lydia Spencer in the pen in Sugar House. I'm not sure how he could bait a trap up here for me."

"Think of it," said Woodside. "All they had to do was persuade him to hire some strong boys. He didn't need to be here."

"You sure?" Sheriff Simms shook his chin in doubt. Except for the money angle, this seemed way beyond the Williams brothers. "James and me even went fishing. We figured they'd all be busy with Clawson. A nothing Saturday. Turns out, not nothing if they stole Sam's flour."

"Boss, it wouldn't be the first time Enos tried to make money off his brethren."

"Could be." Sheriff Simms turned around and looked at Sam. He gave a rueful chuckle. "Hell of a day to go fishing."

Sheriff Simms feared it too late as the sun cast its sheet of gold across the western plateau and dusk settled in, but the news he sought required he try. He raced from Sam's mill along the Weber River through Echo and turned south to continue west of Rabbi Sol's house. He stopped at Sol's gate on the way back to his stall.

"What? Sundown on a Monday. You can't have a new client for me," Rabbi Sol said.

"Could be. I am out here because someone stole a boxcar's worth of flour from Sam Carruth," Sheriff Simms replied. He unlatched the gate and walked toward the porch. "But I stopped by because you were in Salt Lake."

"It'll hold till tomorrow," Rabbi Sol said. "Or at least until after you have dinner with Aryn and me."

"That bad, huh?" Sheriff Simms asked.

"You expected better?" chuckled Rabbi Sol. "Mormons have a lot to learn from Jews."

"Me, especially," said Sheriff Simms. He considered asking again about the news from Salt Lake, but he knew he spoke to a man who had complete control of what he wanted to talk about. "So, what's for dinner?"

After dinner, Sol took him to the rocking chairs on the porch. About halfway to a full moon, the new moon cast plenty of light for Indigo to carry him back to the fairgrounds.

"It's a little cold after dark this late in October," said Rabbi Sol. "Want a blanket?"

"I'll be fine," Simms said, buttoning his coat around him. "Just tell me. If you make it fast, I won't get cold."

"Oh, you'll heat up," said Sol. "There's lots to tell, and you're going to have to hear it in my order. First thing is, you know Judge Charles Zane arrived in September and took the bench."

"Is he the one supposed to set Hopt's date?"

"Like I said, in my order," admonished Sol. "First thing he did was establish open venire. That means anyone can sit on a jury, not only property owners. And it means the marshal can ask if they're Mormon. He can keep asking until he finds ones who aren't." Rabbi Sol bobbed his chin up. "You'll never see another jury like the one couldn't agree on Clawson."

"So, you're telling me everyone was so busy with Clawson, no one dealt with Hopt?"

"I'm coming to that." Rabbi Sol seemed to consider how to continue. "With Zane on the bench and open venire, Clawson'll be found guilty. It's going be a lot tougher for polygs."

"You mean, me, personally?"

Sol continued along the course he appeared to have chosen. "It'll go up to the U.S. Supreme Court, and we know how that'll end. I don't mean to make it personal, and you still live up here in the mountains. I wouldn't be letting my guard down."

"You still haven't said anything about Hopt."

"Oh, but I have. Hopt has a good lawyer. He knows Judge

Zane will not let a killer off, but the judge has other fish to fry."

"So, they gave him another stay," Sheriff Simms said.

"Without even going to open court. The judge issued his order in chambers."

CHAPTER 36:
APRIL 25, 1885

Sheriff Simms giggled with his laughing one-year-old daughter as he held her high in the air.

"I would have been happy enough with a boy." Simms kissed her on the nose. "It's all right to finish our family with little Clara."

Elizabeth swatted him. "Not something that falls under a sheriff's jurisdiction." She beckoned to take Clara back. "Boy or girl, there'll be no talk of finishing our family today."

Sheriff Simms wanted to protest. He kept quiet. Disliking what she said did not mean she was wrong. "We'll see. Life's unfair. We lost our babies, and Woodside lost Angeline when she gave birth to their baby this month. I don't want another baby and lose you."

"You know, it'd be best if you made it a habit to bring Vernon over here more often," Elizabeth said. "It'd be good for him and safer for you."

A comment like that made him wonder how much she knew and never talked to him about. He tested for hidden meaning, saying, "You know there's talk about not reappointing Eire. His special deputies haven't done much of anything. He protests the one and ignores the other by predicting a hundred arrests this year. Tells me the best thing to do is lay low. Even so, Grange showed up on April 1st, again. Seems he's figuring to make it an annual event."

Elizabeth stayed occupied with putting Clara to her breast

and rocking as the baby took the nipple. Successful in her important task, she looked at her husband and smiled before she asked, "I don't imagine you told him you refused to serve the papers?"

"Oh, I didn't refuse. No, sir. A lawyer told me the very best time to serve papers is on a Sunday, so that's when I rode out there. Another example of how useless lawyers are. Blamed wrong. Nobody there. I told Grange that."

She nodded amid an even bigger smile. "Are you going to have more trouble for not serving those papers?"

"That's rich," he laughed. "That's part of what Grange wanted. I gather the Supreme Court had a case a week or two before the Clawson case and decided family was *from the union for life of one man and one woman.* That's a quote."

Elizabeth lifted the baby over her shoulder and burped her. The conversation ended until she put Clara down for a nap. Simms thought about his six daughters as he watched Clara. He saw all six—not very often. Elizabeth stared into his face until she retrieved his attention. "That about the law sounds like a trick. What's it mean?"

"It means Grange knows if the Utah Commission took a mind to it, I couldn't be sheriff," Simms said, and, with a deliberate shift to a light and joking tone, he added, "And it also means I could go to jail for Clara."

She laughed aloud. "Oh, it does not. And that's not something to tease about."

"I'm not teasing. They sent a guy to jail in Arizona in '83. He married his second wife in '68. Almost like us. What's more, he said what I'd say. The judge asked which of his wives he was going to give up. Good man that he was, he told 'em damn straight, 'Neither. I married both in good faith, and I intend to support both.' "

Elizabeth Tonsil never called herself the second wife, and he knew she would never ask any questions. Conversations with his Elizabeths often found John Willford handling both ends of a discussion.

"Looks like women are not being prosecuted," he continued. "I don't know who's behind this, but they're making it into plain licentiousness and making women victims."

"Why that's offensive all by itself. I'm not anybody's victim."

Simms laughed and bobbed his agreement. "Damn right! You're nobody's victim."

Clara had fallen asleep. He leaned over her and kissed his wife on her cheek.

"The newspapers call it 'The Raid.' There's talk of holding a mass meeting at the tabernacle to protest the heavy hand of the federal authorities."

"That would be doing their job," Elizabeth said. "Round you up and lock the doors."

John Willford laughed at the image she created in his mind's eye. "You do me good." He stood and brushed out the bedspread. "I'm not sure I can save those coal lands. What this is about is men who want the church's property. Those men'll find a way without me."

Simms caught himself being too serious. He could feel it in his face. "You know, if it wasn't for Hopt's new stay, all of this should be funny. Somebody wants to arrest me for a law I don't agree with. And the same people want me to enforce an action against the church I don't agree with." He wiped his hand over his face, replacing the seriousness with a look of determination. "President Taylor told us to run, but I'm not going to. Nobody's going to take me until after I have Hopt before the firing squad. No matter how long that takes."

"Do you think you could make it a little longer than that?" Elizabeth asked with a wry smile. "Like, forever?"

Simms's determination dissolved into a smile. "They'll play Billy-hell getting me at all."

CHAPTER 37:
JULY 24, 1886

An army colonel fighting a religious war turned Parley's Park into Park City. The Union sent Colonel Patrick E. O'Connor to Utah Territory in 1862 to keep an eye on the mail routes during the Civil War. Dropping the "O'" to serve his ambitions, the colonel knew the Mormons posed no danger to the mail routes. The danger lay in being Mormons. Colonel Connor ordered the United States Army to camp in a meadow and climb high into the mountains above to prospect for the minerals he averred would destroy the stranglehold of the Mormon agricultural economy. He kept the soldiers digging. Two days before Christmas in 1869, someone filed the Young American Lode claim. Turning dirt into money motivated three thousand newcomers to swarm over the two hundred Saints in Parley's Park. Pioneer Day meant nothing to Park City's gentiles, but they welcomed the annual opportunity to celebrate one more day's survival in the bowels of the mountains.

With no families for whom to save the meager money earned in the mines, these celebrating men spent their wages on the comfort of women and the bottle. In keeping the peace, and to accommodate the need for a place to sleep it off before the next day's labor, the city fathers dug a jail into the mountain under City Hall. Sheriff Luke Willford Simms applauded the decision. Sheriff John Willford Simms played in that jail as a child, took inmates to it as a deputy, and now used it as sheriff.

Ann Cluff's pink curtain in the window surprised Sheriff

Simms. By habit, he had looked but not expected the signal. The Church authorities in Salt Lake City had called the territory to spend this Pioneer Day Saturday in mourning for the one hundred imprisoned and for those in hiding from worse yet. He surmised Ann wanted to express her blessing and support.

"Your deputy's at Street's house in Park City," Ann Cluff said when Sheriff Simms stepped into her lobby. "Three good old boys don't want to pay their fine, and the justice of the peace says the jail over there isn't set up to keep anybody thirty days."

"John Street's a good man. We'll take 'em," Sheriff Simms said. He nodded toward the pink curtain. "Anything else I need to know about?"

"No, only Deputy Woodside's telegram," Ann Cluff said. "Making this a day of mourning aims to slow down that new Marshal Franks. You know he might've come about because of that crossing accident up in Echo. What with all he did, Eire didn't move fast enough. I remember the editorial they wrote about the tragedy: *It is high time to bounce that born and trained scrub J. J. Eire from the office of United States marshal.*"

Sheriff Simms hadn't thought of that. He nodded at this astute woman. "Well, Franks is making his mark. He already has fifty subpoenas from the grand jury."

"Moves fast," Ann Cluff said, "but he won't butt his head against the wall. There won't be polygamists on the street today." She looked at Sheriff Simms, and a smile spread on her face. "Come to think of it, you best be careful over in Park City. I wouldn't put it above those Williams boys to be celebrating in one of the saloons."

Shortly after noon, Sheriff Simms tied Indigo to the hitching post in front of Judge Street's white stucco house accented with brown boards, up and down, sideways, and cross-wise. It spoke of a style that coincided with the money to afford it, money Park City's justice of the peace could earn working as a lawyer down in Salt Lake.

"John," called Judge Street from his porch, "good to see you. I'm thrilled—and surprised—to see you still on the job."

"I hear that from time to time," Sheriff Simms said. "What about you? No problems?"

"I'm not a bishop," Justice Street chuckled. "A lawyer, no more. One wife. They might not have wanted a Mormon justice of the peace up here."

"Today"—Sheriff Simms talked as he strode up the walkway to the porch—"it doesn't seem to matter either way. Pretty subdued."

"Damn lucky no one's mourning for you."

"Some deliberate on my part, too. Hopt finagled another stay last January, until January of '87. Who knows when they're going to send him back to me. I plan to be here when they do." The sheriff shook the justice's hand. "Ann Cluff warned me. She sent her regards. Where's Woodside?"

"Down at the jail. Three of the boys, drunk and disorderly, refuse to pay the price of that ticket. No tickee, no washee. Thirty days if you don't pay your fine, and that means county jail. Their friends promised not to let Woodside take them to Coalville. I imagine that's an idle boast, but I don't want anybody hurt because those three boys are drunk."

Sheriff Simms chuckled. He clapped John Street on the back. "Nobody'll get hurt. A mite sore, but not hurt."

Sheriff Simms had a plan, and he rode Indigo to city hall. My God, all that money and commerce added up to a pretty town, even if tailings scarred the mountain and cribs lined the side of Poison Creek. It made him feel downright cheerful about the prospects of his plan. He left Indigo at the railing and walked through the corridor inside city hall to the stairs down into the jail beneath the mountain.

Two carved-out rooms faced by a single wall of iron bars driven into the surrounding rock created a large and a small cell filled to standing room only by miners. Woodside arose from his chair next to the large cell when he heard the first step on the stairs. He called, "Marshal Bock's down here with me."

"Good to hear," said Sheriff Simms as he cleared the last step into the lantern's glow on the oval space in front of the two cells. "Not to put too much on it, but we've already had a Pioneer Day with three men and a jailbreak."

"Oh, my gosh, Boss, I didn't even think—" said Woodside.

"Don't," interrupted Simms. "We're not going to let anyone get the drop on us. It's nice and dry out there, and we're gonna haul these guys out in their own cloud of dust."

"Hey, it's noon." A croaking voice arose from the small cell.

"No matter how many hours they spend drunk," chuckled Sheriff Simms, "they know when it's time to let them out." He motioned to Bock and asked, "Can you leave them a spell and go with me to fetch three horses from the livery?"

"All of 'em'll be back in tonight." Marshal Bock swept his hand across the inmates. "I'll make it up to them with an hour off tomorrow."

When Simms and Bock returned from the livery, the sheriff hollered down to Woodside to bring up the three miners. The marshal watched the street in case unwanted help arrived.

Sheriff Simms tied the three horses together, halter rope from the third horse to the saddle horn of the second horse, same for the second horse. He held the halter rope of the first horse to walk all three in a line. Woodside looked over the arrangement and waved each miner, one at a time, to climb on a horse. Sheriff Simms looped the halter rope over the hitching rail and took a long rope and tied the hands of the first miner to his saddle horn. Then he strung the rope to the miner's ankles and tied his feet together with the rope running under the girdle. He played the rope out to continue it back to the hands and feet of the second man and repeated on to the third. He looped the extra rope and tied it to the saddle horn.

After he finished the lashing together of men and horses, Sheriff Simms stepped back and looked at his handiwork. "I'm going to take the halter for the first horse."

Woodside nodded and asked, "And I'm to bring up the rear?"

"That," Marshal Bock offered, buoyed by his talk with Sheriff Simms while bringing the horses from the livery, "and making a lot of dust if five horses don't make enough."

"Yep, we're going to run these guys out of town. Right past their friends," Sheriff Simms said, struggling to keep as serious as the moment required. He finally let go with a grin. "I always wanted to see how run-outta-town would work."

"All the way to Coalville?" asked Woodside.

"We'll see. First, past that saloon at the bottom of Main Street with the cute name."

"Wet Your Whistle," offered Marshal Bock.

"That's the one." Sheriff Simms pointed as he stepped into his saddle. "Marshal, I'd be obliged if you kept a watch up the street." He tied the halter rope tight around his saddle horn. He watched Woodside climb up, then reached for his hat and hit his leg with a pop. "Let's go!"

All five horses followed the pace Indigo achieved with her second step, and she continued to pull. They arrived at the bottom of Main Street and passed Wet Your Whistle before anyone except Marshal Bock knew they had left. For several moments after they passed onto Prospector Street and down toward Kimball Junction, the dust cloud continued to hover in the path behind the five horses. If the would-be rescuers ever made it out of the saloon, they could not see their friends disappearing down the canyon.

At the base of the canyon trail, before it turned into the high, wide, and flat plateau that led toward Coalville, the sheriff stopped and checked the ropes. He pulled each miner's legs as tight as he could beneath his horse. "In case anything jumps out at us, I want to make it good and safe for you."

"Jesus, Sheriff, you're crushing my balls."

"I am?" Sheriff Simms asked, moving to the next miner to tighten the lashing on his feet.

Indigo set the pace for the twenty-four-mile trip according to what was best for her. The miners' horses walked from time to time, but Indigo loved to run. The sheriff held Indigo back to a trot four or five times and with that leisurely pace returned to the jail after four in the afternoon. Simms untied the miners. They howled and reached for their crotches. "Follow Woodside," he said amidst the continual moaning. "He'll show you to your home for the next thirty days."

"We want to call the judge," spoke the one whose walking did not take his breath away. "We'll pay his fine if he sends our friends over here with a hay wagon to ride us back to work."

"Park City has telephones," said Simms, "not Coalville. Have money for a telegram?"

Judge Street sent Marshal Bock to make sure all the miners, supine in the hay wagon brought by their friends, returned to Park City.

When the miners left on Sunday, Sheriff Simms waved from the steps of the jail. He recalled the words of Ann Cluff. They forced him to review the increased threat of the past year. Everything had been stepped up a notch after the accident at the railroad crossing and the appointment of that new U.S. marshal. He shook his head and said to Woodside, "Next time I see John Street, I'm gonna thank him. Pioneer Day preys on me. Tomorrow it's back to dealing with Hyer Franks and his fifty subpoenas, but, today, I didn't think about it at all. He gave me the chance for some pure, rich fun doing my job."

CHAPTER 38:
SEPTEMBER 1886

Sheriff Simms awoke Monday after six thirty, burdened by the thought he had disappointed Sam Carruth and, worse, let Emma down. Labor Day had begun to take hold with people in his county these past two years, and knowing the flour was gone, knowing who took it, and knowing he could do nothing about it added up to a late start and a vague wish he could continue his slumbers. Labor Day might be the one good federal law he had seen. He had missed checking the window at the Cluff Hotel on Sunday. He tried to count that as a good reason to stay under his blanket, but it did not suit him. True, he needed to avoid the marshals, but he needed more to resist letting them interfere with his responsibilities. He had to check in on Elizabeth Jensen before he made his wary way to the jail.

Anna made him bacon and eggs, and Sheriff Simms took it to sit on his wife's bed. She watched him without comment or question. He wondered about her condition and discarded the thought of asking her. Certain she had no idea of the world outside her bedroom, he chose a cheery note. "It's gonna be a beautiful day, out there. Good day for a picnic." Simms watched his wife. Her eyes widened. Encouraged, he added, "We could find some place hidden away."

A commotion behind him led to Anna's cry, "I tried to keep them out, Daddy."

Sheriff Simms turned to see Enos Williams holding his daughter by the wrist. Enoch Williams stood behind, and all three filled the door frame.

The sheriff's face filled with rage as he stared at Enos Williams. Enos drew his revolver part way from the holster at his hip.

"I don't approve you took hold of her, but I take that hasty action to be in your effort to surprise me. I don't count you as using her for a shield. You may let her go." Sheriff Simms raised his half-empty plate up as proof of his next statement. "I am here. I never expected you boys here. I'll admit, you appear to have outwitted me." He watched until he saw Enos Williams drop his grasp on Anna's arm. He had left himself no action except to nod toward the door. "Anna, go fetch these men some breakfast."

"We can't eat your food," said Enoch Williams.

Simms raised an eyebrow. "Don't see why not. I'll finish, all the same. Do you mind?"

"Hurry up," said Enos Williams.

"In a hurry, huh? Charge in and threaten my house?" Simms chewed and nodded, carrying his shoulders with the movement. "I see you been busy. I guess I thought you were taking a day off. I been meaning to ask if you were the ones raided Hoytsville, took away Moses Leander and Christian Smith. I imagine you were. I know the both of 'em. Hard-working men, with fifteen or sixteen children between them. So, you sent 'em up for unlawful cohabitation. A term in prison for the fathers, starving for the children, and what was in it for you? The judge makes 'em worth three hundred bucks apiece. What's your split on six hundred bucks?"

"None of your business," said Enos. "They was breaking the law."

"Right. Too bad you couldn't find a grand jury up in these mountains and persuade it to give you an indictment for polygamy. You could have split a thousand bucks."

"Shut up," said Enos. "You get paid in fines; don't be a hypocrite."

Simms remembered years before his father thumped the young Enos with his walking stick. What he wouldn't give to thump Enos Williams. The boy had no spine and no sense.

"Nope. My pa set up as constable with no money from fines, only fees. Now it's two bucks a week plus fees," said Sheriff Simms. "Bounty hunting for cohabs and polygs may look like a pretty good business, but not for a Simms. We split the fees with the deputies, and we don't let anybody collect a bounty."

"Too bad. Show's I'm working for the right man," sneered Enos. "Let's move."

"That's right. You're in a hurry," said Sheriff Simms. "In that case, Anna, send James up to Elizabeth Tonsil. Tell her to have Deputy Woodside take over. He'll know what to do."

"What's that mean?" Enos's hand once again pulled at his gun.

"Best not clear that." Simms pointed at the gun with his fork. "It's bad enough you're in my wife's bedroom; don't add to it."

Instead of leaving, Anna stepped forward into the room. She stood between her father, still sitting on the bed, and the two deputies, still standing in the doorway. Her eyes darted back and forth between these men vying for the upper hand.

Simms watched Enos, waiting until the special deputy realized he would lose what little power he had if he reached for his gun. His hand fell away to his side.

"Did Franks have a warrant for me?" asked Sheriff Simms. "You have one?"

Enoch Williams reached into his breast pocket and pulled a handful of warrants. In the process, he lost his grip. A half dozen uniformly folded sheets tumbled to the floor.

"Don't need one," said Enos. "You know that."

"Didn't think you had one," said Simms. "I been keeping my

ear to the ground. My name don't mean nothing to the grand jury in Salt Lake."

"You're cohabiting," said Enos. "That's all we need. We can arrest you. That's what we're doing. We arrest you under Section 3 of the Edmunds Act for cohabiting."

Sheriff Simms considered disagreeing with young Williams. This attempt to arrest him taking place in the bedroom of his first wife, even if cohabitate had been defined down to mean mere support, might not . . . and he stopped building his argument in his mind. He looked at Elizabeth Jensen, saying nothing and watching nothing, and a suspicion grew in him.

"You plan to subpoena my wife?"

"Mrs. Simms won't be asked to testify against you," said Enoch Williams.

Sheriff Simms frowned at the clever answer, not knowing if he meant Elizabeth Jensen or Elizabeth Tonsil, but unwilling to pursue it further in Elizabeth Jensen's bedroom. "Like I said, I'll finish my breakfast, and we'll go."

"Hand over your gun, first." Deputy Enos Williams stuck out his hand.

"Nah," said Sheriff Simms. "I paid good money for it, and, forgive me, I don't want to risk it going lost. I'll give it to Elizabeth here. You can see she poses no threat to you."

"Give it to me," said Enos.

"That's all right," said Enoch. "It don't concern us, as long as he don't have it."

Simms put his plate on the bedspread. He pulled his pistol with his left hand so it rose in front of him butt first. When he moved to hand it to Elizabeth, she made no response to take it. He placed it next to her on the bed. He looked at Enos and nodded to Anna.

"Go tell James to put that in the drawer. Better yet, never mind what I said. I'll tell him on the way out."

The Williams brothers shared the industrious traits of the Latter-day Saints. Without yet catching a cohab, they stole Sam Carruth's flour under the ruse of smoking one out, and it made more money for them than catching the cohab they were after. Being born LDS conferred the perfect pedigree for the business they now ran—one thousand cattle that belonged to the LDS Church. These boys did not even have to deal with the Branding and Herding Act of 1886, passed by the territorial legislature. Their herd had been driven up from San Juan County, not rustled as defined under the Act. Simms assumed their large herd owed to papers served on the LDS Livestock Company of the same kind Deputy Grange had given him. Those papers languished in his desk. If he could connect with Orson, or pass a message to him, his deputy would make sure those papers ended up lost or destroyed.

"You boys have done well for yourselves," said Sheriff Simms, stepping out his front door onto the porch. "And I see that new marshal has renewed your interest in the cohab business." The sheriff breathed in the cool, dry air of late summer in a mountain desert. He smelled the sage from the plants growing in the foothills after a long, dry summer. Raising his head to look into the blue sky, he saw no horses in sight. He had left Indigo at the yellow house and walked here. He guessed the deputies had done that, too.

Hearing no response from his captors, he continued his survey, looked down the hill, past the jail, and onto Main Street. Of the two people he saw, neither looked like Marshal Franks. He stepped off the porch and walked toward the jailhouse. Sheriff Simms moved along at a brisk pace, buoyed and embraced by the cool air. He made no effort to find out who was keeping up with him. They thought they had a prisoner; let them tell him what to do.

"Where you going?" Enos's voice assaulted his ear from behind his shoulder.

"To tell my deputy I won't be in," said Sheriff Simms, without breaking stride.

"I thought you did that," said Enoch.

"How so? I sent James to tell Woodside to take over." Simms corrected the senior Williams and continued his fast walk downhill. "Clive Orson arrives by seven and sets everything up for the day. He'll be noticing I'm not there."

"If he needs to know anything," said Enos, "Enoch'll tell him."

"Good." Sheriff Simms stopped walking ten feet from the jailhouse steps. He let the Williams brothers catch up to him. "Enoch, you go in there and tell Deputy Orson what I told you. Tell him you've arrested me. Don't let anything he says bother you. He won't be happy. Tell him I'll be a while, and tell him he should clean out my desk. Tell him I want Vernon to take over with a clean slate, sit there without the bother of any of my stuff."

"Now, you're being realistic," said Enos. "Go on." Enos motioned his hesitant brother up the steps and through the door. "Tell him that exactly, because the sheriff won't be coming back."

Hearing no further instructions to him from Enos, Sheriff Simms resumed walking and turned on Main Street toward 100 N. Sheriff Simms walking up Main Street after breakfast made for a common enough sight when the town had sent the signal the marshals were not around. On a new federal holiday, the sheriff with no gun in his holster walking in front of Enos Williams proved interesting enough to send unseen runners who spread the word. Soon people lined both sides of Main Street.

The special deputy U.S. marshal and his prisoner had to walk two blocks. By the time they turned toward 50 E., an anonymous walk swelled into a Labor-Day parade.

The crowd turned the corner with the marshal and his prisoner to the cross street where the yellow house stood. Sheriff Simms saw nothing unusual in the front yard. He noticed three horses and a man he had never met in the back. No surprise to see Franks there. Simms figured the plan had been to catch him at breakfast with Elizabeth Tonsil, in hopes of making a cohab case without her testimony. When leering through the windows at empty rooms had produced dashed hopes for his presence, his pursuers took a stab at the Jensen house. Quick thinking on their part. Slow-witted on his.

"I suppose you'll want me to be going with you." Simms talked as he walked, letting his words stream back to Enos and pointing to Franks and the horses now in full view.

"That's why we arrested you." Enos's voice sounded loud and strained. The sheriff's normal voice boomed as big as all outdoors, never strained. Enos wanted the crowd to hear him, wanted the whole county to share his view of his importance as a special deputy U.S. marshal. Sheriff Simms thought Woodside would never indulge himself in that mistake.

A crowd of young men surrounded Enos Williams. Simms knew all the boys by sight. More than half had experienced his father's, or his, brand of how-to-bring-up-boys—a good thumping and a talk with the parents. That talk coming after Clive Orson had found the father for the long walk to the jail to retrieve his son. Simms recognized the lead antagonist to Special Deputy Williams. The young man's father, Leon, had arrived for the talk. When his son mouthed off, he turned to the sheriff, pointed to the cell, and said, "Lock it good."

"Sheriff," young Leon yelled. "Walk away. We won't let him follow after you."

The sheriff raised his right hand in a staying motion and turned to Marshal Franks.

"I'll need to say goodbye to my wife." His all-outdoors voice did not stray from normal. It was a simple statement of fact.

"Then you don't deny it?" The U.S.mMarshal's tone accused him of an answer to a question not asked.

"What's to deny?" Simms acknowledged the crowd with a wave of his hand. "All these people know I married Elizabeth Tonsil after she lost her parents coming here. That's why she was an orphan."

"No." Hyer Franks stepped in front of him to block the door. "You're not going to have any truck with this woman. I assume you did say goodbye to your wife."

Simms could feel the heat gathering under his shirt, but he said nothing.

Franks bulled through, disregarding the sheriff's silence. "Your wife cannot be happy with this vile institution. This woman is no more than someone you cohabitate with."

Like he was watching himself, Simms responded without knowing the source of the calm in his demeanor. "It is not yours to judge. The bishop married us. She is my wife."

"Not in the eyes of the United States," said Franks. "All you have done is cohabitate, and you have a child to prove it."

"Yes, we do. Clara's about two and a half now."

"See! What'd I say?" exclaimed Franks, not a question.

Sheriff Simms shook his head. "A murderer goes from stay to stay, and all that concerns you is to destroy my family."

Elizabeth Tonsil opened the back door and came out with a basket hanging over her arm. One hand carried a quart of milk, the other a pie.

"Oh, my sakes," she said, nodding toward the crowd that had followed from Main Street. "I didn't plan on so many."

She set the basket on the porch and reached in it to retrieve plates for the apple pie. Enoch Williams arrived from the jail, and she picked him to get the first piece.

"We can't eat your food," said Enoch.

"Oh, fiddlesticks; of course you can." She motioned toward the horses. "Looks like you're planning to go somewhere. Best you have something on your stomach. John Willford loves pie for breakfast. And go back to the shed; you can feed your horses, too."

Sheriff Simms watched the U.S. marshal and his two special deputy U.S. marshals take in the energy and liveliness of Elizabeth Tonsil.

"She's nature's own." Simms nodded and laughed the words and kicked the ground with his heel. "Wouldn't you say?"

No one said anything.

"Well, where are you taking me?"

No one said anything.

"I doubt you're going to ride these horses all the way to Ogden."

"Why not? I rode my horse from Salt Lake," said Marshal Franks.

Sheriff Simms considered the voice he missed these past three years. *Never show off what you know.* He wasn't the only one who knew the railroad built the track down Weber Canyon because it was the best way to travel through these mountains.

"Then, you'll be taking me to court in Salt Lake?" Simms asked.

"What difference does it make?" asked Franks.

"Well, unless you're going to arrest Indigo, I'm still responsible for her. I'll need Seth Parker to fetch her."

The Williams brothers waited in silence, looking at Marshal Franks, until he motioned Enoch over to him and whispered in his ear.

Enoch nodded and turned to take off on his errand and

caught sight of the crowd. He took two steps to stand close to Sheriff Simms. "You might say you and me's of the same opinion. The law we're upholding is all wrong. But we're no different from you, doing our job. It's our duty. Of all the men I arrested, I hated to arrest you more than any of the others."

Sheriff Simms considered the boy as he spoke and thought *how lucky it is you have arrested so few.* He pondered whether to tell Enoch what he thought, maybe say nothing. He could not do that, either.

"It may be your job. It's not your duty." Sheriff Simms shook his head in sorrow. "You're a young man. You made a poor choice. Judas ended poorly."

U.S. Marshal Franks stepped in front of his special deputy. "Get! We can't leave till you're back." He shoved his special deputy by the shoulder in the direction of Main Street.

"I want to stop at Rabbi Sol's on the way," said Sheriff Simms. "He'll know how it works. Maybe he can secure a bondsman so I can go back to work and support my family."

"You're going to be in jail," said Franks. "You should have thought about supporting your family before you started cohabiting."

Simms felt the gathering heat. He waited a long moment. He hoped he could find a piece of calm again. He found it, and, in the search, he found something else.

"You know"—the sheriff pitched his voice way lower than all of outdoors, a confidence he aimed to share—"I figured out you're doing me a favor. As long as I'm not indicted for polygamy, even the Edmunds Act lets me keep my job. So, I'm still sheriff. Go ask for your indictment, Franks. Stop talking about cohabiting."

Franks looked down to confirm the sheriff's empty holster. Bolstered, he asked, "Are you resisting arrest?"

"No, I'm saying we need to stop at Rabbi Sol's on the way to Echo."

"Who said we're going to Echo?" asked Franks.

Simms smiled and cut into the pie that Elizabeth had placed in his hand.

"To put me on the train to Ogden." Once again Sheriff Simms heard *Never show off what you know.* He thought that a caution against bragging. He was not bragging; he was admitting he knew what Franks knew. Simms put the piece of pie in his mouth, chewed, and ran his tongue around the flakes of crust left on his lips. "You sent Enoch Williams to the telegraph office, right next to Seth Parker's livery stable. I imagine the whole town'll know before we even leave."

Sheriff Simms feared he had as much as admitted he had no plan except to cooperate, go along, and escape. Talking too much is always a mistake. The law that bestowed the power to arrest him allowed him to be sheriff until the grand jury indicted him, and that was never going to happen. Practical politicians created laws driven by their vision of gains in store upon breaking the church's hold on the territory. Bountiful ends justified the army of mercenary special deputy U.S. marshals, like the Williams brothers, all raiders employed on contingency to arrest cohabs. It amounted to counting the money.

Marshal Eire had been a good businessman and made good money with the fines and subsistence funds from a hundred-fifty cohabs and polygs. Here was Franks, two months in, with fifty indictments and Sheriff Simms in hand—living proof that Marshal Franks had brought more simple determination than Eire. Summit County added up to thirty thousand dollars as sure as could be if the Williams brothers could catch the cohabs. Franks expected them to do so and leave him to work the grand jury that could net thirty times as much down in Salt Lake.

Sheriff Simms walked past Marshal Franks into the shed where he kept Indigo and his tools. He saddled her and walked her out to the three waiting horses. One man broke from the crowd. Another man walked toward him as stately as could be. Both shook his hand.

"It's an injustice, this crusade against the polygamists," said the man of stately bearing, a bearded elder of the church whom Sheriff Simms knew not to be a polygamist. "Particularly in the segregation of time. The judge put Elder Brown away for four counts of six months, the full time for each wife."

Sheriff Simms didn't know Elder Brown, except to know the elder was a more valuable target than he. Almost anyone would be higher in the church and a more valuable target than he.

"Thanks, Brother Crittenden." Sheriff Simms extended his hand before he mounted Indigo. "I don't mean much to the church, but the Williams boys might make some money."

"Well, don't you worry," said Brother Crittenden. "I own the bank, and your credit is good with me. Marshal Franks shouldn't be too proud he's done something Marshal Eire couldn't do for three full years. Pay the fine if that's what will keep you as our sheriff."

The marshal and his special deputy mounted. By now, a long line waited to shake the sheriff's hand.

"Enough of this," said Franks. "I want to make the noon train." He took Indigo's bridle and turned the horse north. Elizabeth stepped forward and pulled her husband down to kiss her.

"What do you want me to do?" she whispered in his ear.

He read the tight lines and drawn skin on her smiling face. He kissed her on the forehead. She was the wife the U.S. attorney would subpoena.

"Take care of Clara," he said in his regular voice, for all to hear. "I'll see you in Ogden. If anyone asks, answer the truth. We're a family. Even if I go to jail, we'll still be a family."

North of the fairgrounds on the way out of town, Sheriff Simms turned off the road and pulled up to Rabbi Sol's gate. U.S. Marshal Franks protested and cut it short, easier to escort his already walking prisoner to the rabbi's front door.

"That's as far as you go," called Rabbi Sol, standing in his door. "He's my client, and we'll talk in private." The lawyer took Sheriff Simms by the elbow to walk him inside.

When the sheriff re-appeared, Marshal Franks stepped up to him at the door and led him to the gate, where Enoch Williams had arrived after his errand. Marshal Franks watched the stream of passersby. "Did you talk too much?"

"No, sir," said Enoch. "I didn't even talk at the telegraph office. I wrote it out."

"Looks like a lot of people," said Marshal Franks.

"Maybe a lot of people have business in Echo this morning," said Enoch.

"They do now," said Enos.

Sheriff Simms and his three captors followed the trail to Echo across the Weber River. The turn after the grade-crossing led to the steep and narrow Weber Canyon. The marshals and their captive could see the people on the platform. Marshal Franks had instructed Enoch to send a telegram to set up the signals to stop the noon train. Now Enoch counted twenty people who had shown up to take a train that never stops.

Before Enoch counted again, the crowd amounted to thirty people standing in front of the ticket office. The U.S. marshal instructed his special deputies to hold the sheriff at the edge of the platform. As Marshal Franks moved toward the ticket window, the crowd in front of him stayed constant and grew to surround him. He pulled a letter from his breast pocket and stepped out of the line. Brandishing his letter, he marched to the door and knocked.

When it did not open, he knocked a second time. With his third knock, he yelled, "I'm the U.S. marshal. Open the damn door, or I'll bust it in."

While Franks used his letter to secure passage in the ticket office, Seth Parker arrived in his wagon at the edge of the platform. He sat in his wagon and spoke to the sheriff on Indigo. "I heard you asked for me."

"Not so much asked as said you needed to know where to pick her up." Sheriff Simms patted Indigo's neck.

"Well, here I am." Seth surveyed the Williams brothers and let his eyes linger on the U.S. Marshal's horse. "You boys need me to board those horses?"

"Don't know if we're going," said Enoch. "We'll ask the marshal when he gets back."

"Damn straight, we're going," said Enos. "I'm not trusting Franks with my money."

U.S. Marshal Franks returned and looked at Seth Parker. He waved the paper in his hand. "The horses have passage on the train."

"I'll let Seth take Indigo. I won't need her," said Sheriff Simms.

The train whistled from a long way up the grade. The engineer hung out the window and pulled the cord all the way in. When the conductor stepped onto the platform, he looked at the crowd and gave a doubtful shake. "Aboard!" His call lingered on the second syllable.

"Might be a good idea for us, too. You take ours." Enoch Williams said to Seth. He turned to Marshal Franks. "Didn't you say the U.S. government will pay expenses?"

"I'll take 'em," said Seth. "But irregardless the U.S. government pays, you'll get 'em back when you pay me."

Heeding the conductor's call, the crowd milled forward, handing him their tickets. The two special deputies and the sheriff dismounted and climbed onto the platform. Franks stepped to the conductor with his letter and waved the three forward.

"Passage, here," he said. He waved the letter but did not hand it over.

"I'll have to verify that," said the conductor. He continued taking tickets.

"I had it verified in the office."

"I'll have to verify that, too," said the conductor. He continued taking tickets, but now he took the letter and looked at it. "You can wait right here."

"Go," said Franks to Enos and motioned him on board. "Go sit down."

Enos and Enoch walked toward the front car, making slow progress with their prisoner. Everyone who had poured into the car from the platform wanted to shake the sheriff's hand. The special deputies allowed the hand shaking until the conductor returned, holding the letter and shooing U.S. Marshal Franks into the car.

The train began to roll. The special deputies continued to push forward toward the front car. The crowd of people who had climbed on the train without handing their tickets to the conductor now made their way back to him. In the process four men pushed between Sheriff Simms and the Williams brothers. A fifth man, James Bromley, arrived at the sheriff's side.

"John Willford, I haven't seen you since my express office was robbed, and this is a poor moment for telling you: I am sorry about all that happened."

"Mr. Bromley, it's not on your head," said John Willford. "And I still owe you recovering the money. I know where it is, but it'll take another nine years to find it."

"My loss doesn't measure up to yours. I owe you," said James Bromley, pushing the sheriff toward the door, separating him from the four men who made a wall in front of the two special deputies. "It appears the train is moving. You best be moving, too." He reached behind the sheriff, opened the door, and pushed John Willford onto the platform of the car. John Willford felt the rush of air and heard the door close behind him.

By now the train had gained eight miles an hour, about the speed of the trains when boys dared each other to jump off the switching engines up at Wahsatch, a game Sheriff Luke Willford's son had never played. Now seemed like the best time to learn. John Willford jumped.

Sheriff Simms rolled over and down the embankment that held the rails. No wonder kids liked that game so much—what a thrill to stand up and realize he was alive and in one piece.

The sheriff watched the train as he collected himself. He expected to see it slow down and stop. He prepared to run. It continued to gain speed and move away from him. Standing on the parallel road that allowed freighters to take their wares to the loading platform and staring in disbelief at the receding train, he heard a wagon. He turned around. The wagon looked familiar, and so did the blue roan trailing behind.

In the moment Sheriff Simms mounted Indigo, he wondered how had they done this? He planned to escape, and he kept looking for his chance, but when Bromley showed up, he had no thought the community had a full-fledged plan already under way. He guessed it had been done before. It sounded like Apostle Cannon falling off the train last February, except for the Apostle's broken leg.

Simms watched the train gathering speed. He had no idea why it didn't stop. He could imagine the conductor's end of the conversation with the U.S. marshal.

"Your stop put me off schedule. I'm not the one lost him. Now I have to make up time."

Chapter 39:
To Thanksgiving, 1886

Sheriff Simms and Indigo arrived at the jailhouse in Coalville about the same time the train delivered the U.S. marshals to Union Station in Ogden. Woodside had left before the escape and knew nothing about it. He returned to the jail and sat down without a word to the sandwiches Orson's wife had sent. The two deputies ate in glum silence, until the door opened.

"In time for lunch," Deputy Orson said when the sheriff walked through the door. "Mary Beth made enough for all of us today."

The sheriff noticed Orson's lack of expression and that Woodside worked hard to keep his excitement under a firm grip. He played along with Orson's game. "Sorry I'm late; the noon train out of Echo delayed me."

"Now you're back, best I go over to the telegraph office," said Deputy Orson. He put his unfinished sandwich on the plate. "Someone'll send a message up here. I'll wait for it."

"Nah," said Sheriff Simms. "Let Burton bring it to you. No need to let on you know anything." He took a bite of Mary Beth Orson's sandwich. "This good venison reminds me. It's about hunting season. I best take care to store in meat for the winter."

Woodside laughed. "And the place to do that'll be up in the high Uintas."

"Are you saying I'm predictable?"

"Just a little, and just once in a while," said Woodside. "Even if those marshals guess you're up there, they'll never find you."

"More like Franks'll never go up there looking for me," Simms said.

Sheriff Simms stayed in the High Uintas until he looked up in the sky and calculated a week remained before the snows. Except for taking his buck to Trueman over at the Mercantile, he wasn't about to take any chances. He knew a lot of people thought it seemed obvious the marshals could wait for him in town and watch for him to visit his families. He banked on that complacency, but he did not want to test the theory. He kissed Elizabeth Tonsil on the cheek at work and stopped by early the next morning to check on Anna and Elizabeth Jensen. Families attended to, he stayed scarce until the first snows.

With the first snowfall that accumulated above his ankles, he made his way over to Seth Parker and thanked him for the unexpected delivery of Indigo. One of the town's natural resources, Seth could not stop talking. He would have told everyone the sheriff was back, including the special deputies. They had only to show up to retrieve and pay for their horses. Simms knew not to take that risk before he was safe until spring.

"Those Williams brothers arrived here the very next day," said Seth. "At first, Enos tried to arrest me. He claimed I knew something about your escape. Imagine that." Simms could barely hear the words as his mind confirmed his caution. "But he knew there was no bounty for bringing me in, so he tried to bargain for their horses' board. Enos didn't outright say it, but he wanted me to forget payment in exchange for not arresting me. I allowed as how he should do both—arrest me and pay me." Seth chuckled at his own punch line. "Enoch paid up, for his brother, too. Along the way, he told me the conductor refused to stop the train."

"I sort of figured that," said Simms. "What about Franks?"

"Well, he had his horse and his ticket to Salt Lake." Seth paused a moment and laughed with the joy of his next news. "He has so many indictments, them deputies said he was through with Coalville for 1886."

Through with 1886 sounded good to Sheriff Simms. For one, he wanted to be through with the fall. Winter served him better. He chastised himself once again for letting the marshals get the drop on him. Now they had two on him. He knew the Williams brothers had stolen Sam's flour under the banner of law enforcement by way of laying a trap for him. He could know, but he could not arrest special deputy U.S. marshals who were trying to arrest him.

The weeks rolled into Thanksgiving, and he rarely saw the pink curtain or heard a warning the marshals were in town. Sheriff Simms suspected their deal with the cattle kept the Williams brothers occupied. As with every visit to the Jensen house, the memory of September hovered over his afternoon Thanksgiving dinner with Elizabeth Jensen in her bed and their daughters, Anna, Elizabeth, Mary, Helen, and Miarmy. A young lady had invited James, now turned eighteen, to her house. The girls had spread a sheet over their mother's bedspread and made a festive table complete with flowers picked in the summer and dried. Sheriff Simms regretted the distance he felt from the children he had with Elizabeth Jensen. He considered it unnecessary, but he never mentioned it. It seemed to imply a criticism of their mother—something he would never do. He enjoyed what warmth he could find.

The sheriff gauged sunset would be on the land in half an hour when he left to make his way to the yellow house to gather Clara and Elizabeth for a walk over to Sam and Emma's. To tell all he knew and suspected about the stolen flour brought no recovery for the loss. It did not relieve the winter without flour for those families who suffered the theft. He owed this talk to

Sam and Emma, and he looked forward to it. Afterward, he could return with Clara and Elizabeth to the yellow house for a joyous dinner.

Even as disappointment competed with joy to clutter his mind, Sheriff Simms surveyed all Main Street upon his first step onto the porch. No surprise, no one on the street. He walked down the hill, up Main, and right on 100 N. Twilight let him see the yellow house and its front yard. Nothing in the front yard showed any different. He looked again. Something wrong. The windows were darker than the day.

A bright spirit herself, Elizabeth Tonsil set lanterns in the windows and lit the house to make it glow and bring good cheer to the neighbors, more on holidays, most on Thanksgiving Day. When she was home, a dark house was not right.

Sheriff Simms took caution and watched. He thought he saw the front door open, then shut again. His suspicions grew. He kept watching. The door opened once more, and Enos Williams poked out. He looked up and down the street and ran around the corner of the house. As Williams ran he drew his revolver part way from the holster at his hip, not all the way, enough to prepare himself to have it at the ready.

With Enos hidden around the side of the house, his brother Enoch had to be inside. The plan seemed clear, and the thought exploded in the sheriff's mind. Inside meant holding Clara and Elizabeth hostage.

To raid the homes of men whose principal crime had been to become worth an easy three hundred dollars served but the purpose of creating terror in the children. The special deputies justified such disgusting behavior as called for by the investigation, meaning fear instilled in the children was meant to spill out information on their cohabiting father. A good wife knew that. Families who had made it to that mountain desert and survived long enough to have children had faced worse.

Not finding Sheriff Simms, these special deputies planned to lay a trap that worked only by imprisoning his wife and child. Without taking her an inch away from her house, special deputy U.S. marshals kidnapped Elizabeth and her daughter, an act beyond all acceptable limits of what a man should do, an act that claimed authority from the government.

To make money by selling out your brethren could be forgiven if you atoned. Hanging yourself from the redbud tree was not to atone. The tree when it changed its blooms from white to crimson did more to atone for its disgrace than the man who hung from it. In that moment, Sheriff Simms saw that betrayal was not the worst a man could do. Simms had been taught all acts could be forgiven. In the heat of his anger, he did not agree. To terrorize and hurt the innocent in the lust of greed could never be forgiven.

Hopt awaited the firing squad for killing his father. These two deserved the same for kidnapping Clara and Elizabeth. No law he knew meted that justice. Sheriff Simms accepted his calling to uphold the law, but the father to Clara and the husband to Elizabeth felt the need for action like a hot weight expanding against the walls of his chest. He wanted to believe it amounted to a higher calling.

Simms stepped off the street into the trees. He needed to think before he reached the front yard. Like his father, he took great care to avoid even shooting at a man, but he knew, when called upon, he could kill. He revered his calling to execute Hopt, and politics and powers beyond his control had conspired to delay the date. Now circumstances presented the Williams brothers, deserving the same fate. No matter, he could not go blasting into the yellow house.

Every possible action swarmed in his mind. With Enos outside the house, Simms had no way to make it to his horse. He didn't need Indigo, anyway. He could always make it to Woodside's house. He didn't have to do that. He had his gun and his fists. He needed but to disable Enos. He had no doubt he could lay him out with his pistol. Better still, if he needed to use his pistol, he should shoot the bastard. After taking out Enos, Enoch Williams would prove no obstacle.

Sheriff Simms knew why he was not a thoughtful man. It got in the way. This thinking did no good. In all his anger and rage, he knew he would not kill these boys. For damn sure, he would not send them on their way, either. He'd make 'em pay. At least, he could administer a good whipping. Someone would look over his shoulder and declare that idea kind of creepy, but he liked the thought of a good whipping. Boys who behaved like this did not deserve to be called men. Not adults, no need to shoot them, no desire to beat them to death, just whip them. No walking stick; he would have to do it with his fists, one at a time.

Sheriff Simms stepped out of the trees and marched up the street to the front door. If his angry movements alerted Enos Williams in his coward's hiding place, so be it. Simms reached for the door handle with one hand and pulled his Frontier Six Shooter with the other. He had fired one cylinder full, in one round of practice, before he left for Browns Park. He had no plans to pull the trigger a seventh time.

Elizabeth had set the Thanksgiving table in readiness for his arrival. Clara sat in her chair at one end between the two corners meant for her parents. Enoch Williams sat in John Willford's chair, eating pie.

"We have company," announced Elizabeth the moment John Willford walked through the door. "Brother Williams turned down my invitation to dinner, but he's having some pie. The other Brother Williams is outside. I believe he is tending to your horse."

Enoch Williams looked up from his pie at the sound of her voice, one hand on the plate, one hand on the fork.

Sheriff Simms stepped in front of Enoch. "Slide your gun under the table."

He watched the special deputy do what he was told.

"Now put your hands on the table and call your brother."

Enoch Williams complied, "Enos."

Sheriff Simms thought that feeble attempt sounded like a warning. Motioning with the barrel of his pistol, he said, "From the back door. Like you're in charge."

Enoch opened the screen on the back door and barked his brother's name. Sheriff Simms flattened his body against the back wall and waved Enoch back to his pie.

Enos stepped into the frame of the door, his pistol holstered. "What d'ya—"

Seeing no need to tell this sorry excuse for a man to put up his hands, Sheriff Simms crashed the butt of his pistol into Enos's hair, behind the ear.

"Jee-sus, you about killed him," said Enoch. "Now what you gonna do? Whup me?"

"Like as not." Sheriff Simms pulled the pistol from Enos's holster. He gave it to his wife and motioned toward the pistol on the floor. "Take Enoch's gun, too. Tell Trueman to sell them at the mercantile."

"You can't do that."

"That's not all I'm going to sell. Where're your rifles? In here or with your horses?"

"Why you doing this?" asked Enoch.

The sheriff let his jaw drop open in wonderment. "Why? Because no matter how much I tell myself I want to, I can't shoot you . . . And I can't beat you to death."

"We was doing our job," said Enoch.

"And you owe Sam Carruth. It won't amount to nothing to

what you owe those folks, but whatever it is, I am going to get it to him."

Sheriff Simms noticed Enos stirring on the floor. He walked over to him and bent over.

"You gonna hit him again?"

"Not if he doesn't wake up." Simms reached and pulled both hands behind Enos's back and handcuffed him. "Maybe now I won't need to hit him when he wakes up. He'll be vile, but he won't be dangerous."

"You think this is gonna stop us?"

Simms considered Enoch's question. That challenge promised to prove interesting. He pulled his pocket watch and looked at it.

"It's going to stop you raiding my house."

"How?" asked Enoch. "We was doing our job."

"You said that before, and it's no hiding place." Simms waggled his finger, like admonishing a truant boy, or puppy. "And you're not going to hide there anymore. First thing, I'm going to tell your pa when he picks you up."

"He's right proud we're special deputies, and there's no need for him to pick us up. We'll ride home, even if you do steal our guns."

"Confiscate. And that goes for your horses, too. Until the judge decides."

"Judge? What are you talking about?"

"Either you don't listen or you think a special deputy is above the law in this county. Either way doesn't make much sense when you're talking to me."

Enoch Williams made to interrupt. Sheriff Simms held his hand in the air. Each sentence that followed had a little space around it, making it an island of its own.

"I'm taking you two down to the jail.

"Deputy Woodside will arrest you for stealing flour.

"Deputy Woodside will arrest you for breaking and entering.

"And, tomorrow, I'll ask Rabbi Sol if Deputy Woodside can arrest you for kidnapping."

"You can't do that. We was doing our job. Even if you arrest us, they'll let us off."

"Dunno." Sheriff Simms shrugged his shoulders and raised his eyebrows. "The judge'll have to tell the deputy if he did right. For him to do that, you'll have to stand before the judge. He'll ask you questions. He'll ask the deputy questions. Your pa'll be there. Seth'll make sure the whole county knows. I expect the whole county will be there. Like I said, you're not going to hide there anymore."

CHAPTER 40:
DECEMBER 1886

The Williams brothers stood before the judge and what looked like half the county jammed in circuit court to hear the prosecuting attorney. Named as the special deputies of U.S. marshal Hyer Franks—the prosecuting attorney even spelling F-R-A-N-K-S for the clerk—they were charged with cattle running and flour stealing. Given its central nature to the U.S. government's terms of employment, bounty hunting escaped mention. Within minutes, the judge threw out the cattle running charge due to its official imprimatur. When the judge held them over for trial on the flour stealing charge, Marshal Franks seethed. Implicated in open court, he had no fine from the cohab sheriff to show for that caper. The judge did not strip them of their position, but Franks knew he had lost two workers whom he had trained to create good income for him, at least in that county. He had to do something, and he thought he could use the governor to gain his end.

The two special deputies should have been smarter. With a whole government to sponsor their maneuvers against these recalcitrant people, these two had succeeded in losing Franks the income that amounted to nothing more than the government's reward to an entrepreneur who did its bidding. His loss of income coincided with his loss of respect, because he had not brought that high mountain sheriff before a judge to a certain conviction of cohabitation.

Only the lack of snow made the bleak, first Friday in

December bearable. The prospect of Christmas helped some, too. It gave Franks a plan that would work, albeit at the cost of asking the governor for help. Franks wished he could summon Governor Caleb Walton West to meet him in his office. The United States marshal had a fitting office in the federal district courthouse, a luxurious building proper to the federals' superior position, not like the borrowed quarters around the city that had housed the territorial offices since the territory's creation in 1855. The governor and the territorial legislature borrowed space in Salt Lake city hall. West might have been the governor, but the Mormons had him in their building.

Caleb Walton West, a municipal judge in Kentucky, qualified for the president's appointment to be governor of Utah Territory by his friendship with Kentucky's Blackburn, a senator owed a favor by Grover Cleveland. He had been the governor since last May, and, by now, enough people had fawned all over him that Franks doubted the governor would respond well to a summons from a U.S. marshal, however much the marshal was the man in charge. It galled Franks to admit he could not summon the man. What he wanted, only the governor could supply, and he had best not put the obstacle of offending the governor in his way.

Marshal Franks would go see Governor West first thing Monday morning. He would not risk taking up this subject on a Friday afternoon. Governor West might already be in the bottle. Franks did not know, for a fact, the governor to be a drinking man, but with a man from Kentucky, no use taking the chance. He could use the weekend to sharpen his argument. First thing Monday morning would be best.

Like every Sunday morning, Sheriff Simms first thought of how likely the U.S. marshals would invade his family that day. The cold and death brought by snow everywhere justified Marshal

Franks's decision to stay in the valley and do the high value work he could do in Salt Lake City. Though cautious, Simms knew the U.S. marshal from New Jersey had no desire to work in snow. The Williams brothers could no longer run roughshod in Summit County, and the sheriff had heard no word of new special deputies in his county. He could spend a quiet Christmas with his family. Regardless of U.S. government-sponsored harassment, he counted his family as one, his mature one with a son announcing his engagement and his starting-over one with a daughter about to have the first Christmas she would know.

He arose early Sunday morning and decided to go into Elizabeth Jensen's bedroom. "Would you like to go to church this morning?" he asked.

"You know I am in bed," she said.

He looked at her, all white with the pallor of more than three years in bed, and yet still trim, still an attractive woman, her hair brushed and her clothes clean, thanks to the girls.

"Yes, I do," he said. "What I don't know is when it will change, so I keep asking."

"Well, don't ask." Elizabeth Jensen looked at him straight, the first steady gaze in three years. "It won't change."

He nodded, looked around the room to find some way to be of use, and left, stopping first on his porch to survey Main Street. He walked to the yellow house.

"Want to go to church this morning?" he asked Elizabeth Tonsil.

"Of course, I do," she said, her eyes and cheeks as bright as her voice. "Aren't you going to priesthood meeting?"

"You could meet me for Sunday School," he said. "It's the first Sunday of the month. We'll stay and go to fast meeting together."

She looked at him with half a smile and cocked her head into a question mark. "Have you had breakfast?"

He laughed. "No, and I'm not sick."

"Well, there's something wrong with you, all the same. If you want to go to fast meeting, I'm not sure I should fix you breakfast."

"Nothing wrong. Nothing but the circumstances."

She held up an egg in one hand and a pancake spatula in the other.

"Eggs." Sheriff Simms pointed and laughed. "And fast, if you please. After that dustup over Thanksgiving and court, I want people to see me. No one's after me for the moment, and no one'll be after me this month. I haven't been indicted, and I won't be."

Elizabeth cracked the eggs into the black iron pan and worked while she talked. "You sound pretty confident."

"It doesn't take much to understand why. They're better off going after the church authorities, the men who control the properties they're trying to grab. I'm worth no more than my value in cash to a cohab hunter." Though she stood with her back to him, he could see a smile invading her cheeks. "I know that look," he said. "What is it?"

"You're worth every penny," she said, turning the smile full on him. She noticed his blank expression and took it for not catching her joke. "As a cohab, that is."

At that he laughed. "Good thing we're going to church."

"Sunday's a day of rest," she said. "With the marshal in Salt Lake and his Judases out of the question, we owe it to the Lord to rest this afternoon."

To give meaning to her clear challenge, Elizabeth Tonsil swung from the stove to stand close to him, and their bodies touched when she set his plate of eggs on the table.

He looked at the eggs and then at her. "Like we learned in September, it's best not to let our guard down."

Elizabeth poured milk, then hot water into a mug and gave it to him. She stayed at his side. "Maybe, but something's different."

"Getting caught isn't my problem, at least not till New Year's Eve. I'll have to work over in Park City. Snow or no, you can bet the federal authorities will do their duty in Park City's saloons on New Year's Eve."

He looked at her, and she held his look for a while. She always delighted him . . . no, electrified him. He knew she could see right inside him. Whenever she did, it amazed him anew. She said, "You never talk about it either way."

"Well, I do think Eire was the one behind those boys with Sam Carruth's flour. And Marshal Franks hasn't found new special deputies. Franks isn't suited to catch me, not up here. That doesn't make me underestimate him. Marshal Franks will work with what he has. What worries me most is he can work on the one decision I can't do anything about."

"You mean Hopt?" said Elizabeth.

"Yes, I mean crazy Albert Hopt got all those stays and now the last one ends in January. Not so crazy. Hopt's first Christmas down there, the thought of clemency gave me chills. Here we are, coming up on Christmas Eve again three years later, and he's still alive. Every time Christmas rolls around there's a chance he'll be on the governor's amnesty list."

U.S. Marshal Hyer Franks found no guard, no porter, no help when he walked in the front door of Salt Lake city hall. A clerk in the first office on the right told Franks that Governor West sat in an office down the corridor, in the corner, next to the mayor's office.

"I'm not sure the governor has time to see you, Mr. Franks," replied the governor's assistant to the U.S. marshal's request.

"Marshal Franks," repeated Marshal Franks. "I am the U.S.

marshal in this territory, and the governor will have time to see me."

"U.S. marshal or no," said the assistant, "you work for the governor. Of course, the governor has time to see you. I don't know when it will be."

"Actually, I don't," said Franks. "I work for the president, and I have urgent business."

The assistant offered no response and left Franks standing. Before the marshal could engage the assistant in another round of requests for his urgent business, the governor emerged from his office with his arm around the shoulder of the U.S. attorney, William H. Dickson. Now, there was a piece of luck. Dickson had prosecuted enough polygamy cases, he knew Franks, and he would understand the strategy Franks was about to propose.

"Again, congratulations, Governor," said Dickson.

"Well, I am pleased," said Governor West. "The court has assigned Snow's case for argument on January seventeenth. Last May, the day after I was sworn in, I visited the penitentiary and offered Lorenzo Snow amnesty. Very first thing I did. I wanted to set the tone for conciliation with him. All he had to do was give up his polygamous ways."

"No doubt he had his reasons." Dickson's eyes widened with realization. "He was working on this hearing!"

"Maybe so," said Governor West.

"I'm not so bothered by it." Dickson gave a confident nod. "To be honest, it'll be good for us if the court strikes down Zane's notion of the segregation of time. When he propounds that each day with each wife can be charged as a separate count, subject to the full punishment, a man facing time of a year or more multiplied by three or four or how many wives has no choice but to take to hiding out. Now a life in hiding won't look so good. Men will step forward and plead guilty to one offence and pay the penalty. After imprisonment, they'll go forth free men, glad to terminate the constant fear and apprehension."

"That isn't why he turned it down." Governor West shook his head slow and with resignation. "He refused to disavow any one of his families."

"That's the very reason I am here." Hyer Franks inserted himself into the discussion. He knew Dickson and considered interruption of his colleague, the U.S. attorney, to be part of his job. He had met the governor but did not know him and relied upon the municipal judge to recognize that interruption was no act of rudeness at all.

"Are you here to see me?" asked Dickson.

Franks pointed to the governor. "I've holed up a cohabitator I think I can flush out. I'm here to see Governor West about his Christmas amnesty."

"Do the sons bear the sins of the fathers?" asked the bishop in Sunday school. Sheriff Simms heard nothing of the bishop's discussion of the covenant with God and what happened when the father did not make it. The fear that Franks had the power to visit the son's sins upon the father gripped the sheriff. He wondered, *Could Franks make sure the territory never executed my father's killer?* And he would do that because John Willford had plural wives. Jesus, Franks even had him calling it a sin.

Simms lined up the facts straight and simple. His father was dead because of the Edmunds Act. He was a fugitive sheriff because of the Edmunds Act. His father's killer had not had his sentence carried out. That phrase struck Simms as a little mealy mouthed. Hopt had not been executed. Call it what it is. Calling it what it is meant admitting that the killer of Sheriff Luke Willford Simms lived and avoided, maybe forever, the firing squad because of the Edmunds Act.

It could not be forever. This had to end sometime.

★ ★ ★ ★ ★

"I don't know anything about my Christmas amnesty," said Governor West. "Of course, I know the governor has the power, but I have been too busy thinking about how to mediate these hostile camps to consider it."

"I have been the one called upon to prepare the list each year," said Dickson.

"Indeed," said Franks. "And the newspaper announces the list beforehand, sort of a political caution. We should use that tradition to serve our ends. One of the inmates shot a sheriff up in the mountains. The dead man's son is now the sheriff, and he's a cohab. They're all like goats up there. We'll never bring him down. This will smoke him out."

"So, you think if we announce the governor's intention to give amnesty to Albert Hopt, it will bring this polygamist to us?" asked Dickson.

"How do you know the man's name?" asked the governor. "Is this a famous case? Why haven't I heard of it?"

"Not so famous as Lorenzo Snow," said Dickson. "I've been around for two of Hopt's stays. One of them caused a problem, but it's a county matter. Best I remember, his last stay set a sentencing date at the end of January."

"After the Snow argument?" asked West.

"Not sure, maybe, but of no matter," said Dickson. "I don't see how the two are linked. You won't have the decision on Snow's appeal by then."

"And you?" Governor West turned to Marshal Franks. "You think putting this Hopt's name on the Christmas amnesty list will bring this sheriff . . ."

"Simms," said Franks.

". . . to you?"

"No," said Marshal Franks. "To you. Then I will arrest him to take before Judge Zane."

"Well, you'll get a sure conviction from Zane," said Dickson.

Sheriff Simms rode Indigo to Rabbi Sol's house at sunup Monday morning. Suspicious of maneuvering by Franks, he knew the longer Hopt stayed alive, and the more the territory struggled to become a state, the more chance his father's murder would end with the governor pardoning Hopt. He expected Franks to round up people, even Latter-day Saints, to charge that he sought blood atonement. Franks might even pay for that testimony. His accusers didn't need to know the sheriff. They needed only to whisper in Governor West's ear.

God damn it, Hopt's execution was not a religious issue. Simms wanted to lash out again, God damn it. Trouble was, no amount of cursing God took away the political reality he faced.

Riding a horse helped his thinking. Simms settled into the knowledge it had always been a political issue. When Governor Murray sat in office, Sheriff Simms had had no chance to fulfill the legislature's prescription for meting out justice to a murderer in his county. Murray wanted his attacks on polygamy to be so well known that he influenced national policy. Sheriff Simms had no doubt Murray sourced the sympathy for Hopt's stay— and then granted him the stays.

Simms arrived at Rabbi Sol's gate. As he swung it open, he thought about the reason President Cleveland had dismissed Murray. Because he was a Republican, not because he was a rabid anti-Mormon. Unpopular with the Latter-day Saints did not matter a whit. His ways suited the other ten percent. Grover Cleveland's sole thought had been to seat the first Democrat in the governor's chair in ten governors and thirty years. Now, Governor West's first Christmas approached. He professed he wanted to convince polygamists to renounce rather than to punish them. Sheriff Simms thought it wiser to watch what the man did. The best Simms could tell from what he had seen so far, West leaned toward amnesty for crimes against Mormons. Simms had no idea what attitude West held toward murderers. Sheriff Simms feared that West considered the murder of a Mormon sheriff with a polygamous son worthy of pardon.

"What? Not a Saturday?" called Rabbi Sol from the porch. He leapt from it and almost ran to meet the sheriff at his gate.

"Got turned around," laughed Sheriff Simms. "And all I had was Webster. I figure I know how to release the town drunk without your aid."

"Good. Saved me a trip, Saturday night."

"Might 'a done," said the sheriff. "But you know he was back in Saturday night. I think he's looking for a place to stay. It's okay with me."

"Put him in and let him out. Don't even bother writing down his name." Sol left one hand resting on his picket fence and waved at the house. "If you're ever too full, ride him out here. I'll give him a bed."

"Thanks." Sheriff Simms stood at the gate, holding Indigo's reins. "I'll remember."

Sol smiled at the sheriff. "You rode all the way here for the town drunk?"

"Not such a long ride."

"But not why you rode here."

Simms shrugged and answered. "No."

Sol took a step toward the gate and opened it. He made an ushering motion with his right hand. "Come in, and we'll talk about it."

"No need to. I'm here to ask a question."

"I figured that." Sol chuckled. "Saturday mornings, you come because you have a prisoner in your jail. Other days, you come to ask questions."

Simms frowned. He could not afford to be predictable, and he did not like it when a friend pointed out that he was. He liked the friend; he did not like that he was predictable.

"What's the difference between a stay and an amnesty?"

"A stay is a delay, that's all." Sol's flat and straightforward answer gave way to animation in instructing his pupil. "An amnesty is altogether different. It's given to a class of people for political offenses; for the most part, anyway. Are you sure you mean amnesty, or do you mean pardon?"

"Well, it could be political. I'm talking about the Governor's Christmas list."

"That's what I thought. Yes, his Christmas list is an amnesty list, but you mean pardon. An act of clemency."

"Amnesty, clemency, pardon? What the hell does it mean?"

"You are impatient." The rabbi in Sol took over as he patted the air in a downward motion. "There's a lot to say about that."

"There always is." Sheriff Simms did not find this a humorous matter, but he could not help feeling good, almost cheerful, at how complicated his friend made everything. "Just tell me, can he get off scot-free? Innocent?"

"Who he? Hopt?"

"You know damn well that's who I'm talking about."

"Not innocent and not scot-free," said Rabbi Sol.

"Oh, Jesus, Sol." Simms's good feeling shaded into frustration. "Can't you give me a straight answer?"

"Here's the shortest I can make it. Only the chief executive of the jurisdiction can grant a pardon. That means the president or the governor. There's nothing you can do about it."

"I understand that. That wasn't my question." Sheriff Simms pulled on his ear.

"Sure it was," said Sol. "A pardon has conditions. If you're thinking a pardon of a death sentence, that is almost always conditional on serving a term of life imprisonment."

"You mean, ask him to . . . what? . . . agree to stay locked up forever, so he won't face the firing squad?"

"That's what life in prison tends to mean."

"That makes no sense. I'd rather the governor let Hopt go. Then, I'll shoot the bastard."

Governor West watched the U.S. marshal and the U.S. attorney talk about the strategy for this cohab he did not know. The governor frowned a bit before he spoke.

"I want the polygamists to accept an amnesty, but on my terms. You want me to pardon the man who killed a polygamist's father so you can profit from a cohab conviction. That does not seem consistent."

"You don't need to pardon him." Hyer Franks threw off his answer with a wave of the hand. "What I need you to do is put him on your Christmas list."

"What *you* need me to do?"

"That's all. You don't need to let him go." Franks smarted from the barb about profiting from the cohab conviction. He knew for certain the governor served men who sought power; he also knew those men, like him, looked to absorb the property taken. He ignored that the governor waited for an apology. "Even if you do pardon him, you can make it conditional upon life in prison."

"Thanks for the instruction, Marshal Franks. That has not worked with Mr. Snow. I offered amnesty for his brethren and pardon for him in return for a promise to obey the law."

"The rebuff of your gesture, Governor, was to be expected." Dickson tried to soothe the growing tension. "As I speculated, he was already planning his plea to the supreme court."

West had cultivated a bushy mustache that drooped except when he set his jaw. He set his jaw in preparing for his answer. His mustache pointed out at the ends. "I have made clear my determination to build bridges rather than widen the chasm between the Mormons and those of us who are not."

"I think you have to make every example you can," said Marshal Franks. "You can't build bridges with people set upon separating themselves from American society."

"Maybe because I was a prisoner of war myself, in an unjust war, but these people don't need to be prosecuted; these people need to comply." Governor West had a half crown of bald skin that preceded his hair. He drew his hand over it and seemed to lift himself up in further determination. "The Edmunds-Tucker Act passed the Senate last January. It will pass the House, someday. It will become law and once and for all separate church and political power. It will break the political power of this church, and it will pave the way for this territory to become a state. I was sent here to be the last territorial governor before Utah becomes a state. And that's what I aim to do."

Franks looked at Dickson for support.

"Marshal Franks," said Dickson, "I don't know your cohab, but I suspect he's like Mr. Snow. He won't accept an offer of a pardon. It will mean he has to abandon one of his wives and children and grandchildren, if he has any, and cut off all financial support."

"I am not asking Governor West to pardon Sheriff Simms." Marshal Franks stopped talking, and his face lit with a new resolve. "I'm not asking the governor to do anything about Sheriff Simms. I am only asking the governor to put Hopt's name on the Christmas list he publishes the week before Christmas."

"To what end? That publication is to make sure there are no objections of which I am unaware. Surely you know your sheriff objects."

"Exactly!" said Franks. "As an official notice, it will appear in the *Tribune* on Friday, the seventeenth. I will make sure someone takes it up to Coalville by Monday. For sure he'll make a beeline here to see you by Christmas Eve."

Nobody in the jail and, considering he had waited long enough, Sheriff Simms closed the door around five and walked up Main Street. He looked forward to the early Christmas Eve dinner planned with Clara before she scuttled off to bed. He harbored a moment's thought that he would have preferred to begin the celebration at the Jensen house and end at the yellow house. Not a thought allowed to linger long, he considered it good and proper to end up at the Jensen house. It matched with his desire to see the newspaper as soon as Elizabeth Tonsil brought it home.

Sheriff Simms had hung around the empty jail longer than needed in hopes the newspaper awaited him when he arrived home. He had asked her to bring it every day that week before Christmas. It had not yet arrived. The mercantile did not carry the *Tribune,* and the sheriff suspected the slow delivery had been a deliberate effort by Hopt's lawyer to keep him from learning the governor's Christmas list in time to do anything about it. Rabbi Sol had called him paranoid and told him to hold out no hope he could do anything about the governor's Christmas list, even if he knew.

Walking up Main Street toward a family Christmas Eve dinner amounted to the only thing this man of action could do. A man of action, depended on by the whole county for order in the way of things, and he could do nothing to ensure justice served! Active hope amounted to the only action available to him.

Given the governor's well publicized attempts at conditional pardons, Simms felt heavy with certainty that Governor West would pardon Hopt from the firing squad because death by firing squad was an extension of the church's influence. And, to ensure no one called him a coddler of murderers, he would do it with a condition of life imprisonment. The worst result Simms could imagine.

He turned the corner and walked up 100 N. With his first step, he noticed the windows held the lanterns, and the house held the festive and joyful warmth it had lacked in November. He strode the sidewalk to the concrete walkway he had poured from the street to their porch. He paid attention to the snow and the cleared spaces, but he hurried in his determination to reach the information he dreaded.

When he turned into their yard, he could see something pasted or nailed on the front door. He drew near and saw the *Tribune* tacked with a red ribbon tied in bow.

Christmas Proclamation
Governor Caleb Walton West

It is traditional for the governor of the territory of Utah to exercise his power of clemency on Christmas Eve and to announce his intentions in newspapers of record one full week in advance for the purposes of public comment.

With no desire to solicit such comment and with no intention to obstruct the path of progress toward the Americanization of the territory of Utah such that it may one day become the state of Utah,

In recognition of already offered amnesties,

And in further recognition of matters considered and decided by the supreme court of the United States in cases related to those amnesties,

Therefore, I have determined that it would obstruct the path of progress we all so desire and it would obstruct the clear intent of the law on matters weighed and settled before the supreme court to offer clemency when amnesty has been rejected.

My wife, Nancy, and I wish you all a Merry Christmas. We know that 1887 will be a watershed year in the continued path toward statehood.

Signed and sealed,
Governor Caleb Walton West.

CHAPTER 41:
JANUARY 1887

New Year's Day brought joy to Sheriff Simms. In plain words, it snowed like fury.

The sheriff woke in his office after sunrise, the result of moving about in Park City among the revelers on New Year's Eve until all the bars closed. Three celebrants of the evening slept in the dug-in-the-mountain jail, barely enough to keep Marshal Bock from sleeping during his vigil through the early hours. Sheriff Simms ate lunch at the Green House.

"Lunch is my treat," said Mrs. Green. "No fifty-dollar fine on New Year's Eve. The respectable folks call my house a 'shirt-tail factory' and want me out of town. I appreciate you treat me fair."

"I don't treat you any way," said Sheriff Simms. "None of your gentlemen shot up the town or beat on any of your girls. No trouble, no fine."

In the middle of the afternoon, the sheriff borrowed a horse from Seth Parker's Park City livery and left with Indigo and the pack horse to go further south and east to Deer Mountain. A little past dawn the next morning, he shot the buck he needed to add to winter meat and had it dressed and packed before noon. He loved these magnificent mountains around Park City, almost as great as the Uintas he claimed for his own in the northeast end of his county.

Five uninterrupted days spent in the small towns—Marion, Peoa, Oakley—forging his way through flurries in the south end of his county made doing the sheriff's job glorious. He even visited Kamas, happy after three years to reclaim this town fully to his responsibility. That blend of needing to be present and yet invisible had not changed. It ebbed some in the summers with the ever-present threat of the U.S. marshals, and it flowed with the snow, a protection to him and the people of his county from the threat of outsiders. It had been a long time since he had made rounds in his county. He had two good deputies who could take care of everything in town when he rode to Wanship and Hoytsville the next week.

After he spent a full Saturday catching up with the silver freight, he made what rounds he could in town. He waited till dark to do an inventory of work needed at his two houses. He noticed the Jensen house never seemed to need as much work as the yellow house. Sunday morning, he gave out chores and congratulated the children on doing what he had taught them to do. He never thought to congratulate himself, and he never thought the feeling he felt was pride. He thought about the three girls he and Elizabeth Tonsil lost to diphtheria, and he thought about the beautiful new girl who made them a family again. He thought about the girls with Elizabeth Jensen. He thought about the two boys, and he thought about John, who had disowned him. He thought he would like to have another son.

He rode Indigo to the two towns in the south and then through the west end of his county, a lot of country but no towns, and kept a steady pace to make it to Henefer by Wednesday night. Thursday morning, he arrived at the mill and waited until Sam arrived at seven. That night, he slept over in the old schoolhouse in Echo. He made it back to the jailhouse by noon on Friday.

The third week, he rode east to Upton and circled back northeast to Emory, Castle Rock, and Wasatch, determined to cover his county. This conscious effort at patrolling his county served his vision of what it meant to be a good sheriff, and it served its purpose to keep him from thinking about Hopt's stay, up January twenty-eight. Despite all this work, with all the time alone, outside in the cold and snow, how could he not think about one simple fact? He wanted the date for Hopt's execution set. Until it was—no, until he gave the command that was the sheriff's to give—Hopt might steal away with murdering his father. Never mind about life in prison. Hopt had shot Sheriff Simms; Sheriff Simms wanted to shoot Hopt. He knew that, and he knew there was a difference, the difference in civilization. He wanted to shoot Hopt by doing it right, by giving the order to the firing squad.

Sheriff Simms rode all the way back from Wahsatch to make work at the jailhouse for two hours before he walked to the Jensen house for dinner a little after six. On the porch, before opening the front door, he could smell the venison roast he had cut from the deer he shot New Year's Day. He had dinner with the children, and Anna took a plate to her mother in her bedroom. He knew this to be the day of the decision, and he had heard nothing. He returned to more make work at the jailhouse.

It surprised him none to find the jail empty and dark on the last Friday of January. Simms lived among a people bred to follow the rules. Even those of a mind to test that rule found a month of snow every day too much obstacle for hell raising. He sat for a moment at his desk. Lighting a fire in the wood stove would serve against the chill, but he liked better the idea of going to the yellow house, where it was always warm, even if he had yet to light the stove.

Woodside intercepted him on the steps. "I was just to your house."

"Something to report?" asked Sheriff Simms.

"Stayed," said Woodside. No preamble, no extra words. "Until July twenty-seventh."

"When's the twenty-fourth this year?" asked Simms.

"A Sunday," said Woodside.

Simms shrugged his shoulders. "Couldn't shoot the bastard on a Sunday, anyway."

"It's a stay, boss," said Woodside. "That's when they'll set the execution date."

"Yeah, maybe so." Sheriff Simms walked away in the snow. He waved his right hand and let the words float over his shoulder. "Guess so. At least it's not a year. Hope so."

Sheriff Simms found the yellow house colder than he expected. Elizabeth Tonsil had not yet picked up Clara and returned from work. He made a fire. Friday night with Elizabeth and a fire might blanket his disappointment. He felt a twinge of sadness, perhaps guilt, that he faced no risk from the U.S. marshals if he chose to cohabitate. He chided himself as he blew on the tinder in the potbellied stove for being so forthright in his thinking. Cohabitation—the charge, not the act—had been on his mind before he learned of yet one more stay for Albert Hopt.

Before New Year's, John Willford had learned that a man labeled a U.S. marshal, a disaffected Mormon, had shot and killed Edward M. Dalton, down in Parowan, a week before Christmas. John Willford had not heard whether Dalton, a farmer, twenty-four, husband to two families and father to four children, had ever been indicted for polygamy. Dalton had been arrested and had escaped. "Arrested and escaped" could occur from a charge of cohabitation. Marshal Thompson must have been a special deputy, and he had been accompanied by another special deputy, one Enos Williams.

Thompson claimed he had found Dalton at his father's ranch with his father's horse trying to escape. He claimed to have tried to shoot over Dalton's head to warn him and persuade him to stop. Sheriff Simms considered himself no hand with a gun, but even he could shoot a bullet straight in the air without hitting anyone. To aim that close for a warning shot seemed a heavy way to deal with a misdemeanor. To serve what purpose?

Elizabeth Tonsil arrived home from the mercantile to a fire that warmed the house. Snow and cold ushered in 1887 and kept the world outside and protected them. For one Friday evening in January, the world of Hopt and the U.S. marshals could not touch them. They drank in the joy of little Clara at dinner and basked in their warmth together after she fell asleep.

The life created that evening carried on John Willford's calling.

The life they lived faced an even more vicious attack.

★ ★ ★ ★ ★

V: JUSTICE

★ ★ ★ ★ ★

Chapter 42:
March 26, 1887

Sheriff Simms brought news of the Edmunds-Tucker Act to Elizabeth Tonsil on her birthday. Not much of a gift. Passed in the House the year before, surviving the delay caused by negotiating with the Democrats in the Senate, and waiting on President Grover Cleveland's desk for a signature he never supplied, the final encoding of the government's right to strip a religion and its followers of any rights and property beyond mere belief became law.

Elizabeth Tonsil handed the baby to the polygamous, cohabiting husband and father the moment he arrived. "I have asked old Trueman a hundred times to carry *The Salt Lake Tribune*," he said. He carried on talking through play with Clara and through dinner. "I read about the Act in the *Deseret News*, but I want both a pro-church and an anti-church viewpoint. Neither are reliable. With both, I could find a balance."

Elizabeth had made her birthday cake and brought the white cake with thick vanilla icing, his favorite, to the table.

"Grover Cleveland knows this is wrong and was unwilling to sign it. He should have been man enough to veto the damn thing." Simms finished his second piece of cake, and, to punctuate his point, he pushed away from the table and stood.

"You leaving?" Elizabeth reached for his hand. She stood and pulled him toward their bedroom. He resisted, trying to hold back.

"Do you mean going to Mexico?" Her touch still electrified

him, but there was no denying this law had its chilling effect. "Not by a damn sight."

"You know that's not what I meant."

He neither trusted himself nor wanted her to deflect him from his subject. He tried to give her a blank look. "Some more folks've been indicted, and not only bishops. A good many ran off to Mexico, even before this act."

"Not all the news is in the newspaper." Elizabeth smiled and continued to smile as he talked. It occurred to him that he was not sure what she was talking about.

"No one's indicted me. I'm small potatoes. Franks thinks he can use the bastard who shot my father to get to me. He doesn't want to run me off to Mexico, and I won't let him, anyway."

"It can't last forever." Elizabeth continued to pull him by the arm. She had him next to the bed where she sat. "Might be a promising idea to lay low." She patted the bed and lifted the covers to make a tent. "You could hide in here."

"You're right there." Simms frowned. He may have told her she was right about any number of suggestions she was making. "I mean about laying low. From what I read, they've done away with the church. How's that square with freedom of religion?"

"That's too much of a question for me. I'm a little English girl from the country." The little English girl pulled his hand and kept pulling until he lost his balance and landed on the bed beside her.

"It's your country now," said Simms.

"It isn't the country that matters to me. It's you." Her voice softened and her eyes moistened. "You married me when I was in need. I loved you for sure, but we both know the truth is . . ."

"You would have married anyone the bishop told you to marry." John Willford finished the sentence she hesitated to finish.

"I don't like to think of it that way now. But . . . no use denying . . . I was blessed. The bishop made a good pick for me.
God took my parents, and then he took my children. Now we
have a new little family again. All the while you stood with me
because you married me."

"That's what they're calling cohabitation." Sheriff Simms realized he had never discussed the danger they faced with this
strong woman in the belief he should shelter her from it. "Other
people have the same circumstances. We're downright lucky that
it's keeping them away from their families more than me."

Elizabeth smiled. He gaped at her. He knew she didn't want
him to resist her. Hell, she was irresistible. Strong though she
was, he could not have explained it that well. She didn't seem
all that concerned.

"All I'm saying is, it won't last forever." Elizabeth moved
close to his face. Then she kissed him and laughed. "Those men
in charge of the church are running an organization as much as
running a church. I don't know why the people in Washington
are so opposed to the LDS church, but if the government has
found a way to get rid of the church because of polygamy, you
can be sure it would be smart for the church to get rid of polygamy."

"No argument with that." John Willford tried for a tone
unchanged by her kiss. He tried to resist the woman the government called a felony. "I just won't let them get rid of you."

Sheriff Simms held his wife in his arms for a long time. Thinking. Thinking confused him, and it stood in the way of action.
In an intolerable situation, thinking about how he ended up
there did no damn good. It was the action the government told
him to take that made it intolerable. He had made a covenant
he could not break. Living through this situation amounted to
all he could do.

"You're right; there's no need for polygamy anymore. Maybe even the authorities abused it. It's not for me to say. Simply leave us with our families. We're lucky to have a family. A damn miracle you had Clara; thirty-nine's a dangerous age for a woman to have a baby."

"Not so dangerous." Elizabeth cradled her head in his shoulder and brought her mouth close to his ear. "Not if you had one before. Neither's forty-one."

"Well, no one's driving me off. But you don't have to worry. We're not taking that risk."

"Oh, I'm not worried."

The news from Washington had left him angry and enervated and unable to resist Elizabeth Tonsil's calming touch. Now, her words made him suspicious. He rose on an elbow and looked at her.

"Are we still talking about the marshals?"

"Were *we* talking about the marshals?" She sat straight and switched her tone from soft and naive to authoritative, to sound like his. "I agree with you. Always have. I wouldn't let those marshals interfere with a family. And I'm damn glad you didn't."

"I didn't!?" In one swift move, he transformed from propped on his elbow to standing on his feet. In his outdoors voice, he exclaimed, "Jesus, woman, are you pregnant?"

"Yes."

"How can you be pregnant again?"

"Well," she snuggled back in to her pillow, "you were a party to that party."

"Damn it, I know that."

He looked at the woman who made his life glow—and who could die from his touch. He made the decision the U.S. government and the bounty-hunting U.S. marshals had been trying to force on him, and it had nothing to do with the U.S. marshals.

"I love you, woman."

He heard the short gasp as Elizabeth Tonsil caught her breath. From the bishop's parlor to that day, he had never used those words. He could see the fear in her face, and he ignored it.

"This has to stop." John Willford bent to kiss her on the forehead. He stood up and dressed. She stayed in bed.

When he left her bed, he left it forever. He left it to others to think he was protecting her, his family, him from the Edmunds-Tucker Act. He didn't return to the yellow house. He kissed her when he saw her at church. He loved her and needed to explain to no one.

CHAPTER 43:
JULY 1887

July 7, in Salt Lake City, another constitutional convention put the final changes to a document meant to reassure the Congress, the government, and the people of the United States of the Americanization of the Latter-day Saints, who by then had become willing to identify themselves with the pejorative term "Mormons." A Mormon-dominated convention voted a constitution already drafted that proclaimed bigamy and polygamy incompatible with a republican form of government and made both a misdemeanor. Newspapers across the country editorialized that few believed the sincerity of Utah's provision against polygamy.

July 24, Pioneer Day cancelled. Whether its cancellation extended beyond Salt Lake City and Summit County, Sheriff Simms did not know. He felt no loss being rid of a day that served only to remind him of his father's murder—and his murderer's advantaged treatment.

July 25, John Taylor, president, the Church of Jesus Christ of Latter-day Saints, died in hiding in Kaysville, a small farming village in the valley. Death stilled the voice that declared a man faced eternal damnation if he did not observe the law of celestial marriage.

July 28, eighty-year-old Wilford Woodruff assumed leadership of the Church of Jesus Christ of Latter-day Saints as the senior member of the Quorum of the Twelve Apostles. Acting in that capacity from his place of hiding in Sanpete County, where he evaded federal agents who had secured indictments to gain warrants for his arrest, he ordered the body of John Taylor removed from hiding to the president of the church's official residence, the Gardo House, to lie in state.

July 29, George S. Peters, United States attorney for the district of Utah since his May fifth appointment, in his Friday habit of sorting his duties into a list, found that a stay of execution concerning one Albert Hopt had expired the day before. He took it to Governor Caleb Walton West to issue a new stay or to set a date for execution. Governor West liked the new U.S. attorney's attitude toward conciliation. He asked him to discuss a strategy unrelated to Hopt that the governor might undertake using the powers of the Edmunds-Tucker Act.

July 29, at six o'clock a.m., early, though not under the cover of darkness, the Taylor family entered the Gardo House to pay their last respects to their husband, father, and grandfather before the church authorities moved his body to the tabernacle for a funeral.

July 30, U. S. Attorney Peters filed a lawsuit on a Saturday against the Church of Jesus Christ of Latter-day Saints to enforce the escheatment provisions of the Edmunds-Tucker Act. He and Governor West agreed with the act's framers that removing property from the Mormons and the Mormon leaders would prove far more effective and go much further toward gaining co-operation than continuing to try to imprison the members of the church.

The court named U.S. Marshal Hyer Franks to be the

receiver and charged the receiver to secure, hold, and administer all church properties. For this extra burden of effort, responsibility, and time, the court compensated the U.S. marshal from the income of the properties he so administered. Until the court made its final determination, the interim payments for this service as receiver were not to exceed one-third of the cash collected.

CHAPTER 44:
AUGUST 1887

Latter-day Saints drew the ire of mobs in Illinois and Missouri. Attacked, bludgeoned, murdered, and subjected to Missouri's *Extermination Order,* the remaining Saints escaped to pioneer thirteen hundred miles west and established a mountainous desert enclave. These few thousand exiles discovered success bred its own reward—more persecution.

No escaping the Edmunds-Tucker Act, everyone expected the pressure to intensify, and intensify it did—on the church, on the leaders of the church, and on the women. For being polygamous wives, or single wives, or not even wives but unable to escape being women, the United States Congress stripped women of suffrage. The right to stand free, the right to vote, even the right to which American freedom owed its origin all the way back to the Magna Carta—the right to hold property— all rights granted women in Utah Territory rebuked Congress. So long as women held these rights, with special attention to the right to vote, these rights stood in the way of Congress's effort to bring the territory to heel.

Sheriff Simms counted it unfair that his Elizabeth should have no rights unless she ended a marriage she made nineteen years before. Told President Taylor's illness had brought the cancellation of Pioneer Day, he suspected it closer to the truth that the federals cancelled it under their official mandate, legislated by the U.S. Congress, allowed by the U.S. President, to disincorporate the LDS church. Trust the venerable U.S.

Supreme Court to protect the right to believe. Know that believ-
ers have no right to an organized church and no right to a day
that celebrates the struggle of people who enjoy a protected
right to believe in a disincorporated church.

Simms checked his uncontrolled thoughts; better to think
about what he had to do today. Vote on the new Utah constitution and organize his week, about of equal importance in
establishing order in the way of things. The church's existence
mattered more to powerful men than to him, and powerful men
maneuvered to sustain their power. Only the maneuverings
related to Albert Hopt concerned him. Since Albert Hopt's stay
expired, Sheriff Simms had expected to hear something. No
word.

Arrests under the Edmunds-Tucker Act continued to
increase, but Sheriff Simms could see the U.S. marshal had
turned to other, more profitable targets than men who worked a
hundred hours a week, on their farm or in two or three jobs, to
support their two families. The wealth and the polygamous
wives down in Salt Lake had made someone very mad, and now
the act had turned the attention to the real target, the big prize.
Ignoring the ordinary, poor people in his mountain desert
seemed like a practical thing to do.

His ears assaulted by a clatter he had not heard in a long
time, he stopped thinking and looked out the window to see
Rabbi Sol's village cart arrive. Sheriff Simms watched his friend,
dressed as usual in black pants, a black frock coat, and some
kind of special black hat, climb the steps and walk through the
door. Simms made a note someday to ask about that hat.

"You look cheerful. How so? I have an empty jail." Simms
nodded toward the coffee pot and pointed. Sol shook his head,
no. "Not a social call? Business I ought to know about?"

"More like the opposite."

His friend looked cheerful, but he found Rabbi Sol a hard

one to read. Cheerful when bringing the worst news; glum when things seemed to go best. Simms knew Rabbi Sol had driven to his jail to see him for a reason. And, he knew Sol would tell him about it whether asked or not. He waited.

"I took that train to Salt Lake. First time. Not the first time I've been on a train; the first time I have taken the train to Salt Lake. It might be faster to go to Echo and take the train to Ogden and then to Salt Lake, but now there's that train direct from Coalville. So, I took it. For the first time. Oh, I told you that."

Sheriff Simms laughed. He had no idea what was coming nor when. The detour via the train did not surprise him. "Matter of fact, I do know there's a train."

"Left Thursday, in the morning. I didn't trust it would deliver me there by Friday night. If I left Friday morning, that is."

"So, you wasted a day?" The sheriff tried to follow the path of Sol's conversation, expecting some news he had not yet received.

"Not really. Better that than violate Shabbat. I used the time. That's why I'm here."

Before Sheriff Simms could point out he had been waiting to learn why Sol was there, Deputy Orson stepped through the screen door.

Sheriff Simms looked at his pocket watch. "You can set your clock."

"Oh, Rabbi Sol," said Orson. "In time for breakfast. I have sandwiches. No pork."

"Clive," said Sheriff Simms, "before we spread breakfast, I need you to send a telegram. Sol, I want to know what the governor did with Hopt. Where should I send it. The governor? The territorial prison? Both?"

"I told you that's why I'm here."

Sheriff Simms shook with frustration, giving way to a smile. "You did?"

"I told you I made good use of my time. On Friday I visited Hopt's lawyer. He's not Jewish, but he's not Mormon, either. Sometimes he has business for me. Before I left, he asked if I knew the governor had dealt with Hopt's stay."

Sheriff Simms took a moment to decide how to ask what could justify such a long time to arrive at the point of news so important. "Well, are you going to tell me what the governor did?"

"You're gonna get him next week."

Even news that sits atop the list of concerns for four years takes a while to digest when it arrives as good news. Sheriff Simms took a long pause to pick which question to ask next.

"What'd he choose?" asked Simms. To appease sentiment against blood atonement, the territory gave the damned the right to choose his own form of execution.

"Firing squad," said Rabbi Sol.

"After fighting for all those stays? I thought sure he'd choose hanging, to spite me."

"I doubt he thought hanging would spite you."

"You think I'm making too much of myself?" asked Sheriff Simms. "It's my duty."

"Yes, it is," said Sol, nodding in agreement. "Either way. Hopt might see hanging as the common end to an outlaw. The firing squad makes him more important."

Sheriff Simms stared at his friend and tried to understand. He had never been anywhere but these mountains. There might be more hanging, more common, in other places. No need to understand; he had what he wanted. "You say, next week?"

"Governor West set the date for Thursday, the eleventh," said Sol. "He believes those guilty of murder should be punished without warning, but the system's not perfect. The victims never received warning, a chance to say goodbye. That's what he told Hopt's lawyer."

Sheriff Simms couldn't square the governor's opinion with the four years his office helped the marshals use Hopt's execution to get at him. The date set, the governor seemed to agree with him. Different governor, he gave up trying, "When do I pick him up?"

"You're not out of the woods yet," Rabbi Sol said. "The U.S. marshal runs the territorial penitentiary. You don't want to see him or his deputies. Send Woodside."

Sheriff Simms frowned. "That marshal could still use Hopt against me." He looked at Clive Orson spreading sandwiches and pie on his desk. "I'm hungry now." He picked up a sandwich and chewed and tried to rid whatever bothered him.

"Just don't go looking for trouble," Rabbi Sol said. He leaned forward, as if speaking from an invisible lectern in front of him. "Attorney Peters filed on Saturday to enforce the escheatment provisions of the Edmunds-Tucker Act. I think on Saturday because your President Taylor was buried on Friday. An ironic form of respect, you might say."

"He was?"

"You knew he died, right?" asked Sol.

"He must have, if they buried him," said Simms. "Last I heard, Pioneer Day was cancelled because he was sick. Guess that was the truth, then."

"Like I said, died Monday, buried Friday, court Saturday."

Simms tried to understand the meaning implied by the course of events. "You think that's why the governor let Hopt's sentence go through?"

"Don't know. The governor was a judge. He doesn't like murderers." Rabbi Sol's eyes and shoulders added up to a question mark. "For sure, the receiver has bigger fish to fry."

"So, who's the receiver?"

From the moment he arrived, Sol had not touched his black hat. Now, he reached for it. He took it off with both hands. He took a handkerchief in one hand. At a little after seven in the morning, the first day of August had not yet gained sixty of the more than one hundred degrees it would reach that afternoon. The sudden need to wipe the sweatband had nothing to do with heat.

"I told Attorney Peters I represented the county. Eldridge won't be happy, but I arranged for Woodside to pick up Hopt."

Sheriff Simms nodded. "So, are you going to tell me who the receiver is? I have a pretty good idea this hoo-hah means you're not wanting to tell me."

"U.S. Marshal Hyer Franks."

Sheriff Simms snickered. "Sounds like some job. I don't see how he can be paying much attention to me and Hopt now."

"I wouldn't let my guard down," Rabbi Sol said. He reached to shake the sheriff's hand and, before he ushered himself out, stopped to say, "Remember, he has deputies."

Sheriff Simms barely noticed Rabbi Sol's words. His thoughts had gone to the subject he had not allowed himself to think about all these years. Who would he ask to serve on the firing squad? He'd ask Woodside, of course, and Charlie McCormick's name popped into mind. Uncle Frank, too. He should be on the firing squad for the man who killed his brother, but that meant an even longer trip than out to Porcupine Mountain. Rock Springs was too far. He'd make the time to ask McCormick. He'd make amends to Uncle Frank.

That left two. The sheriff considered the meaning of five live rounds and one blank. He and Woodside could do it alone. Hell, he could do it alone. The rest were for show. Nevertheless, he needed five, even for show.

Men who live close to the land, struggle to survive, use a gun to provide food for their table, and allow no man to encroach upon their family, their property, and their safety were the kind of men who lived in Sheriff Simms's county. He felt confident he could find three to serve.

Deciding whom to ask proved to be the hard work. To those he did not ask, he meant no disrespect. Those he asked, he asked for a reason. He never felt the need to tell anyone, asked or not asked, the reason. Requests from those who learned of the firing squad and volunteered their services did not change the process he pursued.

"Yes, I've been thinking of you." He gave the same noncommittal answer to all.

Mayor Eldridge thought no act did him any good unless everyone knew about it. That ruled him out. Members of the firing squad remained anonymous. Simms smiled. He felt downright sensitive to the mayor's dilemma.

He did not ask Sam Carruth. Sam was a good man, and his marriage to Emma Wilde made him family. Sheriff Simms knew complicated feelings awaited the moment he pulled the trigger. He did not want to give those complications to Sam Carruth.

"Yes, I've been thinking of you." He responded to Seth Parker's request when he picked up Indigo from a well-deserved currying. He planned to clear away a concern before he asked Seth. "I need to know one thing: can you keep your mouth shut?"

Seth looked at the sheriff, some stricken. In a voice as aggressive and loud as his normal tone for purveying gossip, he said, "Of course I can keep a secret. I won't tell anybody."

"That's the half of it." Sheriff Simms worked the cinch under Indigo's saddle. "I don't want you to say a word about any of it. Show up at five a.m. on the eleventh, nothing more." He turned around to face Seth. "And *after.* I don't want you talking one word, not a whisper, *after.*" Seth looked startled at the sheriff's demand. Simms continued. "No gossip. When the newspapers show up, no interviews. If you can't do that, you can't help me."

"I can't do nothing more than give you my word, John Willford."

Sheriff Simms continued to look at Seth. He let the silence grow, reminded when Seth used his name like family that he had asked him because his father trusted him.

"I'm not asking for more, but you didn't give me your word. Say, 'I give you my word.' "

"I give you my word."

Simms worked through his decision making and on Wednesday morning still had two left to ask when Clive Orson brought him a telegram.

"I'm coming. Frank Simms."

That left him one more. He turned over every name in the county until next morning he woke knowing it should be a woman in Upton, Kay Jones. She took it very hard when Sheriff Luke Willford Simms died. His distant cold determination had been what she needed when her son-in-law murdered her daughter. He caught the murderer in a month or so and for four years pursued the tortuous effort to bring him to justice. During that time, Sheriff Luke Willford talked often with Kay and even invited her home for dinner. Mary Ann supported him in showing the loving comfort to Kay Jones that she needed.

Sheriff Simms had never heard of a woman on a firing squad, but why the hell not? He could give her the blank. He liked the idea so much, considering it rebuked the Edmunds-Tucker act, he did not spot Marshal Grange approach his jailhouse and walk up the steps. The sheriff first sensed the marshal when the tall man walked through the door.

"Marshal Grange, what a surprise. I haven't seen you in a long time."

"More like, I got the drop on you," chuckled Grange. "August 3rd ain't April 1st, and things seem to be going your way. You weren't watching."

"Well, you might say that," Sheriff Simms said, slow and reluctant. "I mean about getting the drop on me. And about not expecting you. As to things going my way, well, I might agree with you on that, too. Hopt's coming back here next week to face his sentence."

"I been told about that." Grange's smile seemed to hold more information than mere friendliness. He continued. "What with Marshal Franks getting himself appointed receiver for the church property, you don't mean so much to him, anymore."

"I never should have meant much to him."

"He's my boss, now."

From the sheriff's sitting position at his desk, those words signaled the beginning of a disadvantage. He eyed Grange.

"I'm guessing it doesn't make any sense for me to say anything, right now."

Grange laughed. "That'd be my guess. Still, my job's the same."

"Same job, huh? So, you work for Franks, but you're not doing what he was doing?"

"I told you: he has a new job."

Sheriff Simms heard the words meant to reassure him, but he could not shake his feeling disadvantaged. He stood up.

"And you're here to check on me and the church coal lands?" the sheriff asked.

"Hah!"

"You want a sandwich and a glass of milk?" Deputy Orson had brought both to Marshal Grange, making the question something of a formality.

"I always liked coming here, hospitality and disapproval served in equal proportions," said Grange. He watched until

Simms smiled and waved his hand, then he bent to his lunch. "I still have the same problem. I'm an elder, and Franks has already taken the tithing office, the Gardo House, and the church historian's office. If he hasn't done it by now, he's gonna take the stock the church owns in corporations. And it ain't but Wednesday."

"I guess your bishop gave you some justification to go along with that, too." Clive Orson stepped away and sat with a deliberate heaviness at his desk.

"Church property worth more than eight hundred thousand dollars has been confiscated. Franks wants to make it a round million. He told me that's my job. He says it's in the farms and mines and livestock around the territory. Oh, and the land, too."

"What's going to happen with the people who work there, the jobs they do, the good they do? Did your bishop give you an answer for that?" Orson asked from his desk, his voice louder than normal.

"I can see you're upset," Marshal Grange said. "But, listen, my bishop told me the apostles saw this Edmunds-Tucker Act coming. The authorities already transferred most of the church property into the hands of trusted individuals and local organizations. He thinks they protected about three million dollars' worth of property that way.

"So, Deputy Orson, you can see some advantage in that, can't you? All those people are gonna continue to work. Marshal Franks'll rent those properties back to the church, and he'll collect the rent."

"He's probably one—" Sheriff Simms raised a hand to still his older deputy. Orson never showed any excitement about anything, except when one of his brethren was doing harm to his church. No use to let him continue and damage himself with this marshal.

"You in on this?" asked Simms.

"I told you, Franks sent me to work the farms, mines, and livestock around the territory, including the land."

"That's not an answer," said Simms. "Are you going to collect a percentage?"

Grange took a moment before he answered the sheriff. "I'm giving mine to the church."

"Great," said Orson. "Take money from the church so you can pay your tithing."

"Not tithing," Grange said. "All of it."

"I'm sure your bishop approves of that," said Deputy Orson.

"I don't know anything about land," said Sheriff Simms.

"Sure you do," Grange said. "I'm supposed to check out a sizable piece of Main Street."

"That's not raw land. That's tabernacle land. It was finished last year." Sheriff Simms walked around from the back of his desk to the marshal, wagging his chin in disbelief all the while. "You mean you're going to take away the dirt the church stands on?"

Simms stood in front of Grange and let the silence grow. He had something important to do, and he did not want to be in this contest. He wanted nothing to do with this grab of church property, never had. He took charge again. "Why are you here? What do you want me to do?"

"Well . . ." Marshal Grange hesitated to speak, even after the invitation, "you know U.S. Attorney Peters went to court, and the judge gave him an order on Saturday."

"The news made it up here," said Sheriff Simms, recalling Rabbi Sol.

"Seeing as it's the law," said Marshal Grange, ignoring or not hearing the sheriff, "the U.S. owns 'em. The U.S. marshals can take 'em."

"You don't need me for that."

Marshal Grange nodded in agreement. "That's how I make it. Call this a professional courtesy, riding all the way up here to tell you I'm the special deputy U.S. marshal assigned to Summit County." Grange shuffled and grinned. "I'm guessing they won't assign another one."

CHAPTER 45:
AUGUST 11, 1887

The territorial secretary sited the Utah territorial penitentiary in 1853 at a remote but accessible spot with the unlikely sounding name of Sugar House on Canyon Creek next to the southeast limits of Salt Lake City. The territorial legislature supported the commitment to local rule by housing the condemned man in the adobe brick buildings of the penitentiary until the territory sent him back to the county where he had done his deed. There the territory gave the county sheriff the responsibility to oversee society's act of final and just retribution. The first territorial legislature enshrined the individual's right to make the final choice.

Death by beheading

or

death by hanging

or

death by firing squad.

No one had chosen beheading, and Hopt had not chosen hanging.

Six selected, including Brother Crittenden, a bearded banker and unlikely volunteer, who had walked in the sheriff's office and asked to serve as an alternate. Brother Crittenden suggested he keep an eye out for any deputy U.S. marshals who might show up. Remembering the invisible organization around his train ride at Echo, and without asking Brother Crittenden what he would do if any did come, Sheriff Simms accepted the offer. He instructed the volunteers when and where to present themselves on Thursday.

Sheriff Simms sent Woodside to pick up the prisoner at five a.m. on Wednesday. With twenty-four hours to bring Hopt back, upwards of sixteen hours of daylight to make thirty-eight miles, Deputy Woodside and Albert Hopt made the distance on horseback. Sheriff Simms waited at his desk until his deputy and his prisoner arrived. As he closed the cell door, Simms allowed his first moment of certainty that he had Hopt *in my father's jail.*

Six rounds—five live, one blank; that was the law. Sheriff John Willford Simms would hold one live round and hand out the other four plus the blank. In the end, he had decided against singling out Kay Jones to give her the blank. Fair treatment for her and the other five men meant all members of the firing squad treated the same. All faced the same odds. He ignored that he changed the odds from what the law prescribed when he held one live round for himself. So be it.

He had read how a person dies from gunshot. The bullet ruptures the heart or a large blood vessel or tears a hole in the lungs, and blood pours out. The loss of blood supply to the brain causes shock. Consciousness is lost. Bleeding until the heart has not enough blood to beat brings death. Bleeding to death.

Blood atonement.

John Willford had caught the man who shot and killed Luke Willford. Now, after four years avoiding the U.S. marshals, he faced the honor and the duty to carry out the sentence that brought a just end to his father's death.

Sheriff Simms wanted to execute Hopt on the steps of the jail.

He wanted to shoot Hopt the way Hopt had shot his father. And his father would not allow it. The man murdered by the man he was executing would never make a spectacle of bringing justice to a killer, even for family.

Sheriff Simms decided on the county fairgrounds. No one could show up inside the fairgrounds whom Brother Crittenden did not allow. In the ample light of Wednesday night's waning half moon, while Woodside and Orson guarded the prisoner, he prepared the site. He opened the stalls to create a long, rectangular hallway, twenty feet wide, four feet deep. Opposite the front edge of the wide hallway, twenty-five feet away, he set a chair.

He found some wood stacked for the stove in the livestock barn and placed six split sticks as markers about one foot behind the wall of his hallway facing the chair. He stepped up and rested his arms on the cross members of the stall as if he were steadying his rifle. That was the best he could do to create a series of firing ports the length of the stall.

Sherriff Simms turned back to look at the chair. Visible in the light of the waning moon, his mind's eye saw a clear line of sight at sunrise.

He made a note in his little school notebook to bring a pan to set beneath the chair and restraints to fasten Hopt's legs and arms. While he was making notes, he remembered somewhere seeing black hoods, maybe in a book. He made a note to bring a pillowcase.

He looked over at the grandstands, a little far away, still satisfactory. Brother Crittenden would station a man at the entrance and let in no one except the state's witnesses. For a moment, he enjoyed the ghoulish thought of taking tickets at Hopt's execution. The territory had told Woodside to provide seating for the condemned's witnesses and the newspapers. He might as well tell Brother Crittenden to take tickets. An embarrassed conscience stopped him. He sought justice, not to gloat over the man. As to witnesses, this condemned man had none. As for newspapers, Sheriff Simms would allow none through the gate.

The second Thursday in August dawned clear and hot. At five fifty-five a.m. Sheriff John Willford Simms, son of Sheriff Luke Willford Simms, stepped into the stall he had turned into a hallway. Four men and a woman awaited him.

One by one, each volunteer presented his rifle. Sheriff Simms inspected it, placed one shell in the chamber, and handed it back to its owner. He loaded his rifle last.

"Men, take your places."

He had issued each person a number, and, like a well-drilled unit, his firing squad stepped into position with backs to the wall that faced the fenced-in square of the rodeo yard. Simms had kept number four for himself, to the right of center of the line.

"Face the prisoner."

The firing squad turned around. Simms took his place. It was six o'clock and day bright.

The volunteers stood at the wall and watched Orson walk Hopt, dressed in simple dark blue pants and white shirt, in bare feet, to the chair. When he sat in the chair, he stared at the faces of the firing squad across the wall. Orson noticed and raised the pillow case to put it over Hopt's head.

"No, Clive," called Sheriff Simms. "That goes last." He returned Hopt's stare with steady eyes, straight at him. He hoped every person along the line did the same.

Deputy Orson placed the hood next to the chair on the rodeo turf and buckled a leather strap across Hopt's waist. With short lengths of rope, he tied Hopt's hands behind his back and restraints around his legs and chest.

The mayor had found a role with visibility but no responsibility. He stepped in front of Hopt. In a voice loud enough for the grandstands to hear, he asked a question he could have whispered. "Does the condemned have any statement to make?"

Hopt looked at him and grinned. "Ya mean like why I shot him?"

Mayor Eldridge took a deep breath and prepared to answer. Before he could, Deputy Orson stepped in again and pulled the pillow case over Hopt's head with one swift movement that allowed no interruption. He then pinned a red cloth circle over Hopt's heart.

Simms approved of his deputy's judgment but found himself disagreeing with his own idea of the pillow case hood. His father had not had a hood. He saw the barrel coming all the way up and pointing to his chest. John Willford felt the same anger today he had felt for four years. He yearned to feel nothing. He could not. Hopt took away a good thirty years he might have had with his father. John Willford was an adult man of forty-three, and he loved his mother. Those facts didn't change that he still felt like an orphan without a father—a state he would never wish on anyone.

"Let us pray," said the mayor and held all assembled in silence until he broke it with, "In Jesus' name."

Simms sighted. Holding his position, he said in his normal outdoor voice, with no effort to shout, "Men, it is time to do your duty."

He had but one thought, and he never told anyone nor described this moment.

"Ready."

He took a deep breath.

"Aim."

At last.

"Fire."

CHAPTER 46:
OCTOBER 20, 1887

Special Deputy U.S. Marshal Grange proved correct. The U.S. government took the church's property without the sheriff's involvement. Marshal Franks stayed focused on his new opportunities. Arrests continued to increase in the valley, and no one bothered to name new special deputies in Summit County. Sol's words, *not out of the woods yet,* kept Sheriff Simms cautious. Still, it felt different. He had not seen a pink curtain in Ann Cluff's window since August. Only thoughts of the birth facing Elizabeth Tonsil brought concerns.

Sheriff Simms harbored a silent hope that his wife's . . . , uh, size meant she carried a boy, and he feared it added to her risks. Since September he had told Woodside to patrol the county; he took care of the town. He tried to be careful, but he stopped in the jail each morning, regular, and he slept at Elizabeth Jensen's house. By the time his daily rounds took him to the mercantile, it rolled around to nine o'clock, and he checked on Elizabeth Tonsil. Today he planned a cup of coffee and a long visit with his wife.

"I sent the boy to your office more'n an hour ago." Trueman intercepted him at the door with no preamble.

"On my rounds, talking to people." Simms could hear himself defend that he had become careless and predictable. He looked around for Elizabeth as he talked. "What's up?"

"Right!" laughed Trueman. "Go home."

Sheriff Simms left the mercantile and ran back to the jail to saddle Indigo. He had no idea what preparation he made with that caution, and he blessed his sixth sense when he found no one at Emma Wilde Carruth's house. He assumed she had beat him to the yellow house in Elizabeth Tonsil's time of need. From Emma's house, he galloped his blue roan to the south end of town to find the midwife.

"She's not gonna like this," said the midwife to his demand for help with the birth. "How far along is she?"

"How do I know?" Simms stood at the door waving his hat as though he meant her to run out and jump on his horse with him. "Far enough along that Trueman sent a boy to the jail who never found me. All I know is she's forty-one, and you're going to help her."

"This is her sixth." Midwife Martha Ballard had a defiant sound in her voice. "She's never asked for my help before."

"Fifth, and she's never been forty-one before. And she's not asking."

"Well, if by that you mean you're asking, you don't count." Midwife Ballard had said all she wanted to say. Despite her negative response, she picked up a bag that rested at the front door, seeming to be there always at the ready.

"How're you going to get there?" Simms looked around the front yard in his sudden realization that he had Indigo and nothing else to offer. "It'll take too long to walk. Take my horse. I'll walk. Fast as I can. Be right behind you."

"I've done this before, Sheriff." Midwife Ballard patted his cheek with her free hand. "I have my own buggy."

Midwife Ballard and Elizabeth Tonsil Simms shared the same opinion of Elizabeth's ability to bear a sixth child alone. When midwife Ballard arrived, Emma had Elizabeth on the bed, working the birth together.

"Oh, the professional has arrived," called Emma when she saw who emerged from the front door that opened in the middle of their labors. "Here, take over. I'll freshen up the water."

Sheriff Simms stood in the bedroom door, trying to be invisible and out of the way.

"John Willford, you're in the way." Emma pushed by him with a basin of hot water.

He stepped aside and then followed her into the bedroom. Before he arrived at the foot of the bed, Emma exclaimed, "Oh, my lord, he's big. Must be ten pounds." She held the baby boy in her arms and waved John Willford up from the foot of the bed. She handed his father's final grandson to Sheriff Simms. "What will you name him?" asked Emma.

John Willford held the infant, looked at Elizabeth Tonsil, then settled his gaze on the boy.

"Willford, of course." Her smile sparkled. "His grandfather was Luke and his father John. So, he has to be Matthew or Mark."

"My father loved the book of Matthew."

"Matthew, Mark, Luke, and John. I think that makes it Mark."

Sheriff Simms held the boy and with slow deliberation raised him as high as he could. He said to Elizabeth, "A good name to carry on my father's calling: Mark Willford Simms."

★ ★ ★ ★ ★

APPENDIX

★ ★ ★ ★ ★

SUMMARY OF CAMPAIGN
AGAINST POLYGAMY

1862—Morrill Anti-Bigamy Act
Latter-day Saints believed the Morrill Anti-Bigamy Act was unconstitutional and that God would set it right. They were following God's commandments, and he would protect the faithful. Because of this belief and their faith in God, LDS began to live in defiance of the law and hide the law breaking.

The Civil War rendered the government of the United States unable in the short term to address the issue of defiance.

1874—Poland Act
The first law to strengthen the provisions of the 1862 bill, passed by Congress on June 23 and signed the next day by President Grant.

The act abolished the territorial marshal and attorney general of the territory and assigned their duties to the United States marshal and the United States assistant district attorney. Although it dismantled the judicial system in Utah, still there were people in both Utah and Washington who did not believe the bill was harsh enough.

The United States attorney experienced problems when he tried to bring leading church officials to trial. Frustrations at the prosecution of polygamy spurred the Edmunds Act.

1878—Reynolds v. United States, 98 U.S. 145
The U. S. Supreme Court quoted from Thomas Jefferson that there was a distinction between religious belief and action that

flowed from religious belief. The first amendment forbade Congress from legislating against *belief* but allowed it to legislate against action. Religious *practice* may be legislated for/against, and the law is therefore constitutional.

1882—Edmunds Act

Designed to fix problems in the two prior bills and cast as an amendment to the 1862 law. Despite its full-blown name, while it had teeth, it was not a new law. Unlawful cohabitation was defined as, "supporting and caring for more than one woman." After the passage of the Edmunds Act, prosecutors in the Utah Territory focused in the main on unlawful cohabitation.

S1 made polygamy (marriage to more than one woman) a felony, five years in prison and/or a five-hundred-dollar fine. S3 made cohabitation (living with more than one woman) a misdemeanor, six months in prison and/or a three-hundred-dollar fine. S5 disqualified polygamists from jury service and S8 from voting and public or elective office of any kind. S9 threw out all elected officials and set up the five-person Utah Commission to perform all duties relevant to elections.

1885—Murphy v. Ramsey, 114 U.S. 15

This omnibus case concerned the election commission and the disenfranchisement of voters. It held that the Edmunds Act established no *ex post facto* law; rather, the continued polygamous act was the illegal act. To arrive at this remarkable interpretation, the supreme court found: *For certainly no legislation can be supposed more wholesome and necessary in the founding of a free, self-governing commonwealth, . . . than that which seeks to establish it on the basis of the idea of the family, as consisting in and springing from the union for life of one man and one woman in the holy estate of matrimony;*

1887—Edmunds-Tucker Act

The act became law March 3 without the signature of President Cleveland.

A wife or wives were forced to testify against their husbands.

Witnesses did not have to be subpoenaed to appear in court.

Immoralities were defined in the text, and punishments were set forth.

Children of plural marriages were disinherited.

All marriages performed were to be recorded with a probate court.

Probate judges were to be appointed by the president of the United States.

Woman suffrage was abolished.

Service on juries and in public office was conditional upon signing a loyalty oath.

- Pledging obedience to all anti-polygamy laws.
- Pledging support of all anti-polygamy laws.

Utah Commission continued in charge of elections.

- Empowered to administer the loyalty oath.

The Perpetual Emigrating Fund Company was dissolved.

The Nauvoo Legion was abolished.

All local military laws were repealed.

The territorial superintendent of schools was replaced by a commissioner appointed by the Utah Supreme Court.

The Church of Jesus Christ of Latter-day Saints was disincorporated.

- The church property was escheated to the United States.
- The escheated church property was to be used for the benefit of the common schools of the territory.

SIR ROBERT PEEL'S PRINCIPLES OF LAW ENFORCEMENT 1829

1. The basic mission for which police exist is to prevent crime and disorder as an alternative to the repression of crime and disorder by military force and severity of legal punishment.

2. The ability of the police to perform their duties is dependent upon *public approval* of police existence, actions, behavior and the ability of the police to secure and maintain *public respect*.

3. The police must secure the willing cooperation of the public in voluntary observance of the law to be able to secure and maintain public respect.

4. The degree of cooperation of the public that can be secured diminishes, proportionately, to the necessity for the use of physical force and compulsion in achieving police objectives.

5. The police seek and preserve public favor, not by catering to public opinion, but by constantly demonstrating absolutely impartial service to the law, in complete independence of policy, and without regard to the justice or injustice of the substance of individual laws; by ready offering of individual service and friendship to all members of society without regard to their race or social standing, by ready exercise of courtesy and friendly good humor; and by ready offering of individual sacrifice in protecting and preserving life.

6. The police should use physical force to the extent necessary to secure observance of the law or to restore order only when the exercise of *persuasion, advice and warning* is found to

be insufficient to achieve police objectives; and police should use only the minimum degree of physical force which is necessary on any particular occasion for achieving a police objective.

7. The police at all times should maintain a relationship with the public that gives reality to the historic tradition that *the police are the public* and *the public are the police;* the police are the only members of the public who are paid to give full-time attention to duties which are incumbent on every citizen in the intent of the community welfare.

8. The police should always direct their actions toward their functions and never appear to usurp the powers of the judiciary by avenging individuals or the state, or authoritatively judging guilt or punishing the guilty.

9. The test of police efficiency is the *absence* of crime and disorder, not the *visible evidence* of police action in dealing with them.

ABOUT THE AUTHOR

The mountains of Utah and the heritage of pioneer great-grandparents formed **Edward Massey** and created his willingness to take on the unknown. His writing career continues the trek. He has published *Telluride Promise,* quarterfinalist in the 2010 Amazon Breakthrough Novel Awards; *Every Soul Is Free,* League of Utah Writers' Gold Quill Award, 2014 grand prize winner for best novel; and short stories. Consulting and speaking support his writing. Edward and his wife, Anne, live in Massachusetts and Maine. For more on Edward's writing and his life, see edwardmasseybooks.com.

The employees of Five Star Publishing hope you have enjoyed this book.

Our Five Star novels explore little-known chapters from America's history, stories told from unique perspectives that will entertain a broad range of readers.

Other Five Star books are available at your local library, bookstore, all major book distributors, and directly from Five Star/Gale.

Connect with Five Star Publishing

Visit us on Facebook:
   https://www.facebook.com/FiveStarCengage

Email:
   FiveStar@cengage.com

For information about titles and placing orders:
   (800) 223-1244
   gale.orders@cengage.com

To share your comments, write to us:
   Five Star Publishing
   Attn: Publisher
   10 Water St., Suite 310
   Waterville, ME 04901